MW01129152

RIGHT UNDER MY NOSE

ALI PARKER

BRIXBAXTER PUBLISHING

Right Under My Nose

Copyright © 2018 by Ali Parker

First Edition.

Cover Designer: Ryn Katryn Digital Art
Editor: Angela McCallister

1

HOLDEN

"This is going to change everything," I told Raymond as I paced up and down the living room of his place. With tired eyes, he managed to smile at me.

"You really think so?"

"I know so." I turned to him excitedly. I knew I was getting over invested in this, but I couldn't help it. There was so much promise in what was about to happen with the company, with this new job, with all of it. Think of everything I could do with that kind of money—the expansions I could make, the new offices I could rent, the new staff I could put into place....

"So what exactly is it you're doing again?" Raymond rocked his baby daughter, Sasha, in his arms for a moment. She had just fallen asleep. He was keeping his voice low to avoid waking her, but she seemed to sleep best when she was surrounded by people talking, so he didn't return her to her crib quite yet.

"I'm heading down to New York, just for this weekend," I told him. "To meet with the Thanderburgh group. They're looking for a new suite of websites to be designed. And they want me to do it."

"And how much are they paying you again?" he cocked an eyebrow at me, and I shook my head.

"Numbers aren't confirmed yet, but I know it's going to be more than I've been paid for any job before," I explained, and I could hear the overheating in my own voice. That was just the way I got when I talked about this business. I had poured so much of my time into this that I was used to constantly being on the highest levels of energy to make sure I didn't lose patience for the business. Enthusiasm was my default position.

"That's incredible." Raymond shook his head and began walking up and down with Sasha in his arms. She was only a few months old, and he had been having trouble getting her to sleep. I remembered those days. Hell, it felt like yesterday that I had been getting up in the night to take care of Hunter, staring at myself in the mirror and not recognizing the exhausted, baggy-eyed old man who looked back at me.

"How are you doing, by the way?" I asked, realizing I had stormed in here and gotten under his feet when he was taking care of his daughter. "How are things going with you and Olivia?"

"Well." He nodded. "I mean, as well as they can be, given we have this little terror keeping us up most nights."

"It's hard, right?"

"Harder than anyone prepared me for," he confessed. "I knew I would be tired, but I didn't even think this level of tired was humanly possible, you know?"

"It does get better," I promised him. "Give yourself some time. The change is a shock at first."

"I don't know how you did this by yourself." He shook his head. "Even splitting the labor, it feels like I could sleep for ten months straight. And on top of running a business...."

"I was a lot younger then," I reminded him. "Had more energy. I couldn't do all of that now if you asked me to."

"But you still run around like you're twenty and you've got all the energy in the world," he pointed out as Sasha snuffled in his arms. She was a sweet little thing, with a mess of dark hair to match his, and I supposed some part of me did crave that age again a little. But not so much that I ever wanted to go back to the nightly feedings or crawling out of bed in the morning on three hours sleep to go to a meeting with a vital new client.

"Yeah, well, I've got the business off the ground now." I flashed a smile at him. "The success is addictive."

"You need any help with this one?" he asked. The offer was made in earnest, but I wasn't sure he was going to be able to keep his eyes open if he sat down for more than ten seconds. I shook my head.

"No, you're good," I assured him. "Just focus on raising her, all right?"

"Will do." He yawned. Raymond sometimes helped out at the business, putting together banners and sketches for logos when I was coming up with website designs, but I was more than happy handling all of that myself. Especially for a company as big as this one. I wanted to have the final say on every little thing that went into this to make sure that every corner of it was totally perfect. Building this company from the ground up all by myself meant I still had that urge to control, to make sure everything went exactly the way it was supposed to, and that I had a say over all of it.

And to think, I had started Reigns Designs to prove a point to Karla, the mother of my child. We had been together a few months before she got pregnant, but we had both decided to keep it and had begun excitedly preparing for the arrival of my first child. Sometimes, I had caught her looking at me, and the expression on her face would be... well, maybe not disdain but something close to it, like she couldn't believe she was doing this with me. I put it down to pregnancy hormones and did my best to pull together a place suitable for a baby on the limited budget we had. Sure, I had hoped to focus on my career a little longer before my family came along, but I would take what was laid out in front of me and do with it what I could.

She lasted maybe three days after Hunter came along. As soon as I laid eyes on him, I knew what he had to be called. As soon as he entered the world, his gaze was sliding around the room like he was getting the measure of everyone in there and wanted them all to know it. Hunter—it had a sharp, strong ring to it, the kind of name you could trust.

Karla seemed miserable after he was born, and for a while, I was worried it was postpartum depression. But then she took me aside and told me the truth. It was far more to do with me than it was to do with anything else.

"You're never going to amount to anything," she told me. The words had instantly burned themselves into my memory, all my worst fears made reality She'd known I had wanted a career, that I had hoped to focus on getting my work off the ground first, and now here she was, pushing her finger into the open wound of that knowledge till it burned in agony.

"Karla, you don't know what you're talking about," I had protested desperately. "We've just had a baby. I need time to adjust before I go back to focusing on my—"

"You're making excuses," she'd snapped. "That's the trouble."

And with that, she'd left. Or at least, that's what it seemed like. The argument had stretched over a few days, but she was out of there in spirit long before Hunter even came along. I asked her, begged her even, to stay in his life, to do it for him if not for me, but she didn't give a single damn about us. She'd gone, and I was left with this burning desire to prove her wrong. Every single way I could.

In the hours I wasn't taking care of Hunter, I worked on getting the web design business off the ground. And it took so much work, more work than I could handle, more work than I should have been able to do. Raymond put down some money as an initial investment, determined to support me and knowing this was the only way he could do it without me shooting him down, and I slowly began to drag the business up, carving out more time for myself, schmoozing more clients, gathering more intel on the industry at large.

I'd worked my ass off for nearly a full decade straight, and that was how I'd found myself sitting atop a multimillion—soon to be billion—dollar business, with a son I adored and knew I would be able to provide the best for. Raymond, who helped out around the business when and where he could, had seen his return triple on his investment and then some. He had enough cash now that he didn't need to work the rest of his life. Which was lucky, as he had a daughter to focus on now, a kid of his own to raise. Olivia and Raymond had been trying for a long time before Sasha had come along—since before they were married—and I knew it meant the world to him to have a daughter in his arms, even if the look on his face right now might have indicated otherwise.

"You ever think about taking some time away from the business?" Raymond remarked, looking down at his daughter.

"What do you mean?" I furrowed my brow. He laughed.

"Jesus, is it really that foreign to you?" he teased. "I mean, maybe you could start hiring some people to step up and take care of things for you. Just for a while. Then you could focus on yourself a little bit more."

"I'm doing fine." I waved my hand.

"You should get back to dating again," he urged me. We had this conversation pretty often, and I knew how it went. I knew he was right but that didn't mean I wanted to run off and marry the first woman I stumbled across.

"I know you're happy with Olivia," I told him. "I think what you guys have is great. I do. But I don't think I have time for that kind of thing in my life right now. Between Hunter and the business, what woman's going to want to come into my life and take all that on?"

"Someone who's as crazy as you are?" he suggested, and I laughed.

"Look, I actually came down here for a reason," I admitted to him. "I need someone to look after Hunter while I'm in New York over the weekend."

"You know, you could hire a nanny," Raymond pointed out, but he was already smiling. I knew he was always happy to see Hunter, who had followed him around constantly from the moment he could walk and had always spoken highly of his treasured Uncle Raymond.

"Yeah, sure, but then you wouldn't get a chance to catch up with your favorite little guy," I pointed out, and he chuckled.

"All right, I'll do it," he agreed. "Drop him off on Friday evening?"

"Sure thing." I slapped his shoulder. "I have to go pick him up from school now, but I'll see you soon."

"See you soon." He yawned again.

"And try to get some sleep!" I told him as I slipped out of the living room and headed down the steps to my car. Sometimes it felt like I didn't have a moment to myself, but that was the way I liked it. Running around, rushed off my feet, keeping so busy that I hardly had time to think—it was the way I had lived my life for the last nine years, and I couldn't see that changing soon. Which is what made Raymond's suggestion to settle down and find someone special even more ridiculous to consider.

2

AUTUMN

Zoe collapsed into the seat next to me and let out a long sigh, as though being here and not in front of a bad movie with a glass of wine was paining her to her core.

"Has it been that bad already?" I teased, and she held her hand up as though to indicate to me that I had no idea how rough things had been that day.

"I had to deal with two kids freaking sword fighting with crayons this morning," she told me, pulling out her lunchbox. I eyed her carefully packed salad and fruit and wondered if I should make more of an effort to eat like a real grown adult instead of a kid with access to a credit card.

"So? That's not too bad," I protested, and she shook her head.

"And then they tried to hide the crayons up their noses when I went to take them away," she finished up, and I spluttered with laughter.

"Okay, that's a new one," I agreed, taking a sip of my water. The two of us were sitting at the staff lunch table, keeping an eye on the kids around us as they ate and chatted and probably plotted against us.

"Yep, new one on me too," she agreed. She shook her head and glanced around to make sure no one was listening. "I was tempted to let them go for it, though. That would teach them, right?"

"Zoe!" I scolded her playfully. "I'm going to have to put you in time-out if you don't start behaving yourself."

"Oh, please do." She nodded at me. "I could use the break. How long till the end of the day again?"

"Come on, don't talk shit," I protested. "I love these kids. You know that. I can't sit here while you say things like that."

"And yet you're the one saying 'shit' in front of a room full of ten-year-olds." She cocked her head at me, and I laughed.

"All right, point taken," I conceded. I took a bite of my sandwich and covered my mouth as I continued to talk. "You doing okay? Outside the crayon hiding, I mean?"

"Yeah, I'm doing good. Wish I could afford to take a little time off, but no rest for the wicked, right?"

"Guess not," I agreed. I should probably have been craving a holiday as well, but I loved my job so much. I had been teaching elementary for two years now, and I couldn't imagine doing anything else with my life. It might have sounded ridiculous to anyone else, but the thought of spending the rest of my life helping raise the next generation of kids... well, I could hardly think of anything better in the world than that.

"What are you doing this weekend?" Zoe asked. The two of us had met during teacher training, but we had grown close when we had been placed in the same school and both wound up working there full time. She was exactly what I needed, the snarky, whip-smart other side to my ditz and occasional dorkiness.

"Uh, is cleaning out my bathroom cabinets an acceptable weekend activity?" I asked, wincing.

"Only if you do it drunk," Zoe replied, and I laughed again.

"All right, so, I'll bribe you with rosé and you can come around and do it for me?" I shot back. She rolled her eyes at me in that fond way she had.

"You really should be hitting the dating scene," she told me. "You're a total catch!"

"Yeah, I don't think elementary school teacher exactly oozes sex appeal," I said, but she waved her hand.

"Trust me, you're a woman. For some guys, anything you do will ooze sex appeal," she assured me.

"So, what, have you got someone in mind?" I asked her, curious. I wasn't exactly super keen to get out there and date. I had been so focused on getting my job off the ground when I had first started here that I had pretty much forgotten what it was like to go out on actual dates with someone, wearing actual pants after six in the evening when I came home and slipped into sweats or underwear for the rest of the evening. What must that be like?

"Hmm." Zoe tapped her finger against her lip for a moment and eyed me, as though trying to match me up with someone in her head. "I'm not certain. Maybe you could get on some dating apps, see what's out there?"

"I don't think I have time for that." I shook my head.

"Or you're just looking for a reason to keep from having an actual dating life." She could see right through me. I raised my eyebrows at her.

"Yeah, yeah, you got me," I agreed. "Just the thought of actually going out in the evening is making me tired. I'd rather stay at home and get ahead on my grading, thanks."

"Oh, don't be such a downer," she shot back. "How about if I set you up with someone? Blind date. Then all you have to do is turn up at the restaurant and meet him. You won't have to do any of the organizing."

"As long as you pick a place where I don't have to wear heels," I warned her. "Or makeup. Or a dress. Or—"

"So what you're saying is you want some guy who's going to eat on your couch with you?" she finished up for me.

"Yeah, actually." I cocked my head at her playfully. "That would be amazing. In fact, get him to drop off the food and go. That works for me."

"You want me to order takeout for you." She pointed at me, grinning. "That's what you're asking for right there."

"Well, you offered," I reminded her, and she shook her head.

"Autumn, there is no winning with you sometimes," she sighed, and she started in on her salad. "How's the rest of your day been?"

We were chatting away when I found my gaze drawn to a kid sitting behind us at a table by himself. He was one of the younger ones in my class, and he looked it—smaller than the rest of the kids, spindly like he might break if you spoke to him too loudly. I frowned in his direction, even as I tried to tune in to the conversation with Zoe. He had a mop of dark brown hair and beautiful eyes.

"Hey, I have to go get my lesson set up for next period." Zoe glanced at the clock on the wall. "I'll catch you later, though?"

"Sure thing." I nodded.

"And I'm totally setting you up on that date," Zoe reminded me. "Don't think you're getting out of it that easily."

"I never think I'm getting out of anything easily with you," I assured her, and she patted me on the shoulder and vanished to her classroom. I got to my feet and went to join the little boy who was sitting all by himself in that cafeteria.

I had always had a soft spot for the kids who were clearly out of place. Maybe that was why I had gotten into this job in the first place, because I wanted to give those children a sense of place, of home, where they might not have had it before. I had known since I was a kid that I wanted to do this job, and now that I was finally here, I wasn't going to watch some little boy sitting all by himself and not do a single thing to help him.

He looked up at me as I sat down beside him with my lunch. He had a slightly wary expression on his face, as though he was worried he was going to do or say something that would annoy or upset me.

"Hello." I smiled at him. "How're you doing, Hunter?"

"Good." He turned his attention back down to his lunch—sandwiches with the crusts cut off and some chopped apple from a parent who was still clearly hoping to get some vitamins in him. He was at that funny age where they started declaring their independence in silly fashions, refusing food and certain clothes when they felt like it. It was a difficult age for the ones who didn't already have an established friend group, especially as kids started to form their own little cliques It was easy for one of them to get left behind if a concentrated effort wasn't being made to be sure they didn't.

"Cool." I nodded, and I took another bite of my lunch. "What have you been doing today?"

"Uh, mostly math." He pulled a face, and I pulled one back.

"You don't like math?"

He shook his head.

"No," he said, and then he fell silent once more. I spent the rest of the lunch hour coaxing some conversation out of him, making sure he had someone to talk to while he ate. I had been a bit of a loner when I was at school, and I had longed for someone to come and take away the specific torture of sitting alone hoping against hope that someone would come put you out of your lonely misery.

I didn't know who his parents were, which was weird. He had been in my classes for a couple of years now, since I'd started at Portland South Elementary, yet I couldn't remember meeting his mom or his dad in all that time. Which was pretty unusual. Portland fostered a lot of helicopter parents who wanted to be involved in every part of their kids' lives, and that meant sometimes you were deflecting a few emails every week from the same over concerned parental figures attempting to delve into what their kid was getting up to when they weren't around.

But I couldn't even remember the names of Hunter's parents. I would have to check that out later because I was pretty sure I needed to reach out to them. He was a sweet kid. He really was, but I had the feeling he might need a little guidance when it came to finding his place socially in this school, especially as the kids around him started to grow up. I didn't want any of the kids I taught to get left behind if I could avoid it.

"Thanks for eating with me." He smiled at me shyly as he finished up his food. I smiled back. I felt a little sad for him. His manners were impeccable, but that wasn't the kind of thing that impressed the others his own age.

"Any time," I replied.

"See you in class," he told me, his little face so serious and earnest that I wanted to ruffle his hair and tell him it was all right to lighten up and goof around if he was so inclined. I smiled again and watched as he headed away from the table. I made a promise to myself right there and then to reach out to his parents to let them know we should start working together to make sure their son was having the best experience he could. As long as I was working here, I was going to make sure every kid these parents trusted me with got the best experience they possibly could. Especially that serious little boy who looked as though he was doing his best to keep something—maybe everything—all to himself.

3

HOLDEN

I took my son into my arms and held him close. It didn't matter how many times I had to say goodbye to him for trips like this. It never got any easier. I buried my face into his hair and inhaled deeply, as though I was trying to commit him to memory, to take the scent and the feel of him with me to call upon when I needed it.

"I'm going to be back before you know it, all right, buddy?" I told him, ruffling his hair as I got back up to my feet. He nodded but frowned at the same time. It broke my heart to see him like that, to see him as anything other than happy.

"I wish you didn't have to go," he told me, his eyes burning into mine with a seriousness I wished I could ignore. I wanted to be able to go out of town without feeling like I was abandoning my son in the process, but he made that so hard, looking at me like I was personally injuring him in the process of doing this. I remembered the way those eyes had looked at me when we had seen each other for the first time, how I had known Hunter was right for him even then. The way his eyes pierced and penetrated like a bullet or an arrowhead.

"Sunday night, I promise," I told him. "You're going to have so much fun with Raymond. Right?"

I glanced up at my friend, who agreed at once.

"Of course we are!" he agreed, patting Hunter on the shoulder. "You can come and hang out with Sasha. She's starting to get big now. She might even recognize you!"

Hunter managed the flicker of a smile. He would have been reluctant to admit it, but he was already seriously attached to Raymond's little girl. He had never had siblings of his own, of course, and sometimes I wondered if I had denied him something by failing to find him a family beyond just me. But I would never have been able to raise a second child with the kind of life I wanted for him, and I wouldn't have been able to juggle dating, the business, and Hunter when he was growing up. I sometimes felt guilty that he seemed so alone outside of me, but I couldn't have made any other choice. It was the way it had to be, like it or not. At least Raymond and Olivia were awesome with him. That was something.

"I'll be back so soon, I promise," I repeated myself once more. I looked at my watch. I had to get out of there if I was going to make my flight on time, yet every second I spent looking at Hunter was another when I doubted what I was doing. I should have been used to it by now. I had spent so long running all over the city, all over the country, to make sure I could get the clients I wanted. Yet it was getting harder as Hunter got older and he could express how much he was going to miss me with actual words instead of wails like before.

"Holden, you need to get out of here if you're going to make your flight," Raymond reminded me gently. I straightened up once more and ruffled Hunter's hair one more time.

"You have the number of the hotel if you need to call me, right?" I checked with him, and Raymond nodded.

"And your cell number too," he pointed out, trying his best to soothe me. "It's fine, Holden. Really. Go off and get this client. I know you're going to kill it."

"Sure am." I plastered a cocky visage on swiftly so the twinge of sadness at leaving my son behind was buried underneath something. "You guys have a good time, all right? I'll call you when I'm there."

"Sure thing," Raymond agreed, and with one last hug to my son, I turned to head to the plane. I pulled my phone from my pocket as I walked, trying to find my boarding pass and hoping to distract myself from the pain of leaving him behind.

I wouldn't have trusted anyone but Raymond with him, that was for sure, and maybe that was part of the problem. Maybe he'd be more open to people if I let more people close to him. It wasn't that I chased away every single person who even came near us, but ever since Karla had up and left, I had been nervous about inviting someone else into our lives. The thought of hurting my son like that, of allowing Hunter to get attached to someone and then having them drop out of my life, was bad enough. But the thought of falling in love once more and having it slip through my fingers again was impossible to even fathom. There was a reason I'd kept dating on the back burner for so long, and it involved more than only the time it would take to seek someone out and woo them and date them and introduce them into my life. I had plenty of interest, especially once the money had started rolling in. No, it went deeper than that. The thought of being hurt again, of opening myself up to someone and having them hurt me back—I couldn't do it. Not yet. Not so soon. Not when I needed to focus my energy on my business and my son, two things that would never hurt me.

As I looked for my boarding pass, an email popped into my inbox, and I quickly clicked it open. It was from an address I didn't recognize, and the name didn't ring any bells either, but it had the name of Hunter's school in it. I came to a dead halt at once to read what it had to say.

It was from one of the teachers at the school, some woman called Autumn. She was telling me I needed to come in and speak to her. Well, she said both me and his mother needed to do that, but given that I was hardly likely to come stumbling across Karla anytime soon, I alone would have to do the job. She didn't say a lot but implied there was something concerning her about his behavior and wrote that she had never met me in person and wanted to lay some groundwork for our relationship as parent and teacher. My shoulders sank. Hunter had never been in trouble at school before, not once in his life that I could remember, and I was sad thinking that he might have been acting out or playing up. She wanted to see me the next day.

I glanced up at the board in front of me, the one that announced when my plane was leaving and where I had to go to make it to the flight on time. I felt a twist in my stomach. I had to catch that flight. I had to be on it in the next fifteen minutes if I wanted to make it out to New York and confirm this client for myself. But this email, this was enough to give me pause. I shouldn't have let it bother me. I could email her and ask to reschedule for a time that suited me better, but I didn't want to blow her off like this. I wanted to prove to Hunter's teachers that I was actually a receptive parent, that if they needed to talk to me I would be around, and they could rely on me. Besides, what if it was something serious? I would have felt awful if I'd spent all this time running away around the country while there were issues that needed to be addressed at home first.

I turned and scanned the crowd for Hunter and Raymond and found nothing. Shit. I hooked my bag over my shoulder and sprinted back out to the parking lot. I could catch them before they got out of here. Well, I hoped I could since they were my ride home.

I made it out to the parking lot and came to a dead halt as I tried to recall where in the name of holy hell they had parked. I scanned back and forth along the cars in front of me. Then I heard Hunter laughing, and my attention was drawn to the left of the lot. I took off in that direction, and sure enough, after a minute or two, I stumbled across Raymond helping Hunter into the front seat of the car. He cocked an eyebrow when he saw me approaching.

"Everything all right?" he asked, and I nodded.

"I've decided I'm going to stay home this weekend," I told him and gave him a subtle nod to let him know I would explain what was going on as soon as I got the chance. "I'm not going to New York after all."

"Yes!" Hunter punched the air and grinned. "Why aren't you going? What happened?"

"Flight got canceled," I lied to him at once. I eyed him for a second, wondering what exactly it could be that his teacher had seemed so concerned about. He had never been anything other than the picture of sweet, amiable kindness and gentleness with me, but he was getting to that age now where he could show two faces to different people, where he could start to deceive and unsettle. The thought worried me. As if I wasn't constantly worried about Hunter.

I helped him into the back of the car and asked him to plug in his gaming device so I could speak to Raymond for a second.

"What's going on?" Raymond asked, brow furrowed. "Everything all right? I don't think I've ever known you to cancel a meeting before, flight or no flight."

"I know, I know." I shook my head. "But I got this email as I was about to head to my fate."

"Oh? From whom?"

"From one of Hunter's teachers." I glanced over to check that Hunter was all plugged in and couldn't hear a word coming out of our mouths. "She seems concerned about some of his behavior, and she wants to have a meeting tomorrow."

"Jesus." Raymond furrowed his brow. "That sucks. Do you know what it's about?"

"No, but she expects me to turn up with a wife in tow." I sighed. "She mentioned his mother in the email. I guess I never told the school that she's not around."

"Right." Raymond nodded, and he glanced at me as he pulled out of the lot. "Look, you've got to do what you think is right, buddy. The clients can wait. You need to take care of this. Nobody else can."

"Thanks," I said, leaning back in my seat. I might have just shot myself in the foot with the biggest clients who had shown interest in my company to date, but if I'd gone, I'd have spent the whole time away from home convinced I had made the wrong choice. I peered around at my son in the back seat, and he gave me a thumbs-up and a smile. He was glad I was staying home. That was enough to convince me I had made the right choice.

I pulled out my phone and started tapping out an email to let the client know I wouldn't be in New York to meet with them the next day and then sent one to the teacher to tell her I would meet with her on Monday evening. Then I tucked the phone away and promised myself I wasn't going to look at it for the rest of the night. It had already brought enough unsettling news for one day.

4

AUTUMN

I finished writing out the carefully worded email to Hunter's father and read it for what felt like the thousandth time since I'd started writing it that morning. I didn't want it to come across in an accusatory way. I wanted this guy to say yes to this meeting, after all, and that wasn't going to happen if I came at him all guns blazing and blaming him for not being more involved in his kid's life. I had tried to find the mother's email first—they were often more responsive to this kind of thing—but I had come up with a dead blank on that front and had swiftly given up. No point pursuing what wasn't there.

Satisfied that I had been about as diplomatic as I could possibly be, I pressed send on the email and leaned back in my seat with relief. Okay, that was done. That was the hard part.

I stretched and got to my feet, cricking my neck from side to side. I knew I spent too much time with work, that I should have been taking this time to myself to actually relax now that I had finished up grading papers and preparing my lesson plan for the next week, but I couldn't stop thinking about Hunter, poor, sweet little Hunter sitting all by himself with those other kids ignoring him like he wasn't even there. He was like a ghost to them, floating through the school, and his reticence meant he didn't leave an impression.

I couldn't help wondering where that came from. What was his family like? Hopefully, I would get to know firsthand soon enough. I was a little nervous. These kinds of meetings were rarely fun, after all. Still, it would be for the best. For Hunter. Which was what all of this was about at the end of the day.

My phone buzzed, and I snatched it up at once, somehow assuming it must be Hunter's parents calling me up directly even though they didn't have my number. I looked at the screen and found Zoe's name, instead, and answered at once.

"Hey," I greeted her.

"Hey." She yawned down the line. "You feel like going out for lunch? I just woke up, and I don't feel like cooking any time soon."

"Sure thing." I grinned. "Usual place?"

"You know it," she agreed. "See you there in fifteen?"

"Twenty?"

"Deal," she replied, and with that, she hung up the phone and left me to gather myself to meet her. The place we were headed was the same one we had gone to celebrate getting the job at the school in the first place. We had happened to be together when we got the news, and she had insisted on taking me out for a drink to revel in our victory. At the time, I hadn't known her so well, but after that long, boozy lunch, I felt as though she was my best friend, and I couldn't imagine life without her.

Before I headed out the door to Mamas, I noticed the screen of my laptop was lit up like it was trying to tell me something. I turned to check it out and found a fresh email. From Hunter's father.

I quickly clicked it open and scanned through the lines, grinning when I saw he was agreeing to meet me tomorrow at the school as I had first suggested. I would have made it during the school day, but I didn't want to take time away from my day to speak to a parent. Besides, if one of the other kids caught on that Hunter's father was there for a reason, it might make the divide between him and the rest of the kids even more pointed.

I made my way down to Mamas to meet Zoe, who was already sitting there with a green tea in front of her when I arrived.

"Hey." I gave her a quick hug. "You all right?"

"I indulged in a glass too many of wine last night," she admitted. "So I think I'm going to avoid the champagne cocktails for now and stick to detox. How about you?"

"Yeah, I'm actually really good." I nodded excitedly. "I got an email from Hunter's father. You know, the quiet kid in my class?"

"Yeah, I think I know the one." Zoe furrowed her brow as though searching for him in her memory.

"Well, I messaged him right before you called to ask if we could have a meeting to check in on how his son was doing," I explained. "He's not bad or anything, but he seemed a little out of place compared to the rest of the kids."

"Yeah, of course," Zoe said. "Have you met them before?"

"No, that's the thing, the parents have never come to the school before," I shook my head. "Or at least as long as I've been there. That's weird, right?"

"Yeah, that's pretty weird," Zoe agreed. "Why? Did they have a reason, or do they just not turn up?"

"I think they usually have some kind of reason, but it never seems much," I admitted. "Mostly just work. In fact, I've never heard from the mother at all. We don't even have her email on file."

"Maybe she's not around," Zoe pointed out, and I furrowed my brow and leaned back in my seat. I hadn't even thought about that, but it was a strong possibility. Maybe it was just his dad around at home, and maybe that would explain his quietness. Sometimes, with single fathers, kids didn't develop the same kind of emotional literacy they did with both parents. Or maybe he was dealing with abandonment issues and didn't want to let anyone get too close to him.

"Yeah, I guess you could be right," I agreed. "Either way, I'm glad I'm going to get to meet this guy once and for all. Feels like it can only be a good thing for Hunter."

"You're a really good teacher, you know that?" Zoe reached across the table and patted my hand. She was, most of the time, this wisecracking bundle of sarcasm, but occasionally she would come out with something so sincere and so sweet that it would catch me completely off-guard and mean even more thanks to the incongruity. I smiled back at her.

"Thanks, Zoe," I replied. "You know I think that about you too, right?"

"Yeah, but I'm not the one taking time out of my weekend to take care of a kid who needs extra attention," she pointed out, and I chuckled.

"I'll probably be the one nursing the hangover the next time we go out," I warned her. "It's probably going to be a difficult meeting."

"Yeah, there's likely a reason he's been avoiding you so long," She arched an eyebrow teasingly, seeing a chance to get me shifting in my seat with nervousness. "I mean, why wouldn't he come into the school all that time? Maybe he doesn't exist. Maybe Hunter's a figment of your imagination."

"And yours," I reminded her. "Your hoodoo act doesn't work when you told me you know who he is, remember?"

"Darn," she snapped her fingers like a dastardly villain whose plan had been foiled at the last moment. "I forgot about that."

"What do you think his father is actually going to be like, though?" I wondered aloud. "I mean, he's never come in before. That's weird, right?"

"It's weird," Zoe agreed with me. "But I don't think it's automatically something to be freaked out about. It could be a lot of reasons."

"Right." I nodded, glad for her here soothing me before I dived too far down the rabbit hole of overthinking all of this.

"Or he could be a psychopath who doesn't understand human emotion and doesn't want to have to fake it in front of his son's teacher," she jibed, and I shot her a look.

"Oh, come on," I fired back. "You really want me to go in wondering if he's an android? That's going to help nothing."

"Maybe you could check for bolts and wires." She waggled her eyebrows at me. "Single father, remember?"

"We don't know that," I reminded her, but I couldn't help feeling a small flutter deep in my chest. If anything was my weakness, it was men who were good with kids. They just made me swoon. I thought they were the damn sexiest things in the world. There was nothing like seeing a big, masculine guy get down and goof around with their child, nothing like it in the world.

"Let's talk about something other than work," I suggested, and we spent the rest of the brunch talking about a book I had loaned her that she was loving and the movies coming out that month that we wanted to see. I found my mind pleasingly lifted from the worry about what was going to come in that meeting the next day. At least, until I got home.

When I opened my laptop, that email was still sitting there staring me down, and I frowned as I looked at it. I read it through again, trying to find some kind of hidden meaning in the lines, a hint of tone or indication of emotion. But that was impossible through email. This guy was brusque and to the point and wasn't trying to sugarcoat anything, which might have been good or could have been... well, could have been bad. Really bad.

As I got undressed, took my makeup off, and slipped into a bath, I found myself wondering what kind of man Hunter's father was going to be. If he hadn't made it to one meeting before this one, I had to assume he wasn't that involved with his kid's upbringing. Not that it exactly surprised me. More and more parents these days, by choice or not, had to hand over the childcare to other people, whether it was the teachers at the schools or their families and friends. I didn't blame them for that. But something about Holden, Hunter's father, gave me a different kind of vibe.

I closed my eyes, imagined him, and found my mind conjuring up the image of an old, rich man who mostly threw money at his son's upbringing to make sure it went as smoothly as possible without him getting directly involved. That was how he liked it, for sure. But at least he had agreed to come in and meet with me. That was a start, and I had to hope Zoe was wrong, and he wasn't actually a psychopath or an emotionless android in disguise.

And even if he was, I promised myself then and there, I would do everything I could to invest him in the life of his son. Hunter was a sweet kid, and he deserved the people around him to care about him, to feel as deeply as he clearly did. I smiled as I went to apply a face mask, satisfied that by this time tomorrow, I would have done some good in this young boy's life. And I would have done it without quite as many Bellinis in my system as I had right now.

5

HOLDEN

I paced back and forth outside the car for a moment, trying to gather myself. I knew I was being ridiculous, but being here at the school was stressing me out and making me feel like I was about to land in a whole lot of trouble.

"Dad, are you coming?" Hunter asked impatiently, waiting by the gate. The place was nearly quiet, except for a couple of cleaners and some janitors tending the grounds, and I knew I had to go in there and face this teacher, once and for all, to whatever had been going on in my son's life.

"Yeah, yeah, of course." I finally followed him through the gate. I couldn't believe I'd never been here before. Well, not since I enrolled Hunter, anyway. I had liked the look of the place, and he had always been well-behaved and never caused an ounce of trouble until this moment, so I'd never needed to come in. I had read the email the teacher had sent me a good few times through, trying to get a feel for how she felt about him and what exactly this meeting was about. I came up with nothing. As Hunter led me into the main school building, I watched him and found it hard to believe for an instant that he had been causing any real trouble. But I supposed I was the one who had neglected to come in here, who had tucked all the parent-teacher invites behind the clock on the mantelpiece and then forgotten about them. I had no idea how he was doing in school, and I was about to find out, for better or for worse.

I arrived at the door of the classroom he led me to and paused there for a moment as I stared at the woman I assumed was meeting me. She had her head down and was frowning at some papers in front of her, her long, deeply dark hair wrapped into a bun at the back of her head. I cleared my throat, and she looked up—and the jolt of her hazel eyes as they met mine took me by surprise, sending what felt like an electric current across my skin. She smiled and got to her feet, extending her hand to me as she approached. She had a warm, open face, a sincere smile, and I liked the way she looked at me. Made me feel warm, comfortable.

"You must be Holden," she greeted me, and I nodded.

"Autumn?" I asked, and she glanced at Hunter.

"Well, I prefer Miss Becks in this classroom most of the time, but I suppose we can let it slide for now." She winked at my son, and he grinned back. They obviously had a good rapport—that was nice to see. I couldn't help noticing how small the classroom seemed. Or maybe I had gotten a hell of a lot bigger since the last time I had stepped in a place like this. It was all decked out in bright primary colors with various wall charts delivering information about ancient peoples and distant countries and famous authors. The place had a nice feel to it, the same way it had when I had first come here to enroll Hunter.

"Thank you so much for coming in." She took her seat behind her desk at the front of the room, and I sat opposite her. Hunter pulled up a chair to join us. He had a big grin on his face, like his two worlds were colliding and he couldn't have been much happier about it.

"Of course." I shot a look at Hunter. "Are you sure we, uh, all need to be here?"

"I think it's important to keep an open line of dialogue between all parties involved in this kind of situation." She nodded seriously, and Hunter shifted in his seat.

"Am I in trouble?" he asked, and she shook her head at once.

"Not at all, Hunter," she promised him, giving him another one of her calming, sweet smiles. She was striking, and I couldn't help but notice how creamy and soft her skin looked next to the flimsy fabric of the green sweater she was wearing. She reached up to undo and redo her hair, and it briefly swept down to her waist before she gathered it up once more. I caught a whiff of her perfume, which smelled floral but not old-fashioned. It suited her somehow.

"I wanted to bring you in today so we could talk about your social life," she told him, and I raised my eyebrows.

"Is there something wrong there?" I asked. I was on the defensive, and I knew that, but that was what working in business for years had taught me—always come out swinging to defend yourself, just in case you need to. She took a deep breath and continued.

"I'm concerned that Hunter is becoming somewhat isolated from the rest of the students," she continued, addressing me. I could practically feel my son deflating next to me like someone had stuck a pin in him and let the air out. I wanted to cover his ears and demand that she shut her mouth, but that wasn't going to achieve anything. I needed to hear her out. I just wasn't sure my son did as well.

"And what do you mean by that?" I asked, trying to keep my tone cool and collected. Why on earth had she invited Hunter in to hear all of this? I mean, I assumed she knew better than me, but still, it felt cruel to drag him through this pointed attack on his character.

"I mean that Hunter sometimes has trouble connecting with the other kids his own age," she went on calmly, obviously oblivious to the fact that my back was up over what she had told me. "Would you say that's right, Hunter?"

"I don't know what to talk to them about," he replied, his voice small. "I didn't realize it was a bad thing."

"It's not a bad thing," she assured him, and I wanted to reach over and give him a big hug. I wanted to take him out of there and leave and not look back and tell this woman she could go fuck herself if she thought it was all right to talk to my son that way. But I had to sit there and listen to her and take it, that it was my natural reaction as a parent not to want to hear anything wrong about my child. I had to overcome that. I had to prove to her and anyone else who might hear about this meeting that I could handle myself in the face of this.

"No, it's not a bad thing," I followed up, looking at him intently. I turned back to her. "So what is this about? You think we need to address this?"

"I don't want Hunter to feel like a social outcast from the rest of his group," she told me, and the word immediately sent a flurry of irritation through me. Outcast? Who was she to use that word to describe him? She barely knew him. She didn't know him like I did, that was for damn sure. Outcast? The word ran through my mind like it had been lit up in neon, and I inhaled and exhaled slowly to bring myself back down to Earth. I had to remind myself that this woman had my son's best interests at heart, no matter what it might have seemed like to me. She cared about him. It was her job to care. This was what she thought was best, and I should trust her on that.

"And I wanted to see how he was doing outside of school." She pressed her fingertips together and looked at me over the top of them expectantly. I blinked a couple of times, and for some reason, every interaction I'd ever had with my son dropped out of the back of my mind just like that. There was something about the way she looked at me, those hazel eyes burning into mine, that made it harder to think straight than I would have cared to admit to.

"He's going...." I looked at Hunter, and I realized that I couldn't, for the life of me, remember what he had been up to outside of school in the last few months. I had tried to set him up with a couple of clubs—football, drama, that kind of thing but he had seemed reluctant to take any of them on or take any interest in spending much time outside the house. He always seemed bright and sparky when he was around me or Raymond, but he couldn't have us be his only friends. He needed children his own age to connect with, that much was obvious.

"Hunter does really well with me," I told her. "And I have a close friend with a family of his own who Hunter gets on very well with."

"Oh?" Autumn turned to Hunter and smiled interestedly. "Do they have children?"

"They just had a little girl," Hunter gushed, and I grinned when I heard the excitement in his voice. "They said they might let me babysit her sometime."

"But they don't have any children around your age?" She furrowed her brow, and he shook his head. She nodded, and I could see her making an internal note of the information. I shifted in my seat once more. I wanted to know what she was thinking. Usually, I could get a good read on people pretty quickly—years of working in business would do that for you—but she was a different kind of person than the ones I was used to dealing with and I was having a hard time seeing inside her head.

"I think it's great that you get on so well with your dad's friends." She smiled at him again, but this time, it looked more indulgent than anything else. I felt my skin prickle once more, but this time, it was annoyance more than anything else.

"What about your mom's friends?" she asked, and at once I knew I had to put a stop to things there. Hunter froze in his seat, where he had been fidgeting back and forth for the last ten minutes, and he looked to me, clearly expecting an answer of some kind. My heart twisted in pain as I watched him. I knew he was asking me, without words, what the hell his answer to that question should be. Because he didn't have a mother, never had, and I tried to keep the conversation about her to a minimum till I could properly express to my son that her leaving had nothing to do with the person he was and that he should never blame himself for that. But now, here was this teacher, swinging in and talking about her as though she didn't give a damn about our situation. Well, I wasn't going to take a moment more of it. I was fucking done with this.

I got to my feet and crouched down so I could look Hunter in the eye.

"Will you give us a minute?" I asked him, and he nodded, shooting a look at his teacher as though pondering for a second which authority figure he should obey. He went with me. It was the right choice. I watched until he was out of the room and had closed the door behind him, and then I turned to the woman who had caused all this trouble in the first place. Planting my hands on the table, I glared down at her and found her steadily meeting my gaze in return. She didn't defer, didn't look away, and somehow that sent anger flaring through me with even more passion than it had been before. She clearly didn't think she'd done anything at all wrong. Well, I was happy to dissuade her of that. Because nobody got to talk to my son about his mother other than me—and certainly not this schoolteacher who clearly had no idea where the line between appropriate and inappropriate lay.

6

AUTUMN

As soon as Hunter stepped out of the room, it was as though something had snapped inside Holden. I could see it go, my eyes widening as he turned his attention back to me, rounding on me with an anger I wasn't sure I had warranted.

"What's wrong?" I asked him, trying to keep my cool and failing. My voice was high and squeaky, as though someone had pierced me and now I was leaking gas like an old balloon.

"You cannot speak to my son about those things," he told me angrily. I furrowed my brow and shook my head.

"What things?"

"You know what I'm talking about," he told me. "You can't describe him as some kind of... as some kind of social outcast straight to his face. How do you think that makes him feel?"

"Holden, we like to include children every step of the way when it comes to their own education and school experience—" I started reciting the words that I had gone over with the head teacher when I had first started work here, but they didn't seem like enough. Even coming out of my mouth then and there, they sounded insincere, fake.

"Don't start with that." Holden shook his head again. He pushed his hand through his hair, agitated, and I wondered if he was right. Should I have kept this between us? Well, whatever, it was far too late for that now, and we had to run with what we had.

"I didn't mean to make you or your son feel uncomfortable," I told him. "I understand that this kind of thing can be difficult to hear, especially if you're not aware of the problem, but we hoped that Hunter would be able to help us resolve the issue and move forward."

"What issue?" he snapped back. "He's just quiet, that's all, and you're acting like he's a pariah."

I didn't say anything. I didn't want to confirm to this man that his son had been existing on the outside edges of this place for a long time now, longer than even I would have cared to think about. He seemed to be able to read it written on my face, and something between anger and upset twisted his face. Well, I had been wrong about one thing. This man certainly did give a shit about his son, even if I was the one getting chewed out for trying to help.

"It's not like that," I offered in return. I had never been the most socially smooth person I knew, and this high-pressure situation was exactly the time that I would have liked to make a silly joke or thrown in a little gag to break the tension. I knew that was the last thing this situation needed. I had to hold myself together, act professional, and get rid of this guy.

"So what is it like, then?" he demanded. "My son doesn't have a lot of friends, so you drag him in here to make him feel like a freak for it?"

I hated the way he was talking to me. This was my classroom, and I was meant to be the one in charge, and yet here he was coming at me like I was another errant child he had to take in hand. I wanted to remind him of that fact, but it wasn't going to get me anywhere. Best to sit back, try to detach, and hope for the best.

"Hunter is a sweet boy," I told him. "You've done a good job raising him. But he needs people around him who are his own age, people he can relate to at a contemporary level. Not just you and your friends."

I shouldn't have added in the last bit. I knew that as soon as it came out of my mouth. He rolled his eyes and shook his head.

"Maybe he's too mature for all the kids in this place," he remarked. "Maybe he's too adult, and that's why they don't want to spend time with him."

I fell silent. I wanted to point out that this guy was hardly acting mature right now, throwing a tantrum because things weren't going his way, but I figured it was only going to make things worse. If there was one thing I understood well from my time working as a teacher, it was that to treat adults and kids the same was to invite a deep and abiding hatred from adults who hated being talked down to. And right now, I needed to quell this situation before it got any further out of hand.

"Maybe that's the case," I agreed diplomatically, hoping that would be enough to calm him down. "I was simply concerned and wished to make sure there was nothing more going on that I could help the two of you address."

"Why are you talking like that? You sound like a robot." He shook his head. And he was right, I did. It was the only way for me to keep my cool right then and there, the only hope in hell I had of not losing my shit in his general direction. If I could convince myself I was cool and calm and far removed from this, I wouldn't freak out and kick him out of my classroom before we had a chance to resolve this issue with Hunter. Because that was what this was all about at the end of the day, making sure that little boy got the best of this situation, no matter what that looked like for him.

"And another thing," Holden was pacing back and forth across the carpeted section of the floor. "You don't bring up Hunter's mother with him ever again, all right?"

I stared at him for a moment, waiting for him to elaborate. That wasn't the kind of statement people had a habit of dumping into the middle of conversations. It needed a little context.

"All right?" he pressed me again. I glanced down at his hand and saw no wedding ring, so if he and Hunter's mother had ever been married, they certainly weren't any longer. That was interesting. I

wondered what her deal was. Where she had gone to, and why had
even referencing her been enough to send Holden shooting through
the roof? Whatever it was, if it was going to cool the situation, then I
was happy to give him what he wanted.

"All right." I held my hands up. "I'm sorry. I didn't realize I was
overstepping any mark. I'll bear it in mind for the future."

"Thank you," he sighed, and he rubbed his hands over his face. I
could tell this meeting wasn't going to get anywhere further. He was
stubborn, stuck in the ground, and anything that even hinted at the
notion his son might not be perfectly happy and well-developed
seemed like it was enough to set him off. Maybe because he was a
single father who had received enough of that criticism to last a lifetime? I knew how cruel people could be to those around them raising
their children differently, even in a place as allegedly progressive as
Portland.

"Perhaps we could reschedule this meeting," I suggested to him,
pulling out my calendar, "The two of us could talk without Hunter if
it makes you more comfortable. Or—"

"No, I'm not coming in here again if this is the only issue." He
shook his head firmly. "I thought my son was beating up other kids or
something like that. He's fine, everyone around him is fine, and I
don't see the issue here."

"The issue is that his social development isn't keeping up with
that of the kids around him," I argued back. "As a parent, you should
be looking for ways to address that."

I saw something inside him give as soon as those words came out
of my mouth, and I had a feeling that I'd said the wrong thing. Then
he stalked away from my table, as though he couldn't even bear to
look at me.

"And you're his teacher," he reminded me. "That means you teach
him. And that's it."

I fell silent. I realized my hands were clenched to fists at my sides,
which was utterly ridiculous. What was I going to do, throw myself
across the room and start beating on his chest like I was the heroine
of a Regency novel? I crossed my arms over my chest and took a few

long, deep breaths to calm myself, to remind myself that this was my place and that I was the one in control here, no question about it, no doubt.

"Fine," I told him, not giving a shit about the petulance in my voice. "I'll just teach him."

He turned to look at me, and I was suddenly taken aback by the look on his face. It wasn't anger, not this time, but something else entirely, something I was quite sure he had been trying to smother and hide from me this whole time. Exhaustion, maybe, or something that went a little deeper than that. A sadness at something we had been talking about. Maybe Hunter's mother, maybe the way he was developing, but he looked as though he wanted to crawl into bed and stay there for a good long while.

"Thank you." He said, and just like that, the expression dropped, and he was back to being that carefully curated, aloof dude who had walked in here in the first place. The one who didn't seem to give much of a shit about his son's wellbeing. He headed out of the room and left me standing there, and I took a good long while to get my breathing back to normal, feeling like I had wasted my time and his.

"Hey." I heard a familiar voice and turned to find Zoe poking her head around the door.

"What are you doing here?" I blurted, and she shrugged.

"Needed to pick up some papers that I left on Friday, and I remembered you had that meeting today," she told me. "Was that him walking out of here? He looked pissed."

"Yeah, that was him," I sighed, and I leaned back against the table. "It didn't exactly go the way I wanted it to."

"No, I could see that from his expression." Zoe raised her eyebrows. "What the hell happened in here? What was so bad?"

"He was defensive." I shook my head. "Didn't want to hear about anything wrong with his son and when I brought up Hunter's mother, he lost it."

Zoe fell silent for a moment, and she scanned my face. I could tell she was reading me, the way she had always been able to.

"I think you should just leave it, Autumn," she told me firmly. I glanced up at her.

"Just one more email," I suggested. "Just to make sure we didn't get off on the wrong foot—"

"You got off on the whole wrong damn leg judging by the look on his face when he walked out of here," she pointed out. "Don't make it any worse than it already is, Autumn. You don't want Hunter to feel like he can't come to you with shit, and if his dad hates you, that's going to be the case."

"Yeah, you're right." I slumped back against the desk once more. "I just... maybe I could do more."

"I'm giving you permission to leave it all the way alone," Zoe told me. "No, I'm ordering you to. Give it a rest. The last thing you need is to be juggling bullshit from someone who won't even listen to you with everything else."

"Yeah, you're right," I agreed. "I'll leave it alone. I will."

But in the back of my mind, something was ticking, and I wasn't sure it was going to be quite that easy.

7

HOLDEN

"Hi, is this Holden?"

"Yes, it is!" I replied, and I instantly cringed at how overly perky my voice sounded. Did I really have to say it like that? I hated the way I sounded. But I figured it was better to sound a little too keen than a little too removed, so I would roll with it.

"Great to hear from you," Andrea, the CFO of the company that I had canceled the meeting with earlier in the week, greeted me warmly. She had a calm, relaxed voice, and I tried to tap into some of that peacefulness for myself. I was coming to this interview on the back foot, no two ways about it, but I had to convince them that I was worth it no matter how much of an inconvenience I was to them. Which was harder than it sounded.

"I'm so sorry I had to cancel our meeting earlier in the week," I told her. "I had an emergency that had to do with my son, and I couldn't get out of it."

I wanted to roll my eyes when I thought back to what that emergency had been. The way she had been talking in the email, I had been sure Hunter was building tiny little shivs out of sticks and leaves and using them to shank other schoolchildren. As it turned out, he was a little quiet, and she was worried he wasn't spending enough time with people his own age. Which was crazy, because he went to school, didn't he? He was surrounded by kids his own age all the time. She was just talking out of her ass, trying to interfere in his life to seem like she was a good teacher when she really wanted to exert some power and stir the pot a little. Maybe she wanted to delve into my son's personal life for her own gossipy interest.

"I completely understand," Andrea replied, and she sounded sincere. "I have two of my own, six and nine, and they're constantly making it nearly impossible to run a business."

"Oh, what do you have?" I asked conversationally.

"Boy and a girl," she replied, and I could hear the smile in her voice as she spoke. "Boy's older, though he doesn't act it."

"My son is that exact age right now," I remarked. "They're starting to turn into little people, aren't they?"

"For better or for worse," she agreed, and I chuckled.

"So, I want to discuss the proposed contract," I told her, moving on to the task at hand now that I had papered over the cracks that had been left by my cancelation of the meeting. "I understand that it might be easier to do this in person, but if you have your computer there, I can send you everything I think you need to see."

"Honestly, Holden, we're quite impressed with the proposal you put forward," she told me. "We don't need too many more details. Just a time frame and a budget, and then we can get started with the details of the contract for you."

I closed my eyes and punched the air. She couldn't see me, so it was fine.

"That sounds great," I agreed. "Let me run through everything again, so we know that we're both on the same page."

"Never hurts," she agreed, and I launched into my rundown of everything the project was going to be from my perspective. I hadn't half-assed this, knowing I had a point to prove and that I needed to convince them that wherever I was in the world, I could take on this project and do it better than anyone else they could hire. Thank God, they seemed to actually believe me, and after an hour, Andrea was making approving noises down the phone and agreeing with every-thing that was coming out of my mouth.

"Honestly, Holden, that sounds perfect," she agreed. "I'll pass all this along to the legal department and get them to draw up a contract, and hopefully we can start sooner rather than later, huh?"

"Hopefully," I agreed. We finished up the call, and I switched off the phone and dumped it into my pocket, closing my eyes and collapsing into my seat. It hadn't been as bad as doing the presenta-tion in person might have been, but I still felt as though that had taken it out of me. Working on the project was one thing—I could pull that off, no question, no problem—but hashing out all the details was the hard part.

Especially when my mind was lingering over that meeting I'd had with the teacher. I shouldn't have been letting it get to me. I had given her a piece of my mind, and I stood by that, genuinely believing everything that had come out of my mouth that day. She couldn't just drag my son in front of her like he'd done something wrong and then speak to him like he was some kind of socially stunted freak. And she couldn't expect me to stand by and take it. And she for sure couldn't bring up his waste-of-space mother in front of him, not when I had fought so hard to make sure he never felt like anything other than a complete, loved person despite the absence of the woman who birthed him. That was what had seriously pissed me off. She had swung straight into our personal space without a second thought, and I didn't put up so well with that. She was going to learn to keep her nose out of our business. God willing, that would be the last time I ever heard from her.

I headed downstairs, where Raymond was waiting with his daughter and Hunter. I had offered to babysit for the evening so that he and Olivia could go out, provided he was able to keep an eye on Hunter while I was making this call. I grinned when I saw him. She was asleep in his arms, peaceful and pretty, and I could see the relief painted all over his face.

"She's sleeping, so we're being quiet," Hunter told me, lifting a finger to his lips. I mimicked the same motion and nodded in agreement.

"Right." I headed up to them. "You want to hand her over, or you want to wait a little longer?"

"I'll wait a little longer," Raymond remarked, a little gruffly, and I could tell he was trying to play the big tough father but was enchanted by his little girl so much that he could hardly keep a straight face.

"Can I go upstairs and read for a bit?" Hunter tapped my arm, and I ruffled his hair.

"Yeah. Be down for dinner," I told him. "An hour at the most."

"Okay!" he called back down the stairs, and both Raymond and I winced and checked to see if the baby had woken, but she was still passed out.

"What did you do, take her for a six-mile hike?" I remarked. "She's really out for the count."

"I know, thank God," he agreed. "How did your call go?"

"Yeah, pretty well." I shrugged, taking a bottle of water from the fridge and cracking it open. "How about you? How are you doing?"

"Looking forward to getting out from underneath this papoose for a while." He grinned. "Was that call the meeting you skipped in New York?"

"Yeah." I grimaced. "Though now that I look back on it, I don't think I needed to cancel that meeting at all."

"What do you mean?"

"I mean, I went along to meet with that teacher thinking Hunter was beating up other kids or something, and she tells me he's a little lonely." I shook my head. "Can you believe that? She said that in front of him. Then she was asking about his mother like that's relevant to anything in the entire world."

Raymond furrowed his brow and shook his head.

"That is a little weird," he agreed diplomatically. "But maybe she was trying to help?"

"I know that's what she thought she was doing," I conceded. "But that's not how it comes across, you know? Feels like gossip."

"I'm sure it wasn't that," he replied firmly. He fell silent for a moment, eyeing me.

"What?"

"I was just wondering," he said before taking a deep breath. "Have you actually dated anyone since Karla?"

"Hell no." I waved my hand and shook my head. "I have no interest in it either. I'm too busy with the business and Hunter and—"

"It seems like the business is in a good place," he pointed out, cutting through my empty talking in a way that he had plenty of practice doing. "And Hunter spends plenty of time away at school these days. You don't think you should consider getting back out there?"

I sighed heavily. I sort of knew that he was right, that I couldn't spend the rest of my life hiding from romance in my work and in my son, but it had been so long since I had dated anyone even casually that even the notion of it was unsettling to me. What did dating look like now? What did it look like now that I had more money than ever before? What did it look like with a son in tow? I didn't know the answers to any of those questions, but I had a feeling I didn't necessarily want to hear them either.

"Look, I'm not saying you have to run off and get married or something," Raymond continued. "But it might do you and Hunter good if you got out there a little bit more, had a life outside him now that he's old enough to handle it."

"He's nine years old, Raymond. He's not exactly about to put down a mortgage on his first place," I pointed out. He chuckled.

"You know what I'm saying," he replied firmly. "Give you and him a little space, and you never know what could happen. Could make things better between you."

I fell silent for a long moment. He could be right. I hated to admit it, but he could be right.

"Besides, if you did end up meeting someone nice," he went on, "it wouldn't do any harm for Hunter to have a woman in his life, don't you think?"

"I suppose not." I shook my head. "But where the hell am I meant to go about meeting these women? In the line at the grocery store?"

"Hmm." He cocked his head at me, clearly thinking. "Oh, Olivia mentioned to me that one of her friends is looking for a decent blind date candidate. I think you fit the bill."

"A blind date?" I laughed. "I don't think I've heard about anyone going on one of those in years."

"So maybe it's time to bring them back into style," Raymond suggested. "What do you say? You up for it?"

"I guess so." I laughed. "I can't believe I'm agreeing to this. If it's a terrible date, I'm holding Olivia personally responsible. I hope she knows that."

"I'll make sure she does," he agreed. "Say, Friday night? I'll let you know the details as soon as I get them from Olivia."

"Works for me." I reached out for the baby in his arms. "Come on, hand her over. It's time you went out."

"I guess so." He handed her to me a little reluctantly and then grinned. "Thanks for doing this, buddy."

"Thanks for getting me that date," I replied, and he slapped me on the shoulder and headed out the door. I was left wondering if I had just agreed to the date that was going to change my life—for better or for worse.

8

AUTUMN

"**A**utumn!"

I glanced up as soon as I heard her voice. She was excited about something, obviously. It seemed as though this excitement was somewhat aimed at me.

"Hey, Zoe," I greeted her, yawning as I sat up from the table. I had stayed late that day to finish up building the grading curve for the assignments this year, and I felt as though my eyes were going to pop out and roll from my head. I could see a bunch of squiggly lines and numbers in front of me, and I had a sinking feeling that it was all wrong and I'd have to go back and start all over again sooner rather than later.

"What's up with you?" She frowned, stopping dead as she looked at me, and then her gaze lowered to the pages in front of me. She grimaced with a sympathy that could only come from someone who had suffered through the same agony plenty of times before herself.

"Oh, you're doing the grading curves." She sighed. "I'm still putting mine off. I can't face it right now."

"It wouldn't be so bad if we didn't have to wait to receive all the numbers from the different schools by mail," I groaned, pointing to the stack of envelopes on my desk. "I know this is the only way they can do it securely, but surely there has to be some way to actually make this possible without spending hours wanting to throw myself out a window."

"Yeah, I feel like they should have come up with something automated by now," she agreed. "It's crazy."

I could tell that, despite her attempts to commiserate with me, there was something she wanted to share with me. She was nearly hopping from foot to foot in front of me waiting to get the words out, and she looked more like one of my kids than a teacher.

"I have something I have to tell you," she announced and then bit her lip. I looked at her expectantly.

"All right." I waved my hand. "What is it?"

"You remember when you said you would let me set you up on a blind date?" she asked, spreading her hands wide as though she was handing me the best gift she had ever given.

"Nope." I shook my head, casting my mind back and trying to dig that memory up. I came up a fresh blank. My mind was so full of trying to get this fucking grade curve done that it felt as though every other memory had slipped out of my mind all at once.

"Well, you did," she told me, and I giggled. Zoe had such a forthright way about her, there was no arguing with her when she got an idea like this one into her head.

"All right," I agreed. "Say that I did. What exactly has come of this zany scheme of yours?"

"I got a call from a friend of mine," she told me, "and she said there's a single guy in her friend group who's looking to get back out on the dating scene."

"Back out?" I cocked an eyebrow. "And what exactly was keeping him from it in the first place?"

"I don't remember." Zoe waved her hand. "It's not important."

"I think it might be a little," I protested, but she waved her hand again, dismissing my concerns.

"All you need to know is that he's well-off, and he has a great job, according to Olivia," She went on. "He sounds amazing, to be honest."

"So why don't you snap him up yourself?"

"Because I'm such a sweet and generous best friend that I wanted to share my romantic success with you, of course," she replied, as though it should have been obvious.

"You're serious about this," I said, getting up from the table and going to grab some of my stuff.

"Yeah, why wouldn't I be?" She shot me a confused look.

"Because it sounds like something out of a bad sitcom plot, that's why." I shook my head. "I mean, you really think I'm going to go out with some guy I've never met before because you've heard from someone else that he's pretty cool?"

"Oh, come on, it could be fun!" she protested. "I'll have my phone with me that whole evening, so if you're having a miserable time, you can text me and keep me entertained."

"So what you're saying is that no matter what way this goes down, it's all for your entertainment," I said, and she nodded enthusiastically.

"Isn't that what you live your whole life for?" she teased, and I rolled my eyes and shook my head.

"You know, you're damn lucky I don't actually remember that conversation well enough to know whether or not I did agree to go on this date or not." I stabbed my finger in the air. The triumphant smile spread over her face already. Zoe always knew when she had me, and she had me right then and there, no matter how I might have felt about it.

"Honestly, it'll do you some good," she assured me. "When was the last time you were actually on a date?"

"Uh." I cast my mind back and came up with a straight blank. "There was that guy, the one I met at the wedding? We went out for drinks that one time."

"And you said he was the most boring man you'd ever met," she reminded me. "That was nearly a year ago! Come on, you can't spend your entire life in the classroom working on grading curves."

I sighed deeply. I knew she was right, and she knew that I knew.

But that didn't mean I was any keener to get up and out of here, just because she was intent on twisting my arm.

"Can you cancel it?" I asked hopefully, and she shook her head.

"I mean, I could, but you could never go on a date with anyone I knew again." She sighed and shook her head, as though it was a great tragedy. I pressed my lips together and looked at her for a long time, hoping I could change her mind.

"And when exactly is this date?" I asked, already exhausted by the thought of actually spending an evening out on the town and not hiding out at my place with a beer or two and some bad TV.

"Tomorrow night." She spread her hands wide again, and my eyebrows shot up.

"Wow, you're not giving me a lot of time to get used to this, are you?"

"Well, you don't want to overthink it," she explained smoothly. I chuckled.

"You thought that if you booked it close enough to the day, I couldn't back out?" I asked her incredulously, and she shrugged and nodded.

"Well, you're in it now, aren't you?" she pointed out, and I pulled a face. I wished I could have proven her wrong, been a little less predictable, but maybe this was what I needed.

"Fine, I'll go," I agreed. "But if you ever feel the need to set something like this up again, you let me know first, all right?"

"That's half the fun," she replied, and she gave me a quick hug before she headed to the door. "You're going to have a great time with this guy. I know it."

"I better," I shot back, mostly kidding but also a little not. "I'm giving up my Friday night for him."

"It's going to be worth it, trust me," she told me, grinning widely, and with that, she ducked out of the room and left me staring at the pile of tests I needed to work into the grade curve average. Suddenly, my brain felt a little overfull, and I pushed them away and went about tidying the classroom a little to distract myself.

She had meant well, setting me up on a date like this. It had been a long time since I had so much as left the house in heels, and I knew that she was trying to help, to find me someone to get my mojo back. But the truth was, it had been gone so long that I wasn't even sure I remembered what it felt like to have it in the first place.

I had dated a little in high school, less in college, and then, as I had come out into the real world, I had found myself less than impressed with every option put in front of me. I didn't want to be a bitch, but most of the guys I met seemed utterly mediocre. They hadn't achieved anything with their lives and didn't seem to want to. I wasn't talking about needing a mansion and a high-flying international career, just someone with a little ambition who wasn't afraid to share it with me. I worked my ass off and loved my job and went through a small collection of men to whom that notion seemed impossibly far removed. Why would I chase after someone who was so distant from what I wanted, who couldn't so much as wrap his head around the thought of me building a career from the ground up, doing something I loved?

Then there were those, of course, who treated me as though I was a step below them because of my job. They seemed to think elementary school teaching was all about wearing bright colors and smiling all the time and being able to count to ten and identify a triangle. No matter how much I tried to convince these guys there was more to my job than that, they would patronizingly nod and smile and act like I had a hobby instead of a career. They didn't have kids, so they didn't get how serious this work was, how much it took out of me, the skills it required to keep your classroom from descending into utter chaos.

And sure, it would have been nice if this guy my best friend had set me up with was different from them. It would have been nice to spend an evening with a man who respected my work and respected his own. I would have enjoyed a date with someone who seemed like a grown-ass adult for a change, instead of all these boys in men costumes who I'd found myself sitting opposite of at every single date the last five years. But I wasn't holding out a lot of hope. Why would I? I had already been let down enough times as it was, and if I knew anything, it was that keeping my hopes firmly on the low side was going to lead to less disappointment.

I turned my attention back to the grade curves and started working on them once more, letting myself get lost in the fiddly, irritating numbers once more. At least they would probably be more engaging than the man that I was due to go out with the following night.

9

HOLDEN

I checked myself in the mirror for what felt like the thousandth time since I had put on my suit that evening. I felt as though my brain was going to come leaking out of my ears, it was running so fast to try to make sense of what was going on.

"You look fine, Dad." My son appeared at the door, and I stopped and smiled at him in the mirror.

"Thanks." I turned to him and sighed heavily. "I just haven't done this in so long."

"Are you nearly ready to go?" Hunter pointed to the clock next to the mirror. "I think we need to leave soon."

"Yeah, we do," I agreed. "Thanks for reminding me."

With that, I hustled Hunter into the car and started to drive him over to Raymond's house. He had agreed to look after Hunter for the evening while I went out on my date. I had tried to talk him out of it, tried to tell him I needed a little more time to get used to the idea of dating once more, but he had told me cheerfully that if I had too much time to overthink this, I would only find a way to talk myself out of it and he wasn't going to let that happen. I mean, he was right, but I didn't like him pointing it out that way.

So I had left work early on Friday evening and returned home to shower and change into a nice suit. They had at least let me pick the restaurant, and I had chosen somewhere that was familiar to me and that I liked well enough but not so much that it would be ruined if this date wound up taking a turn for the worse. Which I assumed at some point it was going to.

"Are you excited?" Hunter asked curiously as he sat in the passenger seat next to me. I shrugged.

"Not really," I admitted. I wanted to be excited. I really did, and it was sweet that my son wanted me to feel the same way, but I was more nervous than anything else. What the fuck was I supposed to do on a date, after all? How long had it been since I had gone out with a woman? I had done a damn good job hiding out in my business all this time, and I liked it there, frankly. I didn't do dating, didn't do stuff like this.

But Hunter was excited for me. That much was obvious. That was what had kept me from calling up Raymond and telling him to forget about the date once and for all. I could tell my son was excited at the thought of having a woman around the house, even if he seemed to have some misconceptions about how quickly things would happen after the date tonight. All those movies he'd watched over the years had convinced him that we were going to get married on the spot if we liked each other, and nothing I was saying seemed to dissuade him of that fact. He had asked tons of questions about her, not entirely grasping the notion of what a blind date actually was, and I knew that he wanted nothing more than to come along with me and meet her for himself. Which was sweet, in its own way, but also the last thing I needed right now.

I dropped him off with Raymond, and he gave me a quick hug before he sent me on my way.

"Have a good time, Dad," he told me, and my heart melted a little. I nearly called this whole thing off to spend the night with Hunter instead. Then I saw the look Raymond was giving me over the top of his head, and I knew if I didn't go, Raymond was going to drag me there himself. So I turned and made my way to the restaurant and tried to ignore how much my palms were sweating and how deeply I was hoping I would get the call that she had canceled and that, oh well, we would just have to forget all this for tonight.

What had my last date actually been? I cast my mind back and tried to dredge up something and came up with a dead nothing. Before Hunter had been born, it wasn't like I went on anything as serious as a date. You just met up with someone at some party or a bar or a bowling alley, and if you liked each other, you started dating. You didn't whisk people out on full-blown dinners out. Nobody had the money for that, least of all me.

I fidgeted in my seat. Could the people around me tell how out of place I was here? A few other couples surrounded us, and I noticed for the first time that this place was seriously romantic, dim lighting, white tables, glimmering gold accents on the walls. Maybe she would get in here and think I was about to propose to her.

I leaned back and looked around, trying to imagine the kind of woman Raymond and Olivia might have picked out for me. Kind, probably—that would be the first port of call. Back when I was younger, around the time I'd done this last, I likely would have put hot at the top of the list of things I needed from a potential partner. Now with my son in the picture, I needed someone with the patience and kindness to handle a kid who could sometimes retreat into himself.

They hadn't told me much about her, just that she would be wearing a brown jacket and that I would know her when I saw her, which wasn't exactly helping to stem the wild anxiety running through my system at that moment. What if she walked in and I was looking at my phone, and she rolled her eyes and turned heel to walk out of there? What if her main criterion was "hot," and she looked at me and decided I wasn't up to her standards? I wasn't sure my ego could take that. What if she had chickened out and was right now sitting at home with a tub of ice cream on her lap, thanking her lucky stars that she didn't go out on that stupid blind date her friends had set her up on...?

And like that, my nerves went. I had spent the last ten years making risky business decisions to keep my work afloat, but this, somehow, was far too much for me. I reached for my coat and ignored the waiter heading in my direction to take my drink order. I just wanted to be left alone and to retreat from this place in peace.

That, of course, was when I saw her.

Not the woman I was due to go on the date with, of course. No, that would have been far too easy. No, I laid eyes on someone I recognized—and about the last person on Earth I wanted to see at that moment.

I sank back into my seat when I saw Autumn, my son's teacher, for the first time. My pride wouldn't allow me to have her catch me booking it out of there. She might think I'd been stood up, and for some reason, the notion of that made me bristle with annoyance. I could get a date. I would prove it to her. She could watch me on a date with some smart, sophisticated, beautiful woman that my friends had picked out for me. See how she liked that.

I had to admit she looked good as she paused just through the door and scanned the restaurant, looking for someone—was she on a blind date too? If she was, whoever was here for her was going to be pleased with what they got. She was dressed in a deep green dress that hit above the knee, showing off her shapely legs and giving her a generous cleavage to boot. Her red hair was pulled up into a messy bun, but a few artful tendrils had escaped and were framing her face. Her lips were dark, a berry red, and I wanted to sink my teeth into them. I swiftly looked away from her, reminding myself that she wasn't who I was here to see. She was just in the same restaurant at the same time, and it was nothing more than a coincidence—

Then it hit me like ice-cold water dumped over my head. I slowly turned back to look at her and noticed the hue of the jacket she was handing off to the cloakroom guy. Brown. A deep, unmistakable chocolate brown. And she had been looking around the restaurant when she'd come in, as though she'd been searching for someone. It had struck me then that she looked as though she were on a blind date. But there was no way in hell she could be on a blind date with me, could there?

I sat there, frozen at the table, as she looked around the room once more, narrowing her eyes as though trying to pick someone out. Then she saw me, sitting at the table by myself, and I saw the same look of horror, shock, and the desperate urge to race out the door and not look back pass across her face. I got to my feet as she came toward me, and she planted her hands on her hips and stared at me from the other side of the table.

"Please don't tell me that you're here on a blind date," she groaned, and I nodded slowly.

"Afraid so," I replied. "Our stupid friends, huh?"

"Our stupid friends," she agreed and shook her head. We both stood there for a long moment. What in the name of holy hell were we supposed to do now? I wanted to leave, to call the night a bust and chew Raymond out for it later, and to tell him I would need the full name, job title, and preferably social security details of anyone he wanted to set me up with in the future. Not that I was going to exactly be leaping at the chance to take on another blind date after this one had exploded in my face within the first five minutes. I should have gotten up to leave as soon as I had felt the inclination the first time around. Sure, I would have seemed like an ass for standing her up, but at least it would have been better than sitting across the table from a woman I knew didn't like me, from a woman who had dared question my parenting skills to my face a few days before.

"Well, I'm going to get out of here." I went to grab my phone where I had left it on the table. "Sorry to have wasted your time—"

"No, don't go." She cut me off before I could go any further, and I looked up at her, curious to find sincerity in her voice.

"You don't want to do this date, do you?" I asked, raising my eyebrows. I would have been stunned if she'd wanted anything other than to see the back of me.

"Sit down for a minute, will you?" She pointed to the chair opposite hers. "There's something I need to talk to you about."

I eyed her for a moment longer and then carefully sat down on my seat, right at the edge, as though I could leap up and run off at any moment if things took a turn for the worse. But, as I sat there and looked at this woman sitting opposite me and remembered how beautiful she looked when she walked in, I wavered. Maybe our friends hadn't done such a terrible job after all.

10

AUTUMN

I sat opposite Holden, staring at him from across the table, and wondered how the hell I was going to phrase this so I wasn't going to sound like a complete crazy person.

"I can't believe this is happening." He shook his head once more, leaning back in his seat. "Of all the people in the city...."

"And they stick you with the one you never want to see again," I filled in the blanks for him.

"Hey, I never said that." He held his hands up defensively. "I was planning on avoiding the school till Hunter grew out of your class, that's all."

The barest flicker of a smile passed over his face as he spoke, and I knew that was my way in.

"You know, I wanted to apologize for that day," I admitted, running my hands through my hair, knowing that I was messing up the careful updo I'd worked on half the evening getting right. I supposed it didn't even matter now. It wasn't like I was trying to look hot for this guy.

"Really?" He seemed surprised.

"Yeah, I do actually admit when I'm wrong sometimes," I replied.

"Like, for example, I know now that I was wrong to agree to this date."

He laughed. It was a good sound, and I liked it, despite myself.

"But look, I didn't act as professionally as I might have wanted," I went on. "And if I had a chance to do it again, I would change things, for sure. So I'm sorry about that. I really am."

"Thanks." He nodded, and I could tell it meant a lot to him to hear those words come out of my mouth.

"I'm not the most..." I searched for the words and figured we had already long overstepped the marks of pretending to be socially perfect. I sighed and fiddled with my hair again. "I'm not the most socially graceful person in the world," I admitted. "I get that. And sometimes I can get taken over by doing what I think is right before approaching it in the way that's actually going to help, you know what I mean?"

"I think I do," he said with a nod. He paused for a moment, looked at me, and then spoke again. I couldn't help but notice how much softer his eyes looked this time around, now that they weren't all burning with anger aimed squarely at me. His suit was nice too—expensive-looking, just like the rest of him.

"I appreciate where you were coming from," he told me. "I know you wanted the best for my son, and anyone who feels that way is all right in my book."

"Good." I smiled, and my stomach grumbled right then. I looked down at the menu.

"Look, if I told you I was going to pay my own way tonight, would you mind if we ate here?" I suggested. "Not a date, I mean. I just don't want to go home and cook, and I could use the company if you're willing to give it to me."

He paused for a moment, and a smile curled up the corners of his lips. He had a good smile, genuine and broad like it was filling him from the toes up.

"You know, that sounds pretty good," he admitted, and he reached for his menu. "I like the food here a lot."

"You chose this place?" I looked around, taking in the sheer expense of this restaurant. "You must be pretty well-off to afford here."

"I do all right." He shrugged, and I clapped my hand over my mouth and shook my head.

"Oh my God, that's so rude of me," I gushed. "I'm sorry, I didn't mean to be—"

"Hey, it's okay," He held his hand up and chuckled again. "Seems like we're both pretty bad at this, huh?"

"Seems so," I agreed. "Though at least you haven't demanded my salary yet."

"I was going to ask for pay slips and an energy bill with your name on it by the end of the date, but now you've got me thinking that's not the best idea." He tapped his finger against his chin, ponderingly with faux-seriousness, and this time, I laughed. He was actually pretty funny.

"Let's make a night of this to please our friends, and then we can go off our own ways," He suggested, and I extended my hand across the table toward him, relieved that we were able to be adults about this.

"Sounds great," I agreed, and I opened the menu and started scanning down the food in front of me.

We chatted, and he guided me toward the dishes he thought I would most enjoy on the menu. I went with his preferences, and soon enough, we had a small selection of dishes on the table before us that we both chowed down on without pause. At an actual date, I might have been trying hard to play it as dainty, to pretend like I wasn't a starving food hole who would cram herself full of as much as she could get. I didn't worry too much about my lipstick rubbing off or my hair getting out of place or my dress looking too tight around the middle. In fact, I could relax and have a good time, and I found myself doing just that.

"Can I ask you something?" I leaned back from the table and took a long sip of my wine as he inclined his head. "Why did you come on this date in the first place? Forgive me if I'm wrong, but you don't seem like the kind of guy who goes on blind dates."

"What does that mean?" He smiled interestedly, and I shrugged.

"I mean, you seem like everything in your life is just so," I told him. "With Hunter, with your job, with everything. Like you like it your way. I can't imagine that translates well to your friends picking out partners for you."

"If I'm being honest with you—" He leaned across the table, as though he was about to drop some scandalous information on me. "—I haven't been on a date in nearly ten years. I don't know how I'd go about finding someone for myself."

"Ten years?" My eyes widened. "What, since Hunter came along?"

"Pretty much. I was so focused on the business and getting it off the ground that I never had a chance to focus on anything else."

I felt a twinge of recognition at his words. How many times had I wondered if I had been a little less focused on my job if I would have had an easier time on the dating scene? It was different for him, of course, since he was running a whole business, but still. It was a lot for both of us.

"I feel you." I nodded. "I think that's why I ended up set up on this date myself. My friend works with me, and she probably wanted me out of the classroom."

"Well, you're only going to get good at your job by working your butt off there," he agreed. "I get it. Work is easy. You can keep a handle on work. People, not so much."

"So maybe we both start turning down blind dates in the future and find our own people, huh?" I suggested. He shook his head, smiling ruefully.

"Honestly?" He looked at me again, and maybe it was the wine, but the sharpness of his eyes took me aback a little. They were piercing, the kind that seemed to cut straight through you and down into your soul.

"Yeah?" I found myself staring into those eyes, propping my chin in my hand as I waited for him to go on.

"I don't think I would ever come out with anyone at all if it hadn't been for them," he confessed. "Fuck, I was going to get out of this date. If it hadn't been for Hunter, I would have dropped out before I so much as picked the restaurant."

"And Hunter changed your mind?" I asked him. "What did he say?"

"He didn't say anything specific," he said. "It was like... it's just obvious that the thought of me potentially meeting someone really excites him, you know?"

"That's actually kind of sweet," I remarked. "So you think you'll start dating again? For him?"

"Don't get me wrong. I'm sure there's plenty to be said for getting out on the dating scene myself," he remarked. "I'm sure I'll be glad I did it when I actually do. But I guess I needed that little push to make things happen. And Hunter's always been that push for me. For the business, for me as a person, for everything. I just want to give him everything I can."

He came to a halt, chuckled at himself, and shook his head.

"I'm sorry. I guess I've had a little too much to drink," he apologized.

"Not at all," I replied firmly. "It's so nice to hear someone speaking so highly of their kid, especially a dad. You'd be surprised how many think we're going to laugh at them for daring to express an emotion, even if it's about their own son or daughter."

"Thanks," he replied. "Sorry, I haven't talked to anyone new in such a long time, not properly."

"Me neither," I admitted. "But this has been nice. A practice-date, right?"

"I can drink to that," he agreed, and he raised his glass and took a sip.

"Though I'm not sure where I'll be meeting my dates after this," he said. "Most of the women I work with are married, and I'm not sure I'd trust Raymond to set me up again."

"Let me do that for you!" I suggested. "I know you a little better now. I'm sure I could find some women for you to go out with."

"You think?" He cocked an eyebrow.

"Are you kidding?" I waved my hand at him. "Look at you. You're the picture of eligible. Rich, handsome, young, good-looking, kind, a good dad...."

As I listed off his traits, I realized I was having a hard time justifying why I wasn't going for him myself. They were all true, of course, but that didn't mean we had to be together. Did it?

I cleared my throat and shifted in my seat.

"Anyway." I waved my hand. "What I'm saying is, I'll be able to find plenty of women who want to date you. Actually date you, I mean."

"Sounds good." He grinned at me. And with that, we continued to talk until most of the rest of the restaurant had cleared out and the waiters were hovering, waiting for us to move already. We got our separate bills, and I drained the last of my wine.

"Well, this has been a much more enjoyable evening than I thought it would be," I told him.

"It really has," he agreed, getting to his feet and extending his hand to me. "Pleasure to meet you properly, Autumn."

"Pleased to meet you too, Holden," I replied, taking his hand. We must have looked so funny to the people around us, spending the whole night together at a romantic restaurant and closing things off with a handshake. But it felt good, like the promise of a friendship, and I could use as many of those as I could get. Not that I would have minded something more.

I let my hand linger in his a split-second too long, and then swiftly removed it and pushed that thought to the back of my mind. No. That wasn't how this worked. Things with us were fun, that was all, and besides, I had agreed to set him up with someone else. It was just the wine speaking, and I should get out before anything of that nature started spilling out of my mouth as well.

"Good night, Holden." I turned on my heel and made it out of there, not even pausing to hear him say it back to me.

11

HOLDEN

"You all ready to go?"

Hunter was practically bouncing from foot to foot as he waited for us to get ready, and finally, I laughed and ruffled the top of his hair.

"Yes, we're finally ready to go," I told him. "Raymond? You got the keys?"

"Sure do." Raymond held them up. I would have laughed at him in his goofy fisherman's gear if I hadn't already seen it on him a dozen times before. A couple of times a year, the three of us would go fishing down by the lake outside the city, and Raymond would take it as an excuse to put on waders and a giant hat like he was about to go diving in the lake and then scaling a mountain straight after. Truth was, he would probably crack a couple of beers by the side of the water while we caught up on things and maybe caught a fish or two. We rarely came away with anything. Even if we did, Hunter was getting to that age now where he wanted us to throw them back. But I didn't mind that. It was the chance to spend some time with two of my favorite people in the world, and I appreciated any chance I got.

"You boys make sure to stay safe, now," Olivia fussed as we

prepared to head out the door. "I can trust you to take care of them, can't I, Hunter?"

"Of course, ma'am!" he replied, saluting her playfully, and I could see the delight on her face at his sweet old-fashioned manners. If there was one thing that had been a nonnegotiable in raising him, it had been making sure that he was the most well-mannered kid on the block. Manners could get you a hell of a long way if you used them in the right way, and judging by the amusement with which she was looking at him right there, I would have said he was learning what that way was for him.

"Come on, let's get out of here." Raymond pointed to the door, and I grabbed a cooler full of food and drinks and heaved it up to take outside. We had already loaded up the car with fishing stuff, and we were soon ready to go.

Hunter always slept on car journeys, which gave Raymond and me a little time to catch up on what had happened over the weekend. I knew he had been itching to ask me about the blind date they had set me up on, and I couldn't wait to tell them what the hell had really happened that night.

"So you going to tell me how things went with that woman?" Raymond asked keenly, and I grinned and shook my head.

"All right, I admit it. I had a good time," I began, and his face lit up.

"Are you going out with her again?"

"No chance." I shook my head. "Well, not as anything other than a friend anyway."

His face dropped once more, and he furrowed his brow, keeping his eyes on the road.

"What do you mean?"

"That friend of Olivia's friend you set me up with? Yeah, turns out she's Hunter's teacher—the one who gave me the chewing-out the week before about him being too solitary, you remember?" I finished up, and Raymond's eyebrows shut up.

"Holy sh—" He trailed off, eyes going to Hunter in the back seat. "Holy snacks, Holden. You sure?"

"Certain," I told him. "And I swear to God I was about to get up and walk out of there, but then she came over and said she wanted to apologize for how things had gone down between us, that she was wrong to confront me in front of Hunter and that she should have given us all a little space."

"Well, that's good news," he remarked. "You said you had a good time anyway?"

"Yeah, I ended up having a really good time." I smiled, remembering how fun that night had been once we had got past the initial difficulties. "I mean, it was a little awkward at first, but we rolled with the punches, and when the pressure was off, I wound up having a good night."

"And what about her? What did she think?" Raymond asked.

"She seemed happy to have someone to work out her dating stuff on again," I told him with a shrug. "I mean, say what you want, but both of us had been off the scene for a long time. I guess it was nice to hang out with someone else who was as useless as we were."

"And nothing happened?" he asked, glancing at me incredulously in the mirror. "Nothing at all?"

"Nothing at all," I replied firmly. I knew what he was angling for, but that was the truth. Sure, Autumn was cute and all, but she had made it pretty clear that night that we were about as far removed from each other as it was possible to be, and I wasn't going to go and dissuade her of that opinion when it was so obviously true. She was a teacher, good with kids but not quite there with adults, smart and driven in a completely different direction from me.

"Hmm." Raymond tapped his fingers on the wheel. "So, you said you might see her again?"

"I think I will," I agreed. "She said she would keep an eye out for friends to set me up with, you know, now that we had the practice date out of the way."

"Don't get me wrong. That's a very mature way to look at it," he conceded. "But it sounds like you guys had a fun date together. What, was the physical chemistry just not there or something?"

"Oh no, she was—" I stopped myself before I came out with

anything too lewd in front of my son, even if he was sleeping. "She was beautiful. But I don't..."

I trailed off and tried to find the words to describe what was running through my mind. Raymond watched me for a moment as we pulled to a stoplight, and I could see a hint of amusement on his face.

"She's not my type, that's all," I finished up. There, he couldn't possibly need any more explanation than that. There was nothing you could do about a difference that fundamental, could you?

"Right." He pulled the car away from the lights and raised his eyebrows. "Are you trying to convince me of that or yourself?"

I ignored him and turned the attention to fishing as we finally made it out of the city and headed down to our usual spot. It was a little cold at this time of year, but that meant it would be extra quiet around these parts, and we would get all the space and time we wanted to fish and chat and drink root beers together.

I woke Hunter up when we arrived, and he hopped out of the car and helped us get everything set up. He was well-practiced in this now, and every time we came down here, I would marvel at how much bigger and stronger he had gotten. I often forgot, seeing him every day, the changes he went through seemingly overnight some-times. It was wild, noticing those changes come to fruition, how he could easily carry a cooler full of food or sling a couple of fishing poles over his shoulder when the same time last year, he would have struggled to even think of doing the same.

The place was as beautiful as it had ever been. Raymond and I had first come down here the week after I started the business, when I told him I needed nothing more than to catch a break from computer screens and stare at something beautiful for a while. He had taken me down to this lake he and his dad used to frequent, and I had fallen in love with it on the spot. Pine trees climbed up moun-tains around us, and there was a town on the other side that we sometimes stopped at for hot food if things were getting a little too chilly for my liking. The water was crisp and clear and rolled on for miles, and, in the pale, watery sunshine that was managing to come down that day, I just let it take me away. It was good to be out of the city. It had been a stressful week, for one reason or another, and I had sorely needed this break.

We headed down to the lake and took our normal spot there, Raymond and I sipping on a cheap beer and Hunter on a root one. I chatted to my son about what had been going on at school, and he filled me in on all the gossip I needed to know, who was friends with who, who had fallen out with who, who was having their birthday party where. It was fun, the small-stakes stuff, especially because Hunter treated it with such utter and deadly seriousness.

"Oh, hey, I think I got a bite," Raymond told me suddenly, cutting me off midsentence as his line began to twitch erratically. I got to my feet and went to help him, but before we could pull anything up, it got away.

"Ah, well, maybe next time," I said, slapping Raymond on the shoulder. He shrugged. The beer took the edge off any disappointment he might have felt for that, I found.

Hunter headed out to the edge of the water to inspect the stones and rocks there, and as I watched him, Raymond began to grill me once more.

"So you don't have any feelings for this teacher of his?"

"I already told you no." I glanced at him. "Why do you ask?"

"Because you spent this whole day asking him about school." He nodded to my son. "You're trying to find out if he approves of her."

"All right, and where did you get your degree in psychology?" I shot back, glancing over at him. "I really don't feel anything for her. Things aren't that way between us. It's that simple. I liked her, sure, but that was it."

"What was her name?" he wondered aloud.

"Autumn," I replied at once. "Autumn Becks."

And I realized I was speaking the name with some kind of reverence, as though I was worshipping at the altar of the sound of it on my lips. I rolled my eyes, scolding myself for letting the beer get to me and conjure up feelings I was damn sure I didn't have. I tossed one of the empty cans back into the cooler and decided that would be my last one. When I turned back to check on Hunter, he was standing a little closer to me than I thought—and he had probably heard me talking about going on a date with his teacher. To my surprise, instead of acting freaked out or weird, he had a big-ass smile on his face, as though all of this was somehow going exactly according to plan.

12

AUTUMN

"So, do I finally get the inside scoop on that date?" Zoe asked keenly, and I waved my hand and hooked it through her arm instead.

"Honestly, I don't even think you'd believe me if I told you," I admitted. "Can I get a coffee in me first? I feel like I'm going to need one to tell this story properly."

"Oh, that good, huh?" she remarked as we headed down to our usual place. We were heading out to the mall, ostensibly because Zoe needed to get an outfit for a wedding she was attending with her family but really because it was a chance for her to grill me about that date she'd been itching to find out about since I got back from it.

We settled in at our usual table at the coffee shop, and she arched her fingers and looked at me over the top of them like she was a dastardly supervillain.

"Tell me what happened." She smiled at me keenly. "Was it great? I bet it was great. You look like a woman who was on an amazing date in the near past."

"Don't strain something patting yourself on the back," I warned her. "You're not going to believe this, but you actually set me up with

Hunter's dad. You remember. The one I got into it with last week who wound up chewing me out about his privacy? That one?"

"Fucking hell." She slapped her hand over her mouth and widened her eyes at me. "Are you shitting me right now?"

"Nope." I shook my head. "I walked in, and there he was, waiting for me."

"And what did you do?"

"Well, I went up to him, and said I was sorry for what happened when we first met," I told her. "Which sucked because I hate having to admit I'm wrong. But then... I don't know, we were chatting a little, and I decided to stay and eat with him."

"So you actually did get your date after all?" She clapped her hands together. "See, I told you I could tell."

"Well, the thing was, I'm not sure it was really a date." I shook my head. "I mean, given how we met, I don't think we could get over that. And we both hadn't been out with anyone for a long time, so we decided we would treat it as a practice date."

"A practice date?" She cocked an eyebrow. "And what, pray tell, is that?"

"Like, we would get all the awkward stuff out of the way so the next people we both went out with could be totally dazzled by our charm and wit," I explained. "Not that I'm exactly jumping to go on another date again, but you get the idea."

"Hmm." She cocked an eyebrow. "And he agreed to this, did he?"

"Yeah, he seemed to like the idea." I shrugged. "We spent the night together talking, and it was fun. I could for sure see the two of us becoming friends. He has a better sense of humor than I first thought."

"Well, it couldn't possibly be worse," she conceded, cocking her head at me. There was something about the way she was looking at me like she knew something I didn't. "So the two of you had dinner together."

I pursed my lips, trying to figure out her point. She knew all this already. "Yeah."

"And he said he wanted to see you again at the end of it? And that he had a good time?"

"Words to that effect." I waved my hand.

"Are you sure he thinks this is platonic?" she wondered aloud, and I rolled my eyes at her.

"It is possible for men and women to be friends, you know," I reminded her, and she held her hands up.

"Look, I'm not trying to say they can't be," she defended herself. "I'm just saying... give this a little thought, you know? Too many assumptions and all that."

"Huh?"

"The most likely answer is probably the correct one," she explained. "To me, it sounds like you have a man who wants to see you again, no matter what that entails."

"Okay, now I'm certain you just want to have set me up on a good date," I scolded her playfully.

"Yeah, well, I don't like it when I'm wrong." She held her hands up. "And I think it sounds like he actually likes you."

"Well, maybe he does," I said. "But he's so far removed from my type. I mean, he's a high-flying business... guy, that's not exactly going to gel with me having a career all of my own, is it? Especially considering he has a kid."

"You always liked Hunter," she remarked playfully. "Maybe you could be a good stepmom to him."

"And maybe you need to get your head out of your rear end and stop coming up with fanfiction about my life," I fired back, raising my eyebrows at her pointedly. "Seriously, there's nothing going on between the two of us. That's all you need to know."

"Yeah, right, sure." She drummed her fingers on her chin. "When are you seeing him again?"

"I don't know." I shrugged. "When I do, it's going to be so I can get to know him a little better so I can find him someone more suitable to get him set up with."

"Mm-hmm." She sent me an incredulous look. "Right, yeah. Cool."

I could tell she didn't believe me, and pushing any further was going to prove her point inside that head of hers. I should have left it, but I couldn't. I hated the thought of someone walking away from a conversation with me with the wrong idea.

"I think Hunter could use a woman around him," I told her. "Not me but someone who can actually give him all the attention he deserves. Is that so bad?"

"Not at all." She eyed me, clearly amused. "Not at all."

With that, I decided to give up on the conversation and go on our shopping trip. Soon enough, I had forgotten all about Holden and Hunter and everything else. I forgot sometimes how fun it was to hang out with Zoe outside of work and how much fun the two of us had together. She made me laugh so much, strutting up and down in the changing rooms in a variety of terrible dresses that she was never going to buy but couldn't resist trying out. Eventually, she settled on a flimsy green dress that clung to her figure in an almost scandalous fashion.

"You sure that's the right choice for a wedding?" I wondered aloud as she headed to the cashier's desk with it. She shrugged.

"It is if there's someone there I'm trying to hook up with," she told me cheerfully, and I laughed and followed her to the counter. If I could have found my way to a drop of her confidence, I wouldn't have been in such a bad way with my dating life, that much was for certain.

I walked her back to her place and gave her a hug outside the door, where she pulled back and looked at me for a long moment. I knew what was going through her mind before it so much as came out of her mouth.

"Don't even say it." I lifted my finger to stop her talking, but she wasn't having any of it.

"I'm just saying, be careful with Holden," she told me. "It seems like... I don't know, maybe there's more going on there than you know, all right?"

"I know plenty." I waved my hand, dismissing her concerns. "I'm a big girl, and I can take care of myself when it comes to stuff like this."

"Yeah, yeah, sure you can." She smiled at me. "I'm just saying. If he likes you, maybe that isn't the worst thing in the entire world, is it?"

"Maybe so," I conceded to get her to stop talking about it. "All right, I'll see you at work, okay? Thanks for today. I needed it."

"Anytime," she replied and gave me another quick hug before she vanished inside her apartment building and left me to head back home by myself. I didn't mind the walk, though, as it gave me a little time to ponder on what she had been saying.

Holden didn't strike me as the kind of guy who held back when he knew how he felt. He wouldn't have gotten anywhere in business if he had spent all his time dancing around the points in question and not coming outright and declaring what he wanted. He hadn't been slow in telling me what he had thought of me when I had tried to intervene in things with Hunter.

But then, he hadn't dated in a long time, just like me. Since Hunter had come along, he had told me. So maybe he was a little... nervous? Maybe he didn't know how to express himself when he came across someone he liked. Maybe he needed a little guiding. Maybe Zoe was right, and he actually did like me.

I pushed that thought out of my head at once. Even if he did, I wasn't sure anything could ever have worked between us. He had a kid, after all, and while I loved them, I wasn't sure I wanted to step into the mother role at work and at home. And he had shown himself to be defensive before, a little sharp around the edges, and I wasn't sure I wanted to work my way to find his soft center. Besides, he had told me it had been a practice date—and this was real life, not some fantasy where nothing was as it seemed, and nobody could just come out and say what they really wanted.

When I got home, I checked my email and saw his address sitting in my book of recently-used contacts. It would be nice to see him again, just to put my mind at rest about what was actually going on with the two of us. And to get to know him better, so I could be sure that whoever I set him up with would be a good match.

I tapped out an email to him, suggesting that the two of us got lunch together. I made it clear that it was only platonic, as best I could, and hovered my finger over the send button for a moment before I hit it. I had nothing to lose, right? It would just be a nice way to spend an afternoon with a guy I thought was fun. Zoe was talking crazy when she had come out with all that stuff about how he was into me. He would have come out and told me. Kissed me. I found my fingers glancing over my lips as though I was mimicking the sensation of his mouth on mine and quickly dropped my hand back by my side. Man, I really needed to find someone to date properly, sooner rather than later.

I didn't expect to hear a reply from him so fast, but a minute or two later, a response was sitting in my inbox. I hesitated for a moment before I clicked it open, feeling, for some reason, a little nervous at the thought of him turning me down.

"That sounds great," he agreed. "But if you don't mind, I'd like to pick your brains on something different. Shall we say Sunday, at one, at the mall off Bull Street?"

I grinned widely and bit my lip, wondering what on earth he needed to pick my brains about. Whatever it was, I was looking forward to finding out. I swiftly replied in the affirmative and sat back in my seat, grinning. This was going to be fun. I could feel it in my bones.

13

HOLDEN

I waited for Autumn outside the mall, and my leg was jiggling nervously as I scanned the crowds and waited for her to turn up. I shouldn't have picked such a busy day to meet with her. What, did I think I wasn't going to recognize her or something? I remembered what she looked like. In fact, the image of her in that dress when she had walked into the restaurant was seared into my brain, and I found myself coming back to it a lot.

Then, suddenly, she emerged from the throng of people in front of me, and a smile spread over my face. I was just relieved she had turned up. For some reason, I had been nervous all morning about the thought of meeting her here, as though she was going to change her mind and not turn up at the last second. That just told me everything I needed to know about the last time I had been dating, back in the day when getting stood up was a real possibility, when nobody bothered with manners or basic kindness.

Autumn was wearing a green sweater and a pair of jeans, her hair loose around her shoulders, and she beamed when she laid eyes on me. The color of her sweater made her hair glow almost supernaturally around her face, and I moved toward her to greet her as she approached me.

"Hey." She gave me a quick hug, and I was surrounded by the scent of her perfume for a moment. Flowery and slightly powdery, it seemed to suit her, a gentle and delicate scent. I removed myself from her embrace and straightened my shirt, and she raised her eyebrows at me expectantly.

"So, what exactly is it you want me to help you with?" she asked, and I took a deep breath. I had been meaning to do this for ages, and now that I had a woman here to help me, hopefully I would be able to pull it off without picking something totally awful.

"I need to get a new suit," I told her, cocking my head to the side as I spoke so I could get a read of her reaction. "And I was hoping you could give me a hand."

"You're serious?" She laughed, her entire face lighting up.

"Deadly." I shrugged. "I keep on planning on buying a new one, but then it always slips my mind because I'm sure I'm going to pick something crappy. I could use a guiding hand on this."

"Well, I suppose if I'm going to be setting you up, I need to make sure you look the part," she replied playfully, running her hands through her long red hair and smiling. "Buy me lunch after?"

"Sure thing," I agreed at once.

"Then I'm in. Where do you want to start looking?"

"Lady's choice." I gestured back to the mall, and she hooked her arm through mine and started leading me to her first shop of choice.

"This place is pretty expensive, but you can probably afford it," she told me, and she rolled her eyes to the heavens and laughed once more. "I'm sorry, I sometimes hear myself speaking and I know that I come out with the dumbest shit. I don't mean to sound so rude, I promise."

"No, it's fine," I assured her, surprised that I meant it. Normally, I would have been irritated at someone with such loose lips, but on her, it read as charming. Maybe that had something to do with how nice it felt to have her arm through mine like that, the weight of it, the ease of her close to me. Jesus, I needed to get out on a real date, if this level of contact was already getting me thinking twice.

"Okay, but you have to tell me if I'm getting too rude for you," she warned me. "I need you to stop me from making a fool of myself in all these fancy shops."

"I'll try my best," I promised her as we arrived outside the door of a glossy, minimalist place that I had never seen before.

"Are we starting here?"

"Sure are." She headed inside. "I've always walked by this place and thought the suits in the window looked so cool." She sighed as she began to walk a little reverently through the store.

"Uh..." I looked around at some of the mannequins. They were pretty avant-garde, to say the least. It seemed like the kind of thing a young actor might wear on the red carpet, and I wasn't sure I could pull it off as a single dad and businessman.

"Ooh, look at this one!" She came to a halt next to a navy suit with a checked blue shirt underneath and a crisp red tie over the top, and a matching handkerchief tucked into the pocket.

"That's a little forward-thinking for me," I remarked, and she rolled her eyes.

"Oh come on, this would look great on you!" she argued. I could see the shop assistant, a snooty-looking dude a little younger than me, eyeing her with distrust.

"Can we start with something a little more old-fashioned first?" I suggested, and she rolled her eyes again and let out a long sigh.

"I guess so." She grinned, and with that, she headed off to the back of the store to take a look at the suits that were a little more my speed.

She was so into it that I couldn't help getting caught up a little. Most of the clothes I picked out these days were for Hunter, not me, and I had long since forgotten what it felt like to actually shop for myself. I had a few suits I had collected in the early days of running the business, but that was pretty much it, and all of them were hopelessly out of style by now anyway.

"So, tell me about your business," she asked me, as we rounded out of one shop and started to head down to another one.

"What do you want to know?" I asked, and she shrugged.

"Have you been running it since Hunter came along?"

"Since just after," I told her. "I guess I wanted to run my life with a newborn and a business all at once."

"So you run the place all by yourself?" she asked, and I nodded again.

"Yeah, I always wanted to be the one in complete control over there. I know it sounds a little anal retentive, but I like things to be the way I want them to be. I have my reasons."

"Ooh, mysterious," she teased, tossing her hair over her shoulder and waggling her fingers in a witchy fashion. "Am I ever going to find out what those reasons are, by any chance?"

I hesitated for a moment. I had never been forthcoming in telling anyone the truth of what had happened between Hunter's mother and me, why she had left and what about it had driven me to the place I was in my work today, but for some reason, the way she was looking at me made me want to open up. I guessed that was part of why she was so good at her job, because it was so simple for people to tell her the truth.

I shook my head and waved my hand. I didn't want to dump all that on her, not when we were having such a nice day together thus far.

"Maybe another time," I suggested, and she shrugged and turned her attention to the window next to us.

"Oh, I like this shop too." She pressed her finger to the glass. "We should go in and check it out. They're a little more old-fashioned, but maybe that's more your style."

"You calling me old?" I raised my eyebrows at her, and she grinned.

"Just saying that judging by your taste in suits, someone might assume you were," she replied sweetly, and I shook my head and followed her into the store.

Normally, I wouldn't have let anyone talk to me like that. I could be oversensitive, I knew that, but years in business had taught me to try and sense everything anyone was feeling before they even knew they were feeling it. It was what had gotten me so far with the company, but sometimes I found myself overreacting to people when they said benign stuff. But with her, I found myself relaxed enough that I could laugh along to her occasionally blunt comments. In fact, I would even have gone as far as to say I was having something of a good time.

We went through pretty much every store in the mall, and I couldn't find anything that looked right for me. Each one she pulled out for me, I would find a little detail wrong with it. In the back of my mind, I knew it was because I didn't want this day to end yet. I was having a good time with her, and sometimes it was fun to forget about all my responsibilities for a while and let myself goof off this way. And being with her was a good time, a great time, even. If this is what actually dating could have been like, I wouldn't have avoided it for so long.

Eventually, we had made our way around every store in the mall, and I had still failed to come up with something that fit my standards. She planted her hands on her hips and shook her head at me as we came out of the last one.

"Well, I'm not sure what else we can do," she sighed, faux-exhausted. And then a smile spread across her face.

"What is it?" I asked cautiously, and she caught my hand. I felt a buzz of sparks pass from my fingers to hers and tried to ignore them.

"Come and try on that suit in the first place we looked," she suggested. "You've got nothing to lose."

"I'm not sure—"

"Come on, for me?" she pleaded, and I looked into those gorgeous green eyes and found myself wavering. I should have been able to say no, for the love of God, but I didn't want to. I wanted to please her, and she was giving me a straight route to doing so.

"Fine." I nodded. "I'll try it, but I'm not promising anything."

"An open mind is all I'm looking for." She let go of my hand, and I felt as though I had landed back in the real world with a hard thud. I followed her back to the store and stood in front of the suit once more.

"I'm not sure about this," I warned her, and she gave me that look, the one I had such trouble saying no to.

"Just try it on," she ordered, and she waved the assistant over to find me one in my size to test out. I pulled a face when he handed it to me and shot a glance at her.

"If I look like a fool, I'm blaming you," I warned her, and I headed into the changing room. I undressed swiftly and pulled the suit on, and then turned to look at myself in the mirror. And I had to admit, I looked good.

What I had thought would look silly and self-consciously youthful on me actually seemed modern and fresh now that I was wearing it. I looked totally different. Maybe it was more than just the suit. Maybe it was something about the look on my face, the gleam in my eyes. And that had more than a little to do with the woman who had chosen this suit for me.

"Well, how does it look?" she called through the door impatiently. "I'm starting to look creepy hanging around the changing rooms like this."

She spoke so loudly, half the shop must have heard her, and I couldn't help but shake my head and laugh at the thought. I took one last look at myself in the mirror and then pulled open the door so she could take a look at me.

"See for yourself," I told her with a smile, and I watched her for a reaction, feeling lighter than I had in months.

14

AUTUMN

"Well? What do you think?"

As soon as he stepped out of the dressing room, I knew this was the suit for him. He might have pulled a face at it earlier, but it looked fantastic on him, modern and fresh and new, bringing his look to the right here, right now. And hey, I had to admit he looked pretty damn handsome to boot. Not that it bothered me how he looked, but still.

"I love it," I told him firmly, and I reached out to fix the shoulders and dust down the front. I had never done that before in my life, but I wanted to—to touch him? That sounded a lot less creepy in my head. I stepped away swiftly, letting my hands drop to my sides, and nodded with approval at the sight of him like that.

"You look awesome," I assured him, and he looked down at the suit, shook his head, and grinned.

"You know, I would never have thought of something like this if it hadn't been for you," he said. "So thanks. You saved me from getting something terrible."

"It's the perfect thing for whatever date I set you up on," I remarked, and I could see his face drop slightly. I wasn't sure why, since we had talked at length about the dating thing before. Maybe it had been a long day, and he was tired. That could be it.

"Yeah, right." He glanced toward the changing rooms. "I'm going to take this off and get it, and then I think I owe you lunch, don't I?"

"You sure do," I agreed, and I watched as he made his way back into the changing room and pulled the curtain over. I gave him some privacy, wandering away to look at the pocket squares idly. I found my mind drifting to what kind of date I would send him on in a suit like that—something fancy but fun, like a tasting menu at some hip restaurant. I felt my heart twist slightly in my chest and ignored it. I was nervous about setting him up with the right woman, that was all.

He emerged with the suit and paid for it, and I linked my arm through his again as we stepped out of the shop.

"So, where for lunch?" I asked, and he grinned.

"I actually think I have the perfect place," he told me. "I used to go there all the time before the business took off."

"Lead on." I waved my hand, and he took me out of the mall and down a couple of side streets, and before I knew it, I was standing outside a tiny little coffee shop with big windows and comfortable chairs scattered around the floor inside.

"I used to live not far from here when Hunter was first born," he explained as he headed inside. "They had a better internet connection than I did back then, so I would come down here to work all the time."

"And you rate it?"

"Best place in the city." He pulled the door open for me and gestured for me to go in. I couldn't remember the last time someone had held a door for me, but it was the kind of thing a girl could get used to.

We took our seats, and I ordered a coffee and something from the artisan sandwich collection they had laid out under glass at the counter. He joined me at one of the low tables and took a long sip of his latte.

"Man, being here brings me back." He shook his head. I smiled. There was something about this day, as low-pressure and silly as it had been, that had satisfied something in me I didn't even know was awake.

"I still can't believe you started your own business when you were raising a newborn." I still had no idea what had happened to Hunter's mother and, judging by his reaction the last time I had brought it up, I had a feeling it was best for me if I kept any comments on that matter to myself.

"Me neither," he said. "That's what it's like when you're young though, right? Boundless energy all the time, and you can't imagine anything being any different."

"I hear that." I raised my coffee cup to him and took a sip. It spoke well to how much I liked him that I was able to spend time around him without a glass or three of wine. The conversation flowed as easily, maybe even better, than that first night, as though both of us could relax now that we knew we weren't trying to impress the other in a dating sense.

We chatted some more over lunch, about his work and about mine and about how I had ended up doing what I was doing. We had more in common than I'd thought, even though we were at completely different ends of the career spectrum. I would have assumed that he spent as much time as he could at work, but he told me he was working hard on being able to leave the office without stressing and spend more time with his son. I thought that was sweet as hell and likely explained why he had turned to me for dating advice. He hadn't dated anyone since his kid came along, and I couldn't imagine how lonely it must have been for him, raising a child when the rest of his peers were out partying and having a good time. No wonder he wanted to catch up on that life now.

"Well, I can only thank you for all your help." He extended his hand to me when we were outside, and I laughed and knocked it away.

"That's a little formal, don't you think?" I teased him, and I went to give him a hug instead. He seemed a little surprised, but he lifted his arms to wrap them around me for a moment, and I inhaled the sweet scent of his aftershave, masculine and classic, like him. Expensive, like him.

I pulled away swiftly and straightened out my sweater, then returned my attention to him.

"Thanks for today," I told him. "I had a really good time. Better than getting lunch, for sure."

"Thanks for helping me pick out a suit that doesn't make me look a thousand years old," he replied, and I grinned at him.

"You know, I'm going to have to find a woman to go with that suit," I remarked. "I feel like I know you well enough now. I'll start putting some feelers out, see who I can find—"

"Don't you think you should spend a little more time with Hunter and me first?" He cut me off. "Just so you know what kind of dynamic we're working with."

"Uh, I suppose so." I nodded. "Actually, yeah, that sounds like a good idea. Let's do that. You call me up, and we can figure something out, all right?"

"Will do." He flashed me another one of those rare but heart-spinning smiles and turned to head off. I watched him as he went and bit my lip. I had a hard time imagining him struggling with the women, yet he had recruited me for my help. Or something else entirely.

No, I wasn't going to let myself think like that. I was a friend doing another friend a favor. Because that was all it was—that was all I had a reason to think it was anyway. Sure, he had seemed keen to spend more time with me, but that was nothing to read into. He valued his son and wanted to make sure anyone I set him up with was going to be compatible with the kid and with their dynamic as a father-child duo. I got that. I had worked with kids my entire career, and I understood better than most people how difficult it could be to find someone who would fit comfortably into that world.

Yet, as I made my way home, I couldn't help looking forward to seeing him again. Which was, as I said, totally crazy because it was nothing more than platonic. From both sides. Wasn't it? Either way, I was excited to see him again. As a friend, of course.

I arrived back at my place, but my brain was still running at what felt like a mile a minute, and I struggled to keep my head straight, so I decided to give Zoe a call. She was my go-to to get this stuff right, the voice of reason when I needed it the most. And damn, but did I need it right here and now.

"What's up?" She yawned down the line.

"How are you tired? it's the middle of the afternoon!" I scolded her playfully.

"Hey, I had a late one last night," she shot back. "What about you? What are you up to? Want to go out and do something?"

"No, I just got back from doing something actually," I replied, and I could practically hear her ears perk up on the other end of the line.

"Oh?" she prompted me. "Do tell."

"I was out with Holden, remember?" I reminded her. "We went out for lunch, and I helped him pick out a suit."

"So you were on a date with him," she corrected me, and I pulled a face even though she was at least a little bit right.

"I was getting to know him better—"

"By going on a date with him," she repeated, and I laughed and shook my head.

"You're not going to drop this, are you? We're a couple of people looking to help each other out."

"The truth? No, not planning to," she replied and yawned again. I could hear the creak of her old couch as she bounced back against the pillows and waited for me to go on.

"So what happened?" she asked curiously, and I pressed my lips together. I wasn't sure how much of this I wanted to tell her.

"Well, like I said, he needed me to help him pick out a suit, so I did, and we found something really cool," I explained. "Then he took me to a coffee place that he used to go to when he lived in the area."

"Yeah, that's a date," she confirmed. "And a cute one at that. So, what happened after that? You're calling me for a reason, I know that much."

"I was saying to him that I probably knew him well enough to start setting him up with people," I explained. "But then he suggested that I spend some more time with him and Hunter first."

"Because he wants to see you again," she pointed out. "Because you guys are totally dating."

"Right, yeah, I remember now," I replied, knowing she had gotten stuck on this and that there would be no shaking her from it. "So, what did you get up to last night? Anything exciting?"

"Nothing much, but I'll fill you in anyway," she replied, and soon I lost myself in a conversation with Zoe about her night, about work, about the parents we couldn't stand. But at the back of my mind, I was beginning to tip over toward Holden once again and what exactly he had planned for the three of us when we ended up together next. I couldn't wait to find out.

15

HOLDEN

Raymond poured us both a cup of coffee as Hunter helped Olivia in the kitchen. Hunter had always gotten on well with my best friend's wife, and she had treated him like a practice baby, preparation for when their own had come along. They were baking something, I was pretty sure. I could hear them giggling and laughing away as they worked together.

"So, what do you think?" Raymond sat down opposite me and handed me a mug, and I drew my gaze from the kitchen and back to him.

"Hmm? Oh, with the company." I nodded. We had been discussing work, a design of ours that seemed to have caught the eye of a business in the city. They seemed to like the look of it but were going back and forth for a lower price, which I wasn't going to give them.

"I think they're going to take it," I said. "In fact, I'm certain of it. They just need to get their heads around the fact that they're not going to find anyone better for the price, and I think they'll be all right with it."

"Right." Raymond sank into a chair opposite me and pinched the bridge of his nose. I recognized the exhaustion on his face all too well. The baby had recently gone to sleep upstairs, and he was probably glad for the moment's peace he was clinging to right now.

"You tired?"

"I didn't even know it was possible to be this exhausted," he replied, taking a sip of his coffee as though it was the only thing keeping him upright. "I have no idea how you did this with a business to run as well."

"People keep saying that to me lately," I muttered, remembering that Autumn had mentioned it a couple of times when we had been hanging out together. Or maybe it was that her words had a habit of getting stuck in my head. One or the other.

"Yeah, well, I feel like I'm hardly getting a moment to breathe, and I'm not running a business." He leaned back and eyed me for a moment. "You sure you're not some kind of superhuman?"

"I might have been back then, but I sure as hell am not now." I chuckled.

"You ever think about packing the business in for a while?" he wondered. "I mean, you've probably made enough money to have you and Hunter and any kids he might have set up for life, don't you?"

"Yeah, probably." I agreed. "I guess I just... I like running the place, that's all. Gave me a sense of purpose when I didn't feel like I had one."

"You're not planning on expanding, are you?" he pressed, and I shook my head.

"Nah, I don't want things to get any bigger than they already are," I conceded. "It's hard enough as it is now, balancing all of it. I don't want any more than I've already got."

"Right." He shifted in his seat and watched me for a moment. Raymond knew me well enough that I sometimes felt he could peer straight through me, and I wasn't sure if I appreciated that as a skill of his or not.

"I want to make a name for myself, for Hunter," I replied, even though I knew he wasn't trying to come out here attacking me. I didn't know why I felt the urge to defend myself, maybe because I had started questioning my own life choices recently, and it had me second-guessing everything I'd ever done with my life so far.

"I do get that," he replied. Raymond had been around me long enough to know what had kicked me into starting the company in the first place, and that was a wound he didn't want to stick his fingers into.

"But you can't live your entire life trying to make it right, buddy." He leaned toward me. In the kitchen, Hunter let out a burst of laughter, and I smiled as I turned in the direction it was coming from. It was so good to hear him happy and interacting with somebody else. Ever since Autumn had taken me aside and let me know what she thought about his development, I had been hyperaware of the way he interacted with other people. I had been sure it was totally normal for a kid of his age to want to hold back a little, to be his own person before he started involving others. It was what I had been like when I was his age. But she knew better than I did. How many classes had she been through, helping kids like Hunter through the hard parts? I should have taken her seriously right off the bat, not dismissed her out of hand like she was out to get me personally.

"I know, I know." I turned back to the conversation at hand. "And I've moved on from her. I don't even think about her anymore."

"All right." He cocked an eyebrow, and I knew he was incredulous in the face of what I was saying. And I understood. I had spent most of my adult life doing everything I could to prove Hunter's mother wrong about me, about the kind of person she was convinced I was.

"Hey, speaking of women." He leaned forward with interest. "What's happening with you and that woman?"

"Oh, the blind date?" I played it as cool as I could, even though the very mention of her name sent my pulse racing more than it should have. "Yeah, I guess things are going well. As friends, though."

"Hmm." He raised his other eyebrow. "Just friends, huh?"

"Yeah, that's right," I replied firmly, trying to convince myself as much as I was him. "She helped me pick out a suit the other day, says she's going to find me some dates to wear it on."

"Oh, is she now?" Raymond grinned widely. "Sounds fun. How do you feel about that?"

"Honestly, I know I should be getting back out there," I admitted, "but I'm not sure I'll find someone who fits with Hunter *and* me, you know? That seems like a long shot."

"A guy like you, with your success, with a cute son to match?" Raymond remarked. "I don't think you're going to have all that much trouble."

"You flatter me," I replied dryly. "But they haven't exactly been beating down my door the last nine years."

"Hey, it's not like you've ever opened that door to check," he pointed out, and I cocked my head, conceding the point.

"I suppose you're right," I agreed. "But I've been so busy. I don't see that changing in a major way."

"But it will, now that Hunter's older," he pointed out. "You're going to have more and more time the older he gets, don't you think?"

"I guess I don't want that yet," I confessed. "Him growing away from me, I mean. I want him to be his own man, but it's only been the two of us for so long, you know?"

"Well, you might get luckier than you think." He held his hands up. "Plenty of women who would fit with you guys. Someone good with kids. A school teacher, off the top of my head."

"Oh, come on." I rolled my eyes at him. "You know we can be friends and that's fine, right?"

"Yeah, yeah. So, you seeing her again? To convene on potential dates for you?"

"Actually, we are." A smile spread across my face. "I'm looking forward to it, for what it's worth."

"So tell me, what are you doing with her?" he asked. "Something platonic, no doubt?"

"I'm taking her out on the yacht." I shrugged, and he spluttered into his coffee.

"I'm sorry, what?"

"I wanted to get to know her better," I said. "She needs to get to know me and Hunter if she's going to find a woman who's a fit for both of us."

"Taking her out on your yacht, though?" he remarked. "That's tailor-made to impress her, you must know that."

"I'm only showing her what the reality of my life is," I replied calmly. I knew where he was coming from. I could see why he might have thought I was coming out here to make a point about what kind of guy I was, but it wasn't like that. No matter how much he seemed to hope it was.

"Yeah, but the reality of your life is that you don't spend so much time out on that thing, do you?" he reminded me.

"Yeah, but Hunter loves it, and I want to show her what he's like outside of school," I explained. "She only knows him as the quiet kid in her class, and I want her to see that he's so much more than that."

"And show her that you've got more to you than meets the eye as well, no doubt?" Raymond added for me. I shook my head, not wanting to admit he was somewhat right. I mean, if she did wind up liking the yacht, even being a little impressed by it, then that was no bad thing, was it? I was showing her everything that came with my life, so she would be able to better match me with someone who shared or wanted to share the same kind of lifestyle as I did.

"Well, I'm just saying, the yacht is a lot," Raymond said with a laugh. "I can't imagine how I'd react if someone showed me something like that within the first few dates."

"Not dates, remember?" I corrected him. "We're friends. This is all in aid of trying to find me a date in the first place."

"Mm-hmm, yeah, sure." he nodded, eyes wide and faux-serious, as though he didn't buy a word of what was coming out of my mouth.

"You think the yacht is a little much?" I asked. I hadn't been around anyone new in my personal life for so long, I had no idea where the line between appropriate and showing the fuck off was any longer.

"Maybe," he said, lifting a hand to head off any protest. "But if you say it's platonic, and she's clear on that too, I don't see much of an issue. At least you know she's going to remember this."

"Right." I settled back into my seat, somewhat more satisfied than I had been. Still, I couldn't shake the feeling that perhaps he was right that this was a little too much.

"Dad!" a voice came from the kitchen, and I glanced up, pulling out of the weird place in my head I had dropped into for a minute there. I ran my hands over my head and got to my feet, heading to find my son.

"What's up, little guy?" I asked, grinning at Olivia in greeting as I joined them.

"We just finished making cookies," Olivia told me. "And Hunter wants you to try one."

"Let me get my coffee, and I'll be right back," I said, eyeing the fresh-made batch of cookies sitting on the counter in front of them. They did look good, I had to admit. I grinned as I headed to grab my cup, happy to have some time with the people I loved most in the world. No wonder I had never bothered seeking out anyone new. Why would I when I was already surrounded by so many amazing people?

Still, my mind strayed to her and our day on the yacht I had planned. I couldn't wait to see the look on her face when she saw what I had prepared for us. In fact, I just couldn't wait to see her face, full stop. And maybe there was more to that than I would have cared to admit. Even to myself.

16

AUTUMN

I planted my hands on my hips and surveyed the cafeteria. Everything seemed to be as it should be—groups of friends were sitting around, chatting away, laughing and kicking their legs and waving their arms like they were happy to be there. Well, except one kid. The kid who I'd been focused on the last few weeks.

I watched Hunter for a while as he sat at the end of one of the tables, picking at his lunch and staring intently at a spot somewhere off in space across the room. The other kids at the table didn't seem to be saying anything to him, not picking on him specifically. They were acting as though he wasn't even there. He glanced in their direction a couple of times, his eyes hopeful, and then returned to his food, as though he believed it wasn't worth the trouble to try and engage with them. I grimaced, and I knew I had to go over there and talk to him. I couldn't bear the sight of him sitting there all by himself. It didn't seem fair or right.

There was another lunch monitor on that day, and I raised my eyebrows at him and tipped my chin toward Hunter to let him know what I planned to do. He smiled back, letting me know I was good to go, and I headed over to the boy and perched myself down next to him. Jesus, I always forgot how low these seats were. I had to plant a firm foot on the floor to make sure I didn't go careening over on the spot.

"You mind if I join you?" I asked him gently, and Hunter glanced up at me and shrugged.

"No." he shook his head. His food was nearly uneaten, and I felt another buzz of concern. A growing boy like him needed every bit of nutrition he could get in his body, and this wasn't exactly encouraging that.

"How are you doing today?" I asked him, cocking my head in his direction, and he shrugged again.

"Fine," he replied. "How are you?"

"I'm really good, thanks," I told him. He had impeccable manners. I had to concede that—just like his father. I flushed as I thought of Holden and pushed him quickly to the back of my mind. This wasn't about him. It was about Hunter.

"So you like eating by yourself?" I asked. Hunter gave me a look. He wasn't a stupid kid, and he probably knew his lack of enthusiasm for the other kids in his class wasn't going unnoticed by the staff. Plus, he had to be somewhat aware of what was going on with his dad, and he knew whatever was going on between us wasn't exactly standard procedure.

"I guess," he replied, picking up his packet of chips like he had noticed me noticing his lack of consumption.

"Can I ask you something?" I leaned in a little closer as if I were going to share a secret with him and waited for his nod. "Why don't you like to sit with the other kids?"

I furrowed my brow like it was a genuine mystery to me that I needed his help figuring out. He glanced beyond me to the small cluster at the other end of the table, all of whom randomly exploded into laughter at that very moment. He returned his gaze to me and shook his head.

"I'm not cool enough for them," he told me, and my heart sank. It was one thing for children to be left out of some social groups by their peers. Dynamics at this age were hard, and we could at least intervene to make sure they were included where we could encourage it. But it was nearly impossible when that division came from this self-imposed exclusion, when the child in question clearly didn't believe they would ever be able to do anything to make themselves part of the group.

"That's not true," I protested. "You're very cool, Hunter. Besides, that's not the only thing you can do to be friends with someone. There are lots of qualities beyond just coolness."

"That's what they care about, though," he replied, a little glumly. It would have been totally inappropriate, but I wanted nothing more than to give this kid a big hug and tell him everything was going to be all right. But I was already picking him out of the crowd enough. Anything more, and the other kids would begin to notice, and that was only going to make the situation worse.

"I don't think that's true either." I shook my head, but I could see that this conversation wasn't exactly helping matters so I decided to shift toward something a little nicer instead.

"Hey, I'm going to be visiting you and your dad this weekend, right?" I reminded him. Hunter's face instantly brightened, and I felt a wave of relief that I'd managed to move toward something a little more positive.

"Yeah, that's right!" he replied, smiling.

"Are you looking forward to it?" I asked. I knew this was an odd situation, but it wasn't the first time I had followed up with a student's parents outside of school, and it wouldn't be the last either. I knew I was making excuses to myself as to why I felt that zing in my chest every time I thought about Holden and spending more time with him, but that initial attraction would fade eventually. Once we spent more time together, I would be able to see him as the truly platonic friend that he was.

"Yeah." Hunter nodded excitedly. "My dad says we're going to—"

He stopped himself short and narrowed his eyes at me, and I almost burst out laughing. Sometimes, just once in a while, the kids I worked with would do something so strikingly adult that it took me a second to remember they were children, not little adults trapped

inside tiny bodies. This was one of those times, as Hunter silently
tried to parse something without giving too much away.

"Has he told you what we're going to be doing yet?" Hunter asked,
and I shook my head.

"No, he hasn't," I admitted. "Do you know? Can you tell me?"

"It's meant to be a surprise," Hunter replied mysteriously, and I
pulled a face and then grinned.

"Well, I guess I'll have to wait and see then," I conceded. "Is it fun?
Can you at least tell me that?"

"It's really fun," he beamed excitedly.

"That's all I wanted to hear." I patted him on the shoulder and got
back to my feet. I'd noticed a couple of the other kids looking in our
direction, and I didn't want any of them overhearing our conversation
and assuming Hunter was getting special treatment that they weren't.
I went back to my spot at the head of the dining hall, keeping an eye
on proceedings, but I couldn't keep the smile from my face as I imagined what might be in store for me over this weekend.

I headed back to my classroom, where I had a free hour before my
next group came in. I turned my attention back to the grade curves,
the numbers already dancing in front of my eyes before I'd even
gotten started. When Zoe appeared at the door, I closed my books at
once, glad to have a chance to put them off a little longer.

"Hey." Zoe slipped into my room and leaned on one of the little
chairs opposite my desk. "How's it going?"

"Pretty good," I replied. "Got some time to myself and trying to
catch up with those grade curves."

"So what you're saying is, you're looking for someone to come in
here and distract you?" She grinned.

"Please." I smiled back. "How're things with you?"

"Yeah, not bad," she replied. "I saw you talking with Hunter at
lunch. Is everything all right with him?"

"I think so. I'm a little worried about him. You know how it is. He
doesn't seem to have many friends around, and I think it's starting to
get to him."

"Ah, yeah, I noticed that too." She grimaced. "Do you think he'll grow out of it, or do you think it's a more long-term thing?"

"It's hard to say right now." I shook my head. "It seems to be coming more from him than the other kids, so that's at least something."

"Yeah, fair point," she agreed. "You up to anything interesting this weekend?"

"Actually, I'm seeing Holden" I told her, without thinking. I had declined to mention my thing with Holden and Hunter to her earlier, but it slipped out before I could stop myself. She raised her eyebrows at me.

"Oh yeah?" she prompted. "What's going on?"

"Oh, Holden suggested we spend some more time together," I replied with a shrug. "To see the two of them together before I go setting him up with anyone."

"So what you're saying is, he's taking you out on a date," she remarked, eyebrows raised. "What exactly are you guys up to?"

"I actually don't know yet," I admitted. "He says he wants it to be a surprise."

"A surprise date," she continued. I shook my head at her.

"It's nothing like that," I told her off, using my best teacher voice in the hopes that she would get the message. "Do you really think he'd be asking me to set him up with other people if he wanted to date me? Pretty counterintuitive, no?"

"Fair point." She held her hands up. "Or maybe this is a way for him to get to know you better without the pressure of actually dating."

"Look, his son is going to be there with us," I reminded her. "What kind of date would that be?"

"One where he has plausible deniability and can claim it's platonic?" she suggested with a teasing smile. I gave her a look, and she held her hands up.

"Look, I'm just saying, this guy seems to want to spend a lot of time with you and involve you in a lot of his life," she explained.

"Yeah, you do that too," I protested. "It's what being friends is about."

"Yeah, but I don't sweep you out on super-secret special dates," she pointed out. I had to concede that point. I leaned back in my seat and shook my head.

"It's nothing like that," I replied firmly. "He just wants to get to know me better, and I want to as well, to make sure I'm picking the right woman for him."

"And you couldn't be that woman?" She squeezed in one more jibe and then shook her head. "Sorry, sorry, I'm done."

"It's just a get-together," I assured her and realized I was talking as much to myself as well. It was hard for me to convince myself that this really was platonic, but I had to get that through my mind. It was what he wanted, and it was what would be best for me as well. Both of us were so inexperienced with dating, out-of-touch with how it worked. We would surely wind up fucking it up if we tried to hook up with each other.

"Of course." She nodded. "I hope you have a great time."

"Me too," I agreed, and I felt that fuzzy little rush of excitement once more at the thought of spending a whole day with Holden. I ignored it and asked about her weekend plans to distract myself, hoping those feelings would have faded by the time my date with Holden came around.

17

HOLDEN

"All right, you almost ready to get going?"

It was Sunday morning, the day of my trip on the yacht with Autumn, and I was having a hard time containing my excitement.

"Yeah!" Hunter emerged from his room, already in his jacket and sneakers, ready to hit the water for the day. I grinned at the sight of him. He had been talking about this for days, and now it was finally here.

"You looking forward to this?" I asked, and he nodded.

"She's so nice," he gushed. "I want to know what she's like outside of school. I've never seen a teacher out of school before."

"You got a little crush, buddy?" I teased, and he went bright red but couldn't help smiling.

"No!" he exclaimed pointedly back, but I knew he was fibbing to me. It was actually pretty sweet. I didn't blame him for being a little sweet on her. If I'd had a teacher like her back when I'd been his age, I would have felt the same way. And it was nice to see him so excited about something for a change. Sometimes, he would retreat to his room and hang out there for an evening, no matter if I offered him a movie or TV or to spend some time with me. I was looking forward to getting some quality time with him, even if it did include Autumn as well.

In fact, especially if it included Autumn as well. That wasn't the part of this that should have excited me, but I was so looking forward to showing these parts of my life to Autumn. I had worked so hard for everything I had, and it was cool to be able to be a little proud of them, to use them to impress. Not that it mattered if she was impressed or not, of course. I wasn't doing this to make a point to her. But it might raise my stock in the eyes of the potential dates she had picked out for me, and that could only be a good thing, right?

I heard a knock at the door, and I patted Hunter on the shoulder and went to answer it. I had given her my address and asked her to meet me here, so she wouldn't guess what we were doing today. I wanted to see the look on her face when she figured it out.

I opened the door and found her standing there in a pale blue sweater and a pair of jeans. She grinned when she saw me and gestured to her outfit.

"I tried to pick the most all-purpose thing I could think of," she remarked. "But if you're planning on taking us to a fancy restaurant, we might be a little screwed."

"No, you look perfect," I blurted out before I could consider how it would sound coming out of my mouth. I quickly stepped aside and gestured for her to come in. She brushed by me and smiled, so close that I could smell her perfume. I swallowed and tried to keep my shit together.

"Here, let me show you around." I grinned at her, and she glanced around the entrance hall. I was seriously proud of this house, given how hard I had worked for it, and I was looking forward to letting her see it properly.

"Yeah, sure." She seemed a little reluctant despite nodding. I wondered why but didn't linger on it. This was a little unconventional, of course, but surely, she would be able to overcome that. She had been the one to come here in the first place, after all, to agree to this day together.

I showed her around the house as Hunter finished getting all his stuff ready, and I could tell by the time we got to the third room that she was a little bored. She wasn't rude about it, but she simply followed along politely, clearly waiting for it all to be over. I was put out but didn't show it. I knew how expressive and enthusiastic she could be, and this was the direct polar opposite of that. Maybe interior design wasn't her thing. I designed for a living, after all, so I liked everything in my house to be just so.

"Are we ready to go?" Hunter asked, bouncing up and down on the spot as we came back to the entrance hall. I glanced at Autumn, who nodded.

"I am if you are." She grinned. "Can't wait to see what you've got planned for me."

"Then let's get going," I suggested, and we all headed out to the car. She slipped into the front seat next to me, with Hunter chatting away to her excitedly in the back seat. She listened and interjected where she could, and it was clear the two of them had a strong bond. She knew exactly what to say to keep him talking, to get him excited about whatever it was he was enthusing about.

I tried not to let her lack of reaction to the house get to me. It showed that she wasn't a materialistic person, which made sense. She had never come across that way to me before. I hoped it didn't come off as bragging. But I wanted her to see that I was a success, that I had managed to build this life up from the ground for myself and my son, so that anyone she wanted to set me up with would have a better idea of the kind of life I lived, the kind of lifestyle I could maintain.

"So do I get a clue as to what's happening today?" she asked me when we were out on the open road and headed down to the waterfront. "I tried to get it out of Hunter when we were at school, but he wasn't very forthcoming."

"I'm good at keeping secrets!" Hunter exclaimed, and I grinned at him in the rearview mirror. I did wonder if he might slip up and come out with something he shouldn't before I had the chance to surprise her, but he seemed as invested in this day going well as I was.

"Yes, you are," she agreed, and then she turned to me again, raising her eyebrows. "If I'm not much mistaken, we're headed down to the water, right?"

"Right." I tapped the side of my nose and grinned. "But you're going to have to wait and see what I'm taking you to."

"If any of this involves me getting dunked in water, I'm going to be less than impressed," she warned me playfully. "This sweater is dry clean only."

"You're safe, don't worry," I assured her, and a few minutes later, we had arrived at the dock, and I headed down to the cabin where the administrator took care of my keys for me. As I came back from picking them up, jingling them excitedly in my hand, I noticed Hunter and Autumn chatting animatedly at the other end of the pier. Autumn tossed her head back and laughed at something my son had said, and he beamed up at her, clearly delighted by her approval. I paused for a moment, watching the two of them, enjoying their interaction, and then remembered that I was meant to be heading down there to join them.

"We're ready to go." I held the keys up to Autumn, and she cocked an eyebrow.

"And what are those for?" she asked, and I took her by the shoulders, turning her around, and pointed to the yacht we were now facing.

"That," I told her, and her jaw dropped. This was the moment I'd been looking forward to, the one where I got to stun her with something this crazy and luxurious.

"Don't tell me you own that thing!" she exclaimed, a grin cracking across her face.

"Sure do." I held my hands up. "Got it five years ago, but I don't get a chance to take it out as much as I'd like. Though Hunter and I manage a few fishing trips a year, don't we?"

"Yeah, I love fishing," Hunter said, and Autumn smiled down at him.

"Shall we get on?" I suggested. "We can take her out for a spin, see how you like the water."

"I've never been on a boat before," she admitted. "What if I get seasick?"

"We won't take her out too far," I promised her. "If you start feeling bad, you let us know. But I think you're going to like it. It's like nothing else in the world, I promise you."

"I can believe that," she murmured, and I led her on to the yacht and guided it out of the harbor. I had learned to sail on this thing, and I still wasn't the best in the world at it, but every time I got behind the wheel, I felt a little more confident than I had before.

I could hear Hunter explaining all the stuff that was going on in the boat as we sailed, and it was so cute to hear him speak so authoritatively, even when he couldn't quite pronounce every single nautical term correctly. But Autumn encouraged him and continued to chat with him, following him around the deck as he explained this and that to her, and I watched them with a warmth in my chest that mitigated the cool breeze rolling in from the water.

Eventually, Hunter went to get something to eat from the cabin, and Autumn came up to join me. She had her arms wrapped around herself and was gazing out on to the water, a strange expression on her face.

"You feeling all right?" I asked. She blinked and turned to me as though she'd half forgotten I was there.

"Yeah, yeah, I'm doing fine," she assured me. "Just a little overwhelmed, I think."

"What do you mean?" I furrowed my brow at her, and she gestured around us at the boat.

"I guess I never imagined you would have something like this," she admitted. "This is... this is, like, seriously rich stuff. *Really* rich stuff. I knew you were well-off, but between this and the house...."

She shook her head as though she was having trouble wrapping her brain around it. I had a feeling something was off with her again. Maybe this kind of luxury made her uncomfortable. If you weren't used to it, it was a lot to take in. I had earned it from the bottom up, and Hunter had grown up with it, but this was all new to her. No wonder it was a lot for her to wrap her head around.

"But I bet there's plenty of women out there who would love something like this." She smiled at me kindly. I felt a little drop in my stomach. She wasn't including herself in that statement, and that bothered me, even though it shouldn't have—because I'd told myself and anyone who would listen all this time that there was nothing between us, that this was simply a platonic trip out for the three of us. With Hunter right there, how could it be anything different?

"Right." I tried to ignore my disappointment that this didn't seem to impress her. Maybe I had misread her. Clearly, that was the case. I needed to pay closer attention, figure out what would get me in her good books and in with her good friends.

I glanced over at her as she shifted forward to lean on the railing before us, her gaze turned out to the water, which lay out in front of the boat like an endless wash of calm. With the wind whipping through her hair, she looked like she belonged here. Like she was the figurehead on the front of a boat, too beautiful to exist in real life. And once again, I had to remind myself that this was only a friend of mine. That anything more I felt for her was wrong. And that was that.

18

AUTUMN

"So, what about that over there?"

I pointed to a boat about two hundred feet from us, and Hunter narrowed his eyes and gazed at it for a moment, trying to place it.

"I don't know that one," he confessed. "But I'll look it up and find out and tell you at school."

"You do that," I agreed, and I fought the urge to ruffle his cute little head.

"Hey, Hunter, mind if I borrow Autumn for a minute?"

I turned around to find Holden approaching us, a glass of wine in his hand for me. I raised my eyebrows as he handed it to me, and I took a long sip.

"Mmm, that's good," I sighed, as Hunter vanished back into the cabin to give us some space. Probably to look up the name of the ship so he could impress me.

"So, how are you liking it?" he asked, coming to lean on the railing close to me. I was so distinctly aware of how near he was to me right now that I could have shifted and pressed myself against him, and I pushed it to the back of my mind. Useful thoughts only, please.

"Uh, yeah, it's really cool." I nodded, but he cocked an eyebrow, and I could tell that I was hardly convincing him.

"It's not that bad, is it?" he asked. It was obvious he was trying to keep a game face on, but I had seen how disappointed he had seemed when I hadn't been super-impressed with the yacht as soon as we got on it. It wasn't that it wasn't cool. It was incredible that somebody I actually knew was part of the super-rich club to the point that they had their own luxury yacht. But there was something about it that made me a little uncomfortable. It was so conspicuous, like he was making a point about his cash and flashing it around every chance he got.

"No, not at all." I shook my head. "It's very neat, it is. And the fact that you can sail it even more so. But... this wasn't where you were thinking of bringing the women I set you up with on your first dates, was it?"

"It had crossed my mind." He shrugged, furrowing his brow. I took another sip of the wine, letting the flavor linger on my tongue for a moment before I swallowed. It was good wine, expensive, but then that probably went with the territory, right?

"You don't think that's a good idea?" he prompted me, and I shook my head.

"I think it's a little much," I told him gently. "It feels like you're trying to compensate for something. Or that you think they're just in it for the money."

"I guess you're right." He shook his head. "I haven't been dating for so long, it's easy to forget how things come across."

"I mean, some women would go for it," I corrected myself. "But I'm not sure they're the kind of women you'd want long-term."

"Gold diggers, you mean?" he replied bluntly.

"I guess that's one word for it."

"So what do you think would make a good first date?" he asked, turning to me with interest. "Like you. What would your perfect first date be?"

"Wow." I raised my eyebrows. "I've never given it that much thought."

"Don't overthink it," he encouraged me. "Just the first things that come to your mind."

"I think it would for sure have an outdoorsy feel," I began slowly. "Maybe a picnic or something. Oh, and I would love for them to take me somewhere I had never been before—somewhere like a park or a museum or both. Something they were passionate about, somewhere they loved and wanted to share with me. I think that would be sweet."

"That sounds nice," he said. "What else?"

"Hmm." I tipped my head back and let the breeze rush over me. "I think the main thing would be making me comfortable. If they could make me feel at ease wherever they took me, I would be happy with that. Oh, and I don't like it when the guys I date are dicks about me wanting to split the bill. I like to pay my way, and I hate it when they wave me off like I couldn't possibly afford it."

"Guys really do that?" He cocked an eyebrow.

"Oh yeah," I grinned and shook my head. "Like you wouldn't believe. It drives me up the wall."

I fell silent again, the wine settling into my system as I gave the question a bit more thought.

"But I think I'd want someone who was there for *me*, you know?" I emphasized the word. "Not because he thought this is how dating should work or because he thought this specific thing would be enough to impress me. Who listened to me and actually gave a shit what I wanted. I wouldn't mind as long as that was part of it."

"Makes sense," he agreed. "Is it that hard to find someone out there who'll actually listen to you?"

"Oh, you'd be surprised." I held my hands up. "Don't get me started, seriously. Over the last few years, I've had so many dates where I'm pretty sure they didn't listen to a word coming out of my mouth the whole evening. I'm trying to make sure you don't have to go through the same thing."

"Well, I appreciate your effort." He touched his glass of sparkling water to mine and smiled, and I felt that flicker—a flutter, even—in my chest once more. I shoved it down. He was only getting advice, not coming on to me. If he'd wanted to romance me, he wouldn't have brought his son along with us for the whole day.

Hunter returned, and he pointed to the boat I had been asking him about earlier.

"It's a runabout," he told me excitedly, and I nodded to him, glad to have something to distract me from the mess of thoughts running around my head at that very moment.

"Wow, I never would have known that." I cocked my head at him. "Anything else you can name for me?"

And with that, the rest of the day passed pretty well. I had a good time with Hunter, and it was seriously sweet to see him and Holden interacting with such clear affection and kindness. There was no doubt in my mind that Hunter clearly adored his father, and his dad felt the same way about him. Eventually, Holden took us back to shore, and we hopped back in the car to head home. Hunter passed out in the back seat nearly at once, snoring softly, and I grinned as I glanced at him in the mirror.

"He's always tired after I take him out on a day like this," Holden explained quietly. "All the sea air, I think. It suits him. He always likes going out on the water for a while."

"Well, I can see how keen he is on it. Good to see him so passionate about something."

"It really is," Holden agreed, and the two of us chatted about his boat and the trips that he and Hunter had taken on it the last few years until we got back to the house. The drive seemed to go so quickly, and I found myself wishing it could have lasted a little bit longer.

"I guess I should get going," I remarked, as Hunter stirred in the back seat and waved goodbye to me as he headed into the house.

"I guess so," Holden agreed, and he got out of the car and opened my door for me. He was such a gentleman, and I felt my heart flutter as I brushed by him to stand up.

"Well, thanks for an amazing day," I told him after I had called my cab. And, as I stood there, leaning on his car and looking at him, I found something stirring in me—the way he was looking at me, the softness in his eyes, like he was a second away from leaning in toward me and planting a kiss on my lips. What surprised me was that I wanted him to. Badly. He inhaled deeply, and his gaze flicked briefly down to my mouth, and I knew I had to do something to break the tension before one of us did something we couldn't come back from.

"I'll see you soon?" I stuck my hand out to him awkwardly, and he glanced down at it with surprise, as though he wasn't quite sure what to do with it. Then it seemed to click, and he shook my hand firmly, gripping tight, like he wasn't sure he wanted me to let go.

"You sure will," he agreed. "Call me, all right? We'll organize something again soon."

"I can't wait." I smiled at him and realized I was still holding his hand. I dropped it swiftly, ignoring the warmth of his skin against mine, how nice it had felt. I heard the engine of the cab approaching, and I turned to flag it down.

"See you later," I called to him as I slipped into the car, and he closed the door for me, waving through the window before I pulled away. I leaned my head against the cool glass and tried to calm the mess of thoughts running through my head.

I hadn't wanted him to kiss me. I had just wanted to be kissed, period. That was all it was. I hadn't been with anyone for a long time, and I was craving the physical affection. Because Holden was a new arrival in my life, I had just shifted my attention to him, but there was nothing to come of it, nothing to happen because of it.

Even though I had told him I would see him again soon, I wasn't going to wait too long before I met up with him again. I stared out the window at the street whipping by me and wondered if I should pull back a little and, even if that's what I should do, if there was any chance at all that I would.

19

HOLDEN

"Where do you want to go next?" I asked Hunter. I knew he was tired and would have been happy with takeout and TV, but I was buzzing with energy. I would have to work it off if I had a hope in hell of getting to sleep that night. Hunter cocked his head at me.

"Like where?"

"We could go to Dandy's," I suggested. "Get dinner?"

His face lit up. Dandy's was about his favorite place in town, and I loved it too. It was an old-fashioned diner with an arcade section full of classic games, and the two of us would head down there a couple of times a month to play games and eat greasy food. We had already been out today, and I didn't much feel like cooking. Plus, the thought of sitting around this house and thinking about everything that had gone down—no, I didn't need to linger any more than I already had on all of that. I needed to get my head out of my damn asshole and focus on taking care of Hunter. This was what today had been about, hadn't it? Letting Autumn get to know us so she would be able to find someone better suited to my son. Nothing more than that. Nothing less.

Hunter changed, and I threw on an old T-shirt and jeans,

thanking God that the dress code for Dandy's was about as casual as they came, and we headed across town. Hunter was chatting to me the whole time about a series of books they were reading at school, and I tuned in and engaged him as best I could. Soon enough, I found the thoughts of Autumn—the way she had looked at me when she had said goodbye, the way she had let her hand linger in mine—drifting away like debris on the water.

We arrived at Dandy's, and Hunter headed straight over to the arcade as I got us a table and ordered our usual. The wait would be a while, as it was a weekend night and a lot of parents had the same thought as me to bring their kids there. I went over to join my son and found him already deep into a game of Space Invaders.

"I bet I can beat your high score," I challenged him, and he raised his eyebrows at me.

"Try me," he replied, and I saw that flash of competitiveness in his eyes. He got that from me, that spark that made him want to beat out everyone around him any chance he got. We swapped the controllers a few times, and I made sure to fudge my skills to make it so he could win. I loved the look on his face when he punched the air after beating me, the little wrinkle in his nose as he celebrated.

"Did you see that?" he exclaimed after a particularly impressive run. "That's the best score I've ever got!"

"Well, you sure got me beat." I held my hands up and shook my head as if disappointed in myself. "Maybe I'll do better next time, huh?"

"Maybe," he agreed, but he didn't much seem to believe it. He shot a look to the other end of the arcade at his favorite game, Heath Fire. A small cluster of kids was hanging around it right now, laughing and whooping as one of them pulled off an excellent run.

"You want to go over there and wait in the line for it?" I suggested. "I'm sure they won't be too long."

He shook his head, and his face seemed suddenly cloudy, as though there was something bothering him that he didn't want to admit to.

"Why not?" I wondered aloud. "Something up, buddy?"

"No," he replied, but his lips were pressed together like he was trying to keep something inside.

"You can tell me," I told him gently, and he glanced up at me, his eyes suddenly sad.

"They're kids from school," he said, shaking his head. "I don't want to disturb them."

My heart sank as those words came out of his mouth. I wanted nothing more than to be able to go over there, introduce Hunter to those kids, and have the five of them play all together, but I knew he would about expire from humiliation if I did something like that. His shoulders sagged, and I could see this was going to ruin his night unless I jumped in to fix it quickly.

"Hey, shall we go and see if our food's ready?" I suggested. "I got the root beer float, the one you like."

"Sure." He nodded, and I could tell he was trying to hide how hurt he was.

We made our way back over to the booth, and as soon as he had his food in front of him, he seemed to forget all about the incident with the other kids in his class. It concerned me a lot, especially given that Autumn and I had met because she was worried about his social development. But it wasn't going to do a lot of good to try and push him on it right now. It wasn't often I got to spend quality time with him like this, and there was no way I was going to mess that up by forcing a conversation on him that made him uncomfortable.

"How's your food, Hunter?" I gestured to his waffles with bacon and maple syrup. It was the kind of food my mother would have turned her nose up at feeding me when I was a kid, but I knew that denying him these treats would lead him to sneak candy from his classmates when he thought he could get away with it, and I had no interest in that.

"It's good," he said, munching on a bite and washing it down with a sip of his root beer float. There was a time when he would have had to hold that thing up with two hands, and I couldn't help but smile when I remembered how insistent he had been the first time he started eating and drinking by himself. He wanted to be independent, the same way I always had. Except his independence seemed to stretch to include social isolation as well.

"Good." I smiled. "And did you have a good day today?"

"I had an awesome day," he gushed. "It was so fun seeing Miss Becks out of school. I've never done that with a teacher before."

"Me neither." I shook my head. "It was fun, wasn't it? Do you think she had a good time?"

"I think so." Hunter nodded, and I silently scolded myself for needing my nine-year-old kid to confirm that I hadn't completely fucked up the day.

"I'm so glad the two of you are dating now," Hunter continued, and I spluttered into my lemonade.

"I'm sorry, what?" I held a hand up, smiling at him gently. "No, that's not what we're doing. We're not dating."

"Oh." Hunter furrowed his brow. "But you went out with her before, didn't you? And then again today?"

"Yes, I did, but it's not like that." I shook my head. "We're just friends, that's all."

"Oh," Hunter looked a little disappointed. "Oh, okay. I suppose so. It's still nice to have her around."

I took a sip of my drink to clear my throat and wondered if I was going to have to put up with these questions from literally everyone in my life. It felt as though the entire world had an opinion on what I was doing with Autumn whether I liked it or not. I only wanted to spend time with her and get to know her. Was that so wrong? Had I time traveled back to fifty years before, when men and women couldn't spend time together without people assuming they were bumping uglies?

"I really like her," Hunter continued. "Will you start dating her? When would you do that?"

"I don't think that's going to happen, Hunter," I told him firmly. "We're friends. And besides, she's your teacher. It wouldn't be appropriate."

He pulled a face, and his disappointment was obvious. He continued to eat his food and left me sitting there feeling as though

I'd had the rug pulled from under me. Hunter obviously saw something between us, and he was the only person who'd spent time with us together. Kids were meant to have that great intuition, weren't they? Maybe he was sensing something that the two of us, as a pair of adults, were a little too nervous for the time being to acknowledge.

"I hope we get to see her again soon," he replied. "Not just in school, I mean."

"She said she wanted to meet up again," I promised him. "And I'll make sure we get to spend time together, all three of us."

"Yay!" Hunter grinned widely, the sugar rush from his float clearly hitting him. He glanced around at the arcade and saw that the game the other kids had been playing earlier was free now. "Oh, can I go over and play a game? Please?"

"Of course." I waved my hand. "Just stay where I can see you, all right?"

"I will," he promised, and he got up and practically sprinted across the room toward the game. I watched him go and drummed my fingers on the table in front of me. Autumn was in my head again, filling my mind, escaping from that space I had tried to commit her to for the time being.

I couldn't stop thinking about that moment before she'd left when she had shaken my hand and given me that look, as though there was something else going on in her mind beyond the purely platonic.

Or maybe I just really, really wanted her to feel that way. Today had been something more than what we'd had before. She had slotted so well into my little family, getting on well with Hunter and managing to balance the two of us out perfectly. Maybe Hunter was right, and I didn't know it yet. Maybe we really were dating, and I needed to catch up with the game and get on board. And maybe Autumn felt the same way.

I leaned back from the table and sighed. This was all speculation, and until I saw her again, I wouldn't be able to figure it out one way or the other. As far as I knew, we were a couple of friends hanging out together, and that was the way things were going to stay as long as she kept steady in her attitude toward our relationship. What she wanted came first. I wasn't going to do anything to fuck whatever we had up. Because the thought of going on without the promise of seeing her again made my heart sink right down to the bottom of the water we'd been sailing on together all day.

20

AUTUMN

"Oh," I groaned, tipping my head back into the pillow. I couldn't remember how I'd gotten here or even who precisely it was between my thighs right now, but it didn't matter. I was finally getting the release I had craved so deeply for so long, and it was *good*.

His hands sank into my thighs, and I looked down to try and figure out who it was. His face was buried in my pussy, and he seemed to have no intention of coming up for air. I closed my eyes again and let myself get lost to the feeling of it.

He was good at this. So good at it. I couldn't even specify what it was about his technique that was working for me, but it was. It was as though he couldn't possibly get enough of the way I tasted, like my body was a feast and he had been starving for weeks. He was lavishing me with attention, sucking and licking and tasting and trying me like I was the most delicious thing in the entire world, sucking on my lips, on my clit, tracing his tongue over my slit and slipping it briefly inside of me. My entire body was shuddering and shaking, and I tried to remember how I'd ended up here, how I'd managed to convince a man so talented into my bed, but I couldn't for the life of me remember how

I'd gotten him here. It didn't matter. All that mattered was that he was already on the brink of making me come, and my body was grateful for the attention it had been so lacking the last few months.

"Mmm," I reached down and ran my fingers through his hair, silently urging him to tilt his face up to me so I could see him, but he didn't move. He slipped his hands beneath my ass and squeezed roughly, letting out a moan that echoed all the way up through my body. I sank back against the pillow, helpless, and the only thing I could do right now was let him pleasure me. He wasn't going to stop until he was satisfied, until I was satisfied, and I was hardly going to pull away from that to get a look at him.

My legs were beginning to tremble as he drew his fingers to my pussy and slipped them inside, not fucking me with them, but rather stroking the inside of my pussy in time with the strokes of his tongue on my clit. I let out a gasp, and suddenly, the pleasure crested and exploded all over me, cascading over my body in waves, my muscles shaking and my body clenching as the relief finally came. How long had he been going down on me for? I felt like I'd been here for hours and seconds at the same time, the notion of distance distorting in my head.

While my eyes are still closed, he climbed back on top of me and kissed me. I could taste myself on his mouth, taste the sweetness of us all mingled up together, and I pushed my tongue against his hungrily. I hadn't been kissed like this in a long time, that urgent, desperate making out that came from two people who didn't only want each other but needed each other. This strange mix of satisfaction and deep need flooded me, as though I could stop here or go on all night. He was naked suddenly, and I could feel his hard-on nudging up against my thighs. It was thick, impressive, and my stomach fluttered as I realized what I wanted now.

"You're so fucking sexy," he groaned into my ear, and I ran my hands over his back, feeling his muscles move as he shifted to plant kisses all over my shoulder and my neck. His breath was hot, and his need was obvious. I wanted to give him what he so clearly wants. I turned my mouth to his ear, making sure he could hear me, knowing this was the only thing that mattered right now.

"I want you inside me," I moaned, and he didn't need telling twice. He pulled back, but before I could get a look at him, he flipped me over and pulled me up so I was on all fours. Fuck, yes—I loved this position. I wiggled my ass back and forth, wondering if this man could read my mind since he seemed so adept at giving me exactly what I wanted, exactly what I needed.

I felt him pressing against my slit, and I arched my back to make it easier for him to enter me. He slid a hand around my belly and let the other come to rest on my hip as he guided himself inside of me, and I forgot about the fact that I don't seem to know who this man was as we fit together for the first time.

"Oh my God," I groaned. He felt even better than I could have imagined. The warmth of his hands on my skin felt familiar, and for a moment, I tried to place where I might know it from, but then he began to move inside of me, and it slipped from my brain once more.

"Fuck, you're so tight," he murmured, his fingers sinking into my ass as he held me steady. He was as big as I imagined, and I was so full with him inside me like this, like we were perfectly built to go together, as though he were made for me.

He ground himself into me, going in circles, keeping himself deep, and he moved his hand up my back and weaved it into my hair at the nape of my neck, tugging lightly. I went limp, my arms and my legs shaking as I struggled to keep myself upright. How did he know exactly how to touch me, exactly how to get me there? Every move he made, it was like he had crawled inside my head and teased out all those things I had been too nervous to tell the other men I'd been with. Or maybe I had been the one to tell him. I couldn't remember. It didn't matter.

I began to rock my hips back against him, taking him as deep as I could manage as he moved the hand on my belly down between my legs and on to my clit. He let out a low groan when he found my hypersensitive nub, as though my pleasure morphed into his.

Before I knew it, I was growing close again. The mix of stimulation had me helplessly careening toward orgasm once more, and, even though I had just had one, I found my body craving it, pushing me toward him, arching hungrily toward the one that I needed now. I wanted to feel his cock inside of me as I came, wanted to let him know how good this was for me every way I could. I was panting, pushing myself back against him, listening to his breathing as it grew more ragged. I could tell he was getting close too, and I wanted to feel him come along with me, at the same time as me. His hand was still in my hair so I couldn't twist my head around to look at him, but that didn't matter. I could feel him, not just his body but his energy, and that was all I needed.

"Come inside me," I demanded, my voice taking on an edge I had never known I had in me. He moved harder, faster, his fingers moving with more purpose against my clit, and that was when it hit me.

The first orgasm had been intense, but this one was something else entirely. It felt as though my body was having trouble keeping together, the shake spreading out from my pussy and moving across me in waves like aftershocks punching through my system. The noises that came out of me, I had never heard them before, had never had call to make them before. My pussy tightened around his cock over and over again, and he continued to move into me mercilessly, extending the pleasure until I wasn't sure I could take any more. My jaw was hanging open, my lungs gasping for air, my body tingling. I felt as though I had been torched, set alight, and now my body was doing everything it could to make sense of what had happened and to figure out exactly how we could get there again.

A few moments later, he pushed himself hard into me as he came, his body tensing and relaxing as he let out a long, low growl of pleasure. He held himself steady, deep inside me, for a long moment, as though he wasn't ready for this to be over yet. I knew how he felt. I wanted this to go on forever, the two of us never pulling apart. But eventually, with some apparent reluctance, he slid his cock out of me and slid down on to the bed beside me. I collapsed forward next to him, and I felt his hand skim up my back as I leaned in to kiss him—

Then I saw his face, and I woke up with a start.

I was panting hard when I came back to the real world, the memory of the dream so fresh that it felt real. I could feel his hands on my skin, the way they had traced over my body like he was drawing me into existence. I touched my belly, the back of my neck, the places he had laid his hands on me. I wasn't sure if I had come or not, but my body felt limp and satisfied, as though I somehow truly had.

And then his face drifted back into my brain once more, and I clapped my hand over my mouth. There was no doubt who it had been.

Holden.

I stared at the ceiling for a long time, until my breath had gone back to normal, and reminded myself that it had been a dream. I hadn't been fucked in a long time—I had never been fucked like that in my entire life, but still—and Holden was a man in my life, so my brain was extracting the data and offering me up something it thought I would like. Nothing to read into more than that. Nothing serious.

Yet the memory was so vivid, I would have a hard time looking him in the eye next time I saw him, but I would get over that. I needed to push those thoughts to the back of my mind. In fact, what I needed to do was set him up with someone. Now that I had spent time with Hunter and him, I should get a move on and find someone for him to go out with, someone who could act as a block in my brain between the two of us. I couldn't handle having any more dreams like that if I ever wanted to talk to him again without blushing like a damn beacon.

I sighed and turned over in bed, staring at the wall opposite me. Despite it all, as I began drifting off once more, I found myself hoping I would slip into the same dream all over again.

21

HOLDEN

I fidgeted as I sat in the car outside the school. I didn't need to get here this early, but I wanted to make sure I was there to pick up Hunter on time. If I was being honest with myself, it was to make sure I got a chance to see Autumn as well.

I tried not to let that thought stick in my brain too long. I had done a decent job throwing myself into work the last few days, not calling or texting her, waiting for her to reach out to me so we could set up something to do together. I was looking forward to seeing her again, but I also needed a little time to cool off before I let my head get the better of me. The last thing I wanted was to fuck things up with the woman who was trying to help me get back on the dating scene. Even though I was beginning to wonder if it was just her I wanted to date at this point.

Hunter was at an after-school club, hanging out and doing some arts and crafts with his classmates. He hadn't been that keen on going, but I had insisted that he at least try something out to see if he could bond with the kids around him over something new. He had grudgingly agreed to go on the promise that I would take him out to Dandy's at some point soon. If it meant that he actually had the confidence to go up to those kids and hang out with them this time, I was all for it.

Raymond had offered to pick up him, but I had declined, even though it would mean me coming out of work early to get him.

"I know he's nervous, and I just want to be there for him." I shrugged. "Besides, it'll give me a chance to catch up with Autumn again and see what we're doing next."

"Oh, yeah, how was the weekend?" Raymond wondered. "You didn't mention it after you came back. Did it go okay?"

"Yeah, I think it went pretty well." I nodded. "She and Hunter got on well, and I think she had a good time."

"Why just think?"

"I guess she was a little shocked by how... you know the kind of lifestyle I lead," I replied. "She told me she wouldn't want to come out on the yacht for a date. Said she was worried that's how I'd attract women who only wanted my cash."

"Well, that's probably not bad advice." He tapped his fingers on his chin. "I mean, you are fresh back on the scene, and you don't want to get taken advantage of by someone who sees dollar signs when they look at you."

"I'm sure that's not going to happen." I brushed that thought off. "She knows me well enough not to set me up with anyone who might pull shit like that."

"Oh, so she knows you well, does she?" Raymond teased, and I gave him a hard look.

"Seriously, dude, there's nothing happening between us," I repeated myself firmly. "I don't know how many times I'm going to have to say that to you. Or Hunter. He thought the two of us were dating as well."

"Then maybe you should bite the bullet and get it over with." He cocked his head at me. "Would that be so terrible?"

"I'm not just going to date her because you think I should!" I protested, but I was laughing by now. "Jesus, Raymond, you really want me to settle down already, don't you?"

"I want you to have what I do with Olivia," he replied, and I saw his gaze soften as he said her name. I knew how much he adored her, had adored her since the moment they set eyes on one another, and he had made that clear from the start. He wanted me to feel the same way. That was sweet when I thought of it like that.

But either way, I wasn't going to have a happily-ever-after with Autumn. It was clear that the lifestyle I lived was pretty much incompatible with the one she did, and I was going to have to be fine with that. She was entitled to her opinions on my life as I was to mine on hers, and that was totally all right.

I forced myself to get out of the car and stroll toward the door, my head feeling a little fuzzy around the edges, and I did my best to keep myself calm as I headed in her direction. I was just a friend, checking in on another friend. It was casual, that was it. What any friend would have done when given the chance to drop in on an acquaintance. So why was my heart racing, and why were my palms starting to sweat?

I made my way to her classroom and knocked on the door. Her voice came from inside, sounding tired.

"Come in!" she called out to me, and I pushed open the door and waved at her. She beamed when she saw me and got to her feet to give me a hug.

"Holden!" she exclaimed happily, winding her arms around my neck as though on instinct and briefly holding me closer than she needed to. "What are you doing here?"

"I'm picking up Hunter from this after-school club I enrolled him in." I shrugged, ignoring the stirring in my stomach at her closeness. "Thought I would stop in and see you while I was here."

"Well, I always appreciate the visit." She faux-curtsied, and I chuckled.

"I told him to find me in your classroom. I hope that's all right," I explained. She pointed to the one adult-size chair in the room other than her own, propped up underneath the whiteboard, and I grabbed it and brought it over to her desk.

"So what are you doing working so late?" I wondered aloud, and she shook her head and sighed deeply.

"I have to take care of putting these grade curves together," she explained, pointing to papers scattered all over her desk. "Trust me, you don't want to know. They're a total pain in my ass, but I can't get away from them."

"Dare I ask?" I cocked an eyebrow, and she shook her head.

"Trust me, they're about the most boring things in the entire world," she assured me. "I've never been less compelled by anything. I don't understand why they don't automate the system so we don't have to spend three years out of every term making sure we have them ready to go. It feels like such a waste of time, but they say they can't afford it."

My ears pricked up. That sounded like something I could take on. I leaned back in my chair and shrugged.

"If you want, I could take a look at making a program for you," I suggested, and she furrowed her brow at me, smiling.

"I thought you designed websites," she reminded me, and I shrugged and shook my head.

"Yeah, I do, but I had to learn the basics of pretty much everything to do with computers before I opened the business," I pointed out. "I had to be able to run everything myself, and that included making programs that would take care of the tasks I didn't want to pay a real human person to do."

"I'm sure you could do it, and I'm sure it would be great," she said. "But I don't think the school board can afford you."

"You know what? I'll do it for free." I held my hands up, and she raised her eyebrows at me.

"What? No, don't be ridiculous." She dismissed my offer with a wave. "I don't see how we could ask you to give up all that time, just for—"

"Honestly, it probably won't even take me all that long," I cut her off. "If it's just a matter of making a system where you can input the data and it spits out a result, I'm sure I could knock that off in my free time. I haven't done any program design for a while. Could be fun to have something to keep my hand in."

"You're serious about this?" She stared at me for a long moment. "For free? You wouldn't expect anything back for this?"

"Nothing." I shook my head. "Consider it a donation to the school. I mean, this is where my son learns, and I want to make sure all the teachers aren't wasting their time on something I could easily take care of in no time."

"I'll pass along your email to the school board," she agreed. "You can talk to them about it. They'll know more about this than I will."

"Do that," I said. "I really want to help you out with this, Autumn. After everything you've done for me."

"Hey, setting you up on a couple of hypothetical dates doesn't equate to you doing this work for me for free," she shot back.

"I think I'll be the judge of that," I replied firmly, and she smiled at me once more and shook her head.

"If you really can get this thing working, then it's going to change everything for all the teachers I know," she told me seriously. "Really, I don't think I can overstate that. You're going to change the way the school system in this county works and how time is allocated. It sounds boring, but it's so important, trust me."

"I hope I can help." I smiled at her, and then the door opened and we both turned to see Hunter strolling in. He had paint on his hands and a little smudged beneath his right eye, but he was smiling. So that had to be good news.

"Hey, son," I got to my feet. "How about we get you cleaned up, and we can head off?"

"Cleaned up?" He glanced down at his hands, as though he hadn't even noticed. "Oh, right. I'll be back in a minute."

And with that, he had darted out to the bathrooms and left the two of us alone again. Autumn grinned at me, getting up and stretching.

"Well, I guess I have a little more free time on my hands if you really are going to be able to do this for us," she remarked. "So thanks for that."

"How about you spend a little of it with the two of us?" I suggested before I could stop myself. "I know Hunter had such a good time when we all hung out together last. It's all he's been able to talk about since. And I'd love to see you again too."

"Uh...." She hesitated, and I could see her fighting internally with something I hadn't seen in her before. I couldn't put my finger on what it was, but it was clearly unsettling her.

"Hey, Dad, I'm ready to go." Hunter breezed back into the room, and I glanced at Autumn once more.

"What do you say?" I asked her. "Dinner, my place, this weekend? I'll cook."

"Oh, say yes!" Hunter exclaimed. "I want to show you some more of the boats I have in my room!"

She paused for a moment longer and then laughed and shook her head.

"I guess I can't say no to that," she conceded.

"Guess not," I agreed, and I flashed her a smile. "I'll drop you a text, and we can figure out what's going to work for the both of us. Sound good?"

"Sounds great." She planted her hands on her hips and watched us walk out of there. I felt like punching the air as soon as I'd made it outside and out of her sight. Because I was seeing her again. This time, I was going to prove to her I could be as low-key as she wanted.

22

AUTUMN

As I drove down to their house, I found my foot jiggling, the only physical representation of my nerves I would allow. Because I was fucking unsettled right now, and I had to keep my shit together if I was going to pull this night off.

My mind slipped back to the conversation I'd had with Zoe before I'd come out today. She had ducked into my classroom right before I was finished, and she'd given me a once-over and cocked her head in my direction.

"Well, you're looking gorgeous," she'd remarked. "Friday night dinner plans?"

"Actually, yeah." I glanced up at her. "Holden invited me over. Says he's going to cook for me. And hey, I'm not saying no to a free dinner, right?"

"Yeah, of course. That's what this is about," she teased. She took her seat opposite me. "How are things going with the two of you?"

"What do you mean?" I furrowed my brow at her.

"I mean, are you still friends, or is there something else going on?"

I thought back to the dream I'd had about him the week before and shifted in my seat.

"No, we're just friends," I replied. She reached over and patted my hand.

"Of course you are," she mocked, and I shot her a hard look that let her know her spiel with this stuff was starting to grow a little damn tiring.

"I'm just saying." She held her hands up. "The two of you are more or less dating at this point, aren't you? I mean, you know his kid, he's taken you out on his yacht, he's having you over for dinner...."

"I mean, if you want to look at it like that, sure," I sighed. "But nothing's happened between us. Romantically, I mean. I feel like if he wanted to make a move on me, he would already have done it, you know what I mean?"

"Sure, but maybe he's nervous. You said yourself he hasn't dated anyone in a hell of a long time. Perhaps he's not sure what making a move looks like in this day and age?"

"Okay, I think you're being a little patronizing." I raised my eyebrows at her. "He's not stupid. He's just out of the loop. No need to assume he's too scared to hold my hand."

"Fair enough." She cocked her head at me again, and I could see there was something she wanted to ask me, something she was trying to come out with the best way to phrase so as not to piss me off.

"And you're okay with things as they are?" she asked gently. She could talk a lot of shit, but at the end of the day, she wanted nothing more than for me to be happy. She wanted to make sure I wasn't getting strung along, but I wasn't. I was enjoying spending time with Hunter and Holden, but our lives were way too different to make a connection that would stick. At least, that's what I kept telling myself.

"Yeah, I sure am," I promised her. "I would have gone for it if I'd liked him that way. But I didn't."

"And now you're setting him up on dates?"

"Yes. I actually have his first one lined up." I grinned. "Casey, from the teacher training day, you remember?"

"Oh, shit, yeah, I know her." Zoe tapped her finger on the desk to punctuate her words. "Yeah, she's nice. I could see her being a good fit for a single dad."

"That's what I'm hoping," I agreed. If I was being honest, I was hoping that putting a whole person—a person I had chosen and liked and didn't want to wind up hurt, no less—between Holden and me was going to be enough to scrub the last remnants of my attraction to him out of my brain once and for all. I knew it was a little shitty, setting him up to get him out of my head, but I had to work with what I had at the moment, and this was it.

"Well, I suppose you're going to find out how he really feels about you based on how he reacts to the date," she remarked.

"I know how he feels about me," I reminded her, and she gave me a look.

"Well, then it's going to be confirmed for you then," she replied, grinning. She glanced at her watch. "Hey, I have to get going. The takeout place I like closes in an hour, and I want to have my Friday night pizza."

"You get going." I waved my hand at her. "Have a good night, all right?"

"You too," she replied. "And let me know how it goes, okay?"

"Will do." I smiled, and she headed out the door and left me sitting with my thoughts once more. What if he did go along with this date without a question? How would that make me feel? Did I want him to date Casey, or did I want to convince myself that I didn't want to date him?

I went to grab my bag and put on a little makeup for the dinner this evening and didn't let those thoughts stick with me. Whatever happened was going to happen, and I had to be all right with that. I could do this, come what may. It was just dinner, after all. Nothing I couldn't handle.

I arrived outside his house and took a deep breath. I imagined Casey arriving out here, heading up to the door, checking the place out. Would she feel the same way I did about it? Would she think it was a little too much but also be quietly impressed that he had managed to provide this life for himself and his kid? Or would she swoon at his cash, at the promise of all that money?

I climbed out of the car and headed to the door. She would just be glad to have a date, I would bet. It was hard to find people to go out with in this business, given that it was so female-dominated, and she would be glad to find someone who shared her love of kids, her kindness, her compassion. The thought of them spending the night in here, talking about everything and laughing and sharing a bottle of wine, shifting ever closer on the couch—it should have made me happy for my friend. Instead, I felt a stab of jealousy. I pushed it down. No, not now. Not ever.

I knocked on the door, and Hunter opened it a second later, as though he had been waiting for me to turn up. He grinned widely when he saw me, and I smiled back at him. Damn, he was such a cute kid. I mean, I pretty much thought all kids were somewhat adorable, but Hunter was particularly endearing.

"Miss Becks!" he exclaimed happily, and I grinned. It was so weird being called that outside of school, but I didn't mind too much. I certainly wasn't going to encourage him to call me Autumn. I had to keep that line there between us. Just like the line I was trying to maintain when it came to his father.

"Autumn." Holden emerged from the kitchen, wearing a dark gray shirt, jeans, and a dishcloth thrown over one shoulder. "How are you doing? Journey down here all right?"

"More than fine," I told him, and I unhooked my bag and let it drop to the ground next to me. I smoothed out the dress I had put on for the occasion and wondered why I'd felt the urge to dress up like this. Dinner at a friend's place, that was normally a jeans-and-your-baggiest-shirt affair, yet here I was, looking like I was dressed for a date.

"The lasagna's almost ready." Holden nodded to the kitchen. "Hunter, why don't you finish setting the table?"

"Okay." Hunter saluted him happily and vanished off to take care of his task. Holden waved me through to the kitchen, where he had a glass of wine sitting out on the counter ready for me.

"Oh, you have no idea how much I need this." I took a sip of the wine and then inhaled the gorgeous smells filling the kitchen. "Hey, that smells great. Didn't know you could cook."

"I had to learn for Hunter." He shrugged and then checked the food in the oven. "This is my specialty. I hope you like it."

"I'm sure I will," I promised him. "It's nice not to have to cook dinner for myself for a change."

"I can imagine," he said, and I was so distinctly aware in that moment that the two of us were alone in this kitchen together, that I had wine in my hand, and this handsome guy cooking me dinner, and that it would have made every bit of sense if I had shifted myself that inch toward him, moved in close, stolen a little moment of intimacy....

"The table's ready." Hunter appeared at the door, mercifully barring those thoughts from my brain before they went any further.

"I'll take my wine through," I suggested, ducking out of the kitchen and trying to catch my breath. What in the hell was going on with me? It was that dream, that damn dream—but it wasn't real. Nothing had happened between us, no matter how realistic it had felt in the moment. I had to forget it, to leave it all behind. I was here to set him up on a date, after all, and I couldn't very well do that while all those thoughts were running through my mind.

Holden emerged from the kitchen a few minutes later with the lasagna, and he served us all up a generous portion, and we began to eat. The food was good—great, even—and I tucked in happily, glad to have something to distract myself with.

"So, Hunter, I saw that you were in the arts and crafts club earlier this week," I said to him, and he nodded gamely. "Did you like it?"

He shrugged. "It was okay. I don't know if I would want to go again."

Holden furrowed his brow, and I could see that the statement had put him out. I dived in with a counteroffer.

"Hey, so, there's a gaming club that just started at the school," I told him. "I'm helping out with it. Do you think that would suit you more?"

Hunter raised his eyebrows, and his eyes sparkled with interest.

"That sounds good." He glanced at his dad. "Is that okay, Dad? Can I go to it?"

"Sure you can," he promised his son.

"And you'll be there, right?" Hunter asked me.

"For sure." I smiled at him, and he seemed excited by the thought. It was a victory, even a little one, to get a kid like him who had been struggling to find his place in the social scene of the school to come to a club. I knew it wasn't going to be well-populated at first, but maybe that would suit him better, not having a bunch of people around that he felt like he had to live up to.

"Thanks," Holden mouthed at me, and I flashed him a brief smile in return. The way he was looking at me, pure gratefulness in his eyes, it made my stomach twist up. I put down my fork, not hungry anymore, or at least, hungry for something else.

The three of us finished dinner, and Hunter helped me wash up while his dad set up a game of cards for us. I was no good, but they guided me through, so I didn't make too big a fool of myself. I found myself relaxing and enjoying myself, reminded of how much I enjoyed their company. The three of us together, it just made sense.

Soon enough, Hunter was yawning, and it was clearly time for him to go to bed and my cue to get out of there already. I wanted to stay longer, to split a couple of glasses of wine with Holden and catch up adult-to-adult, but that was risking things more than they needed to be risked. Holden set Hunter off to get ready for bed, and I helped him tidy up the cards that were now scattered over his living room table.

"So," I took a deep breath and began to speak, "I think I have a date for you."

"Oh, really?" He glanced at me, eyebrows raised. "Who is she?"

"She's a friend of mine from a teacher training conference," I told him. "Casey Styles. She's really nice, and I think you'll like her. Quiet, sweet, smart."

"Sounds awesome." He nodded after a pause. I felt my stomach drop and realized I'd been hoping, somehow, that he was going to turn down the notion of this date. Which was crazy. This was what I'd wanted for him in the first place, and now that he was agreeing to meet someone new, I was disappointed?

"So I think she's hoping to make it this weekend," I continued. "Maybe tomorrow night, if you can find a sitter for Hunter?"

"Yeah, I think I can," he said. "I'll let you know either way, and we can take it from there."

"Sounds good," I replied, and our hands brushed briefly as I went to grab a card from the spot next to him. I froze for a moment, the connection enough to land me right back in the middle of my dream. I pushed it down. I felt as though I had spent all evening doing that.

"Cool." I pulled back from him and turned away. "I should get going. Thanks for tonight. It was fun."

"Yeah, it was," he agreed. "You're welcome around here anytime. And thanks for letting Hunter know about that club. It sounds perfect for him."

"No problem," I mumbled, going to get my jacket and doing my best not to look him in the eye.

"I'll text you about that date, right?" he followed me to the door. "I'm looking forward to it. Sounds fun."

"I'm sure it will be," I agreed, and suddenly the world felt as though it was tilting to the side, a seasickness taking control of me for a moment. Ironic that I had been out on the water with him for all that time and been fine, but on dry land, I couldn't seem to keep it together.

"Well, see you," I exclaimed, my voice higher than it needed to be, and I headed out the door without so much as a hug goodbye. Because if I touched him right now, I wouldn't be able to keep down those feelings that were no good for me. I closed the door behind me and inhaled a deep lungful of the cool evening air, hoping it would bring me back to earth, to shore. But it didn't, and I was left with the lingering question over whether I had just set up the man I was meant to be with on a date with someone else.

23

HOLDEN

"I don't know what to do," I admitted to my best friend as Raymond sat opposite me and watched me pace back and forth in front of him.

"I thought you wanted her to set you up on a date?" he asked, sounding confused. "That's what you told me the last time we saw each other."

"Yeah, and I guess I did think that's what I wanted." I rubbed my hand over my face. "But now that it's actually here...."

I trailed off and tried to make sense of the mess inside my head. Last night, when we had been tidying the place up after our evening together, I had known. I had known that this was the day I needed to make a move. I wasn't sure what had switched inside of me—maybe the kindness she had shown Hunter or maybe how good it was to have her spend the evening with us—but I wanted Autumn. I didn't want some girl she was setting me up on a date with. I wanted her and only her, and anything else would have been a lie.

But then she had told me that she had someone interested, someone who sounded sweet and good and like a solid match for me, and I felt like the ground had dropped out from underneath me. I wished I'd had the nerve to tell her this wasn't what I wanted, that it would have been silly for me to go out with this woman given what I felt for her, but that wouldn't have gone down well. She had gone to all this effort to find someone for me, right at the moment when I had decided I had already found the person I wanted to date.

"So what are you going to do?" Raymond asked, and I shook my head and shrugged.

"I honestly have no fucking idea," I admitted. "I don't think I can back out of this date now, not when it's all set up for me. I should have turned her down when she brought it up. I don't think I'm ready yet—"

"Dude, I know you probably don't want to hear this, but it sounds as though you have feelings for Autumn," Raymond cut across me. I clenched my fists at my sides. I knew he was right and had been right all along, but I wasn't ready to admit that to myself yet.

"I guess you could be right," I conceded. "But I can't tell her that now, can I? After everything I've done and said in the last few weeks. She's going to think I'm crazy."

"I don't think she is," he assured me gently. "Look, you guys have been pretty much dating all this time, haven't you? All you need to do is tell her you're starting to get feelings for her. Just tell her the truth. I don't think that's so crazy."

"Yeah, but she just set me up with someone else," I pointed out to him. "Those aren't exactly the actions of someone who's into me, are they?"

"I mean, I guess not, on the surface," he conceded. "But maybe it's that she does have feelings for you and isn't sure you feel the same way. This is what you asked for, after all. She's just going along with that. But things have changed now, and you can only try to tell her the truth, right?"

"I don't think I can." I shook my head. "I think I left it too long. I think I've fucked things up between us."

"I think you're catastrophizing because you haven't done this in a while." He cut me off once more, which was the right decision because it felt as though my brain was going to melt and start leaking out the back of my head at any given moment.

"I think I'm going to go out on this date with this woman," I sighed. "I don't want her to think I'm not grateful for it."

"Are you just proving a point?" Raymond furrowed his brow. "Because I'm sure she would rather you tell her the truth than play these silly games."

"I'm not playing games," I replied stubbornly and realized I sounded a little too much like Hunter when he wasn't getting something he wanted. I took a deep breath, raised my hands, and exhaled.

"She's set me up on a date," I told him. "She's gone to all this effort to find me someone. I'm not going to shoot that down, not now. This is what I told her I wanted all along, and it's that simple. I'm going to do it."

"And you're not doing this to spite her?" Raymond pressed. I shook my head.

"I'm doing this because she's trying for me," I replied, and I felt my entire body tense at the thought of what was meant to be happening tonight. Autumn had texted me the address, the place I was to pick this woman up, and I knew I should go there with my game face on and make the most of it. But I could barely even imagine heading out to this woman's place, not when Autumn was spending the night alone.

"Right." Raymond nodded, but he didn't seem convinced. "I'll pick up Hunter, then, and bring him around here."

"No, it's okay. I'll drop him off."

"I think it's important you take some time to think," he replied firmly. "Figure out what you really want, no?"

"I guess so," I sighed. "Thanks, man. I appreciate it."

"It's cool." He waved his hand. "You just make the right choice tonight, okay?"

"Any input on what that is?" I grinned at him ruefully. He shook his head.

"I'm keeping out of this one," he replied firmly. "You have to make this call for yourself."

"Guess so," I conceded. With that, I headed back down to my place to start getting ready for my date that evening.

It wasn't that I didn't like the thought of seeing this woman at all. In fact, in a lot of ways, she sounded pretty great, and I trusted that anyone who was friends with Autumn had to have at least something going for them. I should have been excited at the thought of getting back out there with someone new, even if my last blind date hadn't exactly gone the way I had expected it to. Yet, as I made Hunter some lunch and told him he'd be visiting Raymond later that afternoon, I couldn't shake the feeling that this was wrong.

"Where are you going tonight?" he asked, and I paused for a moment before answering. Should I tell him the truth? No, he was already sure Autumn and I were seeing each other, and the last thing I needed was to confuse him further on that point.

"Just out on a work meeting," I told him. "Nothing exciting. You're not missing anything, trust me."

"I get to see the baby today?" His eyes lit up as it clicked with him that he would be spending the evening with the whole family.

"Yeah, you will." I ruffled his hair, and I felt this sting of sadness knowing that I hadn't been able to give him that same family. I had wanted him to grow up normal and happy, but he had lacked something his whole life, lacked a mother figure in his world. Wasn't that what this dating thing was meant to be about? Bringing him that at last?

Raymond picked him up, and he gave me a hard look and a nod as Hunter climbed into the car. I knew exactly what he was trying to put across. I headed back into the house and started getting ready. I was meant to be picking up this Casey woman at seven and taking her out to dinner. I wondered if she was looking forward to it, if she was excited about what lay ahead, or if she was nervous and wondering if this was the right choice at all. Maybe I should turn up there, tell her the truth, and book it out of there before she could get too mad at me.

I stepped outside to get in my car and found that it had started to rain. Just my luck, as though I needed another reminder as to how this night was going to go. I got in the car and began to drive over to her place, going slowly, but the traffic was light, and I arrived there in plenty of time.

I drew up outside her door—a green one, Autumn had told me—and looked at the house. It was old-fashioned and a little run-down but sweet, and I wondered about the woman inside. Probably kind. Probably funny. Probably smart. Yet I had no urge to pull this car to a halt and go up there and meet her. It was crazy, but there was another woman I wanted to spend my evening with, a woman I knew was funny, smart, kind, beautiful, charming, a little awkward—all those things I had no idea I had been looking for in a partner but had landed in someone right in front of me like she had been dropped from the stars to change everything in my life for the better.

I drove around the block once more and tried to talk myself into going up there. I knew I should. Autumn had gone to all this effort to set this up for me, but the pit in my stomach was telling me this was wrong.

I drove for a while and eventually drew the car to a halt outside the unfamiliar house. My heart was pounding in my chest as I forced myself to get to my feet, to lock the car behind me, to put one foot in front of the other and make my way up there to that house.

I paused in front of the door. There was still time to back out of this, to make things right. But I found my knuckles lifting to the wood and, before I could talk myself out of it, I rapped on the door.

Shifting my weight from foot to foot, I heard someone moving inside, and my heart went double-time, so fast it felt like it was going to pop out of my chest. Finally, she reached the door and pulled it open. And as soon as she did, I knew that I'd made the right call tonight.

24

HOLDEN

When the door opened, I laid eyes on the woman standing in front of me, and I knew I'd made the right decision. It hit me like a wave of relief, the knowledge that I wasn't going to have to lie my way through this. I was meant to be here, but I had to figure out a way to explain why.

"Holden?" Autumn furrowed her brow. "What the hell...? I thought you had that date tonight?"

"I did," I replied quickly. "I mean, that's where I was meant to be. But I couldn't stop thinking about you. I knew I needed to be here instead."

Her eyes widened, and she stared at me for a long moment. Too long. Had I made some stupid, crazy mistake that I wasn't going to be able to come back from? The way she was looking at me—as though I had just come out with the most insane shit she had ever heard in her life—sent my pulse racing through my veins. But I couldn't take it back, so I kept talking in the hopes that I would be able to finally, truly express what I needed to.

"I know I'm meant to be here with you," I continued, the rain still pouring down around me. I was cold, getting damp, but I didn't care.

As long as I got to look into this woman's eyes and tell her how I truly felt, then it was worth it. All of this had been worth it.

Autumn continued to gape at me, as though she couldn't believe what I was saying. I could hardly believe it, either. I had convinced myself for so long that Autumn wasn't the woman I was meant to be with. I'd thought whatever we shared was fleeting and platonic at best, so it felt as though I was reeling back from the truth speaking to her like this. But it was real, and if I had gone out on that blind date she'd set me up on, that would have been the real lie.

I had no idea how she was going to react. I still didn't know her well enough to have a handle on that, not quite yet. Autumn was someone I had known only as a friend for all this time, and I was coming to her, spilling my guts, and admitting I'd had feelings for her all along. If only I had gone along with that first date we'd been set up on together all those weeks ago. If only I had seen then that our chemistry was intense, impossible to deny. Then I could have skipped out of all this fucking bullshit and already had her in my arms.

She didn't speak for a long time, the only sound the rain pitter-pattering around us, but I could see her chest rising and falling rapidly. She was wearing a pair of pajama shorts and a vest top, her skin exposed and so, so fucking tempting. But she had to accept me first. She had to accept what we had between us—if she felt it too. I remembered all those brief touches, those meaningful looks, the way she smiled at me as though I was the only person in the world. I couldn't have imagined all of that. Could I?

And then, all at once, she moved toward me. I wasn't sure if she kissed me first or if I kissed her, but it didn't matter. It was a circuit closing as our mouths met for the first time, the electricity that we had been holding back finally allowed to run wild and free. I wrapped my arms around her, pulling her close against my body, and buried my tongue in her mouth, tasting her, consuming her, needing every single part of her.

"Oh my God, Holden," Autumn breathed as she pulled back. "Are we doing this?"

"If you want to," I murmured back, brushing my mouth against her cheek, inhaling her intoxicating scent, reminding myself of everything I'd been missing out on all this time. How had I held myself back this long? All that seemed distant now, impossibly far away.

"I do," she panted like she was agreeing to a wedding vow, and she kissed me again, pulling me inside the house, out of the rain, and into her warmth.

I gripped her hips and pushed her back against the wall behind us, pinning her there, holding her still. Both of us had been so slippery for so long that we hadn't ever gotten a hold on each other, but now that I had her there, there was no way in hell I was letting her get away. She moaned as I kissed her again, pressing her body back against mine as I skimmed my hands up and over her arms and pushed them up above her head. She felt so fucking good. That was what I couldn't get enough of—how obvious it seemed that we should end up this way, how natural our bodies felt when they were as close as they were.

"Fuck," she groaned as I brushed my mouth over her neck, letting my teeth catch on her skin, feeling her body shiver with need as I caressed her with my mouth. I wrapped my fingers around her wrists and held her tightly, grinding myself into her. I was already hard. How long had it been since I had wanted someone this badly, with this much certainty? My body was pulsing with an impossible need for her, and I could have spent all night exploring every single inch of her body and still craved more the next day.

"Kiss me," she panted, and I turned my mouth back down to meet hers, her soft lips finding mine. She made out with me hungrily, nipping my bottom lip between her teeth and making me groan. She was pushing her hips into me, hooking one leg around me to draw me closer, and every single item of clothing she was wearing was an annoyance between me and her gorgeous body.

I dropped my hands from her wrists and peeled up her flimsy top, tossing it aside. Much to my delight, she was naked beneath it. With one arm around her waist, I leaned back to admire her, to take her in. Her mouth was slightly parted, her breath coming hard and fast, and her body arched toward mine as though subconsciously trying to reach me with every single inch of her body. I trailed my fingers over her throat, watching her eyes drift shut to process the sensation, and then let them go farther until they had found her nipples. I pinched one roughly between my fingers, drawing a sharp squeak from her mouth. It swelled under my touch.

"Jesus Christ, Holden," she moaned as I massaged her breast with one hand, lowering my head down to the other and drawing her other nipple into my mouth. I wanted to consume her, to swallow her whole, to try out and test every inch of her body until I was satisfied. I bit softly over her sensitized breast, and she shivered beneath me. I glanced up to find her head tipped back in ecstasy and her mouth opening and closing wordlessly.

"Good?" I murmured, and she nodded.

"So good," she replied with certainty. I moved farther down, flicking my tongue along the curve of her breast, and then sinking to my knees, I pressed my mouth against her belly, to that soft spot beneath her navel that made her legs tremble with a desperate need.

"Mm," she groaned, running her fingers through my hair, tugging softly at the ends as I moved farther down. I could smell her scent, the rich, tempting muskiness of it, and it took everything I had not to rip off her panties right there and make her come with my mouth. But I wanted to tease her, to let her know every way that I could that I was in no sort of rush.

I ran my hands up her bare thighs and watched as goose bumps appeared where my fingers had moved. It seriously turned me on, seeing how keen she was for me, that my desire for her was reflected in equal measure all over her body. I hooked my fingers around her shorts and pulled them down. She eagerly kicked them away and grabbed my head once more, guiding it toward her panties.

I pressed my mouth against her through the flimsy fabric, inhaling her deeply, letting my breath tease her through her under-wear. She let out a strangled, desperate noise, communicating without words how badly she wanted me down there. I kissed along her panty line for a moment, letting my teeth play at the band, and then I lost my patience and pulled them off. I had to taste her.

I moved my mouth against her pussy at once. She was shaven but for a small triangle on her pubic mound, which I made sure to run my fingers through, the coarseness of her hair contrasting with the velvety-smooth sweetness of her skin. I stroked my tongue slowly across the length of her sex, starting at her slit and moving all the way up until I found her clit She let out a long moan and slumped back against the wall behind us, spreading her legs to make it easier for me to access her. And I took the invitation without a second thought.

I started by licking and sucking at her lips, taking them into my mouth and lavishing them with attention, letting her know that I was here for as long as it took. I couldn't get over how good she tasted. I had gone down on women before, of course, but there was something different about Autumn. Perhaps it was how long I had been craving her, or maybe it was something else entirely, but I couldn't get enough of her.

Eventually, when her thighs tensed and her breath came faster and harder than before, I turned my attention to her clit. I sealed my lips around her and guided it out with my tongue, feeling it swell and harden as I sucked softly. I drew shapes against her, listening to the sound of her moans and her physical reactions to read what felt the best for her, and found that she seemed to like it best when I sucked and lapped softly at the very tip of it. I did just that, moving my fingers up into her as I did so, sliding my fingers deep into her perfect pussy as I ate her out.

"Oh my God," she groaned, and I could tell she was close to coming. I moved a little harder, stroking my tongue with more purpose and getting hard as a rock as the woman before me lost herself to the pleasure I was giving her. There was nothing hotter in the world than making a woman come, except maybe doing it with a woman who I felt I'd been waiting for my entire life.

"Fuck!" she cried out, gripping my head as her pussy clenched around my fingers. Her clit pulsed beneath my tongue, and I pulled back a little, reducing the pleasure so it wasn't so intense. Sneaking a look up at her, I found her cheeks flushed and her nipples swollen, her entire body reacting to the sensations. She looked incredible. Even more incredible than usual, that was.

She reached down to pull me back to my feet and kissed me at once, not concerned about the fact that my mouth was still glistening with her wetness. I could taste the two of us, combined in our kiss, and I pressed hard against her, letting her know I was ready for more whenever she was. She pulled back, looked me dead in the eyes, and grinned.

"Bedroom," she told me. "Now."

And who was I to disagree?

25

AUTUMN

I grasped his hand and dragged him through to the bedroom without a second thought. I couldn't believe this was happening. I wasn't totally convinced yet that this wasn't some hyper-vivid dream—but then, I could have never conjured a man who was this good at getting me off, even in my wildest fantasies.

He pushed me back against the door as soon as we were inside, kissing me again, and I could still taste myself all over his mouth. I couldn't believe he'd dropped to his knees in front of me and done incredible things to me mere minutes after he'd arrived at the door and confessed his feelings to me. I'd never been with a man who seemed to want me this badly, a man who had no trouble worshipping my body.

I was naked, and he was still fully dressed, and something about that dynamic was turning me on and frustrating me in equal measure. I slipped my hand down between his legs and gripped his cock, finding him hard as a rock and ready for me. He growled against my mouth, making it pretty damn clear he wanted me any way he could have me.

"I need you inside of me," I breathed into his ear, hungry for him, starving. I had never wanted anyone with the intensity I wanted him at that moment, and it was hard to keep my head straight, to remember everything that had come before this. All that time, all that waiting, and it had all been building to this moment. And it was going to be worth it.

He pushed me down onto the bed, a little rough with his neediness, but I liked it. I squirmed back on to the covers and watched as he stripped himself down. He was strong and muscular, and as he moved on top of me, I reached out to trace the shape of his arms and his chest. I felt his heart racing beneath his skin, a reminder that he wanted this as badly as I did. That we had waited for one another long enough.

"Condom?" he breathed in my ear, and I reached into the bedside cabinet where I had long kept a small box of condoms in the hopes that one day I might get to use them. Well, that day was here, and it had been well worth the wait. I handed him the small foil packet, and he tore it open swiftly, sheathing himself deftly, and then moved over me. I slid my hands over his shoulders, pulling him close, and spread my legs, surprising even myself with how eager I was for this to finally happen. I hadn't realized until that moment how deeply and truly I'd wanted him all this time, but once he was there in front of me, I knew without a shadow of a doubt that this was right and this was where the two of us were meant to be all along.

He took his cock into his hand and guided it against my slit. He was bigger than I'd realized, and it took a moment to relax into the feeling of him entering me. But I focused on his face, the way he seemed to be consumed with his desire for me, and soon enough, nothing else in the entire world mattered but this feeling, the movement of his body inside of mine.

"Fuck, Autumn," he growled as he thrust all the way inside of me. The sound of my name on his lips turned me on more than I expected, and I soon adjusted to the feel of him inside me. It had been a long time since I'd slept with anyone and even longer since I'd felt a desire that ran as deeply and completely as this one. It was a lot to take in, but it was worth it, every second of it.

I hooked my ankles behind his back and drew him in close to me, letting him know without words that I was truly ready for him. He kissed me softly on the mouth as he began to thrust up and inside of me, going slow, letting me savor the sensation of him buried all the way to the hilt.

He felt so big, and I felt so full like the two of us had been made to go together like this. I rocked my hips back to meet him, loving the way he felt inside of me and craving more of it. I wasn't sure I would ever truly get enough of him. We had waited so long to get to this moment, going back and forth, doubting ourselves and our feelings and our attraction, that I had all this tension built up that needed to be released. And he would be the one I worked it out on.

"You're so gorgeous," he murmured, leaning down to my ear, so I could feel him say the words as well as hear them. I groaned and tipped my hips back a little, taking him deeper, as deep as I could, as hard as he could have me. I couldn't get over how good this felt, how natural and obvious—and how long we'd waited to get to this. How had we held back when this had been waiting for us all along? I flashed back briefly to the dream I'd had a few days before and wondered if it had been my body growing impatient with my doubt and pushing me toward him once and for all.

Another orgasm built deep within me, catching me off guard, as I normally didn't come more than once in a session. But then, the way he touched me, the way he'd eaten me out, he'd made it clear that my pleasure was as important to him as his was, and I was more relaxed knowing I didn't have anything to prove. I clenched my jaw and moved against him, meeting him with every thrust, craving him, needing him.

And then it hit me, the orgasm washing over my body like a wave of relief. The tension seeped from my muscles, and I did my best to keep hanging onto him, to hold him close to me, to surround myself greedily with as much of him as I could get. I never wanted this to end, never wanted the two of us to be apart again.

He moved into me a few more times as the pleasure burst and crested, and a few moments later, he reached his own climax, finishing with a groan and a thrust up to the hilt in my pussy. He held himself there for a long time as though he felt the same way I did—unwilling to pull apart, to admit this encounter was over, and to face up to all the other questions that had come once we had, well, come.

He slid out of me, disposed of the condom in the trash can next to my bed, and then settled back down into the covers with a long sigh of satisfaction. I bit my lip as I watched him. I still couldn't quite believe he was there, sitting across from me, this man who I'd waited so long for without realizing that's what I was doing.

"I suppose you should let your date know that tonight's not going ahead, huh?" I poked his arm playfully.

"Guess so," he agreed, going to grab his phone from his pocket and firing off a swift text. I felt a little bad, but she wouldn't have been waiting too long—and it was hard to feel guilty when I'd just had some of the best sex of my entire life. The bed felt empty until he leaned back into the pillow, still bare ass naked, sprawled across my sheets as though he'd always known he belonged there.

I lay down next to him and watched him for a long moment. I didn't know what to say. I'd never been great at pillow talk.

"I don't know how to say this," I admitted, figuring it was best to shoot for honesty in a situation like this one. "But... what happens now?"

He turned to me, and his eyes were soft and yielding in a way I had never seen them before. I wondered, briefly, how long it had been since he'd shared this kind of intimacy with anyone else. He looked totally at peace, as though everything in the world was as it should be in that moment. I couldn't help but smile.

"What do you mean?"

"I mean..." I hesitated. I was so worried about saying or doing the wrong thing, coming out with something sensationally stupid that was going to ruin what a perfect night this had been so far.

"I mean, what are things between us now?" I wondered aloud. "You ditched your date for me."

"I only agreed to that damn date because I'd talked myself into believing I didn't deserve to be with someone like you." He took my hand and brushed his mouth along the knuckles, making me shiver.

"I think I can change your mind about that." I smiled, a little flut-tery. He smiled back at me.

"You're the only one I want to be with," he promised me, stretching his arm out to encourage me to snuggle into his chest. I hesitated for a moment, though I wanted to do this. I knew that. It was just hard for me to accept it. But I moved into him, pressing my head to his chest, and closed my eyes. This was real. It was happen-ing. I was really here with him, and that was all I needed. He wrapped me in his arms, and I knew that, for at least the rest of this night, everything was going to be fine.

26

HOLDEN

I woke up in a room I didn't recognize, and for a second, I thought that I was still dreaming. I lifted my head from the pillow and blinked a couple of times, trying to place the bedroom surrounding me. Then I heard the woman next to me lightly snoring in her sleep. When I turned to look at her and remembered where I was, a smile appeared on my face. I was with Autumn. So today was going to be a good day.

I'd wondered how I would feel the morning after—if I would feel like I had made a mistake, if now that our chemistry was consummated, I would wonder what I was doing here in the first place. But once I was there, waking up next to her, I knew I'd made the right decision by not going on my date last night. The details of the night before drifted through my mind, and I could hardly keep the smile off my face. It had been good. Really fucking good.

I leaned over to stroke her hair, and she stirred and opened her eyes, offering me a sleepy smile as she came back to consciousness.

"Morning," I murmured to her, leaning over to nuzzle into her neck. She grinned and wrapped her arms around me, letting out a little purr of satisfaction.

"Morning," she murmured back, and she kissed me on the mouth. It was the briefest moment, but it was enough to send my head spinning with excitement, with desire and need for her. I couldn't believe this was happening. I couldn't believe that up until the night before, I had been trying to talk myself into going out on a date with someone else. Hopefully, the woman I'd stood up wouldn't be too pissed off, but honestly, lying there in bed with Autumn like this, it was hard to worry too deeply about what she might be thinking of me.

"Man, I'm starving." Autumn stretched and pushed herself up in bed. She was still deliciously, utterly naked, and it took everything I had in me not to pounce on her right there and then.

"Shall I go make some breakfast?" she suggested.

"If it means putting clothes on," I ran my hand over her thigh, exposed where she had kicked the covers off the night before, "I'm against it."

She laughed, slapped my hand away, and then rolled herself out of bed. In the light of the morning sun, streaming through her window and picking her out to perfection, she looked nearly ethereal.

"Well, I'm hungry, and I'm not getting hot oil all over me just for your viewing pleasure," she shot back playfully. "What do you want? I'm thinking eggs and bacon and hot coffee on the side."

"Sounds perfect," I agreed. I would have said yes to anything she asked for. I reached into my pocket to grab my phone and checked the time. I still had a little bit before I had to go off and pick up Hunter. I was excited to see him, even if I knew Raymond would be gloating about me proving him right by going after Autumn in the end after all.

Autumn pulled on a robe and headed through to the kitchen, and I went to the bathroom to wash up, looking at myself in the mirror. I looked different, or at least felt like I did—lighter, happier, maybe even a little younger. It wasn't only about the sex. It was knowing there was a new romance in the cards, the first romance in forever that felt like it was going somewhere. Who'd have thought the teacher I'd argued with all those weeks ago would wind up to be the woman putting a smile on my face this morning?

When I was done, I went through to join her in the kitchen, inhaling the deliciously savory smell of the food she was cooking. She glanced over her shoulder and grinned at me.

"Feeling a little more human?" she asked, and I nodded.

"Well, you were all animal last night," she teased, and she flushed a little red as she spoke.

"Hey, I can't be a gentleman all the time," I replied, and she giggled and flipped over a slice of bacon, which sizzled satisfyingly as it hit the pan. I couldn't remember the last time I had felt this relaxed, this stress-free. I knew it couldn't last forever, but that didn't mean I wasn't going to enjoy the hell out of it while I still could.

"So, when are you going to be a proper gentleman and take me out on a date?" she asked, cocking an eyebrow.

"Oh, so you're already looking for dates now, are you?" I shook my head. "And here I was, thinking this was a one-night thing."

"As soon as you agreed to breakfast, you forfeited that right," she replied, flicking on her coffee maker.

"Fair play." I held my hands up. "How about Saturday? A proper date, just me and you."

"Sounds fun." She flicked her gaze over to me again, as though she was having trouble keeping her head focused on making breakfast.

"Well, it won't be the yacht," I promised her. "But I'll see if I can outdo it."

"I'm sure you'll come up with something," she replied. "No private planes either, okay? In fact, let's rule out any luxury vehicles at all right here. Probably for the best."

"Probably," I agreed as she served up breakfast, putting a plate down in front of me and pouring both of us coffee.

We spent the rest of our leisurely breakfast together talking—about how she'd ended up in this neighborhood, how long she'd been here, how long she planned to stay. Before I knew it, an hour had gone by, and I had to head off to pick up Hunter.

"Hey, I have to get going," I told her, glancing at my phone reluctantly. "I'll call you, though, okay? We can figure something out."

"Ooh, an actual phone call." She clasped her hands together in playful excitement. "You're old-fashioned, aren't you?"

"You don't seem to be complaining," I pointed out, and I pulled her into a kiss before I left. She smiled against my mouth and wound her arms around me, as though reluctant to let me get out the door.

"Mm, I'm looking forward to that date," she murmured as I pulled back.

"Me too," I replied. "More than you know. And I promise I'm not going to get you to set me up with someone else before I get the nerve to come around here myself this time."

"You better not," she warned, playfully squeezing me close for a moment. "You go pick up Hunter. I'll talk to you soon, all right?"

I planted one last kiss on her cheek and headed for the door, a grin on my face that felt almost foreign, it was so big. Climbing into my car, I started down the road to Raymond's place. I didn't know if Hunter would be up yet, or if he even had a clue as to what I'd been doing last night, but I was looking forward to seeing him either way.

I arrived about twenty minutes later and pulled the car to a halt outside the house. For some reason, even though I wanted to catch up with Hunter again, I wasn't quite ready to get out and see him. It would have been admitting that the night was over, that everything I had done with Autumn was firmly behind me. And that wasn't the case. She had already agreed to a date the next weekend, but still, talking about it with other people would make it seem somewhat real. I wasn't sure I was ready for the rest of the world to know about it yet.

But Raymond had to have noticed my car sitting in the driveway, and he would probably come out and get me himself if I hung around any longer, so I dragged myself out of the front seat, stretched, and headed for the door. Raymond opened it before I got there, raising his eyebrows at me expectantly.

"So?" he asked, stepping aside as I brushed past him.

"So, what?" I shot back, even though I knew what he was asking.

"How much coffee are you going to need to get through today?" he asked, dancing around the question. "You have a late one last night or....?"

"I could use a little." I nodded, and he grinned widely and headed to the kitchen to make us a mug. I followed him.

"Olivia's out with the baby, and Hunter's not up yet," he explained. "So you better fill me in on what happened last night. You stay over?"

"Uh, actually, yeah, I did." I nodded. "But not with the girl Autumn set me up with. With Autumn."

"Holy shit." Raymond slapped my shoulder. "You have to be kidding me. The two of you...?"

"Yeah, I was driving around town, and I couldn't shake the feeling I was meant to be with Autumn and not whoever it was she had set me up with," I admitted. "So I went to her house and told her, and we ended up..."

I raised my eyebrows at him pointedly, not wanting to go into the details. Raymond poured my coffee and handed it to me. It would be my second cup of the day, and I wasn't sure if it was the caffeine that had got me jittery or what had happened with Autumn the night before.

"So you guys are together?" Raymond pressed, and I shrugged.

"We're seeing each other again on Saturday," I replied. "Which reminds me, would you be able to—"

"I'll take care of Hunter, no problem," Raymond lifted his hand up at once.

"Thanks." I nodded. "I know it's short notice, but I don't want to lose momentum on this thing, you know?"

"I knew the two of you were going to get together." Raymond leaned back triumphantly. "Ever since that first date. Can't believe how long it took the two of you to figure it out."

"Hey, let's save the intense gloating until we have a real date, all right?" I suggested, cocking an eyebrow. "I mean, I barely know this woman like that. We just had sex last night, that's all."

"Damn, you don't wait around," Raymond teased. "Well, once you've had the mandatory six-week holding period for somebody, of course."

"Trust me, I know how stupid I was," I sighed. "I can't believe I didn't see it sooner. I was so sure that going for something with her would end badly, you know? What with our first date being such a mess."

"Well, now you get to start over," Raymond reminded me. "Take it from the top. And maybe leave the yacht out of it this time, huh?"

"Don't worry. She's already made her feelings on the yacht very clear," I assured him. "I'm not going to make the same mistake twice."

"So Saturday, right?" Raymond confirmed, and I nodded.

"Saturday."

"And what do you think you're going to do with her then?"

"You know, I haven't given it a lot of thought." I shook my head. And then my mind began to drift back in the direction of a conversation we'd had when we'd taken the day trip out on the yacht, and a smile curled up my face. Okay, so I might have something.

Before I could get stuck on that train of thought any longer, Hunter emerged at the bottom of the stairs, rubbing his eyes.

"Hey, Dad," he greeted me, and I walked over to him to give him a hug. To think, if it hadn't been for him, I might not have stuck things out with Autumn as long as I had.

"How you doing, buddy?" I asked him, and he shrugged and yawned.

"Could I get something to eat?" he asked.

"How about we get breakfast on the way home?" I suggested. "I feel like something big."

"That sounds good." His face lit up, and he turned to head back up the stairs to get ready. "I'll be down in a minute."

"Need to replenish your energy stores, huh?" Raymond teased, and I rolled my eyes at him.

"Yeah, yeah, very funny." I shook my head and finished my coffee. "I'll call you about Saturday, right? We can figure things out from there."

"Look forward to hearing from you." Raymond saluted me casually and then went to clean up our cups. I waited for Hunter to come back downstairs and wondered if this smile on my face was going to stick around all day.

27

AUTUMN

I carefully shuffled and reshuffled the papers on my desk in front of me. I couldn't stop thinking about what had happened a few nights before. I'd barely been able to stop focusing on it since. But who could blame me? That had been about the hottest night of my life, and I wasn't going to be able to let go of it any time soon.

Class started in the next few minutes, and I had to gather myself to be able to deliver a decent hour for the kids who needed it. I'd had all weekend to drift about the house in a happy haze, carrying on a text chain with Holden that lasted all day and all night, drifting from flirty to dirty to prim and back again. I loved having him at my beck and call, loved having him at the other end of the line. No games to play, neither of us working as hard as we could to keep the other at arm's length. It felt like, for the first time since we met, the two of us were on the same page, and I couldn't have been happier.

"Good morning." A familiar voice drew my attention, and I looked up to find Zoe poking her head around the door.

"Morning." I grinned at her, and she slipped in and pushed the door shut behind her.

"What's the weekend gossip?" she asked, waggling her eyebrows at me expectantly. "What happened with Holden and the date you set him up on?"

I took a deep breath. I hadn't told Zoe what had happened between the two of us yet. It wasn't that I didn't trust her or anything, only that I wanted to keep it between us for a little longer. There was something about putting it out there to the world at large that made it seem like it wasn't ours any longer, even though I was going to have to tell everyone eventually. And it would be fun to share it with Zoe, to get her in on the action. How long had she been friends with me, and exactly how much juicy gossip had I delivered to her in that time? I owed her this one, obviously.

"He actually didn't go on the date," I confessed to her, and she cocked her head at me.

"What, like, he stood her up?"

"He canceled with her." I paused for a moment for dramatic effect. "And he came to see me instead."

"No way!" she exclaimed, glancing around to make sure none of our students were hanging out nearby to catch what we were talking about. "He came to your place? What happened?"

"Well, he told me he didn't want to go on that date. He wanted to be with me." I bit my lip, unable to believe those words were coming out of my mouth describing anything other than a fantasy. "And then he came in, and he... uh, he spent the night."

That seemed like an overly careful way of describing what had happened between us. The sex had been pretty much the hottest thing that had ever happened to me, but I couldn't go into details while there were kids drifting around who might have caught what I was saying.

"Oh, did he now?" Zoe's eyebrows practically vanished into her hairline. "And what about the morning after?"

"We had breakfast together, and he said he was going to take me out again next Saturday," I replied, biting my lip. "I'm looking forward to it. I can't believe this is happening."

"Me neither." Zoe shook her head "Can't believe you both finally pulled your shit together and admitted you're meant to be together."

"I wouldn't go that far quite yet," I warned her. "I mean, we only hooked up. Nothing's happened between us yet."

"Yeah, but the two of you have been dancing around this point for, like, six weeks?" she reminded me. "If you haven't gotten sick of each other by now, I'd say you're pretty set for life."

"Well, we'll see." I held my hands up. "Hopefully, this date's going to be a little more successful than the first one I went on with him."

"I'm sure it will be," she promised me, and then she sat down at the desk opposite me, wrinkling her nose up, a look of concern crossing her face.

"Zoe? What's going on?" I asked nervously. I felt as though every single emotion in my body had been racked up to eleven, and I was noticing every little detail of everything people did around me. It wasn't serving me too well.

"I'm just..." She looked up at me. "I'm worried, that's all."

"But you were the one pushing for something to happen between the two of us!" I reminded her. "I thought you'd be happy we finally bit the bullet and did something."

"Trust me, I am," she promised me. "And I hope things work out between you. I do. It's just that..."

She searched for the best way to phrase her concerns that wasn't going to offend or upset me.

"He's got a whole lot of money, right?" she confirmed, and I nodded.

"And men like that, when they come with a whole lot of money, there's some... complications that can run alongside that," she continued, delicately teasing out her actual meaning. "I'm sure he's great, but just... be careful, all right?"

"I will." I furrowed my brow. I wasn't even sure I knew precisely what she was saying, but she was looking out for me, and that was all that mattered. "I appreciate the concern, Zo, but I'm sure I can handle myself."

"I'm sure you can too." She smiled at me. "He won't know what hit him."

She stood up again, glancing at the large clock with the bright red hands above my desk.

"I should get back to class." She tapped my desk a couple of times. "I'll see you at lunch, though, right? And I expect all the gory details."

"I promise there was nothing gory about what happened," I called after her, but she was already gone. The bell rang, and I heard the shuffle of the kids forming a line outside my door. I got to my feet, brushed down my skirt, adjusted my blouse, and went to let them in. It was difficult, sometimes, switching over from weekend mode into work mode, but I would have to find a way to do it. I didn't want anyone, least of all Hunter, catching on to what had happened this weekend.

They were all chatting amongst themselves when they entered, and I noticed Hunter looking at me. For a moment, I panicked, wondering if his dad had filled him in on some of the stuff that had happened that weekend, but he couldn't have been that stupid, could he? Holden and I were still in the very early stages of whatever the hell it was we were doing, and he would've been nuts to go ahead and tell his son all about that. It would have caused chaos for him. I calmed myself as Hunter got closer and offered him a smile.

"How was your weekend, Hunter?" I asked him, and he nodded.

"It was good," he replied, but he was clearly distracted and a little nervous.

"Something you want to ask me?" I wondered aloud, and he nodded, scuffing his foot back and forth on the floor before him.

"I was wondering—" He took a deep breath, as though he had been carefully rehearsing these words since he had gotten out of bed that morning. "—what are you... when do the afterschool clubs start?"

"Next week," I replied. "The gaming one will have the sign-up sheet out soon, and I'll make sure to put your name on it."

"Awesome." He beamed. "Thank you."

I smiled as I watched him head back to his seat. It was so good to see him engaging with something. Yeah, the gaming club might mostly be kids staring at computer screens, but anything that made him feel like he belonged to a group of people was surely a good thing. I was going to get Hunter feeling more comfortable around the rest of the kids in his class before he graduated my year. I was sure of it.

"All right, all right, settle down, everyone." I clapped my hands together at the front of the class. "Take your seats, please."

The kids broke off from their groups and hurried to take their spots at the seats scattered through the room, and there was the shuffle of them grabbing everything they needed out of their bags and lay it in front of them. As I waited, I found my mind drifting back in the direction of Holden, of that night, of how amazing it had been —and the fact that I got to do it all again so soon. That was going to be a hell of a lot of fun. What had he planned for us? Something romantic, no doubt. And probably expensive. I was pretty sure I had run down the list of luxury vehicles that I wanted nothing to do with, but what if he turned up in, like, a tank or something? I giggled at the thought.

And then, I realized I was standing there in front of a room full of kids, all of whom were waiting for me to start their lessons, and I was grinning away like an idiot thinking about something else entirely. I blinked and quickly grabbed my lesson plan, glancing over the words in front of me in the hopes of reminding myself what the hell I was supposed to be doing that day.

"All right." I straightened up and cast my eye around the room, hoping none of them would have picked up on my stutter start right there. "Take out your workbooks and turn to a fresh page."

All of them did as they were told, and I tried to keep my head in the game. I had five days till my date with Holden, and I wasn't going to be able to spend every moment of that time daydreaming about what that night was going to bring. I had to stay focused, and that meant casting him out of my brain for the time being, no matter how hard it was going to be to stop myself from thinking about what we had already shared—and more importantly, what was yet to come.

28

HOLDEN

"Look, I'm sorry, but this isn't what we were looking for." Andreas White sat opposite me, tapping on his laptop screen and shaking his head. "Do you understand where I'm coming from?"

I felt my neck burning with embarrassment as I turned my attention to the website he had pulled up in front of me—the one I had designed for him over the last few weeks. I had been pretty happy with it when I turned it in, but I had spent most of that month completely distracted from the tasks I was supposed to be taking care of. I shouldn't have been surprised he was coming to me with complaints. I should have expected this.

"I'm sorry to hear you're not happy with this." I reached out for his laptop and started clicking through the website, and sure enough, I swiftly noticed a few things wrong with it—a dead link, a graphic that jerked and didn't play properly. This was nowhere near my usual standards, and I was instantly irritated with myself for letting this project get away from me.

"We've already had a few complaints from clients." Andreas shook his head. "And we're going to redesign the website again from scratch. I'm not happy with it, and I know the rest of the team feels the same way."

Part of me wanted to get mad that he was here chewing me out, but that wasn't going to help anything. I needed to stand up and take responsibility for what I'd done, not run away from the problem and hope it fixed itself.

"Of course, I'll do the website redesign for free," I promised him. "I'm more than happy to offer a discount on any future projects you want me to work on—"

"I'm afraid we don't have time for you to do that." Andreas shook his head. "We're already looking at hiring a firm who can get this done quickly and efficiently."

"I understand." I nodded, even though I wanted to slam my fist against my desk in annoyance. I knew he was doing what was right for his company. I had obviously and evidently fucked this one up, and I could have done better if I had given it my full attention.

"I'll refund your money for the original website design," I promised him, hoping I would be able to mitigate the damage to my reputation if I could make it so he hadn't lost anything but time. He eyed me across the table and shook his head.

"You came so highly recommended from several of my colleagues." He sighed. "I expected a better quality of work from you, Holden."

"I can only apologize," I repeated myself, wondering how long I was going to have to sit here and listen to this guy be disappointed in me because it was already getting pretty old.

Mercifully, he had nothing else to say to me. He got to his feet, shook my hand, and left me in that office all by myself once more. I slumped back into the seat as soon as he was gone, feeling like an idiot, wanting to yell curses at the sky, but it wasn't going to help anything.

How long had I been running this business? A decade almost? And this was the first time I had been fired from a project. It fucking sucked. The worst part of it was, I could have done better if I had made more of an effort. I had half-assed that design, and I was losing a hefty amount as a result. I couldn't get the time back I had poured into that project, and I had to give him his money back for a job poorly done. I couldn't believe I'd let a client like him slip through my fingers. He worked for a big ass company, and there could have been ongoing work there if I had managed not to completely fuck it up on the first try.

I leaned back in my seat and stared at the ceiling. I knew I was going to have a hard time focusing on the projects I was taking on unless I put something between me and this meeting. I grabbed my phone, texted Raymond, and asked if he felt like meeting for a coffee. He replied in the affirmative, and a few minutes later, I was walking to the café down the street from my office, the cold air a decent reflection of my mood at the moment

When I arrived, Raymond was already there, and he waved me over, having already ordered my usual.

"Hey, what's up?" he greeted me. "Something go down at work?"

"Yeah, actually," I sighed and shook my head. "I got fired from a project."

"Oh." He furrowed his brow. "Did you fall out with the client, or...?"

"No, he didn't like the work I put in for him, and I have to admit, I don't blame him," I confessed. "It wasn't up to standard. He wasn't willing to wait for me to do a redesign, so I offered his money back. He's going to another firm to get it done, someone who can get it in quicker."

"Has that ever happened to you before?"

I shook my head.

"Nope, but I looked at the website, and I think he's right," I admitted. "When I turned it in, I felt good about it, but I must not have been paying attention. There were rookie mistakes all over that thing, the kind of shit I was doing when I first got started. I don't know where the hell my head was at."

"I think I have an idea," Raymond remarked, as I took a sip of my coffee. "Autumn."

"Yeah, but we only started up this thing last week."

"Sure, but anyone who's been paying attention can see the two of you had something going on a long time before that," he reminded me. "I don't want to sound like an ass, but maybe you've been distracted with everything that's going on with her?"

"I suppose you could be right," I admitted. The thought of it irritated me. I had just gotten something romantic off the ground, and it was already starting to affect my performance at work? What was I supposed to do, choose between having a decent job or a decent love life?

"What are you going to do?" Raymond asked. "Going to keep things up with her, even if it gets in the way of work?"

"I don't want to call things off," I told him firmly, and that was the truth. The thought of breaking things off with Autumn when we'd only recently gotten them going, made my stomach twist up painfully inside me. I had only recently accepted that there was something going on between us, and there was no way I was going to cut that off when it made me feel so damn good.

"So you're going to have to change the way you run the business then." Raymond leaned back in his seat and spoke as though this should have been obvious.

"Like how?" I asked him. He shrugged.

"I mean, I know you've been totally closed off to it in the past, but maybe you could think about hiring some more people to help you out around there," he suggested. I shook my head.

"No, that's too much stress," I replied. "It would change everything. Besides, I don't know if I'd trust somebody else to take on this work for—"

"With all due respect," Raymond said. "If the work isn't getting done up to standard because you're distracted, maybe it's worth hiring someone who can throw themselves full-bore into it?"

"I don't know." I shook my head again. The thought of it didn't suit what I'd been trying to go for when I started up the business.

"All right, what's keeping you away from that idea?" he asked. "Is there something about it that doesn't suit the business?"

"No, it's not that," I conceded. "I just... never wanted to run this company where I had dominion over other people or anything."

"Yeah, I get that," Raymond nodded. "But things are changing for you. When you first started the company, it was only you and Hunter to take care of, right?"

"Yeah."

"So things are different." He shrugged. "Now you have Autumn in the picture as well. And even if it's not her, you said you wanted someone else in your life in that way. You're going to have to accept that you can't juggle all those things at once."

I eyed him from across the table for a moment, annoyed at how much sense he was making at that moment. I had started the business, even if I never would have come out and admitted this to anyone, because I'd wanted to prove a point to Hunter's mother. I'd wanted to show her and anyone else who might have doubted me over the years that I was perfectly capable of building a life for myself and my son that anyone would have killed for. But now that I had done that, and the business was still operating, and my world was changing faster than I could keep up with it, maybe I did need to think about hiring someone new.

"You could come back to the company," I suggested. "Just for a while, until things settle down again. Could be fun, the two of us working together—"

"Yeah, I'm not going to abandon Olivia with a baby while I go out to work again," Raymond told me firmly. "The reason I dropped out of that place was so I had a life of my own, right? I'm sorry, but I'm not interested in coming back to work."

"Of course. Sorry." I held my hands up.

"Not all of us can do the baby thing and the business thing at once," he remarked good-naturedly. "But maybe you can do the employee thing for a change?"

"All right, you've got a point," I said, capitulating. "I have no idea how I should go about hiring someone new, though. Any ideas?"

"I'll keep my ear to the ground and see if we can't figure something out." Raymond nodded. "You've got a reputation in this town. I'm sure plenty of people would be happy to work for you."

"Jesus." I rubbed my hand over my face. "The thought of dealing with someone else at that place is fucking exhausting."

"You raised a kid by yourself while you started that place up, remember?" he reminded me. "So I'm pretty sure you can manage to bring in someone else who can make everything easier."

"I guess so," I admitted. "But if this goes horribly wrong, I'm holding you accountable."

"Good luck with that." Raymond raised his mug to me playfully and downed what was left. I leaned back in my seat and considered what I'd agreed to. It was going to change everything about the way I ran my business—but then, a whole lot had been changing in my life in general these last few weeks, and most of it had been for the better. Maybe I needed to let go of my control freak mentality and accept change when it came my way. Maybe it was for the best.

29

AUTUMN

"The weekend is here at last!" Zoe punched the air as she entered my classroom, not bothering to knock. I might have scolded her for that at some other time, but I was as excited about what this weekend had to bring as she was for a change. But then, I had a damned good reason. My date with Holden was tomorrow night, and I could hardly wait to see what he had planned for me.

"How was your week?" I asked.

She shrugged, shook her head, and made a face. "The less said about that, the better. I felt like a lot of the kids were antsy, you know? Like they needed a holiday."

"Or maybe you're projecting because you need one," I shot back playfully, and she held her hands up in concession.

"You might have a point there," she agreed. "I'm already dreaming about taking a city break somewhere. Preferably with some handsome young thing on my arm."

"Well, good luck with that." I turned back to the papers on my desk, and I knew I wasn't going to be able to get anything done with them this evening.

"Let me know if your man has any friends, right?" she remarked.

"Preferably in the billionaire category too. I can't afford this city break all by myself."

"I'll keep my ear to the ground," I promised her with a chuckle. She did make me laugh. I was glad to have her around, to help assuage some of the nerves running through my system in the lead-up to this date that I was kind of terrified about. No, not terrified. It wasn't that I thought it wasn't going to be fun, or I wasn't going to have a good time. I was just scared at the thought of what would happen now that we were properly together. Would it be different? Would the chemistry be less intense? It was impossible to say, and that was freaking me out a bit.

"So you've got your date tomorrow, don't you?" Zoe raised her eyebrows at me, as though reading my mind. "How are you feeling about it?"

"Uh, a little nervous, I guess?" I shrugged, and my voice was a little higher-pitched than normal, betraying me. Zoe giggled.

"You've got nothing to be nervous about." She smiled at me with a certainty that helped me come back down to Earth. "Really. The two of you have already proven you can spend a day together without getting sick of each other. You're going to be fine."

"Thanks." I grinned back at her. "I needed to hear that."

"What are the two of you up to?" she asked keenly, leaning up against the door. "Has he told you yet?"

"No. He says he wants it to be a surprise." I pulled a face. "I told him no more luxury vehicles, but that's the only thing I'm sure of."

"You spoilsport," she teased. "What are you going to wear? Something cute?"

I shrugged. "Honestly, I was going to shoot for jeans and a T-shirt. I don't know where we're going, and it's not like I have much I can pull out of the back of my closet anyway. He already saw my usual date-night dress the first time we went out together, and I don't want to wear that again."

Zoe looked at her watch and then back up at me, a big smile spreading across her face.

"You know, it's late-night shopping this evening," she said, and I furrowed my brow at her.

"What are you getting at?"

"I'm getting at the fact that you could go out and get something new," she suggested excitedly. "Oh, come on. It'll be fun!"

"I don't need anything," I protested weakly, already seeing she'd firmly made up her mind. "Really."

"Just give me this, all right?" She grinned at me, marching over to my desk and grabbing my hand to pull me to my feet. "I could use a little vicarious living through your dating life."

"Are you serious?" I raised my eyebrows at her. "I mean, we only have a couple of hours."

"More than enough time," she promised me. "I don't want to send you out on your date looking anything other than the goddess you are, you get that?"

"Well, if you insist." I shrugged. There would be no arguing with her.

"Excellent." She beamed. "I'll drive us over to the mall. This is going to be fun!"

I packed up the last of my stuff and headed to the car with Zoe, who pulled open the door for me and playfully bowed down low like she was my lady-in-waiting.

"You're going to have to get used to being treated like that when you marry him," she said as she climbed into the seat next to me. I shot her a look.

"We're not getting married," I reminded her. "This is a date. That's all."

"Yeah, but you really like him, don't you?" she reminded me, shooting me a look. "I've seen the way you get when you talk about him. You're into this guy, whether you want to admit it or not."

"I haven't met anyone I've had this kind of chemistry with for a long time," I confessed as we pulled out and away from the school.

"See, I told you. You're totally going to marry him," she replied triumphantly as we turned onto the main road that led to the mall.

"All right, let's not get ahead of ourselves," I muttered, but the truth of the matter was that I knew things were going well between Holden and me. Really well, in fact. I was starting to wonder if this slow build had been a good thing, if our weird approach to dating would serve us in the long run. I'd gotten to know him before he'd so much as kissed me, and he was more than some overly confident entrepreneur. He was smart, funny, kind, a great father, an ambitious businessman. He was all those things I never would have learned on a simple first date but that I knew coming into our first real evening together as a couple. Which could only be a good thing.

"Here we are." Zoe grinned as we reached the mall. "Come on, I know just the place for us. Let's check it out."

I followed Zoe out of the car and toward the mall, and I was secretly glad she was here with me. I'd always been terrible at shopping for clothes for myself. I didn't know what looked good on me, what was painfully out of style, and what was desperately, obviously hip. I knew Zoe was right. I could hardly turn up to a date with Holden, the man who had swept me out on a private yacht when we hadn't even been a couple, in jeans and a tee. But I had no idea what I should go for instead.

"Oh okay, I think you have to try this one on." Zoe pulled a pale periwinkle blue dress from the rack and held it up against me in the first store we went to. Then she thrust it into my arms—along with another dress and then another. They were all cuts and styles I never would have picked out for myself, but I supposed that was the point of having someone else here with me to make sure I didn't fall back on what I already knew looked good on me. I was striking out into new territory here, and I would need a whole new dress to go with that.

I tried on what felt like fifty dresses from the various stores Zoe dragged me in and out of. She followed me into the changing rooms each time and would give me a cursory once-over, shake her head, and pull me out so we could try something different. My feet were aching as I trailed around after her, but I was grateful to have her eye to guide me through this. I would have grabbed the first one that fit me and gotten out of there if I'd had the chance, but she was making sure I was going to get something gorgeous, something that would firmly fit with whatever evening Holden had planned for me. My heart fluttered as I remembered I was going out with him the following night. Would it end back at my place like it had when he'd come around to confess his feelings to me before? I couldn't wait to get him back into bed, but I was also looking forward to finding out how he was out of the sack as well.

We made our way around about a half dozen shops until Zoe suddenly seemed to lay eyes on something that excited her. Her face lit up as she passed one store, ducking inside and turning to the first shop assistant she could find.

"Hey, do you have that in an eight?" she asked, pointing to one of the dresses on the mannequins in the window. I frowned at them. None of them looked my style, but I would go along with what she thought was right if that's what it took to find something that suited me. Everything I had in my closet was a tried-and-tested cut and color on me, but this weekend was all about trying something different, something new, something I hadn't necessarily believed I would get anything out of before. And Zoe had a better idea of what sexy was than I did, so whatever she had in mind, I trusted her.

The assistant returned a minute later with the dress she was looking for, and she pressed it into my hands and gestured to the changing rooms.

"This is the one," she told me. "I can feel it. Go try it on. I want to see you in it."

I headed to the changing rooms, stripped down, and pulled the dress on over my head. When I turned to look at myself in the mirror, I couldn't help smiling.

The dress was a vintage cut with slightly ruffled sleeves that came down over my shoulders, a nipped-in waist that created a dramatic shape, and a flared skirt that hit above my knees. But the print was what made it stand out. It was a dark, inky blue, and all over it were illustrations of stars and planets and moons. It was the perfect blend of modern and retro, and I twisted back and forth in front of the mirror, checking myself out from all angles. It suited me. I ran my hand over the waist, imagining Holden touching me there instead, and I could hardly keep the smile off my face. This was perfect. Better than perfect.

"Can I come in and take a look?" Zoe asked, and without waiting for an answer, she pulled back the curtain and snuck in. She gasped as she looked me up and down, and I did a twirl in front of her. I was only wearing a pair of sneakers with it, but even still, it looked gorgeous.

"That dress is fucking *stunning* on you," Zoe told me firmly. "You have to get it. Please tell me you're going to get it."

"Yeah, I think I will," I agreed. "It might be a little chilly depending on what we're doing tomorrow night, but..."

"But you'll put up with it because you look amazing." She grinned. I smiled back. She was dead right. This dress made me feel better than anything else I had in my closet, and there wasn't a thunderstorm or a blizzard or a damn hurricane that would keep me out of it for my date the next day.

"Hey, how about dinner?" she suggested. "On me. To celebrate your new dress and your new date."

"That sounds great." I nodded. I looked down at the dress. I didn't want to take it off, but I also couldn't wait to slide it on again the next evening, fresh and new, for my first date with Holden.

"Let me get checked out, and I'll be there in a second," I promised her, and she left me in the changing room once more. I stole one last look at myself in the dress, and I bit my lip as I looked in the mirror and wondered what Holden would think of me in it.

30

"And when are you going to be back?"

"I don't know yet, buddy." I glanced at Hunter in the mirror. He was eyeing me with interest, clearly keen to know how this date with Autumn was going to do. *You and me both.*

"Okay." He furrowed his brow. "Will you say hello to her? From me?"

"I will," I promised him. I had gone back and forth on whether to tell Hunter I was going out with Autumn that evening, but I figured it was for the best to tell him the truth—well, the edited version of it, at least. He didn't need to know I'd been planning out every detail of this date down to the letter ever since she'd agreed to this. I wanted to prove to Autumn that I was able to give her what she wanted, in every sense of that word.

"Oh, look. We're here," I remarked as I pulled into Raymond's driveway. Hunter was looking forward to spending the night with Raymond, but I knew he would have rather come along on the date with Autumn and me. In his head, it would be nothing different from the day we'd all spent together on the yacht, chaste and friendly and involving him. Little did he know everything I had planned for her tonight.

Hunter hopped out of the car, grabbing his backpack to his chest, and made for the door. I followed him. Olivia pulled it open before I got there and gave my son a hug.

"Hey, Holden." She smiled at me. "How's it going?"

"Pretty good." I nodded. "You?"

"Actually starting to feel like I got some sleep for the first time in months." She rolled her eyes playfully. "I don't know how you did it all by yourself."

"Well, I'm a superhero, obviously." I winked at Hunter, and Olivia laughed.

"You joke, but I think it might be true," she remarked. "You want to stick around to see Raymond? He's just finishing up with the baby."

"No, I think I've got to get going." I glanced at my watch. "Don't want to be late."

She nodded. "All right. Have a good time. I'll see you tomorrow."

"See you later," I replied. "And thanks for looking after Hunter for me."

"Always a pleasure." She smiled and then pushed the door shut and left me out there all by myself. Which meant I had no other option but to climb in my car and go pick up Autumn.

I was nervous as hell as I drove over there. I had spent all week putting this together, and I was a little fearful that she was still going to think it was too much. But I had taken in what she said to me when we'd been on that yacht. Surely, she would enjoy herself, given that she had pretty much planned this date for herself.

I arrived outside her place and remembered the last time I'd come here—when we hooked up for the first time, when I sat there in this car for a moment wondering if I was making the biggest mistake of my life. Well, it had turned out pretty well for me in the long run. I grinned as I got out of the car and headed to the door, adjusting the collar of my shirt. I was wearing the suit she'd helped me pick out back in the days when we'd been pretending to be nothing but friends.

I knocked on the door, and a moment later, she opened it. She was wearing a dress I hadn't seen before, dark and sweet, curving in to draw attention to the shape of her body in a way I couldn't tear my gaze from. I looked her up and down, unable to stop myself, and raised my eyebrows.

"You look incredible," I told her, and she bit her lip. For a second, I wanted nothing more than to cancel the date and go into that house to recreate what we shared that first time around, but I knew I had to get her out of the house before we did anything like that.

"Is that the suit I picked out for you?" she asked as she stepped over the threshold, linking her arm through mine happily. I nodded.

"Looks good on you." She briefly leaned her head on my shoulder. "Are you going to tell me what's going on tonight? Or do I have to guess?"

"I promise it's nothing to do with a yacht," I replied. "Is that enough?"

"I guess it's going to have to be," she agreed as she slipped into the car next to me, and I pulled away to head into the center of the city.

We chatted about her week so far, and she told me those after-school clubs would be starting soon and that Hunter had been asking about them. That made me smile. He was starting to open up a little, and that was all I'd wanted from this whole endeavor in the first place. Everything else that had come with it, like her hand resting on my leg as we drove? Well, that was a sweet-ass bonus.

Eventually, I pulled the car to a halt outside a park. I had spent hours trawling for the perfect one, and I was pretty sure I'd found it —big enough that we could get some privacy, but not so big, I was going to end up getting lost in there. Clean and pretty but not over-crowded. She looked into the park and cocked an eyebrow.

"And what might we be doing here?" she asked, grinning. I helped her out of the car and then went to the back seat to grab the picnic basket I'd filled with food for us. She beamed when she saw me pull it out.

"You're taking me on a picnic?" she asked, clasping her hands together with delight. I nodded.

"Like you said you wanted to on the yacht, remember?" I

reminded her, suddenly panicked she would think I'd pulled this out of my ass. She nodded.

"Of course, I do," she sighed happily. "I didn't even think you'd remember."

"Well, I was hardly going to forget." I cocked my head at her. "Come on, let's find a spot, and we can eat. I'm starving."

"Me too," she agreed, and she tucked one hand into mine as I hefted the basket under one arm while we turned into the park. My head felt as though it was spinning, my feet not quite touching the ground. I was so glad she was here by my side and that she liked my date idea. I was pulling this off. I was totally pulling this off.

We walked for a while through the park, and I had to admit, this was pretty nice. I would never have thought to come to a place like this without her, but there was something calm about it. It was hard to imagine the city was ten minutes from here when it was so peaceful out in the park. We made our way down a small lane lined with trees and a few twinkling streetlights as the sun began to set in the distance.

"This is perfect," Autumn sighed as we came to a small clearing slightly off the path and settled down to eat. "Thank you, Holden."

"Hey, thanks for giving me the idea." I held my hands up. "Saved me the trouble of having to come up with something myself."

She slapped my shoulder playfully, laughing, and then helped me unpack the food and the blanket so we could eat. I wasn't sure what she liked, so I went for a mix of anything I could find—fruit, cheese, bread, chocolate, and a couple of pastries.

"This looks amazing," she said when we had it all spread out in front of us. I could see her eyes shining even in the dim light from the streetlamps a few dozen feet away.

"Good." I smiled back at her, leaned over, and stole a brief kiss. We couldn't go any further than that out here in public, but I just needed to kiss her, to touch her. I was already obsessed with how damn good she felt, how sweet it was being alone with her like this. She still had her eyes closed as I pulled away, as though she was savoring the feeling of my lips on hers.

We tucked into our food, and I found myself relaxing a little. I had been so nervous about this date, worried I was somehow going to fuck everything up and make a fool of myself in some way I hadn't anticipated. But this was going well. Really well. We were laughing about something that had happened at her school about her best friend, Zoe, and her desire to land one of my friends. I told Autumn the chances were pretty slim, since about the only friend I had around was Raymond, and he was happily married.

"How did you meet him?" she asked, tearing off a piece of bread and popping it into her mouth. "Oh my God, this bread is so good."

"We met in college." I shrugged. "Ages ago. When I started the business, he invested and helped out a little to get things off the ground. Took his share when they started trying for a baby and now he's set for life."

"Damn." She raised her eyebrows. "Too late to go back in time and invest in you myself?"

"A little." I grinned.

"I thought you ran the business by yourself," she said. "No staff or anything."

"Well, since we were friends, I didn't consider him staff," I replied. "And it's not like he's coming back any time soon. Though it would help me out if he could."

"Why? You looking to hire someone?" She cocked an eyebrow. "And here, I thought you'd be too much of a control freak for that."

"Yeah, you and me both," I admitted. "I've been pushing back against it for a long time, but I think I might have to hire someone soon."

"Oh, yeah?" She raised her eyebrows. "Why?"

"Oh, it's getting a little too much for me to juggle everything," I replied, keeping it vague so she wouldn't catch onto the fact that she was the reason things had started going downhill at work.

"Well, you've got the money to do it, and I'm pretty sure there'd be dozens of people fighting to work with someone as well-established as you," she pointed out. "You should go for it."

"You think so?"

"I know so." She nodded, pulling off a grape from the bunch and slipping it between her lips. For the briefest second, her fingers played over her mouth, and I wanted nothing more than to forget about work entirely.

"But you have to do what you think is right for you," she finished up. "If you don't think you can handle someone else working at the business, then don't do it. It's your place, after all."

"Yeah, I guess so." I had expected her to encourage me to go ahead and hire someone, but maybe she understood better than I had anticipated the passion that came from building something all by yourself.

"Mmm, I'm so full." She slumped back on the blanket and tilted her head toward the sky. There was a smile on her face, and her eyes had drifted shut, and she looked so beautiful, it almost hurt me. I wanted nothing more than to lean over and plant my mouth against hers, to move on top of her and render that gorgeous dress pointless, but there was something else I had in mind first. We had done her part of the date, and next, we were going to do mine.

"Got room for a little something extra?" I asked, and she opened one eye and looked at me.

"I'm listening."

31

AUTUMN

"Ice cream?" I laughed as we pulled the car to a halt on the pier. "This is where you wanted to take me?"

"Yup." Holden grinned as he pulled the car to a halt. "I'm not coming all the way into the city and not getting ice cream from my favorite place now, am I?"

"And what if I had said no? Would you have picked it up on the way home?"

He shrugged. "Probably. Come on, it's only open for another twenty minutes. We can get one and walk down the pier. It's pretty this time of night."

"And you're not going to spring a last-minute boat ride on me, are you?" I asked him playfully. He held his hands up.

"Well, now you've called me out on it..."

"Holden!" I exclaimed, tapping his shoulder playfully. "Come on, I want to try this ice cream. Or should I say... cone on?"

"Okay, that was the worst joke I've ever heard in my life," Holden told me as he climbed out of the car.

"You totally thought it was funny," I replied. "Besides, you better get used to them. Terrible jokes are sort of my specialty."

"Why do you think I keep feeding you?" he teased. "I don't want to hear any of your puns anymore."

"Bold idea, but it's not going to work." I tapped my finger on my chin, as though pondering on it. "Nothing stops me when I have a terrible joke the world needs to hear."

"A national service, is it?" he asked as we headed toward a small, old-fashioned looking ice cream shop.

"I'm only doing my duty for my country." I placed my hand on my heart. "The world can't be denied my awful sense of humor."

"Of course." He opened the door for me and swept his hand ahead of him to indicate I should enter. "After you."

I brushed by him and had to smile when I caught a whiff of his aftershave. There was something so nice about being out with him like this, after all that time I'd spent trying to ignore that I was developing a serious crush on the guy. I didn't have to hide it anymore, didn't have to hold back. We were out together on a real date, and he was treating me like the perfect lady to his perfect gentleman. Though I was hoping he would drop that act as soon as we were alone together once more.

"What do you recommend?" I asked as I scanned through the list of flavors. There were the usual ones there—vanilla, strawberry, chocolate—as well as some more out-there ones. I was pretty full, but my mouth watered when I caught sight of a salted caramel espresso one.

"Well, I can see which one you're going to go for," he teased, noticing the way my eyes lingered on the sign of the ice cream that had caught my attention. "I'll get a ginger-orange one. You can try some if you want."

"All right, but I'm not sharing mine," I warned him playfully. He paid for the couple of cones, despite my protests, and the old man behind the counter loaded up the waffle cones with a scoop of our chosen flavors and handed them to us. Holden led me back out on to the pier, and I paused for a moment, looking out over the water, catching a drip of melting ice cream that was making its way down my cone already.

"This place is so pretty at night," I said. "I've never come down here this late in the evening before."

"I used to bring Hunter down here a lot when I didn't have much cash and was trying to find stuff for the two of us to do," he explained, joining me and leaning on the railing in front of the water. "It was cheap to get a little ice cream and take him for a walk down here."

"And now he only comes for the ice cream, right?" I finished up for him.

"How did you guess?" He raised his eyebrows and took a bite of his cone. "It is really fucking good, after all."

"Yeah, it is," I agreed, as I started in on my scoop. "I'm looking forward to having Hunter in that after-school club thing. I think it's going to do him good."

"Me too," Holden agreed. "I'm glad he seems so enthusiastic about it. It's been hard finding stuff that appeals to him outside of going out with me, but you seem to bring out that side in him."

"He's at that funny age now." I shrugged. "Sometimes they go out and make their way in the world without any help needed, and sometimes they need a little nudging in the right direction. He's trying to figure himself out. It might take a while, but he'll get there."

"I'm so glad you're there to give him a hand," he told me, looking at me seriously. "I know it's been hard for him, but having you around has made it a lot easier."

"He's the one putting in the work too," I replied. "Hey, does he know we're out together tonight?"

"Yeah, I mentioned it to him. He kept asking me if we were going out together, and I just told him finally. Is that all right?"

"He's young enough that he won't think much of it." I shrugged. "Maybe jealous he didn't get to join us for ice cream, huh?"

"Oh yeah, that's for sure what he's going to be the maddest about," Holden agreed. "I told him not to talk to you about it, though. He knows that much."

"That's a relief," I replied, planting a hand on my heart. "I don't want to have my dating life come up at school, not when Zoe's around on gossip high alert."

I think my friends are the same way." He grinned. "They want me to get together with someone already, and they've been hearing about everything that's been happening with us all along, so they're feeling pretty smug now that we're on a date."

"Well, they should," I agreed, flashing him a smile. "You're doing pretty well."

"Pretty well?"

"Pretty well," I repeated playfully. "Room for improvement, but the night's not over yet."

I slipped my arm through his, and we made our way down the pier while a question crossed my mind. I knew it was the kind of thing I should have kept to myself on a first date, but since we'd known each other a while, I figured I had a right to ask it. And besides, I wouldn't be able to shake it from my mind if I didn't.

"Hunter's mother," I asked, hesitant. "What's the situation there?"

"Hey, don't hold back, huh?" Holden shot me a look that was one part playful and one part defensive. I winced.

"Sorry, is that kind of a sore spot?"

"No, it's fine." He rubbed his hand over his face and paused for a moment. "Look, I don't want to talk about Hunter's mother if I can avoid it. All you need to know is that she's not in the picture, and she's not going to be. Ever."

"Okay." I let out a breath. My curiosity was piqued, but pressing any harder was going to wind up in me ruining this date, which had been going so well thus far. I didn't want to put a downer on our night, so I changed the subject.

"Oh, I have so many grade curves to do this week," I groaned. "I'd rather be out here with you, trust me."

"You know, the offer's still on the table if you want to take it," Holden said. "I could come up with a program that forms them for you. Might take a bit of time, and I'm sure I'll need your input on it, but if you're game..."

"You're serious?" I cocked an eyebrow at him. "For free?"

He nodded. "Yeah, of course. I told you, anything I can do to make the lives of the people who look after my son easier."

"Well, aren't you Mister Generous," I teased, nibbling on my ice cream. "Don't you have proper clients you'd rather be taking care of? Ones who pay?"

"Maybe I'm looking for excuses to spend more time with you," he shot back, and I couldn't help but smile.

"I'm sure I can find some way to help you indulge that," I replied, my pulse racing a little as I saw his gaze move down to my mouth for a moment. Even though we'd already hooked up before we'd so much as planned our first date, I still found our sexual chemistry burning as brightly as it had ever been. If this pier hadn't been so damn family-friendly, I would have been tempted to have him push me up against the railings and take me right here.

"Glad to hear it." He took a bite of his ice cream, and we continued down the pier, looping around the far end and starting slowly to make our way back toward the top.

"Even if it didn't give me a chance to spend time with you," he said, "something like that could be big if we could pull it off. I know it may not sound like it, but if lots of teachers are having trouble like you—wasting their time putting together something that a program could do for them—it could be a big win for me."

"Oh, so you do have some selfish reasons then," I teased. "Thought so."

"Hey, are you calling me selfish?" He raised his eyebrows. "When I got this ice cream for you?"

"Yeah, like you haven't wanted to steal a bite since I picked it up," I shot back.

"Sure have," he agreed, and before I could even think about what was happening, he leaned forward to loop an arm around my waist, pulling me close and pressing his mouth to mine. His lips were cool from the ice cream, distantly sweet, and my heart fluttered in my chest as our mouths found one another. I felt as though my feet were barely touching the ground, my entire being spinning in the air as he kissed me.

When he pulled back, he smiled and lifted his hand to brush the tiniest smudge of ice-cream from my face.

"Not so selfish now, huh?" he remarked, and he kissed me on the cheek once more before he turned to lead me back down the pier. I didn't have the words to fire back some smart comment in his direction, as much as I wanted to. Because my heart was too busy racing in my chest, my mind too preoccupied with trying to make sense of everything that kiss had meant to me. I paused for a moment, watching him walking in front of me, and it was as though clouds had cleared from behind my eyes, and I could finally see him properly. The man I was looking at was a man I was beginning to fall for, harder than I'd ever expected to.

"Hey, wait up!" I called after him as I hurried to catch up with him while a sticky line of ice cream made its way down my hand, cool on my skin like he had been.

32

I glanced up at the clock on the wall and pulled a face. I would have to go and pick up Hunter from his after-school activities soon, but I was on a roll with the project, and I didn't want to take a break.

I leaned back from the computer and closed my eyes for a moment, but the letters and numbers still danced behind my eyelids like they were imprinted there for good. It felt nice to be working on something that I wasn't churning out for any old client, something that I was putting together for a damned good reason. Autumn was much easier to work with than most of the people I'd had on my roster in the last few years. I also got to make out with her once in a while, which was a new one on me. And the longer I spent putting together this program to help her produce the grade curves for the school year, the more I started to believe this could be something good for the business. I didn't know anyone else in the city who was working on stuff in the education sector. Sure, I didn't know if they would take it or not, but with Autumn championing the cause, there was a good chance, right?

I was working from home while Hunter was out at his gaming club. It was the second one this week, and he had seemed to enjoy the first one well enough. I was hoping he would start making some friends there soon. Autumn was there to keep an eye on him, and she would report back to me with the ups and downs for my son so far, but it was up to him to strike out on his own and make some new buddies. She could only guide him so far, and I hoped his case of self-imposed social isolation wasn't permanent.

I closed my laptop, got to my feet, and stretched before reaching for my car keys. It always sucked to break off a project when I was right in the flow of it, but at least I got to go see my two favorite people in the world to make up for it. I grinned as I headed out to the car. Autumn would be there. I would get to see Autumn again.

Our date over the weekend had gone so well, I hadn't been able to stop thinking about her since. She was smart, charming, delightfully awkward, and a little blunt in her own unique way—and a great kisser too. If I'd had my way, I would have taken her home and fucked her senseless all over again, but Raymond was set to drop Hunter off early the next morning and the last thing I'd needed was for my son to catch Autumn making coffee for us the next day. Hunter wasn't dumb, and it wouldn't take him long to catch on that there was something going on between me and his favorite teacher, but that didn't mean I had to hand it to him on a plate yet. Not before I knew where I stood with her for sure.

I drove up to the school and found myself humming along to the radio, something I hadn't done in years. I normally found most of the modern pop songs that got airplay a little dramatic and silly, but I was in a better mood that day than I had been in a long time. I drummed my fingers on the wheel and thought about Autumn, fitted the lyrics of the silly love song crackling over the air to everything we'd been through so far.

We were still at that early, nebulous stage of the relationship when it felt like anything at all could happen. We could stick together forever, or she could vanish tomorrow, for all I knew. Though I hoped she was going to pick the former. There was something about her that made me feel buoyant, as though I was about to float up and climb a hundred feet into the air without even realizing.

I arrived at the school and checked myself out in the mirror. I couldn't help noticing that I looked a little different than normal. Not physically, but something inside me seemed to have lit up, my eyes brighter. I liked it. If this was what Autumn did to me, then damn straight I would be keeping her around as long as I could.

I hopped out of the car and headed up to the school, cutting around the back to get to where I needed quicker. I was a couple of minutes late, but I doubted Hunter would notice, given how involved he'd been in his game the last time I'd come around.

I paused when I laid eyes on him, and I smiled when I saw who he was talking to. It was a kid his own age, a little girl, and the two of them were waving their arms around and laughing at some shared joke. I didn't want to cut him off yet. It was so nice to see him interacting with another kid, having a good time and not forcing it.

"Dad!" Hunter spotted me suddenly, and he came barreling toward me as though I was the most exciting thing he'd ever laid eyes on.

"Hey!" I waved to him and headed toward him.

"This is Amelie," he gestured to the girl standing next to him, looking up at me a little bashfully. "We did a campaign together today. She's really good! Better than me!"

"Well, that's pretty impressive." I nodded down at her with a smile. "Maybe you could train Hunter up, huh? Get him up to your level?"

"She says she's going to show me some tricks next time we're in the club." Hunter nodded, and he glanced around at the door. "I just need to get my bag."

He headed through to grab it in a little buzz of overexcited activity, and I began to relax. He was doing well. I'd wondered if these clubs might be a little too much for him, but he seemed to be getting along great—and hey, he'd already made a friend who he wanted to see again. That couldn't be so bad, right?

"Hey."

I heard the familiar voice behind me and had a smile on my face before I so much as turned around and confirmed the source.

"Well, hello there," I greeted Autumn, who flushed a little and smiled back at me as soon as our eyes met. I knew exactly how she felt. Being in her presence sent little sparks of electricity racing all over my body. There was so much I wanted to do to her, so much I wanted to say, and it felt like those urges were all climbing on top of each other in my brain.

"Seems like Hunter's getting along well." I nodded to the spot my son had been standing in, as Amelie's mother appeared and led her away.

"Yeah, I wondered if he and Amelie might click," she said. "They're both a little quiet, but they're both *obsessed* with games. I'm not surprised they joined the club and enjoyed it so much."

"You're doing such good work here, Autumn," I told her fervently. "Really. I can't thank you enough. I know he's had a hard time making friends and socializing, but... well, you've helped him through it. That's more than I ever could have asked for."

"Just doing my job." She smiled modestly, though I could see the pleased little flush move a little farther up her neck.

"Speaking of," I changed the subject so as not to sound like I was heaping her with praise, "I've been working on that program to figure out the grade curves for you."

"Oh, really?" She perked up. "How's it going?"

"It's coming along well." I nodded. "I had to drag myself away from it to come down here. I'll probably be in touch for a little advice in the next few days. Maybe you could test run it for me sometime?"

"Well, I'm pretty crappy with technology, but I'll give it a go," she agreed. "Maybe we could make a night of it?"

"A night?" I cocked an eyebrow at her playfully. "My, my, a little forward, aren't we?"

"You're the one who came to my house that night," she reminded me, raising her eyebrows in my direction.

"And I didn't hear you complaining so much," I shot back. I glanced over my shoulder, where I could see Hunter chatting to one of the other kids back in the computer room, and I swiftly moved toward Autumn, took her hand, and pulled her into the classroom behind us.

"What are you doing?" She giggled, but she didn't protest as I pushed the door shut behind us and then pressed her up against it.

I kissed her swiftly, knowing this was likely all I would be able to steal for the foreseeable future. I wasn't sure when the two of us would find the time to hang out again, and I wanted her, wanted every little piece of her I could get my hands on. Her fingers traced a formless shape over my neck, and she let out a little moan that sounded like relief as much as anything else, as though she had been craving this as deeply and as keenly as I had. I pushed my tongue into her mouth, pulling her body against mine, feeling her begin to soften, to fit against my form...

And then I heard a door outside click open, and I swiftly pulled back from her. She was panting, catching her breath, and she raised her eyebrows at me.

"I don't think that's appropriate school behavior," she remarked playfully, and I brushed my mouth over her neck, greedily inhaling her familiar scent.

"Well, you'll have to find a way to punish me." I cocked an eyebrow at her, and she giggled and touched my cheek.

"When do I get to see you again?" she asked.

"Anytime you want," I replied at once. "Seriously, text me and let me know when you're free. I want to see you again."

"Me too," she agreed, and she glanced around. "Hey, I should probably get back out there, make sure the rest of the kids get home all right."

"Of course." I pulled away from her reluctantly, and she shot me one last smile before she headed out the door. I lingered for a moment, gathering myself, making sure it wouldn't be too obvious what I had been up to when I went to pick up Hunter. After a second, I stepped out through the door and went to grab my son.

"Dad!" Hunter called to me. "Where were you? I was looking for you."

"Oh, I had something to talk about with Aut—with Ms. Becks," I replied. "Come on, let's get home, shall we? I'm starving. You can tell me all about your campaign on the way there."

"Sure!" Hunter sounded excited as he followed me back out to the car, and I glanced back into the building one last time to steal a look at Autumn. And, of course, I found her looking in my direction, staring at me like she was trying to drink me in before I got out of there for good. I smiled at her and then turned my attention back to Hunter.

"What are you smiling about?" He furrowed his brow at me suspiciously.

"Oh, nothing." I waved my hand. "Come on, tell me about your campaign with Amelie. I can't wait to hear about it."

33

AUTUMN

I watched as Hunter and Holden left the school, and I wrapped my arms around myself and smiled. That kiss was still lingering on my mouth, and I was so glad he'd come in to pick his son up today. I couldn't get enough of him. I felt like I was drunk on Holden, constantly needing more to keep up the feeling. The tips of my fingers tingled as I remembered the way his stubble had felt beneath them. Man, if I could have gone home with him tonight...

"Hey there." Zoe appeared in the door of the computer room, which I realized was empty except for me as all the kids had been picked up and taken home.

"Oh, hey." I glanced around at her. "Didn't realize you were still here."

"I had to work on those fucking grading curves." She shook her head. It still felt dissonant to me to hear her swear on school property, even though there was no one under the age of eighteen to keep it PG-13 for. I grinned.

"Yeah, I feel you," I sighed. "Why do you think I started these after-school things? I want to avoid having to do my actual work."

"Did it go well today?" she asked. "The computer club?"

"Yeah, I think it did, actually." I nodded, remembering Hunter and Amelie chatting to each other as they ran some campaign together. It was good to see the two of them interacting, and they seemed to get along well. Maybe they could cultivate that outside of the club tomorrow at school.

"Well, you're a braver woman than me, taking on more work on top of everything else we have to do," she said. "I can barely keep up with everything as it is."

"It's no trouble." I waved my hand, and she cocked an eyebrow at me.

"And that wouldn't have anything to do with the fact that you get to see your beau every time you do it?" she asked. I grinned at her, holding up my hands in concession.

"All right, maybe you've got a point," I agreed, glancing out the window again to see if they were still there—they were long gone, but my head was still full of Holden.

"Hey, you want to go grab dinner?" she suggested. "I'm starving, and I don't feel like cooking."

"The Indian place off Languin Street?" I replied at once. My stomach was growling, and I didn't have the energy to come up with anything myself when I got home. Besides, I was in the mood to be with people tonight. I would have spent the entire evening lying in bed and thinking about Holden if I didn't, and no matter how much fun I was having with him, I didn't want to sour it by letting my brain wander.

"I'm in." Zoe nodded. "I'll drive. Come on, let's get out of here. I'm starved."

We headed down to the restaurant and got the last table, squeezing into what was meant to be a romantic two-seater at the dim end of the dining area. They lit a candle between us as they delivered our menus, and Zoe laughed.

"Hey, just because I asked you on this date doesn't mean you don't have to pay, all right?" She pointed at me seriously.

"Where's your sense of chivalry?" I teased, and I turned my attention to the menu, my mouth already watering. This was our usual place to come after a long day, and it had never let me down. The food was always excellent.

We ordered a selection to share, as well as a bottle of wine to split between us, and we enjoyed the food for a while, chatting about our days thus far. Then Zoe cocked her head at me, and I knew at once what question was coming next.

"So," she began, rubbing her hands together. "What's going on with you and Hunter's dad?"

"Well," I smiled, glad to have someone to talk about it with. I didn't want to gush straight off the bat when nobody had asked about it, but it felt like the only thing I'd been able to wrap my head around in the last couple of days.

"We went out on a date over the weekend—a real one," I told her. "It was really nice. When he took me out on the yacht a few weeks ago, he asked me what my idea of the perfect date would be, and he pretty much made that happen."

"Oh my gosh, that's so romantic." She clasped her hand to her chest. "What did you do?"

"He took me out for a picnic at this gorgeous park in the center of the city," I continued. "And then he took me to this old ice cream place on the pier, and we took a walk."

"Okay, now that's super cute." She nodded approvingly. "Since then?"

"Not much." I shook my head. "We've both been busy. But he told me today that whenever I want to see him, he's free, so I'm going to take him up on that soon enough."

"Ooh, that sounds so cool." She clapped her hands together and grabbed a bite of her vegan samosa.

"And we've been in touch about what he's working on at the moment," I continued with a shake of my head.

"Oh, what's he putting together?" She furrowed her brow. "He's a website designer, right?"

"Yeah, but I mentioned to him how much I hate putting together all the grade curve stuff, and he basically suggested that he come up with a program to do it for me," I explained. "I thought he was kidding around at first, but he told me today that it's coming along pretty well. He asked me to take a look at it and try it out for him soon."

"Okay, as soon as he gets that thing up and running, I'm first in line to try it out," Zoe stabbed her finger in the air decisively. "I can't believe nobody thought to do that before now. He could make a lot of money off that if he marketed it right."

"Yeah, he could, but I think he's only doing it to help me out."

"Which is pretty damn sweet all by itself," Zoe finished up for me. "Things sound like they're going well then."

"Really well," I agreed, taking a sip of my wine. I couldn't tell whether it was the alcohol or talking about Holden that was spreading warmth through my chest, but either way, I would happily take it.

"Can I ask you something?" She cocked her head at me.

"Sure thing."

"What's the deal with Hunter's mom?" she asked, and I wrinkled my nose up.

"You know, I asked him about it on the date, and he seemed pretty... I don't know, like he didn't want to talk about it," I replied. "I know she's been out of their lives for a while and that he doesn't consider her involved with them at all."

"Hmm." Zoe tapped her fingers on the table.

"What?" I prompted her.

"I mean, she is the boy's mother," she pointed out. "I wouldn't trust in her ever being out of the picture for good, would you?"

"I don't know about that." I shrugged. "I don't think she's been in the picture for much of Hunter's life, if at all. And I don't think Holden would lie to me about that."

"Oh, I don't think he's lying or anything." She waved her hand, dismissing the notion at once. "But Hunter's still got a lot of childhood left, and the mother could roll in whenever to try and get custody. Or Hunter could go looking for her himself. He's a curious kid, and he'll start wondering at some point."

"I suppose you're right." I leaned back from the table, my appetite suddenly vanishing.

"Hey, I don't want to put a downer on anything," Zoe swiftly jumped in to assure me. "I was just wondering, that's all."

"Yeah, well, as far as I know, she's out of the picture for now," I replied with a hopeful smile. "I have to keep my fingers crossed that it stays that way."

"I'm sure it will," Zoe replied, but the seeds of doubt were already sewn in my head. I would have to hope they didn't have any reason to start sprouting anytime soon.

We finished our dinner together, shifting the conversation to some of the gossip around the teachers at our school, and said our goodbyes outside the restaurant. Zoe dropped me back at the school, and the whole time, everything she had said to me was running around and around in my head.

What if she was right about Hunter's mother? What if she suddenly decided she wanted to be part of her son's life again? Or, as Zoe had pointed out, what if Hunter went looking for her? It would complicate what was happening between Holden and me so much, and that wasn't what I wanted. If she came back into the picture, I would have to take a step back from the two of them and give them some space to figure out what they wanted to be, how they wanted to operate as a family. That conversation had come as a stinging reminder that, no matter how well things were going, there were a whole lot of variables at play with dating a single dad like Holden, variables I didn't have any control over.

I arrived back at the house still mulling over the conversation and went straight for a shower and climbed into bed. I needed to get some sleep to push those thoughts out of my mind for a while. I didn't want to get overstressed about something that wasn't even happening, not when things between Holden and me were going so well.

My phone buzzed on my bedside table where I'd dumped it when I came in, and I reached over to check who was messaging me. Despite everything that had stuck itself in my mind that evening, I smiled when I saw it was Holden.

"Hey. Just wanted to say I'm thinking about you and that kiss, and I can't wait to see you again—X."

It was enough to temporarily banish the doubts that had been running through my brain to somewhere I couldn't get to them, and I bit my lip as I quickly responded.

"Me too. Miss you—X."

I placed the phone down next to my bed and snuggled down, letting my head sink gratefully into the pillow. It had been a hell of a long day, and I had an early start tomorrow. The most important thing for me was to get some rest and not spend the rest of the evening mulling over things I couldn't control.

34

HOLDEN

"Uh, I'll have a coffee, please." Raymond glanced up at the waitress as she approached. "Black. And strong."

She smiled and nodded, jotting down his order on her pad, and wandered off again. Raymond bounced his daughter in his arms, and she let out a little snuffle and a squeak.

"Tired?" I asked, and Raymond nodded and yawned.

"I didn't even realize it was possible to be this damn tired," he replied. "I feel like I've been up for three months straight."

"Yeah, that doesn't go away for a while," I told him, and he shook his head and glanced down at his daughter.

"You couldn't lie to me and tell me it's going to get better tomorrow?" He jibed.

"Okay. Yeah, I promise." I nodded to him seriously. "It all gets easier in precisely an hour's time, and then it's a cakewalk from there until college."

"Oh, don't make me think about sending her off to college," He made an anxious face. "I can barely handle being out of the room without her these days."

"Trust me, it does get easier as they get older," I promised him, hand on heart. "I know it seems impossible, but when they start striking out on their own, you'll want them to. You'll encourage it."

"Okay, I'll believe it when I feel it." Raymond grinned as the waitress returned with his coffee and placed it down in front of him. His daughter had dozed off in his arms, and Raymond lowered his voice so as not to wake her.

"What about you? How are you doing?" He gestured to me as he carefully replaced his coffee cup in the china saucer so it wouldn't make a clink and wake up the baby. I nodded.

"Yeah, I think I'm doing really well at the moment," I replied.

"Think?"

"I know," I corrected myself. "Sorry, I'm not used to feeling this good about things. I'm still getting used to it."

"I feel you on that," he agreed. "What are you up to these days? Made any decisions about hiring someone to come work for you?"

"Well, I've been giving that a lot of thought," I replied. "Lots. But for the time being, I've decided to shift away from all my client projects and work on this idea Autumn had for a program. Well, an idea she gave me, at least."

"All of your clients?" He raised his eyebrows. "Is that a good idea?"

"It's not as scary as it sounds." I waved my hand. "I'm up-to-date with all my projects for the time being, and I let them know I'm not taking on new work in the next couple of weeks. I don't think any of them are going to jump ship when there's nothing they need to be done in the first place."

"I guess you're right," he conceded. "What's this thing you're working on with Autumn?"

"Well, she was talking about what it's like teaching, right?" I leaned forward, pleased to have someone to talk to about it. "And she mentioned to me that one of the things they all hate the most is putting together those grade curves. As in, they have to input all the data by hand and come up with grade curves to mark all the students based on the results from the years before."

"All right, so that's just begging to be updated," Raymond conceded. "How long have you been putting that together?"

"A week or so," I replied. "I think it's going pretty well, though. I've been talking to Autumn a lot to get an idea of the kind of programs they already use down there, so I'm not putting together something that's too out there for most of the staff."

"And she knows about this?"

"She's excited about it." I grinned. "And so am I. I think it's a big gap in the market, and the worst they can say is they don't want it, right?"

"Bit of a change from website designing," Raymond pointed out. "You sure that's what you want to be doing?"

"I know it's unorthodox, but the program—"

"No, I meant, are you sure website designing is still what you want to be doing?" he corrected himself. I fell silent and leaned back in my seat. If I was being honest, I hadn't considered anything else in my adult life. Sure, occasionally I got frustrated with a project or a client and thought about what it would be like to work a different job, but this was what I was good at. This was how I could build a life for my son, and I was hardly going to double back on that just because I was working on something different.

"I..." I wasn't sure how to answer him. Raymond had this habit of seeing right through me, an annoying little trick he'd picked up since we worked together. If I lied to him and told him I was still dead set on the web designing business, he would see it for the lie it was.

"I don't know," I confessed. "I like working on this program, especially with Autumn. Maybe I should take a step away from the business for a while. After that client left..."

I stared into the last few sips of my coffee, as though I could divine the answer to my question in there. Though I was pretty sure that was meant to be tea leaves.

"Or maybe you're enjoying spending time with Autumn," he suggested. "Maybe that's what it is. Do you think you'd be as committed to this project if it weren't for her?"

"I honestly have no idea," I admitted. "I like being around her so damn much, Raymond."

"Yeah, I can tell," he teased, kicking me under the table. "The way you talk about her, I think it's pretty obvious to everyone in this place."

"Yeah, well, I haven't had a date in nearly ten years. Allow me to actually enjoy one when it comes along," I shot back, finishing up my coffee and gesturing to the waitress for another.

"Hey, I'm not holding it against you," Raymond assured me. "I think it's cute that you've found someone after all this time. And I'm a little smug that it was Olivia who set the two of you up."

"I don't even know if I could count that first time as a date." I shook my head.

"Hey, don't try and take all the credit here," Raymond shot back. "It was totally Olivia's doing."

"All right, I concede." I held my hands up. "Your wife gets the credit."

"Damn straight." He leaned back in his seat triumphantly, but the sudden movement jolted the baby, and she snuffled and woke up. She stretched slightly, pushing her little fists away from her body, and I couldn't help but smile. I could still remember my son at that age when he'd been so tiny, I'd been terrified at the thought of letting him out into the world at large because he seemed too vulnerable and delicate.

"So things are going well between you and Autumn," Raymond finished up, and I nodded.

"Sure are," I agreed and reached over to touch his daughter's little hand. "Though I can't take my eyes off this little lady at the moment."

Raymond watched as she shuffled and sniffed again in his arms at my touch, and I leaned back before I woke her up entirely. He returned his gaze to me and cocked an eyebrow.

"You ever think about having any more kids?" he asked. "With Autumn, maybe?"

"Hey, hey." I held my hands up. "We've only been hanging out a few weeks. Let's put the brakes on the wife and two kids for now, all right?"

He grinned. "All right. But it must have crossed your mind. I mean, she's so good with kids, being a teacher and all, and it seems like Hunter loves her."

I eyed him for a moment and shrugged. If I was being honest with myself, I had allowed my mind to stray a little bit toward what a future with Autumn might look like. How would it feel to be working from home and hear her come through the door, toss her shoes off, and throw her coat onto the rack and then find me for a kiss? How nice it would be to take her out to Hunter's favorite spot and play games together all evening as a family—and yeah, sure, maybe even having another kid when the time was right if she was open to it. But we hadn't so much as talked about what a future would look like between the two of us, and I would freak her all the way out if I was to suddenly start talking marriage and kids. When you had a child, it felt as though all dating automatically clicked up to the next level of seriousness whether you liked it or not. Autumn had to know that, but that didn't mean I had to slide straight into "but where is this going?" mode when we hadn't even had our second official date yet.

"Yeah, sure, but things are still so fresh," I pointed out. "I think it would scare her off if I was to start trying to pin her down to a commitment in the next few dates, don't you?"

"I don't know, man." Raymond shrugged. "I mean, when I met Olivia, things got serious pretty quickly. I knew she was the one, and that was it for me."

"Yeah, but I bet you weren't talking about getting her pregnant on the second date," I pointed out, and he chuckled.

"Okay, point taken." He raised his eyebrows. "I was wondering if you thought about it yet."

"You've got babies on the brain, that's the problem," I remarked. He glanced down at his daughter, who had slipped back to sleep in his arms.

"I mean, can you blame me, when she's the introduction I've had?" he replied. I knew exactly what he meant. No matter how hard it was, no matter how little sleep you got, no matter how crazy you felt as you were trying to keep yourself together sometimes, parenthood was addictive, thrilling, and impossibly fulfilling. I would have done it all again if I had gotten the chance, if the right person had come along at the right time and had wanted the same things I did. Maybe that was Autumn. Or maybe I needed to get to know her a little better before I started jumping to those conclusions.

"Yeah, I get it," I agreed, and both of us fell silent for a moment, reflecting on the place fatherhood had in our lives. It was so strange to see Raymond at the start of his journey when I felt as though I was a veteran of mine, but I was proud of him. He was going to be an amazing dad to that little girl. I could see it in the way he looked at her as though he couldn't believe his luck. Besides, he'd basically been a second father to Hunter his entire life, so it wasn't like he was coming to this totally fresh.

"Hey, speaking of Autumn," I began, and he glanced up at me as though he had forgotten I was even there.

"Yeah?"

"I was planning to take her out again this weekend." I grinned. "Think there's a chance you could watch Hunter?"

"You know we're always happy to," he replied. "Olivia loves having him around."

"Excellent, thanks." I smiled at him. "You know, if I didn't have you around, my dating life would be a hell of a lot harder."

"So what's your excuse for the last ten years, huh?" he teased. "We've been around all this time, and you've barely made it out of the house."

"All right, point taken." I shook my head at him, laughing. "Isn't it enough that I'm getting out there now?"

"Sure is." Raymond nodded. "And I have a good feeling about you and Autumn. I think you're going to go all the way. Really."

I shrugged and took a sip of my fresh coffee. I didn't want to admit it for fear of jinxing what I already had, but deep down in my gut, I felt that way too.

35

AUTUMN

"Hey, what are you guys up to?" I asked, crouching down next to the row of computers Hunter and Amelie were working on together.

"A campaign in Breadsticks." Hunter pointed to the screen, and I creased my brow as I peered at it, trying to make sense of what was going on in front of me. If I was being totally honest, most of this stuff sailed straight over my head, but as long as they were enjoying it and it seemed age-appropriate enough, I was fine with it.

"Wow, looks great!" I remarked enthusiastically, and Amelie and Hunter exchanged grins and turned back to their screens. I got to my feet to leave them to it and wound around the rest of the room, where about a half dozen students were hanging out in small clusters on computers and playing their favorite games. They all looked as though they were having a great time, and that was the main thing. I glanced at the clock. Only a few minutes remained before I had to call time on this, which was a shame because it was getting better every time we met.

I was surprised by how well the after-school activities had taken off, especially the game club, which was a new addition to the roster and not something the school had experimented with before. I was glad the club I'd chosen to run was going down pretty well so far, that everyone seemed to be having a good time and making new friends. All I'd needed to get the quieter kids to interact was some video games and some quiet time. Who knew?

I had been keeping an eye on Hunter in particular since he'd been one of the kids I'd been most worried about when it came to socializing with his peers. Amelie, the girl who seemed to have taken him under her wing, was smart and outgoing and didn't have trouble making new friends. Perhaps if they got along well together, she would be able to draw him into her wider group.

A little zing of excitement flashed in my chest at the thought of seeing Holden soon. He always came to pick up Hunter from the activities, even though he could probably have afforded to pay someone to do it for him. A lot of the parents in this city did when they could. I thought it was sweet he still made the effort to come in and get his son himself, and hey, it gave me a chance to catch up with him before our date tomorrow night. I wondered what the hell he had planned, what could top what he had come up with last time. I bit my lip as I considered a night in instead. Yeah, all that time alone together, to do whatever we wanted? That would work for me.

"All right, guys." I clapped my hands together, drawing the attention of everyone in the room and pushing those age-inappropriate thoughts to the back of my mind for the time being.

"That's it for today," I told them to a chorus of groans and some muttered protestations.

"But you'll all be back next week, right?" I smiled at them and found a few faces peering up at me with excitement at the thought of it. Yeah, they would be back. And that was the most important thing.

As they all went to gather themselves up, I headed over to talk to Hunter and check in on how he was doing.

"How's it going, Hunter?" I asked casually, as though I'd happened to pick him out of the rest of the group because I wanted someone to chat with. The last thing I needed was for any of the kids to feel like I was treating him differently or with some kind of special attention because of his problems.

"Good." He grinned up at me. "I can't wait to come back next week."

"What are you working on with Amelie?" I asked. I was sure I wasn't going to understand a word that came out of his mouth, but there was no harm in asking, right?

"We're building a town together." He glanced over at her, and she held up her hand for a high-five. He gave it to her and then laughed.

"I wish we could stay longer," he admitted.

"But it gives you something to look forward to next time, right?" I pointed out, and he shrugged and nodded. For a second, he looked so much like his dad that it caught me off guard. It wasn't in the way his face or his body was arranged, but in a gesture he made, a movement that reminded me he had been raised by Holden and had spent his whole life absorbing his habits and eccentricities.

"Yeah, I guess so," he agreed, and he went to grab his bag. As he hitched it onto his shoulder, he glanced around to make sure nobody else was going to hear him and then turned to me with a serious expression on his little face.

"Thank you for doing this club." He gestured around. "I really like it."

"I'm glad to hear it." I smiled at him, and he nodded at me again and slipped his arms through the straps of his bag, gripping them like he was going on a mission. Before I could say anything else, he ducked away, as though he was a little embarrassed by the admission that he liked the gaming club and was grateful to me for starting it. Kids his age were so funny. Sometimes they seemed like real children, and other times, they had that overtly self-aware teenaged thing going on like a reflection of the adolescents they were going to be. I shook my head as I watched him head out, glad I'd made an impression on him. He was talking to me a little more than he had before, and I knew that had to be a good thing in the long term. If this thing with Holden and me was going to work out, I would need to get along with his son.

As though I had conjured him with a thought, I suddenly looked up and noticed Holden standing in the door, watching me. He was leaning on the doorframe with a smile on his face and looked as though he could have stood there all day taking me in.

"Dad, can I go talk to Amelie for a minute?" Hunter asked, looking up at his father with wide eyes. "I want to work out what we're going to do next time we get on the computers."

"Go ahead, Hunter." Holden nodded, and Hunter hurried off to find his friend, leaving the two of us alone.

"Of all the after-school clubs in all the world, and you had to walk into mine." I grinned at him, knowing I was mangling the quote and not caring one little bit. I was just glad to see him.

"Seems like he's been having a good time." Holden nodded after Hunter.

"Yeah, I think he's enjoying it more every time he comes in," I said. "Seems like he and Amelie are getting closer, and she's got a lot of friends in the school. It'll be good for him if she takes a shine to him, and I think she's getting a little crush on him."

"Why wouldn't she?" he replied playfully. "Takes after his father in the looks department, after all."

I laughed and felt that tingle deep down in my belly. Being around him felt like a gift, any time that we could steal together a thrill, even when I knew he would have to be off again soon to get Hunter home.

"So are we still on for tomorrow night?" He cocked an eyebrow at me. I nodded.

"Sure thing," I promised. "And can I ask what you have planned for me?"

"You know I like the surprise." He tapped his nose.

"Yeah, I do," I groaned. "But I never know what I'm supposed to wear!"

"Anything you want," he assured me. "Trust me, I'm not taking you to the opera."

"Oh, and here I was sure we were going to take in some actual culture this time around," I shot back.

"What about ice cream isn't cultural?" he protested.

"Fair," I conceded, and we smiled at each other from across the room. I wanted to steal another kiss, to make out with him like we'd done in my classroom before, but that was a little risky given that there were still a bunch of kids milling around, and their parents could have stuck their heads in at any moment to talk to me.

"I guess you'll have to wait till tomorrow to find out, huh?" he remarked, cocking an eyebrow.

"Guess I will," I agreed. "I can't wait."

"Well, I suppose I should leave you wanting more," he said with a sigh, and I laughed again.

"Oh, so you're suddenly playing hard to get now?" I teased. "Very good."

"Hey, a gentleman always has his tricks." He shrugged and smiled. "See you soon, right?"

"See you soon," I agreed, and I watched as he headed out of the room and left me to my own devices once more. I let out a breath. When I was around him, I felt as though I was filling up like a balloon, drinking in his flirtation and our chemistry until I was brimming over with the stuff. I had a big, goofy smile on my face, and it was going to be sticking around there for a good long while. Up to and including our date tomorrow night, I would wager.

Zoe brushed into the room, glancing over her shoulder to watch as Holden walked off. She raised her eyebrows at me and closed the door behind her, cocking her head to the side as she did so.

"Well, well, well, looks like you're getting some after-school action at the moment," she teased. I rolled my eyes and laughed.

"We're not getting up to anything on school property," I replied, conveniently choosing to forget our hot little make-out session the week before.

"I would be if I had my claws in someone like him," she replied bluntly. "He's super hot, Autumn. You're a lucky woman."

"Yeah, I know." I nodded. "Guess I attract the hotties, right?"

"Well, someone has to," she agreed. "Any luck finding out if he's got any billionaire buddies he feels like sharing with me?"

"I don't think you're going to have much luck there, but I'll keep my ear to the ground for you," I promised. She shrugged.

"Guess I'll have to take the initiative and go out and find one myself." She sighed as though it was some terrible chore. "You guys going out again soon?"

I nodded. "Tomorrow night. I'm looking forward to it."

"I'll bet he's got something ridiculous planned," she said.

"I have no idea. He won't tell me." I pulled a face.

"Ah, a little bit of mystery only adds to the romance." She wiggled her fingers in a mystical fashion. "Text me tomorrow and let me know how it goes, okay? Or the morning after if it goes well."

"Will do," I agreed, and I turned to start tidying up the classroom. Zoe helped me, chatting about the day thus far. But my mind was on everything tomorrow evening—and tomorrow night—could bring, and that buoyancy began to fill me up once more. It was going to be amazing. I knew that much.

36

HOLDEN

I heard a knock at the door and got to my feet. She was here. She was finally here. I felt as though I had been waiting for this for months, even though it had only been a couple of hours since Hunter had left and given me time to prepare for my date. I was cooking a selection of Chinese dishes and had laid out the wine and the candles in an attempt to set the mood. I had no idea if it was coming across as cheesy or romantic, but as long as she was there, I didn't give a damn.

I went to the door and pulled it open, finding her standing there in a pair of jeans and a light T-shirt that hung off her body in the most perfect way, drawing attention to her delicate collarbones and soft, creamy skin. I wanted to lean forward and take a bite of her, but I figured that might have been a little forward.

"Hey." She smiled at me, and she leaned forward to plant a soft kiss right on the corner of my mouth. It sent a flood of electricity through my entire body, and it took everything I had in me not to grab her, drag her to the bedroom, and work out all the tension that had been building between us all this time. Instead, I stepped back and gestured for her to come in.

"Man, it smells great in here," she said as she came through the door. "Are we eating in tonight?"

"Sure are." I nodded. "I made Chinese food."

"From scratch?" She raised her eyebrows. I nodded.

"Okay, when are you going to stop being the perfect man?" she asked playfully, tapping me on the arm. The way she was touching me, it was like she couldn't get enough of me, and I knew exactly how she felt.

She headed through to the living room, and she turned to me and grinned when she saw all I'd laid out for her.

"Trying to seduce me, are you?" she asked, moving against my body, wrapping her arms around my neck. The feel of her next to me like that was almost a relief, a release of tension I'd no idea I'd been holding until that moment.

"Is it working?" I asked, and I moved in to kiss her, brushing my lips lightly against hers, promising her there was far more to come that night if she was open to it.

"Might be," she murmured as I pulled back, and I noticed a flush to her cheeks that hadn't been there before. I stepped away from her, heading through to the kitchen to serve up, that heat between us growing so much, we wouldn't even make it to dinner if I didn't cut it off.

I brought the selection of plates through, and she raised her eyebrows as I laid them down in front of her.

"You're going to need to show me how to make all this stuff," she remarked, grabbing a spring roll and dunking it in the peanut-chili sauce I had made to go with them. She took a bite, closed her eyes, and groaned.

"Oh my God, that's so good," she sighed, leaning back in the seat as I poured her a glass of wine and handed it to her. Our fingers touched for the briefest moment, and I found myself looking forward to what was to come the rest of this evening.

We ate and drank our wine and talked for a while about nothing in particular, catching up on what we'd been doing, sharing funny little anecdotes and stories from our week thus far. I enjoyed her company so much, we could have been talking stock projections, and I still would have been having a good time. She was so expressive, waving her arms around as she spoke, her face lighting up when she got onto something she was excited to talk about. She was reading a new book, a piece of journalism she enjoyed, and the way she was speaking about it, she could have earned a pull quote on the back cover.

"Man, this wine is good." She took another sip and finished off her first glass, and I leaned over to top her up.

"Trying to get me tipsy?" she teased.

"And why would I need to do that?" I replied. She cocked her head to the side and watched me for a moment. I could tell there was something running through her mind, something she wanted to come out and ask me.

"What is it?" I pressed her gently, shifting on the couch so I was fully facing her.

"I just..." She shook her head. "I don't know if this is too personal. I don't want to pry."

"Pry away." I waved my hand. I was feeling loose myself after the first glass, and besides, I wanted her to know me. That was what dating was for, right?

"Okay." She furrowed her brow and hesitated a moment before she spoke again.

"I was wondering," she began slowly, "what happened with Hunter's mother. Why isn't she part of your lives? Or is she, and I just don't know about it?"

"She's got nothing to do with either of us." I shook my head. This was a sore spot, but I knew the question was going to come up at one point or another. It was the same question everyone had for me when they first met me, the wondering why I was a single dad, what had happened to Hunter's mother. Most people assumed I'd been widowed, and sometimes I would let them believe that because delving into the truth was too complicated and too rage-inducing for me to bother with.

"Why did you guys split up?" she asked, and I looked at her—

really looked at her, this woman who only wanted the truth from me. She had never asked for anything more than that. She wanted to get to know me better, to understand those things that had driven my life the last few years, and I figured I would have to tell her at some point. A couple of glasses of wine in, hanging out together at home with no one else around, this was as good a time as any.

"She left me not long after Hunter was born." I sighed deeply. I usually kept these memories locked away, buttoned up so I didn't have to think about them, and delving into that part of my brain wasn't the best feeling in the world.

"She told me I would never amount to anything," I continued, "that I was a loser. Which I was, at the time, but I was also this fucked-up kid who was trying to deal with the fact that I was about to have a damn baby. I was a mess, but she acted like that's all I was and all I would ever be. Said she didn't want to stick around after he was born. I think she would have taken him in if I hadn't been able to cope, but as it was, I wanted to step up and look after him."

I finished up the second glass of wine, grateful for it taking the edge off the difficulty of this conversation.

"I thought, well, she's flaky enough to walk out on me, so what would she do if she decided Hunter wasn't worthy of her either?" I explained. "So I took him. I insisted on it. I think she was relieved, more than anything, because she didn't have to worry about being a mother. She was young—we both were—and I don't think she was ready to raise a kid. I mean, I wasn't either, but I don't think she was capable of it, so it fell to me instead."

"Oh my God." Autumn shook her head. "I had no idea it went down like that. I'm so sorry."

"No, it was for the best in the long run." I shrugged. "I don't think the two of us would have stuck it out for any length of time anyway. She could be a massive bitch, and I didn't like the way she was with my friends, so I really believe we would have moved on from each other. I think whenever that happened, she would have used it as an excuse to get out of Hunter's life."

"Jesus, she sounds like a nightmare," Autumn muttered, and I could see the anger in her eyes. "Just leaving you and Hunter like that..."

"That wasn't the bit that really got me," I confessed. "I mean, yeah, it was fucking hard raising that boy all by myself, but I loved him the moment I set eyes on him. I was all the way in from the second he was born. It was... it was that she told me I was a loser and that I'd never amount to anything. That was the part that fucking stung."

I trailed my finger around the top of my glass and sighed, shaking my head.

"I started the business not long after she left," I continued. "I was so determined to prove to her I wasn't what she thought I was. I guess it worked out for me in the long run because it took off, and Hunter's turned out pretty all right, and she's still far away somewhere at the other end of the country."

"I think you won that breakup." Autumn smiled at me, leaning over to touch my knee. "I'm still sorry, though. That's an awful way to be treated by someone you're having a baby with."

"Hey, it's not the worst breakup I've ever heard of." I shrugged. "And I wouldn't be where I was today if I hadn't tried to prove a point to that woman, so I guess I've got something to thank her for, at least."

"Guess so," Autumn echoed, and she eyed me from her end of the couch.

"What is it?" I asked again. Whatever it was, I knew it would be easier to talk about than what I had shared with her.

"I can't believe she would look at you and see a loser," she replied. "I know... hell, I know you were probably different then, but I can't think of any word less suited to you."

"Oh, no?" I cocked my head at her. Sure, I was looking for an ego boost, but that was all right, all things considered, given that I'd shared the most painful part of my life with her.

"Oh, no." She put her glass of wine down and moved toward me. She ran her hand over my chest, letting her fingers slip under my shirt and against my bare skin. "Anything but."

Our faces were so close, I could almost taste her and suddenly I couldn't take it anymore. I pushed toward her, grabbing her and lifting her onto my lap, and pressed my mouth to hers.

The connection was a release of tension. I'd never felt this kind of need for someone, not just desire but a stone-cold *need* for them. The way her body rocked against mine, the way her hands seemed hungry for me as they ran through my hair and over my neck and down my arms, I had been starving for it all this time. I pushed my tongue deep into her mouth, and she moaned softly, stroking my hair gently, twirling strands around her fingers and tugging lightly. The sensations charged out over my entire body, waking up every inch of me again.

"Mmm," she moaned softly, smiling as she pulled away. Her hands moved down and between my legs, finding my swiftly growing erection. A smile curled on her face as she found me, and she kissed me on the corner of my mouth as she had done when she'd first arrived.

"Now, what do we have here?" she breathed in my ear, and I closed my eyes and let her take control. It was what I needed and, most of all, what she wanted.

37

AUTUMN

I kissed my way down his neck, unbuttoning his shirt so I could move my hands and my mouth down his chest. He was so strong, and it made me feel so safe, as though he could have fought off any threat that might have come near us, drawn himself up and taken care of me no matter what. But tonight, I wanted to take care of him and wanted to show him I saw the pain from his past and rejected it completely.

I slid down his body until I was between his legs, my fingers shaking a little as I went to undo the zipper of his jeans. He had put so much effort into this night, and the least I could do was return that favor. His eyes were burning as he watched me, reaching out to brush a strand of hair back from my face. His fingertips against my skin left trails of electricity behind, tingling my nerve endings wherever they touched.

Finally, I managed to pull his jeans off, followed by his under-wear. He looked so hot like that, naked but for that shirt pulled open over his torso, and I leaned back to take him in.

"Like what you see?" he teased, and I raised my eyebrows.

"Let me show you how much I do," I assured him, and I leaned forward, wrapped my hand around his cock, and took him into my mouth.

I sealed my lips around the head of his cock and swirled my tongue around him for a moment, lapping at him hungrily, tasting the hint of precum already oozing from his erection. He groaned and let his head sink back into the couch while I focused my attention on lavishing him with pleasure, showing him I appreciated all he'd done for me tonight and wanted to return the favor. I closed my eyes and began to take more of him, inching down slowly until I'd taken nearly his full length into my mouth. So many of the guys I had been with before, they would push back, thrust up into me before I was ready to get me to gag on their dick, but he was different. He let me set the pace, take control, and even though I was the one between his legs servicing him, I felt utterly at ease.

I worked my tongue up the underside of his cock as I slid my mouth languidly up and down his full length, wrapping my fingers around the base to hold him steady as I did so. His body tensed, his breath coming a little faster than it had before, and I knew I was doing a good job. It wasn't exactly something I could stick on my resumé, but I had always known I was good at giving head—and Holden didn't seem in any rush to dissuade me of that notion.

"Look at me," he breathed, and I lifted my eyes to meet his. Something about that connection, the acknowledgment of what we were doing and that it was seriously getting him off, sent a shiver of desire through my body. I slipped my hand down between my legs, popping open my jeans awkwardly and pushing my fingers into my panties to play with my clit. I was grinding against my hand as I went down on him, my own pleasure as important as his, and I began to suck softly on his dick, applying that gentle pressure I knew would push him closer to the edge.

"Fuck," he groaned, and I looked up at him once more, meeting his gaze, staring into his eyes and watching every single reaction he had to me, every single twitch, every single rush of tension, every single time his lips parted as though he was trying to express a pleasure he couldn't put a name to yet. I worked him with my mouth, going fast and then slow, hard and then soft, switching it up so neither of us got bored. I loved this. I could have done this all day. The mixture of the power of having him in my mouth and the pleasure of my fingers against my clit was an intoxicating mix that I could never imagine getting enough of.

Suddenly, he leaned down and lifted me up to face him, so I was on his lap once more. He kissed me hard, his teeth catching on my lip, his tongue meeting mine in a moment. I groaned and started to kick off my jeans and my underwear, letting him help me.

"I need to be inside you right now," he panted into my ear, and I squirmed against me.

"Anything you want," I replied sweetly, acting as though I was doing this for him and not because I was getting off on this just as much.

He grabbed a condom and returned, sheathing himself swiftly and tossing his shirt aside. Sliding down on top of me in one swift movement, he pushed my legs apart. The couch was soft and comfortable, his body hard and needy, and the combination of the two sent desperate shivers all through my system. I spread my legs and lifted my hips to him, my mouth parting into a gasp as I watched him move into me for the first time.

"Oh, God," I moaned, tipping my head back and closing my eyes, my body taking every inch of him in one smooth motion as he thrust up and into me. He worked in long, slow strokes at first, burying himself all the way inside of me, his mouth on my neck, his breath hot on my skin, his hands quick as they moved over every inch of my body like he was charting me, making a map of me, learning my contours and curves.

And then he began to move faster, pushing harder as our hips came together with more purpose. I lifted myself off the couch and started to push back against him, drawing him deeper into me so hard and so fast, my entire body began to tremble. I hadn't realized how much I needed this, but I was close to coming already, my body teetering on the edge of this delicious precipice that I was perfectly happy hanging out on for a while.

"You're so fucking gorgeous, Autumn," he murmured into my ear, and his voice was as layered with lust as it had been the first time we'd done this. I had wondered, somewhere in the back of my mind, if he wouldn't be as interested in me once we had consummated the relationship, but he was proving to me every way he could that he wanted me as much as he did then. I wrapped my arms around him, sinking my fingers into his back, tracing lines with my nails, unable to vocalize what I needed to say but telling it to him anyway.

He moved relentlessly inside of me, and I shifted so I could play with my clit once more. I needed both of us to come, and I had to come soon or else I'd explode. I closed my eyes, letting the sounds and the sensations take me over, listening to his breath as it tore from his lungs, listening to the slight creak of the couch below us as he moved hard into me, taking in the long washes of pleasure that seemed to consume me as he fucked me roughly, his body owning mine, my entire being wrapped up in this moment.

"Ah!" I cried out as the orgasm hit me, tossing me over the edge of that cliff once and for all where there would be no going back, the pleasure exploding through me, running from between my legs and out, fire tearing through my very being. I pressed against him, needing to feel his body on mine, his skin next to my own. He thrust twice more, the last time holding himself still as my clenching pussy massaged his cock, and then he came.

"Fuck," he growled against me, right in my ear, the sound of the word as it came out of his mouth instantly burning itself into my memory. There was nothing better in the world than knowing that the person you were with had been so helpless to you that they'd come. I let my eyes stay shut as I ran my hands gently over his body, reminding him I was here, that I wasn't going anywhere. He kissed my collarbone and my neck, telling me the same thing.

After a moment, he pulled out of me and went to dispose of the condom. My eyes eventually fluttered open to find him offering me a fresh glass of wine.

"Why, thank you." I laughed. "But you don't have to get me tipsy now, right?"

"Trust me, if you think I'm done with you, you're totally wrong."
His eyes flashed playfully at me, and I shifted in my seat. I grabbed
my panties and slipped them back on, tucking my legs up and underneath me. He grabbed his boxers and flopped down on the couch,
nearly naked, his chest still rising and falling sharply as he caught his
breath.

I reached out to run my fingers over his chest. I could feel his
heart beating fast. He closed his eyes and shifted his head so he could
lay it against the couch like he had done before, and the two of us sat
like that in that moment of silence.

It all began to click into place for me, the reason he had worked
so hard, had thrown himself into his job to the detriment of practically everything but his son. He had been trying to prove himself to a
woman who had never wanted him, who hadn't even stuck around
long enough to help him raise their son. And my heart ached for him.
Nobody deserved to be treated that way, and maybe I was biased, but
Holden was certainly at the bottom of the list of people who had
earned the title of "loser." It made sense why he'd been so keen to
show off his lifestyle to me, to prove he was a wealthy, successful man.
He wanted to show me what he was capable of, to escape that name
once more.

When he opened his eyes, he smiled gently at me and then
reached out to tuck a stray strand of hair behind my ear.

"You all right?" he asked, and I cleared those thoughts from my
head, not wanting them to get in the way of the rest of the night we
had ahead of us. I knew the truth about Hunter's mother, and that
was all I could ask for.

"Yeah, I'm fine," I replied.

"Just fine?" He cocked an eyebrow playfully. "Let's see what we
can do to make that better, huh?"

38

HOLDEN

As I stirred the next morning, I had a smile on my face. I turned in bed, facing Autumn, her hair splayed wildly over the pillow, her clothes from the night before tossed on the floor next to us. She looked gorgeous fast asleep, so peaceful, her usual animated expression quiet and still for a change. I ran my hand down her bare back where she had tossed aside the covers early in the morning, and her eyes fluttered open and she looked at me.

"Hey," she greeted me sleepily, her voice a little croaky. "You okay?"

"Sure am," I assured her, and I laid my head back down on the pillow so I could look her in the eye. The night before had been perfect, totally, utterly perfect, and getting to wake up beside her like this was the cherry on top. I knew we wouldn't be able to do this a lot —I didn't want to dump Hunter on Raymond and Olivia a couple of times a week—so I savored the moment while I could, the intimacy of coming back to the real world to find one of my favorite people there next to me.

"Mmm." She wriggled against the sheets as I continued to trace my fingers over her back. "That feels nice."

"Don't tempt me," I warned her, and she giggled, flicking her eyes open and meeting my gaze.

"Spent from last night?"

"I don't think we have time this morning before I have to go pick up Hunter." I made a face. "But trust me, I want to."

"Well, save it for next time, huh?" she suggested, pushing herself upright. She was utterly naked, and the sight of her stripped bare like that was more intimate than sexy, knowing she felt comfortable enough not to hide from me.

"Do we have time to make some breakfast before we go?" She pushed her closed fist into her stomach. "I'm pretty hungry."

"Well, you did work up one hell of an appetite last night," I teased her gently, and she shot me a look.

"Hey, don't strain something patting yourself on the back," she fired back, grinning and stretching.

We both got dressed and headed to the kitchen to make ourselves something to eat. Nothing major, just some fruit and toast and yogurt, but once again, it felt so nice to be able to share the simplicity of an act like this with her. It felt as though it had always been this way, as though she had always been around like this was some Sunday morning tradition we'd been carrying on for years.

"What do you want to do today?" she asked casually, and I glanced at her in surprise. I'd assumed she would want to head home, given that I was going to pick up Hunter.

"I have to go collect Hunter after this," I told her, "from Raymond's place. But you could come along if you want. Raymond and Olivia would love to meet you."

"Olivia's the one who set you up with me, right?" she asked. "I suppose I owe her a thank-you, at least."

"Oh, trust me, they haven't let me forget they were the ones who stuck us in the same room together." I rolled my eyes playfully.

"I'd love to come with you if that's all right," she suggested hopefully. "Maybe I could spend the day with the two of you? Get to know Hunter a little better?"

"That would be awesome." I nodded. "I mean, maybe I'm a little biased, but I think he's great company."

"Yeah, he's a good kid," she agreed, taking a bite of her toast.

"I'm sure he'd love to spend the day with you," I said. "He's been enjoying your after-school clubs so much. I think he might even have a little crush on you."

"Well, can you blame him?" Autumn gestured playfully to herself, and I gave her the once-over, taking the opportunity once more to check out the outrageously beautiful woman I was currently dating.

"I think I can give him a pass on this one." I grinned. She chuckled, and we finished up breakfast and finished getting ready, heading out across town to Raymond's place to pick up Hunter.

"So how do you and Raymond know each other?" she asked as we drove, her window down an inch so her hair was flailing wildly around her face. She didn't seem to care. And why should she?

"We went to college together," I explained. "We got close then, but he was one of the only ones who stuck around after Hunter was born. Most of the rest of the people I knew around that time didn't seem to know what the fuck to do with a baby, so they avoided me, but he was there through all of it. He helped me with the business when things got going, and he's had a kid of his own, so now I'm the one helping him where I can."

"That's sweet." Autumn smiled, turning her head to absorb the cool air pouring in through the window. "Girl or boy?"

"Girl. Sasha," I replied. "She's a cute little thing too."

"Well, I look forward to meeting her," she remarked, and my mind drifted back to the conversation I'd had with Raymond at the coffee shop recently. Did she want any kids of her own, or would Hunter be enough for her? I eyed her for a moment, considering how cute her beautiful red hair would look in little tufts on a baby's head.

We arrived at the house, and I headed to the door, not even landing a knock on it before Olivia pulled it open. She beamed at the both of us, her eyes sliding over to Autumn at once and taking her in.

"You must be the famous Autumn!" she exclaimed, and she

stepped aside to let her in. "Come in, come in. Raymond's feeding the baby, and Hunter's upstairs getting ready to go."

"Good to meet you too." Autumn smiled back at her, a little nervous, and I took her hand and squeezed it as we headed through to the living room. These two were my best friends, no doubt about it, so no wonder she was feeling a little anxious about making a good impression.

"Oh, hello!" Raymond cocked his head at Autumn as he spotted her entering the living room. Sasha was in his arms, awake but quiet, and Autumn's eyes practically bugged out of her head as soon as she laid eyes on her.

"Hi." She nodded to Raymond and then turned her attention to Sasha, squeezing her little hands into fists in his arms. "This must be Sasha. Holden was telling me you guys had a baby recently, but I didn't realize how little she was!"

"Yeah, she's a tiny thing." Raymond looked down at her lovingly. "You want to hold her? She's pretty calm right now. She just got fed, so she won't cause much of a fuss."

"Sure." Autumn reached out for her, and Raymond carefully deposited the baby into her arms. At once, Autumn cradled her close to her chest, and Raymond shot me a meaningful look, clearly thinking about our conversation as well. I ignored it. Yeah, Autumn looked cute with a baby in her arms, but that didn't mean I was looking to get her pregnant in the next five minutes.

"You're an elementary school teacher, right?" Olivia asked as she bustled into the living room with some coffee for all of us.

"Yeah, that's right. For about five years now. I love it and can't imagine doing anything else."

"I can hardly manage one kid, let alone a whole class of them," Olivia said. "I don't know how you do it."

"Hey, there's a reason we have to go through so much training," Autumn answered, getting a laugh from Olivia.

"I suppose you're right," she agreed. "We've been learning on the job."

"Well, she's gorgeous." Autumn cooed at Sasha. "You've clearly been doing a good job."

"And I suppose you'd know," Raymond said.

"Yep, you officially have my seal of approval." Autumn grinned at him. "Here, take her back before I try to steal her."

Raymond eased Sasha out of her arms, and Autumn reached out to touch her little hand. I was so glad they were getting on well. Autumn was totally charming in her own specific way, and I'd had no reason to think they wouldn't get on well. Still, it was a relief that she seemed to get along with all the important people in my life. I could already imagine taking care of Sasha for an evening with her. That could be fun.

"You have any kids, Autumn?" Olivia asked. Anyone listening in might have assumed it was a casual question, but I knew her well enough to guess she and Raymond had been discussing the same thing Raymond had with me earlier. I wanted to leap in and shut the conversation down, but it would have seemed so obvious that I didn't want to talk about it. I left it, hoping it would fizzle out quickly enough.

"Uh, no." She shook her head. "Just the ones I'm teaching."

"You ever think about having them?" Raymond asked, and Olivia tucked her arm through her husband's, the two of them watching Autumn expectantly. A pair of interrogation-bots, here to make my day that much more awkward.

"Uh..." Autumn trailed off, and she shot a look at me, begging me to jump in and remove her from this conversation. I tried to catch Raymond's eye and let him know I didn't want to talk about this, but his attention was focused squarely on Autumn, pretending I wasn't even in the room.

Thank goodness, Hunter came bounding down the stairs and into the living room at that moment. He glanced around, and his face lit up when he saw Autumn standing there.

"Miss Becks!" he exclaimed happily. "I didn't know you were going to be here."

"Well, here I am." Autumn spread her arms wide, throwing in

some jazz hands that made Hunter laugh. I silently thanked the gods that I wasn't going to have to stall that awkward conversation any further. My son had excellent timing, even if he had no idea of it yet.

"We'll finish our coffee and get going." I clapped my hands together. "We're spending the day together, right, Autumn?"

"If that's okay with Hunter." She glanced at my son, who nodding enthusiastically at once.

"Of course, it is!" he agreed, and he stayed on his feet as the rest of us sat down to drink our coffees, obviously ready to go right then and there. I waved him over to my side, and he leaned against my chair, staring at Autumn with a smile on his face so big, it looked set to split his face in two.

The conversation turned to what they had been up to the night before, and I thanked my lucky stars I wasn't going to get stuck talking about Autumn's prospects for kids in the future. We had barely been on a handful of dates, and I had a feeling pushing that on her so quickly was going to freak her out. She wanted to spend more time with Hunter and get to know the two of us better. That was all I wanted and all I needed for the time being. Sure, those were the kinds of questions we were going to have to think about at some point, and I knew that. But for right now, I wanted to enjoy dating once more, having a woman I adored by my side, and the future could wait. As long as Autumn was close to me, nothing else mattered.

39

AUTUMN

W ith my hand tucked happily into Holden's, I headed out the door and to the car waiting outside. Hunter hopped into the back seat, practically dancing where he sat, and Holden turned around to face him.

"So what do you feel like doing today, buddy?" he asked. "Autumn's going to come with us, so make sure it's something cool."

Hunter opened and closed his mouth, overwhelmed by all the options surrounding what he was going to get me to do today. I grinned at him.

"Where's the most fun place in the city?" I asked him, and he beamed at once.

"Freddie's!" he replied excitedly.

I turned to Holden and raised my eyebrows. "And where might that be?"

"A place down by the pier," he explained, shaking his head with a smile on his face, as though that's precisely what he'd expected his son to say. "Lots of games and junk food."

"Sounds great." I turned to smile at Hunter, whose face lit up as soon as he met my gaze.

"How about we hit the science museum as well?" Holden

suggested as he pulled the car out of the driveway. "Then we can at least pretend we're doing something educational."

"Yeah!" Hunter squealed excitedly from behind us. It was about the most animated I'd seen him in the whole time I'd known him, and it was distinctly adorable to see him expressing so much excitement about something like this.

"Lead on." I waved my hand and leaned back in my seat, as Holden drove us across town to the science museum. I rolled my window down and let the cool air blow in, enjoying the way it bathed my face and the calmness it brought me. But I was excited too—maybe not quite as much as Hunter, but I was getting to spend the day with the two of them together. It was an extension of our date in the best way. I couldn't imagine how this could get any better.

"Come on, I want to show you the bird exhibit!" Hunter exclaimed as he climbed out of the car, and he grabbed my hand and hurried me into the large, modern building that housed the science museum. I glanced over my shoulder at Holden, who waved me ahead.

"I'll pay for the tickets. You go on ahead," he told me. I grinned and let Hunter lead me into the building.

"They have all these bird skeletons," Hunter explained to me enthusiastically. "They're so cool. I love them."

"That sounds very interesting," I agreed, as he paused for a moment to figure out where he wanted to take me. He ducked off down one corridor, and I hurried to keep up with him, and just like that, the day had begun.

I was surprised by how much I enjoyed the science museum. I had never much been one for the nerdier side of things, but they had everything set up to make sure it was accessible to even complete dunces like me. Hunter clearly loved it there, bouncing between exhibits and pointing out details to me that I might have otherwise missed. Holden caught up with us within a few minutes, knowing exactly where his son would have taken me on my first trip, and I watched as the two of them admired a deconstructed motorcycle. I loved Holden when he was with his son, loved the way they interacted, how utterly Holden gave himself over to whatever it was his son was excited about. He was an amazing father, one of the best I'd ever seen. Though perhaps I was a little on the biased side.

We went around what felt like every exhibit in the place until my legs were aching, and my stomach was growling.

"Freddie's?" I suggested, and Holden shrugged, a smile on his face.

"If you want to put away fifty pounds of terrible food, sure," he agreed.

"The food isn't terrible!" Hunter protested, and Holden held his hands up.

"Well, we'll have to get Autumn's vote on that one." He winked at Hunter and then turned to glance around the foyer. "I'm going to grab a bottle of water for the ride. I'll be back in a minute."

"Sure thing." I waved him off and sank down gratefully into the stone seat behind me. My feet were sore, and I needed to get the weight off of them. I wasn't used to standing up for such a long time. Damn, I needed to hit the gym.

"Are you having a good time?" I asked Hunter, and he nodded excitedly.

"I still think I like the birds best," he told me. "But the cars are cool too."

"Any of them catch your eye?" I remarked. "For when you're old enough to have one of your own?"

"All of them," he blurted out at once, and I couldn't help laughing. It was awesome seeing him so enthusiastic, so passionate, so engaged. But as he stared up at me, I could see something else lurking behind his eyes, a question, a concern. I had worked with kids long enough to know when they were holding something back from me, and the last thing I wanted was for Hunter to feel as though he couldn't say whatever he needed to say.

"What's up?" I prompted him, and he twisted his mouth up and shook his head.

"I don't know if I should ask it."

"Come on, it's okay," I assured him. "What's bothering you?"

He took a deep breath and then finally came out with it.

"Do you know my mom?"

I fell silent for a moment. That wasn't the question I had been prepared for, although I supposed I should have expected it. Here I was, a woman in his life, someone dating his dad when he'd never had anyone fulfill that role before. Of course, he was going to have questions.

I shook my head at last, glancing over at Holden and wondering how long he was going to be. I didn't want to come out with anything he didn't approve of, but I couldn't deflect the question, especially not after pressing it out of Hunter.

"No, I don't," I replied.

"Neither do I," he said with a sigh. "I've never met her. And my dad..."

He looked over at Holden, and a brief flash of sadness passed over his face. I wanted to give him a big hug, but kids could pick up on when you were feeling emotional, and I didn't want him to think this was a huge deal.

"He never talks about her either." He shook his head. "I don't know why. But I know I'm not supposed to bring her up."

I fell silent. I didn't know how to respond to that. Hunter was old enough to have noticed he didn't have a mother around when a lot of the kids his age did and to start having questions about it. But it wasn't as simple as that when it came to explaining why. This woman, Hunter's mother, had hurt Holden badly, and bringing her up would be a painful memory for him, no matter how much his son needed to hear the truth about her.

Before I could say another word to him, thankfully, Holden turned up next to us, swigging from a bottle of water.

"Everything all right?" he asked, seeming to notice the odd atmosphere between us. "What were you two talking about?"

"Nothing," Hunter replied quickly, shaking his head, and he gave me a quick look to indicate that I should agree with him.

"Nothing important," I said with a nod. I got to my feet. "Are we ready to go? I'm starving. And I want to see the most fun place in the city!"

With that, the conversation seemed to be behind us—well, behind Hunter, at least, as he got to his feet and skipped to the exit. Holden and I followed behind, and I wondered if I should tell Holden what his son had been asking me. But he had already been through enough, with everything that was happening with me, and I didn't want to stress him out more. Raising kids was a trial at the best of times, and I wanted today to be fun for all of us.

We arrived at this goofy little diner with a bunch of old-fashioned arcade games, great boxy things that looked as though they would need industrial cranes to move them, and Hunter showed me his favorites and his skills. Holden ordered a selection from the menu, and I sat down at one of the little booths next to him. The seats so small, we were all pressed up against each other.

"See? The food is good here," Hunter fired in his father's direction, taking a sip from an enormous chocolate milkshake and reaching for the plate of pancakes.

"Sure is," I agreed, and Holden cocked his eyebrow at me playfully.

"Taking his side over mine? Duly noted," he teased, and I grinned as I started to tuck in.

As we ate together, and Holden and Hunter chatted about the high scores on his games and how Hunter planned to beat them, I let myself settle into the moment. I hadn't realized how much I had needed this. I could never have imagined being this close with a family other than my own, and I certainly had never guessed I would get involved with a single father. I might have worked with kids, but that didn't mean I wanted them in my personal life as well. But this was... good. Easy. Fun.

And then Hunter's question from before drifted back into my mind, and I tensed slightly. It wasn't that I was worried I had said the wrong thing. I had hardly said anything at all, and I couldn't imagine that I would spark something awful with the vagueness I'd offered him. But he was without a mother. He had always been without a mother.

Now that I was here, that was going to change a little bit. Whether I liked it or not, it was clear that motherhood was the role Hunter wanted me to play for him—maybe even needed to. And Holden being open to me spending time with the two of them together as a family meant I was already slotting into that position. Which was flattering and thus far, I was enjoying my place with Hunter and Holden, but what if I wasn't enough? What if, when things got hard, I didn't know what the fuck to do? I had never done anything like this before, and I was so scared that I was going to do or say something that hurt one of them. They were so wrapped up in each other that to hurt one would be to hurt both.

"You okay?" Holden nudged me, and I blinked and remembered where I was. No time for drifting off into neuroses.

"Yeah, I'm fine," I assured him, and I smiled and grabbed a handful of curly fries. I had to keep focused on the here and now, what was right in front of me, and stop my brain from straying to places it had no right going. I was having a good time and so were they. For the time being, that was all that mattered.

40

HOLDEN

I was pouring myself a coffee as a well-earned break from work when I got the call. I wasn't expecting anything from anyone. It was the end of the school day soon, and I would be going to pick Hunter up from one of the clubs he was part of, but I grabbed my phone anyway and answered at once.

"Hello?" I greeted the person on the other end of the line, pinning the cell between my shoulder and my ear as I poured my coffee.

"Hello, Holden?" A man's voice I didn't recognize came down the line, and I furrowed my brow.

"Yeah, that's me," I replied. "Who's speaking?"

"This is Paul Robertson," the man replied, and it took me a moment to place the name. I knew it from somewhere, and then it hit me. Hunter's principal.

"Is everything all right?" I asked, concerned. I had never had a call from him at home before.

"Hunter's safe," he promised me at once. "But he's in some trouble. We need you to come by the school to pick him up and so we can talk."

"I'll be right there." I hung up and dumped my coffee down the drain. Hurrying to the car, I wondered what in the name of hell he could have gotten wrapped up in. I had never known Hunter to be anything other than a model student before. I hoped he hadn't gotten into a fight. Maybe some other kids had started picking on him, bullying him, and things had gotten out of control? My mind was racing as I hurried to make it to the school, and when I arrived, I went straight through to the principal's office.

"Hello?" I opened the door and found Hunter sitting in a small chair in the corner waiting for me. I instantly went to him, checking him all over to make sure there were no visible injuries, but he seemed fine. He squirmed away from me, as though he wished he could have been anywhere else but there.

"Hello, Holden. Take a seat, please." Paul pointed to the chair opposite him. I did as I was told, straightening my jacket and looking at him expectantly.

"We called you in today because Hunter was caught painting his name on the side of the school building with another boy." He sighed, sounding as though he was already exhausted with this and wanted to go straight home.

"What?" I glanced around at my son, hardly able to believe what I was hearing. He looked away from me, going bright red as he did so.

"We caught him about an hour ago," Paul continued. "We wanted to call you in to discuss the best mode of discipline going forward."

"I'll pay for any damages," I assured him at once, "and Hunter will come in over the weekend to paint over anything he left there. Right?"

I turned to Hunter, who nodded. He was still squirming in his seat, as though he couldn't wait to get away.

"He'll also receive a week of detention from the school," Paul replied. "Since this is his first incident, we'll leave it to you to discipline him the best way you see fit. For future incidents, though, he will receive a harsher punishment, and we'll expect to meet with you again to discuss options going forward."

"Of course." I nodded, and I did my best to keep my brow furrowed and my face serious in light of what he was telling me. Of course, I was angry. Hunter shouldn't have been pulling shit like that, and he knew better than to deface property in that way. But at the same time, there was some part of me that didn't mind his acting out as much as I perhaps should have. After all, how long had I been hoping he would start acting like a kid his age?

"Thank you for coming in." Paul shook my hand and glanced over at Hunter to give him one last long look. "You're both free to leave now."

Hunter hopped off the seat and trailed behind me out to the car. He didn't say a word, probably thinking I was mad at him and he was in for a chewing-out as soon as he opened his mouth—which I would give him, of course, because I didn't want to be caught in the middle of raising a little vandal. But it was hard to be too cross with him.

He climbed into the seat next to mine and turned to look out the window. Despite the downturned corners of his mouth, there to convince anyone looking that he felt bad for what he'd done, I could see a glimmer in his eyes—something like amusement, as though he was going over what he'd done in his head and couldn't get over how fun it had been. I had pulled plenty of stunts like that one when I was a kid and I had turned out all right. I had done them alongside all my best friends, all the kids who'd made my life worth living when I was growing up. If he could be a part of some of that energy, then I wasn't going to begrudge him a little bit of nonsense in the process.

"Are you mad at me?" Hunter asked quietly as we pulled in to the driveway of the house. He had been silent the entire trip back home, as though he was under the impression I might up and forget about what he'd done while we were on the way back here.

"I think what you did was very wrong," I told him firmly as I switched off the engine. "And I'll be driving you there on the weekend to clean it up. If I ever hear about you doing anything like this again, there's going to be real trouble, all right?"

He nodded. "All right. I'm sorry. I know I shouldn't have done it."

"Who was the boy you did it with?" I asked, and his face lit up at once.

"Jason," he replied. "We were playing with the paints after school, and he said we should see what happened when we put them under the sunlight, so we decided to paint our names out there together."

Okay. That didn't sound too nefarious.

"And what did happen?"

"We got caught, and they took us to the principal's office." He made a face.

"Well, that's what's going to happen if you deface other people's property," I told him sternly. "Don't let your new friends lead you astray. I know some things can seem fun on the surface, but you have to make sure they're not going to hurt anyone else. Otherwise, they're not fun for the person who's getting hurt."

"I get it." He nodded, clutching his bag close to him on his lap.

"Good. Now, get inside and finish your homework before dinner. Think about what you've done. Try not to paint on any of the walls in the process."

"Okay, Dad." He hopped out of the car and hurried into the house. I followed him after a moment or two. He was likely embarrassed and probably wanted some time to be by himself after what had happened. I could remember what it was like to get caught at that age when you felt as though every idea you had was the greatest in the world right up until the moment some big boring adult came by to dissuade you of the fact.

When I made it back into the house, he was already upstairs in his room, the door shut behind him, and finally, I allowed myself a smile. I sincerely hoped this would be the last bit of trouble he got into—hell, that he would learn to be smart enough to keep himself from getting caught the next time.

I should have been more mad that I'd had to come down to the school in the middle of the workday to pick him up, mad that he'd been pulling a stunt as silly as that one. But I couldn't find it in me to feel that way. The way he'd told the story, it didn't sound like either of those boys had intended anything nasty with the painting. They'd been curious and too silly to consider what the consequences of that curiosity might be.

Even if it had sprung from somewhere a little more rebellious, I found it hard to mind too much about that, either. I had spent so long worrying about Hunter, worrying that he wasn't acting like other boys his age. This kind of troublemaking, the kind where a kid and his friend put their heads together and came up with an idea that they were both too dumb or too excited to notice would get them in trouble, that was an integral part of being a kid. It had been to me, at least. I would never have been able to become the man I was today if I hadn't spent my growing-up years taking silly risks and reaping the rewards—or the punishments. It was the only way he was going to learn how the world worked, this kind of low-stakes boy stuff that he had seemed to hide away from for so long.

And he'd been doing it with a friend. That seemed, to me, the most important part of this. He was coming home and telling me about the friends he'd been making, even if he was doing dumb stuff with them. I couldn't wait for him to start bringing them around, so I could see him surrounded by all his companions, the people who made him feel valued and special and safe.

I headed to the kitchen and went to have that coffee I had been so rudely interrupted from when I had received that phone call. This time, I had a smile on my face as I was making it. Yes, I would have to sacrifice my weekend to teach my son a lesson about respecting other people's property, but if it meant he had friends by his side, I would have given up every weekend for the rest of the year. He was turning into the boy I'd always dreamed he would be, and nothing was going to get in the way of how good it felt to finally see him come out of his shell.

41

AUTUMN

I waited in front of the main window in my house, looking out to the street and waiting for Hunter and Holden to get there. Any other weekend, I would have been mad at the thought of heading back to school and giving up my Saturday, but as long as the two of them were there, I had no problem at all heading back in.

Besides, a member of the staff had to oversee the detention they'd given Hunter for the little stunt he'd pulled during the week. I still couldn't believe someone like Hunter could do something like that, but then I'd found out Jason Mann was involved, and it all slotted into place. Jason was a bit of a rebel, not much bothering to let the rules get to him wherever he could, and he was popular for it. I was surprised when I heard the two of them were spending time together, but I supposed it was sort of sweet too. They were bonding, even if what they were bonding over was painting their names on the back of the school's janitorial shed.

Holden was making the right choice by sending him back to the school to clean it up, though. It was exactly the sort of thing that would keep him from doing it again without going overboard. I had no idea how Jason's parents were dealing with it, but they seemed content to give him a longer rope than he should ever have. They were probably talking up their son's latest modern art installation, knowing them, instead of teaching him that people weren't going to be so impressed with this play once he got a little older and grew out of his cute little chubby cheeks and cheeky smile.

I saw Holden's car pulling up the driveway and headed outside to meet them. It was a cool day, colder than I'd expected, and I wrapped my coat tightly around myself as I slipped into the front seat next to Holden.

"How's it going?" I asked, fighting the urge to lean over and give him a kiss to greet him hello. We weren't quite there yet, and Hunter certainly wasn't. The last thing I wanted was to make this day any more uncomfortable than it already was for him.

"Tiring." Holden glanced in the mirror at Hunter. "Had a little trouble getting this one out of bed to take care of his mess this morning."

"I feel you." I flashed a smile at Hunter. It was a little weird for me, given that I was his teacher, but this also felt like a date with his dad. We hadn't seen each other since the weekend before when I'd slept over and we'd gone out together afterward. I'd missed him more than I should, especially because he'd been busy with work and sorting out everything with Hunter and hadn't had much time to keep in touch.

We headed over to the school, and I went to grab the paint can and painting supplies that the janitor had left out for Hunter to use over the weekend. I handed them to him, pointed him in the direction of the shed, and planted my hands on my hips.

"Off you go!" I told him, waving my hands, and he trudged over to take care of his graffiti. There was hardly anything, really, a few tiny smudges of paint, but I wanted to see him deal with it anyway. The only way to stop this kind of thing from happening again was to nip it in the bud early, before he got it in his mind that it was worth doing.

Holden and I took a seat on the small bench at the other end of the playground, and we kept an eye on Hunter while he worked. Holden slung his arm casually along the back of the seat, and I found myself shifting back against it, wanting to feel the weight of him near to me. I had missed him so much, not only talking to him but his presence, being near him, feeling his softness and his warmth coming off him in waves.

"What do you know about this Jason kid?" Holden asked as Hunter began to paint. "Hunter says that was the boy he did this with."

"Yeah, Jason's all right," I said. "Popular. Bit of a troublemaker but nothing bad, just a kid who probably gets encouraged in everything he's ever thought of at home."

"Popular?" Holden raised his eyebrows.

"Yeah, he's always got his little crew around him."

"And now Hunter's part of that?" He grinned. I could see how excited he was at the mere thought. I supposed it was a big deal, once I thought about it. Only a few months ago, I never would have known Hunter to do anything like this, let alone doing it with one of the most popular kids in his class.

"Well, if this doesn't do it, nothing will," I replied, gesturing to the cleaning operation taking place in front of us.

"That's good to hear." Holden leaned back and grinned, stretching his arm over his head before he let it come to rest behind my shoulders once more. I shot him a look out of the corner of my eye and raised my eyebrows.

"You're totally pleased about this, aren't you?"

"Well, we met because you said he wasn't making any friends," he replied. We were far enough away that Hunter couldn't hear us, and I let out a laugh.

"Okay, but this wasn't precisely what I had in mind." I waved my hand in the direction of Hunter and the paint smears on the walls, which were rapidly disappearing under the busy hand of his paintbrush.

"Yeah, but it's something, isn't it?" Holden pointed out. "Look, I know it sounds weird, but he seems like he's had such a hard time finding people he connects with. Then you come along, and he gets on so well with you, and then the after-school clubs, and now this..."

As he trailed off, I could see him getting a little misty-eyed.

"Look at you, getting all soppy." I nudged him.

"This is my son we're talking about," he pointed out. "I think if I'm allowed to get a little soppy over anything, it should be him."

"Fair point." I grinned. "And I guess you're right. He's been doing well on the social front the last few months, better than he has in the whole time I've known him, at least."

"I think it's going to get better," Holden replied. "Him getting involved in silly boy stuff like this—it's good news, I think, in the long term."

"If not for our weekend plans."

"I can live with it if you can," he shot back, and he briefly traced his fingers across my neck. I shivered, and it had nothing to do with the cold that time around.

"I'm sure I'll find a way to push through." I sighed like this was all some deep struggle I could barely handle, and I was doing some great noble task by going through with it.

"I appreciate the effort," Holden grinned. "And I'll have to find a way to pay you back later."

"Mmm." I shivered on the spot again and gave him a look. "Maybe save this till later, huh? Don't want us getting into trouble for inappropriate conduct on school grounds."

"It'd be totally worth it," he protested, but then he shrugged and held his hands away from me to show he wasn't putting the moves on me. "But whatever you think is best."

We turned back to watching Hunter, who was moving in small, careful strokes to make sure he'd covered every inch of the painted words he and Jason had left behind. I smiled as he turned to us expectantly, pointing to the bare wall.

"Is it done?" he asked, and I got to my feet to take a look. Inspecting the wall closely, I made sure every drop of the paint they'd put there was invisible, and only the new application was noticeable on top of it.

I nodded. "Looks good to me. We'll let this dry and then see if it needs another coat of paint, all right?"

"All right." Hunter nodded and just looked glad it was all over. I waved Holden across to us, disappointed by how quickly this had all been over and done with. We barely got to spend any time together, and no doubt Holden would want to take Hunter home so as not to prolong his punishment.

"Looks good, son." He nodded to the wall proudly. I grinned. It was good to see a parent who cared about their kid learning the difference between right and wrong, but at the same time, I loved seeing one who supported and complimented everything their child worked on too. It was the perfect balance, the balance Holden seemed to have no trouble finding when it came to Hunter.

"What now?" I asked, raising my eyebrows at Holden, and he grinned at me.

"I was thinking," he began, flicking his tongue over his lips as though he was about to make a huge announcement. "Ice cream?"

"Little cold for that, isn't it?" I pointed out, and he shook his head.

"Not if we get it with hot fudge sauce, right, Hunter?" he asked, and Hunter's face brightened.

"Yeah!" he agreed, and they both turned to me expectantly. I planted my hands on my hips and stared them down for a moment. If I kept going along with all these spontaneous trips, I was going to end up blowing my nonexistent diet and not being able to fit into that beautiful dress I'd bought for our first date all those weeks ago. But as I looked at their faces, I knew it was worth it. Totally worth it.

"Let's get out of here." I waved my hand toward the parking lot of the school, and within a few minutes, we'd dropped all the painting supplies off inside and were on our way down to the ice cream shop Holden had taken me to the first evening we'd spent together.

"Have you been here before?" Hunter asked, and I glanced at Holden. I had no idea whether he'd told the boy about our first date or the details of it or where he'd taken me. I shrugged.

"Once," I replied vaguely. "But I don't remember much about it."

"No?" Holden remarked, stealing a pointed glance at me.

"No, I was pretty distracted," I replied, flashing him the briefest smile to make sure Hunter wouldn't catch on to what we were actually exchanging.

"Hmm, what's distracting about an ice cream shop?" Holden shook his head. "Can't imagine what you might have been focused on."

Before he could tease me any further, we pulled to a halt outside the shop, and Hunter scrambled out to race inside. There was a cold breeze coming in from the water, and Holden wrapped an arm around me as we walked into the shop. I knew we should have played it a little more cool and casual than that, but Hunter wasn't looking our way, and it had been a whole week since we'd seen one another. I think we were allowed to steal these little moments where we could.

We ordered our ice cream and all squeezed into a booth that looked over the sea beyond us. I snuggled close to Holden, pretending it was the cramped size of the booth but enjoying the feel of his body next to mine.

"Now that I've done the painting..." Hunter took a deep breath, suddenly glancing up between the two of us, as though we were the arbiters of whether or not he would ever have fun again.

"Yes?" Holden prompted him, and Hunter looked down at his ice cream, placed his spoon down next to it, and then spoke quickly like he was worried he might run out of nerve if he lingered on it too much.

"Jason invited me to his house tomorrow evening," he blurted. "Can I go?"

Holden glanced over at me, clearly checking in as silently as he could as to whether this was a good idea. Jason's parents were a little lax, but he was a good kid if a bit of a kooky one. Him inviting Hunter around to his place was a big deal, and I nodded briefly, letting Holden know it would be a good idea to let his son go out on this occasion.

"As long as his parents can pick you up and bring you back, that's fine," Holden replied. "Do you want to call him when you get back so the two of you can work out the details?"

"Sounds great." Hunter nodded, beaming. "Thanks, Dad."

"No problem." Holden watched Hunter slip from his seat and dart off to find more sprinkles for his ice cream, and then he turned to me with a smile. "Gives us a chance to spend the evening in together, huh?"

"I guess it does," I agreed, happy his mind had gone to the same place mine had. I was so looking forward to a whole evening, just the two of us, without having to worry about babysitters or what was to come the morning after. Before I could lose the nerve, I leaned over and planted a brief kiss on his mouth, stealing it fast enough that I was sure Hunter hadn't caught me. Holden closed his eyes for a moment as if savoring the taste of me on his mouth.

"Can't wait." He grinned as Hunter turned to join us back at the table.

"What are you talking about?" Hunter asked curiously, and Holden shook his head.

"Boring adult stuff." He waved his hand. "But we'll try to keep it interesting now that you're back."

Under the table, his hand slid onto my leg, and I grinned knowing that tomorrow night was going to be a hell of a lot of fun.

42

HOLDEN

As I stood outside the house, scanning the street and waiting for the car to arrive, I couldn't help feeling a little jolt of sadness in my chest. I mean, I knew I shouldn't have been sad. I should have been happy my son was finally growing up, spending his first night away from home out of choice to sleep over at his friend's house, but still, it was going to be weird saying goodbye to him and knowing I wouldn't see him until I picked him up the next morning.

I'd spent an hour on the phone with Jason's parents the night before and texted Autumn to check in on what she thought of them. I was nearly satisfied at the thought of leaving my kid with them for a night. Just a single night, but still, it was more than I could have managed a few weeks before. But Hunter and I were both making progress. Besides, a whole night where someone else had offered to take care of him, no questions asked? That meant I got to spend an evening with Autumn on short notice, which felt like the kind of gorgeous luxury I had to indulge in while I could.

An expensive-looking car pulled up the driveway, and I smiled when I saw the kid, Jason, waiting in the front seat. He was a goofy-looking little thing with big glasses, slightly messy hair, and long, gangly arms on a short torso, as though bits of him were growing out of sorts with one another. He hopped out of the car and waited for his father to join him, and the two of them made their way to the house.

"You must be Jason." I smiled at my son's friend. "Hunter's upstairs, I think, if you want to go find him."

"Thanks!" Jason replied, and he darted inside the house, leaving me and his dad standing out there in the cool evening together.

"You must be Logan." I extended my hand to the father, who shook it.

"Holden, right?" He nodded.

"That's me," I replied. "I'd hoped my first time meeting other parents from the school wasn't going to be after our sons mutually defaced some property, but I guess I can't win them all, right?"

Logan chuckled.

"You know, I have to admit, I don't see it as that big of a deal," he confessed. "I mean, I know they shouldn't have done it and all that— and we told Jason off for it—but it seems like boys being boys, you know?"

"I have to agree with you." I nodded. "It's hard to be mad when you can remember doing a bunch of stuff like that yourself when you were a kid, right?"

"Agreed." He nodded, rubbing his hands together to ward off the cold. "Is this the first time you've let Hunter sleep away from home?"

"Yeah, at least it is with one of his friends," I confessed. "Is it that obvious?"

"No, I just remember how I was when Jason first went somewhere else, and I recognized it when you were talking to us last night," he replied with a kind smile. "I know how hard it can be, but we'll take good care of him. And I know Jason will too."

"Thanks." I smiled back, glad to have someone around who seemed to get where my nerves arose from.

Hunter and Jason burst out the front door of the house, both of them laughing loudly. Hunter had a bag slung over his shoulder, one I'd helped him pack earlier in the day.

"I'll see you later, buddy." I ruffled his hair as he sprinted past to get into the car. As soon as he was situated in the back seat, he waved to me and rolled down the window.

"See you later, Dad!" he called back, and with a flurry of activity, all three of them were gone, leaving me alone at the house once more.

I turned back inside and wandered around for a while, not quite sure what I was supposed to do with myself. Autumn was going to be getting here soon, but until then, this place was just... empty. Sure, he had stayed over with Raymond and Olivia before this, but that was different. I knew them inside out, and they had known Hunter his entire life, pretty much acting like his extended family. I had never handed him off to someone I'd never met before and let them whisk him away for the evening. It felt weirdly wrong, but I had to let him go if I wanted him to grow into the kind of kid he needed to be.

I settled in on the couch and stared off into space, trying to enjoy the quiet and struggling to find a way to get my head around it. Parents were meant to crave this kind of peace and quiet, but there was almost nowhere I'd rather be in the world that sitting opposite Hunter, listening to him tell me all about some new obsession that had him lost down a rabbit hole.

I heard a car pulling up outside, and a tiny part of me hoped it would be Hunter coming back to spend the rest of the evening with me. I knew it was ridiculous, but I wanted nothing more than to kick back with him and remind myself exactly what a great kid he could be. But when I got to the window, I found Autumn climbing out of her car and heading toward the door, and I grinned. I supposed that was just as good.

I opened the door, and she pushed two bottles of wine into my chest, brushing past me and hanging her coat up.

"I wasn't sure whether I wanted red or white, so I got both," she explained, and I looked down at the bottles and grinned.

"Either works for me," I told her, heading through to the kitchen to pour us each a glass. She followed me through and paused in the doorway, looking at me.

"Fuck, it's good to see you," she murmured. Then she wrapped her arms around me and pressed her head into my shoulder from behind. My heart swelled with the happiness of having her there. Maybe this night could be just as good without Hunter here.

"It's good to see you too," I agreed, and I turned to kiss her, to properly kiss her—not those stolen little pecks we got when people weren't looking at us, but a real kiss, our tongues finding one another, my body against hers and hers leaning into mine. When I pulled back, her cheeks were flushed, and she brushed her nose against my jaw.

"Okay, I *really* missed you," she murmured pointedly, and I knew exactly what was going through her mind. But I wanted to tease her a little, to watch her squirm for me, and besides, I was hungry and needed something to eat before she drained my energy for the rest of the night.

"You want some dinner?" I asked.

"What were you thinking?" she replied. "Because I'm pretty sure my fingers are way too clumsy for the stuff you made last time I was around."

"Some pasta," I replied. "Nothing too difficult, I promise."

"Well, nothing that's so difficult, I can't take it on after a glass of wine, okay?" she warned me, and I pulled out the chopping board and handed her a pan.

"Can you put that on the heat?" I asked her, pointing to the stove, and she fiddled around with it for a minute before she found the right switch and turned it on.

"Perfect." I grinned, and she snuggled up next to me as I began to chop vegetables for a simple Bolognese.

"Yeah, it is," she told me, planting a kiss on my cheek. And at that moment, I felt such utter contentment that I could almost feel the words swelling up and out of me, the words I knew it was far too soon for, the words I'd been doing my best to hide from for a long time. The words I knew I couldn't dump on her lap in front of her while the two of us were cooking dinner.

It was too soon for "I love you." I knew that much. I might have been out of the dating scene for a long while, but throwing that at her when we had only been together a few weeks would have been way premature.

I hadn't said those words to anyone but Hunter's mother in the last ten years—well, said them in a romantic sense, of course. And they held so much power, even I could see that. They contained multitudes, not least the indication that this relationship was deadly serious. As I watched her put some olive oil into the pan and swish it around to coat the bottom, humming quietly as she worked, I knew it was true, but I didn't want to come out and hit her with it yet. I wanted both of us to be totally sure so I could know she was going to say it back to me when the time came.

"What are you thinking about?" she asked, and I shook my head and went to grab a few cloves from the head of garlic that was sitting out on the counter.

"Nothing much," I lied, as I took a sip of my wine in the hopes I could distract myself from the thoughts running around my head. Though there was a chance the alcohol would make me more likely to blurt out what was in my brain.

"So what are we cooking tonight?" she asked, bumping her hip against mine and lifting her glass to her lips. I glanced over at her, at those big eyes shining at me over the top of her wine, and I couldn't help smiling. I had never been so sure of anyone in my life before. For as long as I could remember, as an adult, I'd pushed away the people close to me, determined to keep safe from the same kind of heartbreak I'd been through with Hunter's mother. But with Autumn, it was different—so different. She never looked at me and saw a man who would let her down, a man who would never live up to his potential. I knew she looked at me and saw hope, a future, a grounding that she had been craving for a long time. I would work my hardest to prove she was right to see all those things in me.

"Something awesome," I promised her, and I reached over to kiss her wine-stained lips before I continued. I couldn't get enough of her tonight, and I had a feeling it was going to be hard to get this meal on the table with all the trouble I was having keeping my hands to myself.

43

AUTUMN

As he poured the pile of onion and garlic into the pot and shifted me out of the way so he could stir, I leaned against the counter and watched him. He had a funny look on his face, as though he was doing his best to contain something he didn't want to make a big deal out of.

"How are you doing with Hunter being out of the house?" I asked, and he shot a look at me and shrugged.

"Is it that obvious?" He made a face. "It's weird, you know. I haven't had him out of the house like this, not with people I don't know, in the whole time he's been alive."

"Well, I know Jason's parents pretty well," I assured him. "And they're good people. A little kooky but harmless, and they adore their son, and they'll be working their asses off to make sure Hunter has a good time tonight."

"I'm still going to pick him up first thing tomorrow morning, though."

"Yeah, you'll be there at the break of dawn, leaning on the horn," I teased, and he grinned and shook his head.

"Thanks for coming over tonight," he told me. "I could use the company. To get me out of my head, you know."

"And to spend the night with your beautiful, charming lady of choice?" I reminded him.

"But of course," he agreed, and I shifted back along the floor so I could stand next to him again. I was feeling so fluttery in my chest like a thousand butterflies had sprung to life as soon as I'd walked in here.

"How long till dinner?" I asked him. My stomach was starting to grumble, and whatever he was cooking smelled so delicious.

"Not long," he promised me. "Fifteen minutes at the most?"

"Perfect." I loved watching him make dinner. There was something underrated and sexy about watching a man who could cook work his magic in the kitchen. He had to have such confidence, such sureness in what he was doing, and I found myself watching Holden's hands intently as he went about his business.

He finished cooking and served up the meal, taking us to the small dining table in the living room. I grabbed our wine and followed him, and he laid out the food for us, taking his seat opposite me. I could still see the Hunter thing was weighing on him, the way his eyes darted around as though he was looking for someone he knew wasn't going to be there, and I reached across the table and patted his hand.

"Hey," I told him gently. "He's going to be fine. Really. You can always give them a call if you want to check in."

"Is it that obvious?" He grinned at me, a little ruefully, and I cocked my head at him.

"Hey, he's your son," I pointed out. "I think it would be a little weird if you were totally fine with him skipping off and spending the night with someone you don't know."

"Don't put it like that." He lifted his hand. "Or else I'll go down there and pick him up right now."

"Hey. And leave me here all by myself?"

"Who knows what kind of mischief you'd get up to?" He managed to smile, and he took a sip of his wine.

"This smells awesome," I told him as I went to tuck into the food. "Thank you for this."

"Thanks for coming," he replied, and he touched his glass to mine.

And with that, he seemed to relax a little bit. I knew it was hard for parents to send their kids off like that, and especially so for someone like Holden who was the only caretaker Hunter had ever known. It was natural for him to be feeling a little out-of-sorts, wondering if he'd made the right choice in sending him away. But he unwound as the evening went on, and we made it through a bottle of wine together, chatting about my work friends and the gossip from our separate friend groups. The conversation flowed so easily that I barely even noticed the time passing, the sun dipping in the sky until it was dark outside, and I could convince myself we were the only two people left in the world.

"I have something to show you." Holden got to his feet when we were done.

"If it's another glass of wine, I think I'm good." I held my hand up, but he shook his head

"Trust me, it's better than that," he replied, and he took my hand and tugged me to my feet. When he led me upstairs, for a moment I thought he was about to launch some kind of seduction on me, but he took me in the direction of his office at the last minute instead of the bedroom. Which was a relief because I was full of pasta and wasn't sure I could have handled anything other than cuddling at that moment.

"Look, if you want help with your programming, I'm probably going to come up a little short," I warned him. "I can just about do enough to teach the kids some basics, but other than that—"

"No, I don't need your help with the programming." He guided me into the seat in front of his computer. I leaned back against the leather and looked up at him.

"I think I've finally finished putting together that program for the grade curves." He grinned at me. "You remember? You were telling me what a pain in the ass it was for you to have to put out all that time and effort for them?"

"Holy shit, I can't believe you finished it," I exclaimed. "I didn't think it would be done so soon."

"I've put some of my other work on hold for the time being." He shrugged. "I wanted to get this done."

"You didn't have to." I smiled at him. "But if this works, you've made the lives of every teacher in the county a million times less irritating."

"Well, then, I totally had to do it." He booted up the computer and clicked on the program icon. He pulled it up, and I squinted at the screen. It looked like a bunch of boxes to me, and I wasn't sure what to do to get it to function.

"So how does it work?" I asked, looking up at him hopefully.

"You just have to input the numbers here." He highlighted one column with the cursor. "And then you press calculate there."

I put in a selection of numbers, remembering what I could from the grade curves I'd been trying to make all this time, and clicked the calculate button. In a moment, a beautiful graph popped up, the numbers plotted out carefully onto it. My eyes widened.

"Oh, Holy shit, it works!" I exclaimed, peering closer to make sure the numbers were where they all should be. "And how many numbers can it take at a time?"

"As many as you need," he replied, and I could tell he was trying to play it modest but was secretly pleased with my reaction.

"Honestly, you have no idea how handy this is going to be," I told him excitedly. "Wait till I tell everyone at work about it. Zoe's going to be pumped."

"I'm glad it's working," he said. "I still want to do a few more tweaks to make it more user-friendly, but I think this is a good jumping-off point—"

"It's perfect," I replied, and I leaned up to plant a kiss on his lips like I was giving my handsome knight a token for his efforts.

"Good." He grinned and caught my head in his hands to kiss me again, harder this time, a teasing little moment that made my heart pulse with excitement in my chest. He pulled back, and I stood up again.

"I think that's enough computer programming for tonight," he murmured, taking my hand and leading me back downstairs.

We curled up on the couch together, and I nestled into his chest, feeling sleepy and happy and a little tipsy. I loved these quiet little moments we spent together. They were the ones I came back to when I needed a boost, when I wanted to let myself revel in a little pop of happiness when I was having a hard day. He stroked my hair gently back from my face, and I laid my head on his chest, listening to the steady beat of his heart beneath my cheek.

"You didn't have to go to all that trouble for me," I told him. "With the program, I mean."

"Well, it seemed like a gap in the market, and I had to take it," he replied, and I could tell he was holding something back. I lifted my head to look him in the eyes, and he shrugged and smiled.

"And I wanted to do something nice for you," he admitted, brushing his fingers over my mouth for a brief second. He paused, took a deep breath, and then continued.

"I don't think... I don't think what I feel for you is something I can put into words right now," he confessed. "I haven't felt this way about anyone in a long time, Autumn, not for years. Doing this for you— well, it's some way I can show you how important you are to me. I know things were weird starting out, but I wanted more from the beginning. And now we have it..."

He trailed off once more, and he was looking at me so intently, I nearly let the words slip out of my mouth. They hadn't occurred to me until that moment, the big *I love you*, but the way he was looking at me, the things he was saying, they only had one real end. I caught my breath and drew my gaze away from him, cooling myself off. It wasn't the time. Not quite yet. We hadn't been together long enough, and besides, it seemed as though he was still getting his head around actually having feelings for someone.

"I know exactly what you mean," I murmured, and I nestled back into his chest, noticing that his heart was beating a little faster than before. I knew that had been his way of telling me he loved me, the closest he could get to those words for the time being. And I smiled, inhaling his scent, as he wrapped his arms tightly around me. We were both barreling toward admitting how we felt for one another once and for all. And I was okay letting him take his time to get there. He had been through a lot the last ten years, and it made perfect sense that he wouldn't be forthcoming with those words. But he was showing me they were true, every way he knew how. That made me happier than I could ever imagine.

We lay there together, holding each other, the words unspoken but solid in my mind. I felt so safe in his arms, so safe in his affections, so sure we were doing the right thing by sticking this out. As the light dimmed outside, my eyes grew heavy, and I fell asleep, warm and comfortable, on his chest.

44

HOLDEN

"T his is going to change everything," Zoe exclaimed with excitement as I headed over to their computers and started to install the new systems. Autumn had invited me in that morning to apply the new grade curve program to the computers, and I had agreed, happy to see if it worked or not and get some hands-on testing for the work I'd done. This thing could look as pretty as it liked, but if people couldn't use it, then it was back to the drawing board for me.

"I hope it does." I nodded to her with a smile, and I noticed her shooting a look at Autumn and raising her eyebrows at her. I hoped that was a good sign. A *you got a good one* sign.

"Well, I was playing with it last night, and it seems to work well." Autumn nodded to Zoe. "I'm hoping it'll go fine with actual data this time around."

"No reason it shouldn't," I offered hopefully, and Autumn smiled at me. I was glad to be helping out where I could, and if that meant getting on the good side of Autumn's best friend as well, that was a bonus.

"So the files are copied over, and now I boot it up?" Zoe asked as I handed her laptop back to her.

"Yeah, that's right," I agreed. "Just put in the data points in the—look, it's pretty self-explanatory. I'm not going to patronize you by explaining it all. If you have any trouble getting it to work, let me know. I'll help you out."

"Sure thing." Zoe nodded, and she shot another look at Autumn before she ducked out of the room. Autumn grinned as she pushed the door shut behind her. We still had a few minutes before class was due to start, and the two of us were all alone in this little classroom, nobody here but us. The air was still as I moved toward her, double-checking that the door was shut tight before I went to her and wound my arms around her waist.

"Mmm." She grinned, as I nuzzled into her neck, inhaling that impossibly specific scent she had, the one that seemed to fill me from top to bottom every time I caught a hint of it. I could have lost myself in there, hidden in the depths of it. My next project would be finding a way to commit her scent to a bottle just for me so I could have her whenever I wanted.

"Thank you so much for putting the program together," she sighed as I pulled back. "Seriously, this has been a thorn in my side and for all the people who worked with me the last few years. Loads of people have been talking about making something to have it run a little smoother, but you just up and did it."

"Hey, it's only an act of charity to my local school system," I replied gently, and she grinned

"And not at all an attempt to get on my good side?" she teased.

"The thought never so much as crossed my mind," I replied as I nuzzled myself into her neck a little farther, letting my lips brush up and over her skin. She softened in my arms, even knowing that someone could walk in and catch us at any moment The chemistry between us was hard to resist or ignore, even when the circumstances were less than ideal.

"You need to get out of here," she told me, but there was no conviction behind her voice as she spoke. I turned my head to find her mouth, kissing her gently, and she let out a soft moan and wrapped her arms tightly around my neck. She kissed me back, briefly but deeply, enough to let me know that what had been on my mind lately had been on hers.

When I pulled away, her eyes were still closed, and she was swaying slightly in my arms like someone had run a jolt of energy through her, and she was figuring out what to do with it

"Mmm." She purred, kissing the corner of my mouth again. "Okay, now you really need to get out of here before someone catches us."

"Fine," I replied, reluctantly pulling away from her and heading to the door. I paused for a moment, letting myself come back down to earth, and I could feel her watching me as I made my way across the room. Fuck, if I'd had a few minutes longer, I would have grabbed her, pushed her over that table, and fucked her hard—

"Catch you later," I told her, cutting off that train of thought in my head before it went to places I didn't want it to go. Not then, at least.

"See you later," she said. "You're coming back after school to pick Hunter up, right? After the club?"

"Yeah, that's right." I grinned. "So I'll see you again then."

"Can't wait." She beamed, and I ducked out of her classroom and turned to head back to my car. I felt as though I had an actual skip in my step as I headed to make my way home. I had never imagined, not once in a million years, that things with Autumn would end up where they were. Not just the two of us together, but the two of us unable to get enough of one another, drinking deep from the well of our mutual adoration for each other. I wanted to do everything I could for her, to make her life easy any way I knew how, and for me, that was love. To show her how good her life could have been with me, that was my way of telling her how I felt, proving to her that she was making the right choice by staying.

I drove back to the house and considered the fact that I would have to get back to my real, regular work since I was done with the program. That was a weird thought after I'd poured all that time and effort into putting it together. Maybe Raymond was right, and I should start thinking about hiring someone new to step up to the plate and help me out. It certainly wouldn't hurt to have someone keeping my projects ticking over while I was working on other things. Even just a person to touch base with my clients and catch them up on the state of their projects. It was certainly something to think about. Perhaps I would place an ad when I got home.

And as I turned the corner to draw up outside the house, my thoughts stopped dead in my tracks when I saw a car there I didn't recognize. I wondered, for a moment, if it belonged to someone from the school, if Hunter had landed in more trouble, but I had only just left. Anyone coming from there would have been forced to overtake me to get back here. It wasn't Autumn, it wasn't Raymond, and it wasn't anyone from the school, so who in the hell was sitting outside my house, waiting for me to arrive home?

I pulled my car to a halt behind the one already parked there and peered out at it through the window. It was beaten, a little battered-looking, the paint job needing another go over sooner rather than later, and there was a small crack running up one of the side windows. Whoever it belonged to, they were a little down on their luck. Maybe looking for a handout? Some help? A job? I had no idea how they would have found my place, or what—

And then I saw her.

I recognized her at once. Her face had run circles in my mind when she had first left me, when I'd been convinced all of this was an attempt to prove a point to her. And there were flashes of her in Hunter as well, little moments when he would turn around or laugh and frown, and I would see, with a certainty that I often tried to ignore, that he was her son as much as he was mine.

Karla, standing there on my doorstep and pressing the bell, looked a little different than how I'd remembered her. The image I had of her in my mind was a young woman, messy hair with bleached-out ends, eyebrows plucked thin, with that enormous belly where she had been growing our son and those sharp eyes as she picked holes in me. She had aged a little—hadn't we all—with her features growing a little softer around the edges, her jawline not quite as sharp, her cheekbones fading under a little fat.

She heard me getting out of the car and turned around, her eyes lighting up when she saw me standing there.

"Holden." She came down the steps. "I'm sorry to turn up like this, but I didn't know where to find you, so I thought—"

"I was dropping Hunter off at school," I told her carefully. How could she not have thought of that? It showed how out-of-touch she was with our own son, that something as basic as that wouldn't even cross her mind.

"Of course." She slapped a hand to her forehead. "Sorry, I didn't even think about that. But I guess… the important thing is that I have you here in front of me, right?"

"Karla, what are you doing here?" I demanded. When she had first left, I would have given anything to have her come back, to have her turn up on my doorstep like this, but so much time had passed, and I had firmly grown out of desiring her back in my life. In fact, I knew I was better off without her. Yet, here she was, sniffing me out from God knows how far away.

She took a deep breath and twisted her hands around one another, smiling and shaking her head.

"I can't believe I'm going to say this," she confessed. "But I want… I want to see Hunter. I want to have him as a part of my life."

I stared at her some more, unable to believe the words coming out of her mouth. Did she think it was that easy? That she could walk back into my life, my son's life, and act as though she hadn't missed a beat?

I thought back to Autumn, how good she had been with Hunter when we'd been out together, and I knew I couldn't give in to this. I had seen what Hunter had looked like when he was with people he liked, who he trusted. He'd never met this woman, not really, even if she was his mother. Why would I let her back in after everything she'd done—and failed to do?

I wasn't sure how to tell her, so I stood there for a long moment, letting the shock wash over me and waiting for it to dissipate. But before I could reply, she seemed to take my silence as an opening for something else.

Stepping forward, she pressed her hand to my chest, through my jacket, her touch familiar but completely unexciting to me. I looked up, and she was gazing deeply into my eyes, staring as though I was the only living thing in the world.

"And you as well," she finished up. "I want you in my life too."

And time seemed to fall away as I looked into the eyes of the woman I'd loved before Autumn, the mother of my child, the girl who'd turned back up into my life after nearly a decade. And I couldn't think of a damn thing to say to her.

45

AUTUMN

"How's it going, guys?" I asked as I wandered over to check on Hunter and Amelie. They had been playing on the computers together from the moment school had ended and the club had picked up, and it was clear they were intently focused on the campaign they were working on.

"Good!" Hunter grinned at me. He had practically been pinned to my leg all day at school, telling me about the sleepover he'd had with Jason and how much he'd enjoyed it, and I was delighted to see him doing so much better. I glanced at the clock. It wouldn't be long until Holden got here, and I couldn't wait to see him again. Even these little moments we managed to steal together were enough to sustain me, enough to remind me totally what I was doing with him. I missed him, even though he'd only been away a few hours. Which was a little silly, but I couldn't help how I felt.

The program had worked beautifully. Zoe had come running to me at break time to tell me as much, waving her hands around and exclaiming as though this was truly the most exciting news in the world.

"I'm glad it's working," I told her. She nodded and ran her hand through her hair.

"Ah, it's going to come in so useful," she sighed. "Seriously, what can't that guy do?"

"I know, I know." I shook my head and smiled. I'd been thinking that myself. He seemed so utterly perfect, filling in all these gaps in my life without me even having to ask him. Because he wanted to show me how much I meant to him. That's what he'd said. It felt so good to have someone, a real boyfriend, who seemed to want to remind me every chance he got that he felt like the luckiest dude on earth for dating me. I had never felt so valued in a relationship, so important to the person on the other side of it.

"You should marry him and lock it down now," she told me, heading back to her classroom. "He's amazing. If you let go of him, I'm going to be pissed."

"I've got no intention of breaking up with him, trust me," I assured her, and she paused in the doorway and cocked an eyebrow at me.

"Things going well?" she asked, and I nodded effusively.

"So well," I gushed. "I think... I really think I'm falling for him."

She planted a hand on her heart as though touched by the sentiment.

"I'm so happy for you." She smiled, and even though she was usually all sarcastic quips and snarky comments, I knew she meant this.

"Me too," I replied, and she laughed. As she left, I bit my lip, excited to have a chance to talk about Holden, about us, about how brilliantly things seemed to be going between us. And with Hunter too. Hunter seemed to be warming up to me, and he was connecting with his peers in a way I had never seen him pull off before. Things were looking up for all of us.

I smiled as I watched Hunter and Amelie confer over something and then turn back to their individual screens. I'd be damned if I had a clue what was going on in front of them, but it looked PG, and they seemed to be having a good time, so I wasn't going to get in the middle of it.

I glanced at the door and spotted Holden striding toward the room. We still had a few more minutes before the club was officially done, so I could steal a little time with him for a split second. I stepped out, shutting the door behind me so nobody else could get in, and grinned at Holden.

But as soon as I was face-to-face with him, that smile slipped off my face at once. Something was wrong. Seriously wrong. I scanned him up and down for any obvious signs as to what the problem was, but I came up with a straight blank.

"Holden?" I reached out to him, touching my fingers to his arm, and he pulled away at once, turning his back to me.

"What's wrong?" I demanded, striding toward him, my heart pulsing hard in my chest. This had all been going too well. I should have been more suspicious. I shouldn't have let myself get comfortable, fall for him, I should never—

"I'm sorry, it's nothing to do with you." He shook his head and grimaced. "I just... something happened. When I was back at the house today."

"Is everything all right?" I widened my eyes, and Holden pressed his lips together and looked as though he was going to slam his fist into the wall next to us.

"Karla was there," he told me, looking up into my eyes as though this should send a shiver of horror down my spine. I furrowed my brow.

"Karla?" I prompted him.

"Hunter's mother," he explained—and my stomach dropped to my shoes.

"I thought you said she wasn't a part of your lives anymore," I reminded him, and he rubbed his hands over his face as though trying to make some sense out of this situation.

"Yeah, well, she wasn't." He held his hands up. "She hasn't been for almost ten years. She left after Hunter was born. I wasn't lying about that."

"Then what is she doing back here?" I furrowed my brow. "I don't understand."

"Neither do I," he replied. "She was there at the house when I got back there, and she told me she wanted to be part of Hunter's life again. And—"

He cut himself off as though he didn't want me to hear that next part. His face was overwritten with tension, anger—maybe even something close to fear. I wanted to reach out and hold him, but his hard edges wouldn't soften for me. I knew how hard this had to be on him, and I had no idea how I should deal with it.

"She wants to be a part of Hunter's life?" I focused in on the positive. "That's a good thing, right?"

"She signed over all her rights to him the day he was born," he snapped back. I knew his irritation wasn't aimed at me, but it still made me jolt, to hear him talk to me that way. He had never been anything other than kind and soft with me this whole time, but the fury in his system was taking control.

"She doesn't have any right to come back into his life and act like she's been anything other than utterly absent all this time." He shook his head.

"But surely, it's something positive for both of them if she wants to see him again, right?" I pressed him. At the front of my mind was the conversation Hunter had with me at the museum when he'd made it clear he'd noticed his lack of a second parent. He might have never expressed those kinds of feelings to Holden—he'd said his father shut down all conversation about Karla—but there was no way Holden hadn't picked up on it at some point, right?

"I don't know." Holden shook his head. "I don't think her intentions are exactly pure here."

"What do you mean?" I wondered aloud. I couldn't imagine anything but good coming from a mother wanting to reconnect with her son, no matter how long it had been since she left.

"I mean..." He took a deep breath as though he couldn't quite believe that he was truly going to come out and say this. "I mean, when I was speaking to her, I let her into the house. I didn't think I had a choice, but I'm pretty sure she wasn't in it just for Hunter."

My heart dropped.

"You as well?" I whispered. How could I compete with the woman who was the mother of his child? They would have a connection that ran deeper than mine could ever hope to. If she made it clear she wanted him...

"My money," he replied, and I felt my heart rate smooth out once more, return to something more normal.

"How would she get that?" I furrowed my brow.

"I don't know," he admitted. "But I don't know her. I know the kind of person she is, the kind of person she's always been. I wouldn't have put it past her to have found out about the money I've made since she left and for her to try to finagle her way into a big chunk of it."

"I think you should give her a chance," I told him. "I mean, she can't take anything you don't give, you know?"

"You don't know her like I do," he growled. "You don't know how she is when you give her the chance—I can't talk about this right now." He shook his head and headed to the door. "I'll see you tomorrow."

And with that, he went to pick up Hunter. Hunter was disappointed at being dragged away from his game, but the club was over, and other parents were starting to arrive as well. I chewed on my lip as Hunter waved goodbye to me, and Holden nodded his farewell without saying a word. I knew this was big, bigger than anything we'd had to deal with before. Even if I hadn't known the history between them, it was easy to see how something like this could fuck Holden up. He'd raised his son for so long with it being only the two of them, and it had been hard enough for him to open that up to even me. For another woman—a woman who had some true biological claim over his kid if not a legal one—to come into his life and demand that he find her a place in it? He must have been freaking out. I knew I certainly was.

I sent all the rest of the kids home with their parents and hung back to tidy up after the club was out. My mind was racing. I wished I could talk to someone about this, but I could tell Holden didn't want anyone else knowing the truth of what he was dealing with. I wanted to go to him, to comfort him, to tell him it was all going to be all right, but it wasn't the truth. He wouldn't believe it, even coming from me.

I stood there, staring at the blank screen on one of the computers, and ran through everything he'd told me. And doubt began to rise in my chest. What if he was keeping this woman at arm's length for my sake? What if he was worried that taking her back into his life would get in the way of the two of us? If I stayed in the middle of this, would I be getting in the way of a true family?

The questions barreled through my mind so fast I could hardly keep on top of them, and I did my best to push them down. What I wanted wasn't important. What mattered was Holden, Hunter, and that woman. I was an outsider to this family, a newcomer, someone who would never truly share the bond I wanted with them. And I had never felt that more intently than this very moment.

46

HOLDEN

"So what the hell are you going to do?"

The question hung in the air between Raymond and me for a long time, and I let out a sigh and tossed my hands in the air. I had no fucking clue what I was going to do, and he knew it.

"I don't think I can turn her away." I shook my head and picked up where I'd left off pacing up and down his living room. "Because if Hunter gets older, and she comes back, and he wants to see her, and he finds out about this, it's going to come across like I was trying to keep his own mother from him. The last thing I want is him believing something like that, you know?"

"Well, that is what you're doing," he pointed out bluntly. I grimaced. I knew he was right, but I didn't want to hear it.

"I know, I know." I shook my head. "But I have my doubts about why she's coming back. After all this time? What could her motivation be for that?"

"Maybe she feels like she's grown up enough to accept having a child now and wants to be part of his life?" Raymond suggested hopefully, but I could tell from the look on his face that he sure as fuck didn't believe what he was saying. He had been there through all of it, through all the shit that had gone down with Karla when she'd first left me, and he knew how badly it had hurt me and how hard it would be to forgive her for everything she'd done—and everything she hadn't.

"I think it's got to do with money," I replied. "She turned up in a car that looked pretty beaten-up, and she couldn't stop pointing out how nice the house was when she was inside it. She already knew about the company when she arrived, so she's clearly been doing some research on me—"

"Or maybe she was curious and wanted to see how the two of you were doing," Raymond pointed out. I knew he could be right, that perhaps I was being too harsh on Karla, but I couldn't shake the feeling there was something wrong about the way she was approaching me. About the timing

"I'm mostly worried about what this is going to do for me and Autumn," I confessed. "I know that shouldn't be at the front of my mind, but the last thing I need is to fuck things up with her when it's all going so well."

"How do you think it would fuck things up with her?" Raymond asked, furrowing his brow. I shook my head.

"I can't help wondering if Karla's going to try to push Autumn out of our lives," I replied. "You know how she was—possessive. She's not going to be happy when she finds out there's someone else in all of this, you know?"

"Does Autumn know she's back?"

I nodded.

"I told her about it the day it happened," I replied. "I think I was a little harsh with her. I was still so shocked."

"And what did she think?" Raymond asked.

"Same as you, that I should give her a chance," I sighed. "But I don't know if she understands the impact that could have on us. Not really."

"You should credit her with a little more foresight." Raymond raised his eyebrows at me. "She's not stupid. And I'm sure she was prepared for something like this, even if you weren't. She knows she's not Hunter's mother, and—"

"And she'd be a better mother to him than Karla could ever dream of," I finished up for him, the words catching me off guard. I hadn't realized the conviction with which I believed them until that moment. I mean, I wouldn't have been with Autumn if I didn't think she would have made a good mother to Hunter, but at the same time, hearing those words come out of my mouth with such conviction made this situation even harder. Just when I'd found someone who could give Hunter what he needed, what we both needed so badly, and Karla came drifting back into our lives like she'd always belonged there.

"I think you have your answer then," Raymond pointed out gently. "When are you seeing Autumn next?"

"I'm seeing her when I pick up Hunter from school today." I glanced at my watch. "Shit, I should get going."

"Don't let this get to you," Raymond told me, getting to his feet to walk me to the door. "I know this is a lot for you to take in, but it's workable. You know what you want, and that's the most important thing."

"I sure as fuck hope so," I replied, managing to smile in thanks for his kind words. "I'll let you know how it all goes, all right?"

"All right." He nodded. "And if you need any help with Karla, you let me know."

"Thanks, man," I closed my eyes for a moment. "I'll see you again soon."

I headed out to the car, my mind still racing, trying to make sense of everything swirling around in my brain. I wanted to be with Autumn. I'd known that for so long that it felt like second nature, like a fact that had always been true in the back of my mind. But at the same time, I knew keeping Hunter from his mother would only come back to bite me in the ass years down the line. I didn't want him to think I'd been trying to keep them apart, divide them. I was wary of Karla, more than I realized I was, and I didn't want her anywhere near my son, nor the life I had so carefully built for him. I didn't want her sticking her nose in and messing everything up, which is exactly what she would do if I gave her the chance.

And she said she wanted me. I had been firm in shutting that down, but what if she wouldn't let it go? What if she saw us as a package deal? That was going to be hard to shut down, especially if I did decide to let her have some contact with Hunter. I wasn't sure what to do. I felt as though every avenue open to me was the wrong choice, the choice that would leave someone close to me hurt in ways I never wanted to inflict on them.

I arrived at the school and waited outside in my car for a few minutes. I wanted it to go back to being like it had been before Karla had shown up again. Things had been going so well for a change. After so long feeling like I was fighting to keep going, life had been happy, easy, fun. And that was all threatening to be pulled out from under me.

I forced myself out of the car. I had to pick up Hunter, and I didn't want to be late and tip him off that there was something serious going on. He was a smart kid, a sensitive one, and the last thing I wanted was for him to catch on to what was going on with Karla. I winced as her name crossed my mind once more. I hated this. I hated that she had come back to make everything harder, to make me second-guess every decision I'd made over the course of the last ten years. I had done well enough without her, but all these questions were rising, unanswered, and hanging out at the back of my mind. It was an uncomfortable feeling, to doubt myself after so long, and I didn't want to have to get used to it.

I headed inside the school, and Hunter was already there, waiting for me. He ran up to me and gave me a hug, and I held him close, savoring these moments with him. I wasn't sure how long they would stick around before everything changed again.

"I need to talk to Jason," he told me firmly, as though he was informing me about an important business meeting. "Can I have five minutes?"

"Of course." I smiled at him and watched him run off to be with his friends. At least that was something that had changed unarguably for the better, Hunter having people around who cared about him beyond me. I glanced up and saw Autumn leaning in the doorway of her classroom, an expression on her face that I couldn't quite read.

"Hey," she greeted me, making her way to me. "I think we need to talk."

"I think we do too." I sighed. I knew I'd come down too hard when I'd seen her before, and I needed to let her know there was no problem with her, just with Karla.

"I've been thinking about what you told me." She took a deep breath, her brow furrowing. "And... and I think we should take a break."

"What?"

My heart dropped. This couldn't be happening. This was what I'd been afraid of, the direct opposite of what I wanted from this conversation.

"I don't want to get in the way of whatever's happening between you and Karla." She glanced over to where Hunter had scurried off, and I saw the flash of pain pass over her face. I realized this was real. She was truly walking away from this, from us.

"Autumn, that's not what I want," I told her desperately. "I know things are going to be complicated, but the last thing I need right now—"

"The last thing you need right now is having to consider my feelings on top of everything else that's going on," she told me gently. "I know it sounds crazy, but Holden, I don't want to get in the way of your family."

"Karla's not my family." I shook my head. "She left us when he was born. She signed away all her rights—"

"She might not be your family, but she's Hunter's," she replied softly. She was smiling, but it seemed to be a ploy to keep the tears from coming. Panic was rushing through my system. Why had I told her about it? Why I had come in all hot-headed and forced her to deal with this? I should have held back, waited till I had things figured out.

"And I don't want to get in the middle of this," she told me. "I don't want to complicate matters any more than they already have been."

"You're not complicating anything," I replied desperately. "You make everything easier. Autumn, please—"

"Holden, please don't make this any harder on me than it has to be." She held her hand up and looked away from me. "I know this is hard, but we both need space. It's better in the long run."

And with that, she turned to head back into the classroom, closing the door behind her. I stood there, speechless, trying to take in what she'd said to me. Hunter came running back up to me and nudged me.

"Dad?"

I looked down at him, blinking, trying to come back to reality.

"Can we go home now?" he asked brightly. His face was clear and serene, no idea of the mess going on around him at that moment.

"Yeah, we can go home," I replied, and I turned to walk out of the school—and couldn't help wondering if I was walking out of Autumn's life for good as well.

47

HOLDEN

I stared down at the photographs in front of me. I'd been looking at them for so long, they started to blur around the edges, but I didn't care. I couldn't look away.

I was leafing through some pictures of Hunter from the last few years of his life especially. It was crazy how much he had grown up in that time, how he had gone from being a boy to a little man, and I couldn't help smiling as I traced his growth from baby to the ten-year-old he was now. How could that much time have passed already? It didn't make sense to me. Yet as I looked at him like this, a pang of sadness overwhelmed me.

I had missed so much of his life while I'd been setting up the business. It had been the right thing at the time, of course—or at least I had managed to convince myself that was the case. But looking at these photos, I couldn't dismiss the fact that I didn't remember every single one, every single occasion. I wasn't even in a lot of them, probably off taking a call or checking my email while Raymond had been snapping the photograph. Perhaps I should have been there for him more. If I could go back in time and do it again, I would have shoved to the back of my mind the urge to prove Karla wrong above all else and would have focused on being the father my son needed.

He was out spending time with one of his friends that afternoon, and I was glad for a little peace. It had been such a hectic week, and I felt as though my brain was going to start leaking out of my head. Seven days before, Autumn Becks, the woman I was falling in love with, had told me that we needed to take a break, and I'd been reeling from the shock of it ever since. Even thinking about her hurt me in a visceral way, a way I'd never prepared for. There was something else I had taken for granted, something else that had slipped through my fingers before I had a chance to take hold of it. If only I had made it clearer when we first got together that I didn't care about Karla, Hunter's mother. If only I had made it more obvious that Autumn was the only woman I needed. Maybe she would have stuck around even after Karla appeared in my life again. Instead, she had taken a step back from me, and I hadn't heard from her since. I was giving her all the space she needed, but I craved her there by my side to help guide me through this strange new place I found myself in.

I had barely left the house all week, focusing all my energy on work and Hunter in the hopes of shutting down those panicked thoughts about the two women in my life who wouldn't give me a moment's rest inside my head. One of them, Autumn, was new and fresh and exciting, the kind of woman I could see myself with in any serious way, the woman who had turned me around on the thought of dating again. Then there was the woman from my past, the last woman I had dated before Autumn, the mother of my child and the person who had spurred me to become the man I was today by telling me she never thought I would amount to anything. They were both important in their own ways, but I didn't have space for both of them in my head at once.

A knock came at the door, ringing through the quiet of the house and taking me by surprise. I lifted my head up from the pictures and tried to remember if I'd invited anyone over that day, but I couldn't remember suggesting anyone come around. I got to my feet and headed to the door, peering through the keyhole, and found Raymond waiting on the other side for me.

I opened the door, and he grinned at me. He knew what was

going on with Autumn and Karla, and he'd been there from the start for all the bullshit with my ex. Being the good friend that he was, he was likely here to get me out of the damn house and make sure I didn't spend my time festering and hiding from all the trouble chasing me right now.

"Well, good day to you, sir." He raised his eyebrows. "Been a while since I saw you last. You doing all right?"

"I'm doing okay," I lied. He cocked his head at me.

"Are you?" he remarked, giving me the once-over. "Because you look like a hermit."

I ran my hand over my unshaven chin and sighed. He was right. I needed to get out of the house and have an excuse to clean myself up a little. But I didn't want to go anywhere.

"Come on, I'm taking you out to lunch," he told me firmly, brushing past me and into the house. I shook my head.

"No. I mean, I have work to do."

"Yeah, like you haven't been using that to distract yourself all week," he said. "Come on, just for an hour. I know a place close enough. I won't take up much of your day, I promise. Besides, seems like you could use the trip out, huh?"

"Fine." I sighed. "Can you give me a minute to shave and get myself ready?"

"I think you'd better," he teased. "You really think I'd be seen out with you looking like that?"

"All right, point taken." I waved my hand at him and retreated to my bedroom to get myself dressed and cleaned. I felt like a slob. I usually took a great deal of pride in my appearance, but now that Autumn was out of my life, I didn't have much reason to any longer. I had even avoided picking up Hunter at school when I knew she would be there, and I waited outside the gates so he could come out and find me. The thought of looking her in the eye and letting her see the mess I had become within only a few days without her was too humiliating.

I headed out to meet Raymond, and he clapped his hands together.

"There, you're already looking more like yourself." He jerked his head toward the door. "Let's get going. I'm starving."

I followed him out to the car and let him drive me to this place he wanted to take me to. It turned out to be a quaint little seafood place near the water, which would have been perfect if driving this way didn't remind me so instantly of my date with Autumn. We'd come down here to get ice cream. We had kissed on the pier, and it had been so perfect, it made my heart hurt a little to know I wouldn't get to do it again any time soon. I asked Raymond about Olivia and the baby to distract myself, and he happily chatted to me about fatherhood and how he was adjusting having a newborn. It was good to talk to him, to get my mind off the constant thoughts that had been running around in my head since last week.

"What are you going to have?" I asked him as we took our seats and looked down at the menu. My stomach was growling. I was starving, having not eaten nearly enough these last few days. I had been too distracted and depressed. Thank God Raymond was here to try and help make things better.

He shrugged. "I don't know yet. You want to split some stuff?"

"Sure," I agreed, and I found myself relaxing. It was nice to have some human company after everything that had happened—adult company too. Hunter was awesome, but he was hardly what I needed to help talk me through the intensity of everything that had happened the past few days. He didn't have a clue his mother was anywhere near us, and he'd been cheerfully asking when we were going out with Autumn again.

"How are you doing?" Raymond asked once we'd ordered, sitting back in his seat and giving me a hard look across the table. I shrugged.

"Yeah, fine, I guess," I replied, and he shook his head.

"Come on. I know you've been through a hell of a lot these last few days," he told me gently. "How are you coping with it? How's it going with Karla?"

"She's tried to call me a few times, but I haven't picked up." I shook my head. "I don't want to have to deal with her at the moment.

I'm too... I don't know. I just never thought I would have to handle her or her bullshit ever again. I need some time to wrap my head around the fact that I do now."

"And what about everything with Autumn?" he pressed. I snorted, but there wasn't much actual amusement in my tone.

"Okay, now there's someone I'd actually like to hear from, but I haven't," I admitted, letting out a long sigh. "I've tried to get hold of her, but she's not replied to any of my calls, and I don't want to push her further than she's already been pushed. You know what I mean?"

"Fuck." Raymond shook his head. "This is one hell of a mess, isn't it?"

"Sure is," I agreed, trying to keep my voice upbeat but knowing it was reading as depressing. I didn't want to bring him down, but he was insistent on pushing the issue.

"Have you thought about talking to Karla?" he asked. I lifted my eyes to his and gave him a long look.

"No." I shook my head after a pause. "I don't want anything to do with her if I can avoid it. She just... no. I can't stand the thought of having her in my life, in Hunter's life—especially because she told me she wants the two of us to get back together as well."

"Okay, you don't have to go that far," he conceded. "But maybe it would be worth talking things out with her a little? Seeing where she's coming from?"

I fell silent. I knew he was right, and that was the frustrating part. I wanted nothing more than for Karla to drop out of my life and out of my son's life and leave me alone once more, but that wasn't how this worked. She was back once and for all, and she wasn't going to leave us alone until she got what she felt like she was owed, a relationship with her child.

"I guess I could," I muttered, and Raymond nodded.

"Only way to deal with any of this is to jump into it head-on," he said, and I grimaced.

"Yeah, well, I'm still going to be over here trying to avoid everything if I can." I cocked an eyebrow, and he chuckled.

"Good luck doing that when I know where you live and need you for babysitting duties," he warned me, picking up his cutlery as the waiter approached. I managed a smile as he placed our food down in front of us. Sure, this whole thing was more than a bit of a mess, but Raymond was right. The only way through it was to throw myself in headfirst and hope I could find a way out the other side. That meant listening to Karla and finding out precisely what she wanted from me.

48

AUTUMN

"Miss Becks?"

I looked up from my computer, and my heart sank when I found my gaze meeting Hunter's. School had gotten out, and he'd ducked back into the classroom for a moment to talk to me. He was the last kid I wanted to see at that moment but at the same time, the only one. I managed to smile at him.

"Hey, Hunter." I greeted him with as much lightness as I could muster. "Are you all right?"

"I made you this." He reached into his bag and thrust a piece of paper in my direction. I picked it up and checked it out, turning the orange card over in my hands, and my heart sank when I saw what it was. Just a card, a little one with his spidery handwriting over the front, telling me that he missed me.

"Thank you, Hunter." I smiled at him, trying to keep the rush of tears that were threatening to take me over at bay. "I really appreciate this."

He smiled, but he didn't look satisfied yet.

"I don't know what my dad did wrong," he said, "but I'm sorry. I hope you come back soon."

My heart twisted, and before I could stop myself, I got out of my seat and went to give him a quick hug. I knew I should have sent him away to meet Holden at the gates, but he looked so forlorn standing there in front of me that I couldn't leave him to it.

"It's all right, Hunter," I promised him. "Thank you for the card."

I drew back from him and found him gazing at me expectantly. I knew he wanted me to tell him I was about to come back, that all of this had been a mistake and I was going to turn around and head back home with him and his father. But I couldn't as much as I wanted to.

"Spring break's coming up soon," I reminded him, trying to cheer him up before he left. "Do you have anything planned?"

"Nothing yet." He shook his head, still looking a little down.

"I'm sure your dad has something awesome planned for you." I smiled at him, squeezing his arm. He managed to smile back, but I could tell it was strained.

"You should get going," I told him, nodding toward the door. "I'm sure your dad will be waiting outside to pick you up."

With that, he ducked out of the classroom and left me all alone. I had been working on some of the grade curves since class had let out, and it was so much easier now that I was using the program Holden had made for it. Every time I booted up the website he was hosting it on, I felt a little pang, remembering how we had gone through this in his study after he'd cooked me dinner. I just wanted to be near him again, more than anything else in the world. I wanted to feel his arms wrapped tight around me, wanted to rest my head on his chest and tell him I loved him, those words I had been too nervous to say before, certain it was too soon.

"Good evening." Zoe breezed into the room, flashing me a big smile that dropped suddenly off her face when she saw the expression on mine. "Hey, are you all right?"

"Yeah," I said with a sigh. I had caught Zoe up with everything that had happened, and she had been so supportive all that time, but it would be impossible to express the mess I found myself in right now.

"You working on the grade curves?" She came around my desk to get a look. "I was too. But mine got done so quickly. This program works so fuckin' well. I can actually take some time off for spring break this year for a change instead of being stuck at my desk churning out those godforsaken things."

"Yeah, I'm getting my last few done," I told her. I had no plans for spring break. I was only planning on lazing around at my house feeling sorry for myself and mulling over what had happened between Holden and me. It was far from healthy, but I needed time to process it properly. I had been throwing myself into work to avoid thinking about it, which was only going to make it harder in the long run. Especially since Hunter was right there every time I came to my job, a potent reminder of what I'd walked away from when I ended things with Holden.

"You going to take some time off?" Zoe asked, flopping down in the seat opposite me and crossing her arms over her chest. I knew she was trying to distract me, and I appreciated the effort to help me out, even though I was having a hard time thinking about anything but Holden and what had happened between us.

"I mean, I guess I should," I admitted, and I could see her eyes shining with—well, I wasn't sure what it was, but I had a feeling, given that she was here, that it had something to do with me. I cocked an eyebrow.

"What's going on?" I asked, and a huge grin spread across Zoe's face.

"I..." She shook her head and closed her eyes as though savoring this moment before she dropped the news on me. "I want to take you on a trip, Autumn."

"Like where?" A smile spread over my face, despite my mood.

"Vegas." She raised her hands as though offering me some sacred gift. My eyebrows shot up, and I burst out laughing.

"Vegas?" I giggled. "You've got to be kidding."

"You've never been, have you?" She leaned forward eagerly.

I shook my head. "No, and I can't say I've ever been that interested."

She lifted a hand to stop me in my tracks. "Trust me, you've got no idea what you're in for. It's the most fun you'll have in the states. And it'd be good for you to get away."

"I'm not looking to go get drunk and sleep with strangers." I shook my head again. "It's not my style."

"Oh, fuck, me neither," she agreed. "But there's so much more to do out there than that. I spend most of the time there lazing around beside the pool and drinking cocktails."

"Then you actually do the getting drunk bit?" I waggled my eyebrows, and she rolled her eyes playfully.

"So sue me, I like a few mimosas by the water." She grinned. "Come on, Autumn. We'll both have the time to spare. Just for a few days. I've already booked the hotel."

"What? Without speaking to me first?"

"Because I knew you'd find some way to talk yourself out of it," she pointed out. "Like you're doing right now."

"Yeah, well, maybe because—"

"Maybe because you were hoping to spend that whole week sitting around at home and mulling over everything that happened with you and Holden?" she asked. I fell silent. She was right. I would have hung around my house feeling sorry for myself and wishing I could be somewhere else. Well, Zoe was offering me that chance for something else. I would have been crazy to turn it down.

"I suppose you're right." I finally gave in, and I felt a little flutter of excitement at the thought of it. It could be fun to get out of town, to blow off some steam. It had been a hell of a stressful few months with everything happening, even if most of it had been good stress, and I was already looking forward to leaving that all behind right here and spending more time than was strictly necessary lying around in a bikini and sipping on expensive cocktails. I had a little savings put away, and they weren't doing anything right now, so I might as well tap into it to show myself a good time for a change.

"We should think about looking at those red-eye flights," I suggested. "Get something really cheap."

"Plus it'll cut the cost of the hotel room if we get in there early,"

Zoe pointed out with a smile. "More money for cocktails and cheap bikinis."

"Okay, that does actually sound pretty good," I conceded, and she clapped her hands together.

She beamed. "I knew you'd come around to it. It's going to be so much fun. That place is built for blowing off some steam and having a good time. It's totally where you need to be right now."

"All right, but if I go bankrupt gambling, I'm holding you personally responsible." I leveled my finger at her across the table.

"I solemnly swear that I'll keep you away from any and all casinos." She planted her hand on her heart like she was making the Girl Scout pledge. "Unless that's where the cheap drinks are."

"I can't believe I'm agreeing to this." I shook my head. "Just to be clear, this doesn't give you the right to start planning trips for me all over the place."

"I promise." She flashed me a smile, and I could already tell she was planning where to take me next now that she'd managed to twist my arm into going to Vegas with her.

"Thank you for this." I reached over and touched her hand. "I really needed to get away. I feel like I'm going crazy, you know? With all this stuff that's been happening with Holden, especially with Hunter around on top of everything."

She smiled at me sweetly. "You're welcome. Anything to help you out. You know that."

"And when it comes with a trip to Vegas as well—"

"All the better," Zoe finished up for me and got to her feet. "Let's go get some dinner, and we can start looking at what flights we're going to take out."

"Sure thing." I closed off my computer, and a weight lifted off of me. It wouldn't last forever, but I would take it for now—the relief, the briefest little moment of peace from the maelstrom that had been consuming my brain these last few days. I paused for a moment, took a deep breath, and then followed Zoe out of the room. I was going to be all right. All of this was going to be all right. Or, at least, that's what I had to keep telling myself until it became true.

49

"Hey, buddy, are you almost ready to go?" I asked, waiting by the door for Hunter to come downstairs so I could drop him off at school. He had been a little lethargic lately, as though he was coming down with something, but I had a feeling it had more to do with the fact that Autumn wasn't in our lives anymore. He hadn't had any explanation for it, and he must have questions about what happened between the two of us, questions I had no idea how to answer. I didn't even have those answers myself. How was I meant to articulate them to my son?

"Yeah." He emerged from the top of the stairs and headed down to join me. He looked tired like he'd struggled to sleep the night before. I knew how he felt. I had been up most of the night wondering if I was doing the right thing today in meeting with Karla.

"Let's get going, shall we?" I opened the door for him, and he headed outside to the car. I watched him as he went. Once in a while, it struck me how little he was, how delicate and small this entire boy's existence seemed. I wanted to take care of him, to protect him from the world at large, but I had no idea how to do that anymore. I had been sure Autumn was a way to help with that, but these days, I wasn't so sure.

I climbed into the car next to him, and we pulled away. Normally, Hunter took these opportunities to chat away to me about what he was doing that day and about everything he was looking forward to, but that morning, he was curiously silent.

"You okay?" I asked him, and he shrugged. "What are you thinking about?"

He turned to me with a long sigh, as though even letting himself linger in this place in his mind was painful to him.

"When will Autumn be coming back?" he asked me, and my heart dropped. It had been the one question I had hoped to God he would never ask of me. I swallowed heavily, knowing I had to come up with something.

"I don't know, Hunter," I admitted.

"Did I do something wrong?" He frowned.

"No!" I exclaimed at once. "No, buddy, you didn't do anything wrong. Things have just changed a bit. But Autumn still cares about you a lot and so do I. You know that, right?"

"I guess," he agreed, but I could hear the doubt in his voice, the second-guessing. I hated that he felt that way, hated that it had been my choice to bring Autumn into our lives that had caused him this kind of pain. If I could have gone back in time, knowing what I did now, perhaps I wouldn't have gone through with any of it.

I dropped him off at school and frowned as I watched him make his way into the building. He was clearly unhappy at the moment, and I would have done anything to make it right. Maybe this meeting with Karla would be what I needed to get things moving again? Maybe Hunter needed a mother in his life more than I had known. Now that Autumn had opted out, perhaps his real mother was my best choice.

I headed home to change and prepare myself for this meeting with Karla. I was nervous beyond belief, my hands shaking as I went to button up my shirt. I had shared so much with this woman, and she had walked away from me when times had been hard. How could I look her in the eye again and find any sort of kindness when she had failed to do the same for me?

I drove out to the diner where we'd agreed to meet, and I felt a flicker of guilt for not letting Hunter know about any of this. She was his mother, after all. Perhaps I owed him that much. But the thought of inflicting more hope on him only to drag it away after what he had already been through—no, I couldn't do that to him, not again. I had to handle this myself, as his father.

I arrived outside the diner and brought the car to a halt, closing my eyes and trying to swallow the last vestiges of my nerves. I felt like I was going to throw up. For a moment, I considered turning around and getting out of there, forgetting this whole thing had ever happened and rewinding time to before she had turned up at my house. But I had to face this. Once and for all.

Forcing myself out of the car, I headed up to the diner. I could already see her sitting in a booth on the far side, looking out over the street beyond. I pushed open the door, and she looked up into my eyes, and I felt a jolt as though I had been knocked backward through time.

I headed over to join her, taking my time, and took in Karla properly for the first time since her reappearance in my life. I had been so shocked the first time she had come by that I hadn't had much of a chance to really get my head around her again, but now I was a little calmer and could take her in.

She was still beautiful, still had that long, thick dark hair that fell in waves over her shoulders. Her eyes were a sharp and piercing gray, always looking fascinated by everything that was going on around her. She didn't miss a thing, for better or for worse, though sometimes I felt like it was the latter. But her beauty wasn't enough to distract me from the memory of everything she had done, from the snake she really was beneath that flower. She had abandoned me to raise our son alone, and she had to have a good reason for wanting back into his life after all this time.

"Holden." She smiled at me as I took a seat opposite her. She was sipping on a coffee and seemed totally at ease, in direct contrast to me. "You want something to eat?"

"No, I'm fine." I shook my head. I couldn't even think about food at that moment. My stomach was churning with nerves.

"How are you doing?" she asked conversationally. I couldn't believe she was approaching this with such casualness like we were a couple of old friends meeting for breakfast.

"I'd rather skip the niceties and get straight to the point," I told her, and her eyes flickered with irritation. She never liked feeling out of control of any situation, so this had to be frustrating her. But I wasn't here to indulge her anymore.

"Fine," she snapped back at me. "If you want to do it like that, so be it. I want to see my son again. I want to be part of his life."

"Why do you feel that way now?" I demanded. "After everything that happened?"

"Because I can't live without seeing him anymore," she told me, her eyes wide and playing at sincere. "I miss him so much, Holden. You don't even know—"

"No, you don't know." I stopped her in her tracks. "You don't know him. How can you miss someone you don't know?"

"You couldn't possibly understand." She shook her head and gestured to her belly. "I carried him for all that time, and I've never stopped missing him since, never stopped wondering how he was—"

"But you never bothered to check in on him until now," I finished up for her. "And what exactly brought you here this time? Why now?"

"Can't I just want to see my son again?" she demanded, her voice rising a little so that it attracted the attention of a couple of people sitting in the booths around us.

"I've been raising Hunter by myself for nearly ten years," I reminded her. "I'm not letting you walk back in and play at being this perfect mother."

"I know things will be hard at first," she confessed, and she reached across the table to grab my hands as she spoke. I let them lay there in her grasp, not having the energy to pull them away and have her make a scene about my rejection.

"I don't think they're going to stop being hard," I pointed out to her. "I mean, you don't think Hunter's going to want to know why you weren't there for most of his life?"

"Then we tell him the truth," she replied as though it should have been obvious. I raised my eyebrows.

"Let me get this straight." I leaned toward her. "You want me to tell my son that you left him when he was a baby and never came back because you couldn't be bothered with him?"

"Tell him that people change," she protested desperately. "Things don't always stay the same. Holden, I've changed so much in the last few years. You don't even know."

"And let me guess, something happened to push you all the way back here?" I demanded, pulling my hands away from her.

"Holden, my life has been a wreck these last few months," she confessed, as though I hadn't put those pieces together already. I had assumed something had to have happened to drive her to do something as extreme as this, but I couldn't, for the life of me, figure out what it might have been.

"What happened?" I sighed. I figured I had to find out the truth if I had any hope of understanding what it was she was doing here and what she really wanted from me.

"I was with this man," she admitted. "We were together for a long time, Holden. You would have liked him. He took care of me, he made my life so easy for a while, and we were so happy together..."

Actual sadness filled her eyes—not a play at it but some real pain. I would have felt bad for her if I didn't know she was using this to get something out of me.

"He told me he would support me doing anything I wanted," she continued, her eyes snapping to anger instead. "But he left me. He dumped me. With *nothing*. No money and no job and no notice. I don't have anything, Holden, and I thought... I thought maybe the three of us could have *something*."

So this was a rebound. That made a lot of sense to me. She was coming here in the hopes of putting back together the pieces of her life she felt she had lost control of.

"I'll give you money," I told her bluntly. "Is that what you want? Call it child support. I don't mind."

"It's not about that." She shook her head, but there was a hint of something in her eyes—greed maybe—as though she was edging toward something she really did want.

"I'm not letting you into his life just like that," I told her firmly. "I'm sorry things have been hard for you, but they've been hard for us, too, and I think you coming back is only going to make things harder."

"I'll take you to court over this," she threatened me, flattening her palm on the table. "Don't think I won't."

"I'll be happy to see you there," I told her, trying to keep my voice steady. "But you can't walk back into Hunter's life and act like everything's going to be fine. I can't have that. I've worked too hard to make things secure for him."

"You don't know what you're doing." Her face twisted up into a mask of anger. "You have no idea how hard it is for a boy to be raised without his mother."

"You're the one who made that choice," I reminded her. "You had all this time to make things right, and you never did. You can't undo the past, Karla."

Before she could say another word, I got to my feet.

"You're not even going to hear me out?" she exclaimed, sounding pissed. I closed my eyes for a moment, gathered myself, and then looked her dead in the eye.

"I've given you the chance," I told her. "If you want to work out something more long-term and stable for Hunter, I'd be willing to talk about it. But you can't expect both of us to drop everything and let you act like you were never away. That's too much of an upset for Hunter."

"And what about me?" she demanded. "Don't you care that you're keeping a mother away from her son?"

"About as much as you cared about it when you left us ten years ago," I told her. Her jaw dropped, and she had nothing else to say.

Before she could come up with something, I turned to walk out of the diner.

As soon as the cool air hit me, I felt a wave of relief. It was over. I had known she was doing this to make a point, to grab our lives and insert herself into them so she could finagle some form of stability from somewhere. But I wasn't going to let her do that to my son. Or to me. Things had been wild enough as it was without her, and I wasn't going to put either of us through any more. And I sure as hell wasn't going to let her manipulate her way back into my life. Not without a fight.

50

AUTUMN

As I stepped off the plane and inhaled a deep lungful of the crisp morning air, I felt a little waver in my stomach. Had this been the right choice?

"Come on, come on. I want to get to the hotel." Zoe grabbed my hand and tugged me along impatiently, and I hurried to keep up with her. She was wearing an enormous hat that drooped down around her head, a pair of shorts, and a strappy top, and she looked like she'd been plucked from the poster of an old-fashioned, risqué vacation flick.

"Hey, hey, I'm going as fast as I can," I protested as I hurried to keep up with her. "I got up in the middle of the night to make it here, remember?"

"Oh, enough of your complaining." She rolled her eyes playfully. "We're in Vegas! Aren't you excited?"

"Yeah, I am," I assured her, even though I wasn't certain I was telling the truth. Sure, it was nice to get away somewhere new for a change, but some part of me felt... uncomfortable? Maybe it was because I hadn't been anywhere but Portland for so long, but I couldn't fight the feeling that I was in the wrong place, that this city wasn't right for me.

We collected our bags and bundled into an overpriced cab to our hotel not far from the center of the city. The separate rooms had been cheap, and I was glad I would have somewhere to rest up soon. But Zoe seemed to be buzzing with excitement, ready for us to take on anything Las Vegas had for us.

"Okay, when we get there, we get something to eat." She ticked the ideas off on her fingers. "And we get changed, go down to the pool, and start drinking."

"And then?"

"And then we see where the night takes us!" she exclaimed, her eyes glinting with excitement at the thought. "Oh my God, it's going to be so much fun."

I was exhausted by the thought of it, but she had gone to such great lengths to organize this for us, and I didn't want to let her down, so I ignored the nagging little voice at the back of my head. I told myself I was here to have a good time, not to sit around brooding on whether or not I had remembered to turn down my thermostat before I'd left home.

"I'm going to dump my stuff in my room and take a shower," Zoe told me excitedly as we arrived at the hotel and picked up our keys. "I'll meet you downstairs for the buffet soon, all right?"

"Sure thing." I nodded. My stomach was grumbling, and eating a damn good breakfast was at least something I could get behind. I went to change and wash up and arrived down at the bar area not long afterward. Zoe, as she usually did, was taking a while to put herself together, so I ordered a coffee and took a seat at the bar, scanning the surrounding area and trying to get myself to kick back and actually fucking relax since I was all the way in Vegas.

The place was nice if not super glamorous. It was certainly built for the less discerning tourist, which was fine since that was precisely what I was. Clean but unremarkable. I took a sip of my coffee and began to brighten up. I was so far from home, maybe I could actually let go of some of the shit that had been plaguing me the whole time I was there and have a good trip with Zoe.

I felt a pair of eyes on me, and I turned around, expecting to see

Zoe bouncing toward me from the entrance arch to the bar. Instead, I found a man looking at me. If I had been in the mood for flirtation, he would have been precisely the kind of person I would do it with. He was handsome, a few years older than me, with some streaks of gray in his hair and a dark beard that suited him well enough. He was grinning at me as he slid over to join me at the bar, taking the seat next to me.

"Well, hey," he drawled, in a voice that was attempting to sound sexy, I assumed. I stifled a giggle.

"Hey," I greeted him.

"You just arrive here?" he asked, and I nodded.

"Thought I would have noticed you at the hotel if you'd arrived before this," he said, letting his eyes swim all over my body. I tugged down the hem of the short teal dress I had thrown on over my bikini and shifted in my seat, not sure how to react.

"You come here often?" he asked. "To Vegas, I mean."

"No, this is my first time." I shook my head. "My friend brought me out here. She said I'd love it."

"Oh, wow." He nodded. "There's so much stuff to do, especially around here. What kind of things are you into?"

"Uh..."

"Like food, music, movies." He cocked an eyebrow at me. "That's what I'm asking about."

"Oh." I laughed. "Uh, I guess food. Or maybe that's on my mind because I've not eaten any breakfast yet."

"There's plenty of places around here I'm sure you'd like," he said. "I could show you if you like."

"Oh, no, it's fine." I waved my hand, not wanting to put him out. "I get a free breakfast as part of the deal with the room. You don't have to worry about that."

"Or maybe I just want to take you out," he said. I made a face. "Is it that awful a thought?" He half-laughed, and I felt like an ass for reacting the way I had.

"I'm sorry. I'm not really out here looking for... anything."

"You came to the city of sin with the plan not to commit a single one?" he shot back, and his voice was a little barbed as if he didn't like that I wasn't receptive to his advances. Did he often chat up women at hotel bars like this? Did he often do it *successfully?*

"Yeah, I guess so," I conceded, shrugging cheerfully and taking a sip of my coffee. I kind of wanted to be left alone, but I got the feeling this guy wasn't going to let it go that easily.

"Sure I can't tempt you to a drink, at least?" he suggested. "On me. To celebrate your first time in Vegas."

"Really, I'm fine," I replied firmly. I craned my neck around to see if Zoe was anywhere near arriving yet. I just wanted this guy to fuck off and leave me the hell alone, but he didn't give off the easygoing vibe that he had at first.

"I'm not asking for much of your time," he told me, and my opinion of him soured swiftly.

"Yeah, and I'm not asking for any of yours," I snapped back. He raised his eyebrows.

"Damn, I like a bit of feistiness in my women," he remarked, grinning widely as though he had achieved something by getting me to respond that way. I wanted to kick myself. To this kind of man, any reaction was still a reaction he could hook into, proof that he was getting under my skin and could get what he wanted.

"I'm going to leave now," I told him. "If you see me here again, don't bother talking to me."

"Fine, fine." He held his hands up, acting shocked by my lack of interest and apparent irritation.

As I walked off, I heard him speaking to the bartender, and I did my best to tune him out, but he seemed determined to make sure I heard him.

"And there I was thinking she would be an easy lay," he commented. I felt my cheeks burn hot, and I wanted to turn around and scream at him, chew him out in front of everyone in this place for acting like he could speak about me that way when I was right there in the room. But letting him rile me up would be enough to start the conversation again, and the last thing I wanted was that. I paused for a moment, gathered myself, and marched out of there, trying to ignore that my cheeks were burning with rage.

Before I got all the way out, I bumped into Zoe, who had a big, breezy smile on her face and looked about as full of the joys of life as I'd ever seen her. I instantly felt a twist of guilt. She had gone to all this effort for me, and I was already letting some jerk-off with a complex about winning me over get under my skin?

"You okay?" Zoe asked, grabbing my arm and leaning away from me to take me in. She could obviously read the anger on my face, and I worked hard to clear it away as fast as I could.

"Yeah, yeah, I'm fine," I promised her. "Just hungry, that's all. Let's get something to eat."

"Yeah, agreed." She nodded, rubbing her closed fist into her stomach. "I could really use some breakfast."

We ate together, and thankfully, the man who had been at the bar before didn't so much as bother to make eye contact with me this time. Probably because I wasn't as easy a lay as he'd imagined. We ate way too much, and I was starting to feel a little better.

"Hey, walk me back to my room?" Zoe asked. "I want to brush my hair before we go to the pool."

"Sure. I need to charge my phone anyway."

I followed her back up the stairs, and I ducked into my room as she headed into hers. Plugging my phone in, I went to check my makeup, and that's when I heard my cell buzz to life on the counter next to the bed.

I went to pick it up, assuming it would be some spam from my cell provider. Instead, I saw a number I recognized, a number I had done my best to forget.

"Hey, Autumn. Hope you're doing well. I miss you. H x"

My heart sank, and just like that, all the hard work I'd been doing to convince myself I was doing all right seemed to slip away from me. How could things be okay when he was all the way back in Portland and missing me? I ached to have him close to me, and I held the phone up to my chest, pressing it to the spot above my heart. I knew I was acting crazy, and I didn't care. No matter how much space I put between the two of us, I was still going to miss him. Nothing could change that.

I stared down at the message for a long time and chewed on my lip. I should have ignored it and gotten on with the rest of my trip. But I couldn't. I opened a new message, hesitated for a moment, and then tapped out a response of my own.

51

HOLDEN

When my phone buzzed on the desk, I practically jumped out of my skin and snatched it up from the spot where I had left it. I had tried to talk myself out of texting Autumn, but I figured one little message would be permissible—nothing too intense. But I didn't realize until I got that response right back how overly invested I had been in hearing from her as I scrambled to open the reply she had sent me.

"Hey," it read. "I miss you too. X"

My heart leaped when I saw it, and I couldn't stop smiling. I knew I wasn't exactly doing a breakup properly, but I didn't care. I just wanted to hear from her, about her, anything like that—get the chance to talk to the woman I missed so much, there was a great big hole in my heart where she had once been.

"You want me to come and see you?" I shot back, knowing I was pushing my luck. Hunter was on spring break at the moment, and though I had offered to take him off for a trip somewhere, he had insisted on staying home, probably worried he was going to miss Autumn if he got out of there. I decided not to push my luck and let him hide out in his room while I got some work done. I knew how he felt. Sometimes, I wanted nothing more than to lock the door to my room and pretend the world at large couldn't find me.

"Can't really manage that," she shot back. "I'm in Vegas."

"Vegas?"

"Vegas. Zoe took me out here to cheer me up, but it's not really working."

"Cheer you up?"

"After what happened with us."

I closed my eyes and ran my fingers through my hair. She was just being nice, that was all. Just sharing a little conversation. But to me, it felt like a lifeline, something to hook on to, something I could use to pull us back together where we belonged.

"I've been thinking about you so much," I replied.

"Me too," she agreed. "I wish I could see you right now."

The words glared up at me from the screen, and an idea bounced into my brain—an idea I instantly recognized as totally mad, of course, but an idea nonetheless. I put my phone into my pocket and began to pace the office for a moment, trying to figure out if this really was the stupidest idea I'd ever had or if there was something in there worth chasing down for a change.

Fuck it. I loved this woman. I knew that for sure, and here she was texting me to tell me she missed me and she wanted to see me. Why would I run away from that? I had spent the last ten years trying to keep everyone but my son at arm's length, and I was so done with that right now. I needed to see her, even if that meant flying all the way to Vegas to do it.

I tapped off a text to the company who ran my private jet. I didn't use it often, but like the boat, it had been an indulgent purchase I couldn't say no to when I'd gotten the money together to finally buy it. I thanked God for it right now because the thought of spending another second away from Autumn when I knew she wanted me was impossible to wrap my head around at that moment.

"Hunter?" I strode out of the office, and my son poked his head out from his room.

"Yes, Dad?"

"You want to grab some things?" I suggested. "I'm taking you down to stay with Raymond for a couple of days."

"Why?" He furrowed his brow.

"Because it's spring break, and you should be doing something," I told him firmly, figuring it was for the best not to get his hopes up about Autumn. Hell, I wasn't sure I should even be getting my hopes up yet, but here I was, letting them bubble over deep down inside of me to those places in my mind I had done my best to duck since she walked away from me.

I texted Raymond quickly and thanked God when my best friend agreed at once to take Hunter for a few days. That was the good thing about Raymond wanting to practice his parenting skills. He was always willing to take Hunter for me to squeeze in a little more rehearsal. Hunter grabbed his stuff and threw it into a bag, and I paced the hallway excitedly as I waited for him to come out.

"Ready to go?" I asked as soon as he joined me. He nodded.

"Awesome." I grabbed his hand. "Let's get out of here, shall we?"

"Where are you going to be?" Hunter asked as we climbed into the car. "Will you be visiting Raymond and me?"

"Of course I will," I told him, ruffling his hair. "I'm going away on a business trip, Hunter, but I won't be gone long. I'll be back before you know it."

"Okay." He eyed me curiously, and I could tell he knew there was something else going on. I turned my eyes to the road and pulled out of the driveway. I didn't want him to guess, and I certainly didn't want him getting his hopes up about Autumn coming back to us before it was totally confirmed one way or another.

I arrived at Raymond's place in record time, and Hunter hopped out of the car to head straight to the guest room to dump his stuff. Raymond leaned on the doorframe as I headed up the steps, and he raised his eyebrows at me.

"You going to fill us in on what this is all about?" he asked teasingly.

"What do you mean?" I replied, not sure I wanted Raymond being able to guess the crazy shit I was about to pull. If he figured it out, he would tell me I was off my rocker and needed to calm the hell down before I scared her off for good.

"Dropping Hunter off here with such little notice?" he pointed out. "Come on, I know you well enough to remember that you don't really do things spontaneously. Is everything okay?"

"Everything's fine," I assured him, and excitement flooded me at the thought of what I was going to do. "I'm actually—I'm going to see Autumn."

"She's right across town, isn't she?" Raymond frowned. "Why do you need a sitter for Hunter?"

I shook my head. "She's in Vegas right now."

"Vegas?" Raymond exclaimed, and I gestured for him to keep his voice down.

"Hey, hey, Hunter doesn't know about it yet," I warned him. "And I don't want him to. Not until I'm back at least."

"You're flying to Vegas to see her?" He looked skeptical, his eyes narrowed. "Is that a good idea?"

"Look, she was texting me earlier about how much she misses me and how much she wishes she could see me," I told him. "I'm not pulling this out of my ass here. I want to see her so fucking much, and I'm not going to turn down the chance now, no matter how crazy it might seem, you know?"

"Fuck it." Raymond shook his head, chuckling. "Sounds kind of wild to me, but you go get it, man. Just don't have a shotgun wedding in Vegas, all right? At least without inviting us."

"Who's getting married?" Hunter appeared next to Raymond.

"Nobody," I told him quickly, and I leaned down to give him a quick hug. "I'll see you soon."

"See you soon." He smiled at me and then wandered back inside the house. Raymond wished me good luck one more time, and I turned back to the car to shoot over to the airport. I was so beyond ready for this. The thought of seeing her again and holding her in my arms was making the soles of my feet prickle with excitement.

I texted her after I arrived at the airport to ask what hotel she was staying in. She replied with the address and some curiosity.

"Why do you need to know?"

"You'll see," I told her.

"Can't wait to find out. X"

I grinned at the kiss at the end of her message and slipped onto my private jet. Soon enough, I was shooting off across the country toward the woman I loved.

I arrived a few hours later after trying to get some work done on the plane but failing because I was so distracted by the notion of seeing her again. I got her room number and hopped a cab across the city to her hotel, my heart pounding in my chest the entire way. Please, let this be what she wanted. Please, let her be glad to see me.

I arrived at the hotel and began having second thoughts. What if it had been mild flirtation over text, a little bit of teasing to see how far I would go? The thought of that stung, and I pushed it to the back of my mind. No, no. She wasn't like Karla. I was getting the two of them wrapped up in one another, and there was no good reason for that at all. They were utterly different people, and I was going to remind myself how utterly different they were once and for all.

I headed up to her hotel room, giving the front desk my name and letting them know who I was there to visit. I wasn't sure they would let me through, but they must have seen the certainty in my eyes and understood there was no way in hell I was backing down, no matter what anyone said. I arrived outside her door and took a deep breath. I could do this. I had come all this way just to be close to her. And I was tired and jetlagged and nervous, but I wasn't going to walk away from this now, no way in hell when I was finally so close to being with the woman I loved.

I knocked on the door, and she pulled it open almost at once like she had been waiting for me. She was wearing a large hotel robe, her hair wrapped up in a towel on her head, and her eyes practically bugged out of her face as soon as she saw me.

"Holden?" she exclaimed. "Holy shit, I didn't think you would actually come."

"I couldn't wait to see you," I told her, reaching out to clasp her face in my hands. I couldn't believe how good it felt to be in her presence, to have her in my arms again. I had been sure I'd pushed things too far or freaked her out with my forwardness, but here she was with a smile spreading across her face.

"I missed you so much," she breathed as she pulled me over the doorstep, yanking me inside the room and pushing the door shut behind me.

"You have no idea," I agreed, as I leaned down to kiss her for the first time in what felt like forever.

52

AUTUMN

As soon as our lips touched, I knew I had made the right choice replying to that text. I had second-guessed it a few times when he'd been messaging me since, wondering what the hell I was encouraging with this, but I couldn't resist the thought of pushing things as far as I could. I wanted to see him, wanted to feel his strong arms around me again, wanted to know that he had ached for me the same way I had ached for him. I missed him so badly, but he was with me again, and we could work out the details when this part was over.

"Mmm," he moaned against my mouth as he slipped his hands beneath my robe and let it fall to the floor. He moved his fingers over my bare waist, my hips, my thighs, and I silently thanked God that Zoe was spending the evening down in the pool and sauna area. We had decided to take some self-care time individually, so she wasn't going to come in and disturb us. The last thing I needed was to have to explain what the hell my recent ex was doing in my hotel room where I had come ostensibly to catch a break from moping over him.

The towel slipped from my head as he pushed me onto the bed, and I pulled him on top of me, our lips not breaking for a moment. It was as though we were trying to make up for lost time. That was certainly what it felt to me, as though both of us were doing our best to remember how good it felt to be together, how hot our chemistry still was even after all this time.

I could feel him getting hard, and I moved my hand between his legs to squeeze his cock through his jeans. As soon as I touched him, a deep need rose within me. I needed him inside me more than I needed anything in the world. He bit down softly on my lip, teasing me, and I wriggled beneath him and wrapped my ankles around him, pulling him down close.

"I want..." I moaned in his ear, but I couldn't find the words to tell him what I needed from him. He kissed down my neck, across my breasts, drawing each of my nipples into his mouth in turn. My mouth hung open uselessly, any attempts at speech vanishing as I watched him pleasure me with his tongue.

"Tell me what you want, baby," he whispered, moving back up to look me in the eye. One hand was stroking my hair and the other was slipping down between my thighs, and the blur of sensations was making it hard to think straight.

"I want... you," I finally managed. "Inside me."

"How?" He dipped his fingers down against my slit, tracing them around my entrance before he pushed them briefly inside. "Like this?"

I groaned and pushed my head back into the pillow behind me as he penetrated me with his fingers. It wasn't quite what I had been talking about, but it felt so fucking good that I didn't care. He was grinding lazily against my thigh as he moved his fingers into me, reaching his thumb up to play with my clit as he did so. My legs began shaking, and he kissed me again as he played with me as if bringing me back down to Earth where I belonged.

"You feel so good," he murmured against my mouth. "So wet."

"Ah." I groaned once more, lifting my hips and grinding back against his hand with more purpose, but I needed more than his fingers. I needed him to fuck me, to give me what I had been missing since we had last seen each other.

"I want you inside me," I told him. "Fuck me, Holden, please."

"Anything you want." He brushed his lips over my cheek in a gesture that would have been almost chaste had it not been for his fingers in my pussy, and he reached into his pocket to pull out a condom. I was so wet, my pussy aching and throbbing to feel him inside of me.

He unzipped his pants, took his cock in his hand, and sheathed himself quickly. I was wriggling with excitement on the bed below him, trying to remember the last time I had craved someone as deeply and fully as this. I was going to burst with need for him, with want. He guided himself toward my slit, and I spread my legs and tilted my hips back so he could push into me more easily.

We both let out long breaths as he penetrated me, as though the two of us had been waiting for this for a long time. I knew I had. Until I had seen him standing there at my door, and my body had exploded with that visceral reaction to his presence, I hadn't noticed how badly I had missed him. How badly I'd missed being with him in this way.

He drove deep into me, pushing all the way inside of me in one long thrust, and I sank my fingers into his back and pulled him down on top of me. I wanted to feel how our bodies fit together. I wanted, more than anything, to feel the weight of him bearing down on me as he moved inside me, how natural we felt together, to scrub all those doubts from my mind and leave behind everything that had been wrapped up in these last couple of weeks.

"I missed you so much," he murmured, turning his head so he could say the words straight to me.

"I missed you too," I replied, and he kissed me once more, his tongue in my mouth as he slowed his thrusts and apparently took a second to savor the moment. I wrapped my legs tighter around him and pulled him into me, rocking my hips back to meet him, insisting on deeper, harder, more, more, more.

I moved my hand down between my legs and began to play with my clit as he fucked me. He pushed himself back up from being on top of me and looked down at my hand, a grin spreading across his face as he took me in.

"I love it when you touch yourself like that." He watched my fingers as they moved across my delicate nub. "You look so fucking hot."

"Not so bad yourself." I giggled, and then the smile was wiped off my face as he plunged deep into me and sent a shudder of pleasure through my body, contorting my muscles for a moment.

"Fuck," I moaned as he moved into me, and suddenly he dropped down on top of me and wrapped his arms tightly around me. He ground his hips into mine, desperate, hungry, and I pushed back as best I could, needing him, the pleasure building and growing and swelling.

When I came, I didn't make a sound. I couldn't have if I had wanted to. All nonessential systems in my body shut off for an instant, the pleasure taking control as my pussy clenched around his cock, and the lust transformed into satisfaction. He held himself deep inside of me, letting my pussy massage his dick as I lay helplessly back on the bed while the pleasure coursed through me. A few seconds later, I felt his cock twitch inside me, and he came himself, his body shuddering from head to toe as he reached his climax.

He held himself there for a long while, probably knowing we were going to have to talk about things after he pulled out and no doubt as reluctant as I was to do so. But after a moment or two, he slid out of me, pressing one last kiss to my lips as he did so. He got rid of the condom and rolled back on to the bed with me. I was stark naked, and he was still mostly dressed, and I giggled as I noticed the difference between us.

"I feel very exposed right now," I remarked, grabbing the covers and pulling them up over my body. He tucked them in around me and handed me an extra pillow for my head, stroking my hair back from my face as he did so.

"I can't believe you're here," I murmured.

"Me neither." He grinned at me. "But as soon as I got your text, I knew I had to see you again. I just missed you so fucking much."

"I missed you too," I agreed, and he lay his head down on the pillow next to me, caressing my stomach and watching the way I reacted to his touch.

"So what do we do now?" I asked, my voice tiny. I wasn't sure I wanted to hear an answer to that question. Yet here, I knew we couldn't hide from it for much longer.

"I met with my ex while we were apart," he told me, pushing his head up so he could look me directly in the eyes. I felt my stomach clench at the thought of it.

"Oh?"

"And seeing her..." He shook his head. "It made it crystal clear to me that you're the one who's supposed to be in our lives. Mine and Hunter's. It just makes sense. I know it might be hard for you, and I respect that, and I'm not going to push you to do anything you're not comfortable with."

"I'm comfortable with this," I assured him, and he smiled at me.

"I'm not sure if things are all wrapped up with her now or not," he confessed. "But I don't want to be apart from you. If you're ready, I am."

I looked deep into his eyes and felt that rush of love for him, that certainty that came with knowing I was with the right man and that having him lying next to me was the only way I wanted to spend the rest of this evening.

"I think I am," I agreed, and he smiled into a kiss, moving his hand up to cup my face gently like he was touching something impossibly precious.

When he pulled back, he brushed his nose against mine and raised his eyebrows.

"I didn't expect to find you in Vegas, though," he said. "Doesn't seem like your kind of place."

"Yeah, I'm not sure it is," I admitted. "Zoe booked the trip for us after what happened, and I figured it was better to come out here than to spend all that time lying around at home feeling sorry for myself."

"Well, I don't care where you are as long as we're together." He grinned.

"Trust me, I'm looking forward to getting back to Portland," I told him. He raised his eyebrows.

"Hey, there's some fun stuff to do here," he pointed out. "It would be a shame to miss all of it, right?"

"You've been here before?"

"I did some work for one of the hotels down here, and I figured it would be fun to stay for a few days just to say I had." He shrugged. "And yeah, it was pretty cool. You just have to know where to go."

"Well, I'm all ears," I agreed, and he kissed me again like he couldn't resist for a moment longer.

"I can't wait to show you this place," he murmured, looking deeply into my eyes, and a thrill ran through me. This trip was going to be fun. As long as he was by my side, everything seemed like a good time.

53

HOLDEN

When I woke up, the weight of Autumn's head rested against my chest, and I was convinced for a moment that this was all a dream. There was no way I could have come all this way on a whim in the hope of reconnecting with this woman, and even if I had, there was no way she would have taken me back like that.

But I looked down and saw her head against my chest, her face nuzzled into my skin, and I grinned. This was real. I leaned down and smelled her hair, closing my eyes and letting the scent of it wash over me. Real as day. Real as anything.

I didn't want to wake her up, so I was happy to lie there and come to wakefulness slowly, letting the reality of the situation wash over me. It was real, and it was happening. I was with her again, and the two of us were happy.

I wrapped my arms around her and felt that swell of love for her once more. I knew it was love. It had been so long since I'd felt that way about anyone that some part of me had been afraid before that I was wrong and that I was going to blurt out something I didn't really mean. I knew now, though. I wanted to tell her, but I was worried it would scare her off, given everything else that had already happened so far. The last couple of weeks had been a lot to take in, and I didn't want to overwhelm her with anything too intense when things were going so sweetly between us.

Suddenly, a knock on the door rang throughout the room, and my head snapped up. That had to be Zoe, Autumn's friend who had brought her out here. I had a feeling she was going to be less than impressed if she found me sleeping in Autumn's bed.

Autumn's eyes flickered open, and Zoe knocked again. Autumn sat up in bed, yawning, and ran her hands through her hair.

"Stay here," she told me. "I'll be back in a second."

"Okay," I agreed, and I grinned as she went to the door, grabbing the robe from where we had dumped it the night before. She pulled it open, and I ducked beneath the covers so I wouldn't be visible to anyone standing out there.

"Morning," Zoe greeted her. "You don't usually sleep in this late. Everything okay?"

"Everything's great," Autumn assured her. "Did you have a good night?"

"Yeah, I really did," Zoe confessed excitedly. "I went to the bar and met this guy. I really like him. He's taking me out today. You can come with us if you want?"

"No, no, I don't want to cramp your style," Autumn replied, and I could hear the relief in her voice. "You go out and have a good time. I'm going to relax in here for the day and maybe go to the pool."

"All right, well, keep in touch," Zoe told her firmly. "And don't spend too much time lying in bed thinking about Holden. You're here to get your mind off him."

"Of course," Autumn agreed, and I heard the door click shut and lifted my head from beneath the covers.

"So you're not going to spend too much time in bed with me?" I cocked an eyebrow, and she giggled and slipped beneath the covers.

"Hush. I don't want her to hear you," she scolded me, snuggling up against my body. "I just want to enjoy it being the two of us for a while."

"I feel like a teenager," I said, wrapping my arms around her again. "Sneaking into bedrooms I shouldn't be in."

"Oh, come on, you're a grown-ass adult," she threw back at me. "I think you're allowed to hang out in bedrooms these days."

"Let me have my fun," I protested teasingly, and she laid her head back and let out a satisfied sigh. I knew how she felt. I couldn't have asked for this to go any better, and it felt so perfect to have her here next to me. Everything on the outside world could wait for a while as time seemed to slow down to make room for us.

"We should do something while I'm here," I suggested. "It would be a shame to have both of us in this place and spend the whole time in the hotel room."

"Oh, would it, now?" she teased, cocking an eyebrow.

"Come on, get dressed." I lifted myself out of bed. "We could go for a walk down the main street. Trust me, there's always something cool going on there."

We shared a shower, got dressed, and then headed out for something to eat. There was a quaint little diner not far from the hotel, and since we had missed breakfast service, we happily stuffed out faces with some delicious junk before we hit the town.

"So what happened with your ex?" she asked me, furrowing her brow as she took a sip of her coffee. "You said you met up with her?"

"Yeah, I did." I sighed. "I don't really know what I expected. But she just got dumped by this guy who was taking care of her for the last few years, and I guess she's looking for some money to get by while she tries to get back on her feet. Or find the next unsuspecting victim to pay for her entire life."

"Did you offer her money?"

"Said she could have as much as she wanted, pretty much." I shrugged. "But as soon as I told her I didn't want her near Hunter, she got difficult again. Really difficult. I think she saw me turning her down as taking her power away, and she hates that."

"What are you going to do? Do you think she's going to back off now that you've told her it's not going to happen?" Autumn asked.

She was trying to keep her voice casual, but I could tell she was heavily invested in my answer.

"I honestly don't know." I shook my head. "I haven't heard from her since then, and she hasn't come by the house or anything like that, so I guess maybe she's dropped it."

"Well, that's good—"

"Or she's going to come back and take me to court to try and get custody of Hunter," I finished up. Her face dropped.

"Do you think that's likely to happen?" She pulled a face. "You really think she'd go that far?"

"I have no idea. I haven't seen her in such a long time, and it's hard to know what she might actually do to get one over on me."

"Shit." Autumn leaned back and shook her head. "She sounds like a nightmare."

"Yeah, she's not great," I agreed, the understatement of the year. "And it's just so transparent as to why she's doing all of this. I think that's the hardest part. If she had come to me and asked for money, I could have dealt with that, but she got so up in arms about Hunter not having a mother."

"But she's the one who left him," Autumn pointed out, and I held my hands up.

"Trust me, Autumn, I know," I agreed. "But she still might want to make a point out of this. She does that sometimes, or at least she did back when we were dating."

"Jesus," Autumn muttered. "You really think she'll take you to court over it?"

"She might," I replied, and I noticed the way her face dropped when I said that. "But it's going to be okay. I have this under control. Besides, I don't want to bring down our trip with this shit. She's all the way back in Portland. We don't have to concern ourselves with her right now."

"I guess you're right," she agreed, and her face cleared and brightened. "So what do you want to do today?"

"Well, when we're done here," I dusted my fingers off on my napkin and scrunched it up and placed it on to the empty plate in front of me, "I thought we could go to this cocktail bar not far from here. It does really good, cheap drinks, and they have cheesy old arcade games there as well."

"Like father, like son." She cocked her head at me, smiling. "Now I know where Hunter gets his love of games from."

"Well, maybe when he's old enough, I'll take him to this place." I laughed. "But I don't think it's exactly family-friendly."

"Even better." She raised her eyebrows. "Let's get going. It sounds perfect."

We spent the rest of the day together, and she seemed to be having a good time. Maybe Vegas was more suited to her than she thought. She kept in touch with Zoe throughout the day, half to make sure she was doing all right with her new man and half to make sure we weren't going to run into her at any of the spots we ended up. When she was on a call to her friend, I checked the tickets for shows that were on that evening, and I grinned when I saw there was an internationally renowned circus troupe in town. Sure, it was a little cheesy, a little tacky, but I wanted to indulge all of that with her. I wanted to blow off some steam and take on some of the sillier stuff this town had to offer. Things had been so serious lately, I felt as though we both deserved some pure fun.

"Hey." She greeted me with a kiss when she returned, picking up her drink and taking a sip. "Zoe's doing great. I'm pretty sure she's going to get shotgun-married to that guy."

"Well, as long as she doesn't do it tonight," I said, and she raised her eyebrows expectantly.

"And why might that be?"

"I just booked tickets for us." I held out my phone so she could get a look at the site.

"Oh my God!" she exclaimed. "I've never seen them before, but I've always wanted to. Is it tonight?"

"Sure is." I nodded, and she tossed her arms around me and gave me a cosmopolitan-flavored kiss.

"This is going to be perfect." She beamed at me. She was a little tipsy—I was too—but she was happy, and that was all I cared about.

"Yeah, it is," I agreed, slipping my arms around her waist, not caring one little bit who was looking or how mushy we looked together. I was a great big pile of mush when I was around her, and there was no point in hiding it.

"Thank you so much for coming here." She kissed my cheek. "This place is so much fun when you're here."

"Same goes for you." I grinned. And it was true. The last time I'd been down here, I had enjoyed myself, but it was nothing compared to this. I was never going to forget this trip with Autumn because it was the start of something—the start of us once and for all.

"I think I have another game to win." She pointed to the cheap old basketball machine that was sitting next to the wall. She had already beaten me a couple of times, and I was convincing myself that I was just being nice and letting her take the victories.

"All right, bring it on." I rolled up my sleeves and followed her over there, unable to keep the grin off my face. Yeah, I was never going to forget this trip. No matter what happened.

54

AUTUMN

"I can't believe we're actually going to see them in person," I gushed as we waited in line to take our seats for the circus. "I've never done anything like this before."

"It's going to be great fun, I promise," Holden assured me, wrapping an arm around my waist and pulling me close. He had been like this all day, really touchy-feely like he literally couldn't bear to keep his hands off me. I liked it. I nuzzled into him, smiling, glad he was here with me after all. And Zoe was off with her new man having a great time. She likely wasn't even thinking about me right then, and I could fill her in on the whole situation with Holden at some point when she was back. For now, I wanted it to be just the two of us, stealing away in the city together, our little secret.

"Oh, we're moving." Holden pointed forward, and the crowd was finally pouring through the gates and into their seats. I hurried forward to take mine, inhaling the scent of popcorn and sawdust that filled the place. I felt like a kid again, giddy with excitement at what we were about to do.

The day itself had been perfect enough so far as it was. He had taken me to a bar where we'd spent the afternoon getting tipsy and playing games and blowing off some steam. I was still worried about what he'd told me regarding his ex and her appearance back in his life, but that felt so far away from us right now that it was hard to get too upset about it.

He led me to my seat, and I looked out over the space in front of us. The place was packed, and the room was rich with anticipation. I didn't even want to think how much it must have cost to get us in here on such short notice, but then money had never been a problem for Holden. He had flown all the way to Vegas with no notice, for goodness' sake, it was obvious that he didn't care much about spending cash if it meant we could be together. Which made me so happy—not that he treated me to so much but that nothing got in the way of the two of us being together.

The lights dimmed, and I took Holden's hand as the show started, and soon, I was caught up in the incredible act taking place before our eyes. I had watched some of this stuff online, idly checking ticket prices and assuming I would never get to see it in person, but it was stunning the way they moved, the artful control they displayed over every part of their bodies. I wished I could have that kind of grace, but if I had so much as thought about doing something like that, I would have tripped over my own feet before I got my hands on the trapeze.

"Oh my God!" I gasped as one of them flew through the air, letting go of their platform to catch the hands of someone else dangling from their trapeze. I turned to Holden, eyes wide, and found that he was already looking at me. In fact, I had a feeling he hadn't taken his eyes off me since the show had started. My heart warmed, and I almost said it then, almost told him I loved him. But the music swelled and drew my attention back to the stage, and I promised myself I wouldn't wait much longer before I came out and told him the truth.

We took in the rest of the show together, and I got completely caught up in the performance. The entire crowd was equally caught up, and it was awesome to be surrounded by people who were so engaged with something as whimsical as this. I couldn't remember the last time I had allowed myself to get lost in something so utterly beautiful, and it felt good to let go of all those stressors I'd been carrying around the last few weeks and fill my brain with something incredible instead.

"That was amazing," I said with a sigh as soon as we were outside, surrounded by the excited chatter of the crowd who had watched the show.

"It really was," Holden agreed. "I didn't think it would be that cool, but they were so talented."

"I would love to be able to do stuff like that." I kicked one leg up in the air in a mimic of one of the moves they'd made on stage. Me being me, I instantly lost my balance, and Holden had to grab me to keep me upright.

"Hey, whoa, there." He laughed. "Maybe hold off on the acrobatic career for a little while longer."

"You can't keep me from my passions," I declared dramatically, but I stopped dancing in the street and let my feet hit the sidewalk below us once more. "What do you want to do now?"

"Shall we just take a walk?" he suggested. "I think I need some fresh air."

"I'm not sure any of the air in this city could be described as fresh, but I'll see what I can do." I smiled, and the two of us turned to make our way back to the hotel. It was quite a way across town, but I was fine with that. I would have been happy to talk to him all night if possible. I couldn't get enough of him and of what it felt like to be a real couple.

I took his arm as we walked, and I noticed a few people glancing in our direction as we made our way down the street. I couldn't help smiling. They thought we were nothing more than a normal couple in love enjoying an evening out in Vegas, which is what we were, and it was what I needed right now. The feel of his body next to mine was intoxicatingly good, the way his pace fell in time with my own reminding me he was paying attention to every little detail. I could have walked all night with him by my side.

"Where's Hunter right now?" I asked. I hadn't given Hunter a lot of thought today, but I didn't know who he was with or if he understood that his dad had come to Vegas to see me.

"He's with Raymond." Holden shrugged. "Dropped him off there yesterday."

"Does he know?" I asked nervously. I wasn't sure what I wanted here, if I would have preferred him to hold back a little or push forward and make it real to everyone. The thought of being all trussed up in this safe little bubble in Vegas where nobody knew what we were doing was appealing, I had to admit that, but we couldn't stay that way forever. At some point, I was going to have to concede that the world beyond this city existed and give in to the fact that we had to return there, no matter how fun hiding from it had been.

"About us? No, he doesn't know." Holden shook his head. "He's been missing you like crazy, but I didn't want to say anything about coming down here before I knew for sure what was happening one way or the other."

"That makes sense," I agreed. "I'm glad you didn't come out swinging with everything. Things are still so fresh."

"Yeah, I get that." Holden nodded. "I didn't know whether you were going to kick me to the curb as soon as you set eyes on me here."

"After I texted you all that stuff?" I reminded him. "You really think I'm that heartless?"

"Sure," he shot back playfully, and I slapped him gently on the arm.

"Oh, come on, a little credit here," I protested. "I'm not that bad, am I?"

"Of course, you're not," he assured me, and I nestled against him.

"What are you going to do with Hunter the rest of spring break?" I asked him. "I guess you could go back whenever you want, what with the jet and all."

"Sure can," Holden agreed. "But I thought we could have another day here at least. Maybe head back on Tuesday?"

"You sure you want to leave him that long?" I furrowed my brow, and he smiled at me.

"Trust me. There's nowhere in the world he would rather be than with Raymond and Olivia right now," he assured me. "He loves it over there. I doubt he'll even notice I'm away as long as he's got them to distract him."

I laughed. "Oh, come on. You really think he won't want to do something for spring break?"

"I suggested a few things to him, but he didn't seem that taken with any of them," he replied, shaking his head. "I think he was pining after you. I know how that feels."

"Well, maybe we could do something together when we get back," I suggested as we turned the corner on to the street with the hotel on it. "I wouldn't want him to miss out on a fun break just because you were all the way out here romancing me."

"Don't worry. When he finds out we're back together, he's going to be the happiest kid in the world," Holden remarked.

"Oh, we're back together now, are we?" I raised my eyebrows at him. "Little presumptive, don't you think?"

"I didn't mean to jump the gun," he blurted out. "I just thought since we were—"

"Of course, we are," I soothed him, giggling at his reaction. "Sorry, I didn't mean to worry you."

"You need to stop playing me like that." He grinned, a look of relief on his face, and I took his hand.

"Couldn't resist," I replied breezily. "God, I'm looking forward to seeing Hunter when we get back. Maybe we could go out together, do something with the three of us?"

Holden didn't reply for a moment, and I turned to him to see him smiling at me.

"What is it?" I asked.

"Just..." He shook his head. "You always think about Hunter. It's never just about you. That's why I lo—"

He cut himself off and quickly picked up the pace, but that couldn't scrub the reality of what he'd nearly said from my head. My eyes widened, and I silently implored him to pick up where he'd left off. But he didn't.

"That's why we love spending time with you," he finished up carefully. "Hunter and I both. You're so thoughtful of the both of us, and I know he appreciates it as much as I do."

"Anytime," I replied, and in my head, I pleaded with him to say the words I knew had been on the tip of his tongue. They had been so close, I could almost taste them, could almost feel them rolling out of his mouth and into my mind, the words I had longed to hear for so long. *I love you.* But I knew there was no point pressing the issue. He would come out with that when he was good and ready, and it was clear he wasn't quite there yet, for whatever reason, which I had to respect. No matter how much I wanted to grab him and tell him I felt the same way.

"Come on. Let's get back to our room." He tugged on my hand and flashed me a smile. "The night's not over yet."

Returning his grin, I followed him back to our hotel room, knowing he was right. There was still a whole heap in this relationship that we had ahead of us, and I made a promise to myself right there and then that I was going to sit back, enjoy the ride, and not push for things to go any faster than they already were. We would get there in the end, and that was all that really mattered.

55

HOLDEN

I pressed my ear to the bathroom door to make sure Autumn was in the shower and not about to burst out on me. Satisfied by the sound of the gushing water, I snuck out of the hotel room and headed down the stairs to reception. I hoped my surprise had already arrived by now. I'd ordered it for express delivery, and I wanted it here by tonight to prove to Autumn that I had been paying attention to her wants and needs on this trip.

I had so nearly said those powerful words the night before, nearly let it slip out when I wasn't ready for it. That was crazy because the last thing I needed right now was to come out with something as bold and big as *I love you*. It wasn't the kind of thing I let slip out at random. When I said it to her, I was going to be sure she would say it back, and I was going to be dead-certain she knew I meant it. It wasn't something to blurt out after a night on the town together when we'd spent the most of the day drinking and goofing off.

I had noticed her eyeing a dress when we walked to the hotel that evening—a red number in the window of a boutique down the street from the hotel as we were passing. I knew at once that she had to have it. I would have done anything to make it so she had everything she wanted, not to mention that I thought she would look incredible in the red dress. My mind drifted back to our very first unofficial date when she'd taken me shopping for a suit, and I grinned. How the tables had turned.

I arrived down at reception and waited patiently for the woman to turn her attention to me. I smiled when she did, unable to keep the grin from my face.

"Hi. I think there's a package here for me?" I told her. "Holden?"

"Oh, right, sure." The woman reached beneath the desk and handed me a small, slim, soft package. "Here you go."

"Thanks." I nodded to her and headed back up the stairs to the hotel room. Autumn had been complaining about not knowing what to wear earlier, given that we were headed to one of the fanciest restaurants in the city, but I had the perfect solution to her problem. I couldn't wait to see the look on her face.

I opened the door and found her sitting on the edge of the bed, wrapped in a towel, her arms wound around herself protectively. She looked nervous, and she gazed up at me as soon as I walked into the room.

"I thought you'd left." She furrowed her brow. "Where did you go?"

"I was just picking this up for you," I assured her, handing her the package.

She smiled at me and took it with a shake of her head. "What is it?"

"Open it, and you'll see," I told her with a grin. She did as she was told and then gasped and laughed when the red dress fell out into her hands.

"Is this the one I was looking at yesterday?" she asked, passing it back and forth in her hands. I nodded.

"I just wanted you to have it," I told her.

She gave me a kiss on the cheek before heading into the bathroom with the dress. "Well, you've solved my problem of what to wear this evening. How long before we need to go?"

"Half an hour," I called to her as she closed the door behind her. I went to grab something to change into myself. At least I'd grabbed a suit earlier in the day, so I had something presentable to take my lady out in. I wanted to show her a seriously good time tonight. Yesterday had been fun, but tonight was going to be incredible.

She emerged from the bathroom twenty minutes later, transformed in her red dress and a pair of black heels with her makeup dark and smoky. She twirled before me with a giggle.

"What do you think?" she asked.

"You look good enough to eat," I replied, and she flushed a little.

"Well, save it for the restaurant, yeah?" she teased, taking my hand as we headed to the door. "I like the new suit."

"I like the new dress," I replied as we stepped into the elevator. She snuggled into me once more. She had been doing that a lot, as though she couldn't keep her hands off me. It was a good feeling, one that I shared with her.

"Where is this place that you're taking me again?" She furrowed her brow as we headed out of the hotel and climbed into a cab.

"I did some website work for them a good few years ago," I said. "When I was done, I came down to take a look at the place, and I fell in love with it. I've never seen anything like it. I've wanted to take someone I was dating there ever since, so you earn the honors."

She grinned. "Well, I'm touched. You saved this for me, and you hadn't even met me yet."

"Sure did," I said as I watched the Vegas streets whip by outside.

We arrived outside the building the restaurant was in, and she frowned when we stepped out of the cab. I had to admit, from the outside, it didn't look like much—but then, that was part of its charm.

"I know it doesn't look like a lot from out here," I assured her. "But when you see the inside..."

"All right, show me." She waved her hand for me to lead on. "I've got to see this amazing place already."

I headed into the building where a host was waiting by a sleek glass elevator. He glanced up when I walked in and offered us both a welcoming smile.

"Holden," I said. "We have a reservation for seven."

The host turned his gaze to the pad in front of him, his eyes scanning over it quickly, and then he pressed his finger into the paper and nodded.

"Please, take the elevator to the top floor." He gestured to the elevator beside him. "You'll be taken to your table from there. Enjoy your evening."

"Thank you." I nodded to him, and Autumn gave me a wide-eyed look of "what the hell is going on?" as we slipped into the elevator that whisked us up to the top floor. When we stepped out, her jaw dropped.

"Oh, you have to be kidding me," she murmured as she looked around the place. Even I had to admit, the restaurant looked even better than I remembered it.

Huge windows looked out over the sparkling city of Vegas laid out below us. Shimmering glass chandeliers dripped from the ceiling and cast a cool, expensive glow over everything. There were only a handful of tables, and all of them were full except one, which we were swiftly led to. Autumn took her seat opposite me and turned to take in the view.

"How do I not know about this place already?" she asked, turning back to me. "Why doesn't everyone come here? It's amazing."

"It's the sort of place you have to know about already," I explained. "They don't advertise a lot. I think they like to keep the clientele small and exclusive."

"It's incredible," she dragged her eyes away from the view to look at me. "Thank you so much for bringing me here. You have no idea how much this means to me."

"You have no idea how much you mean to me." I took her hand as the waiter approached with the wine list and a menu, and she beamed across the table in my direction. My heart swelled with love for her, and I almost dropped the words right then and there, but the waiter passed us our menus and let us know the specials, and the moment wasn't quite right. Yet.

"Oh my God, all of this looks so good," she said as she cast her gaze over the food on the menu. "What do you get when you're here?"

"I try to get a mix of everything," I replied. "They had some incredible chefs here. It'd be a shame to miss out on anything they're cooking up."

"Then let's do that." She nodded, closing her menu. "You choose what we have. I know you'll make the right choice."

"Bold," I teased her. "What if I make the wrong one, and the entire night is ruined?"

"I guess I'll just have to hold it against you," she teased, leaning forward.

"As long as you're not wearing that dress when you're holding yourself against me." I raised my eyebrows at her playfully, and she let out a burst of laughter that attracted the attention of the other patrons. She slapped her hand over her mouth and glanced around apologetically, but most of them seemed more amused by her outburst than anything.

"Stop it. We're in a classy establishment," she scolded me. "I don't want to get booted out because you can't keep it in your pants."

"Hey, I'm just making the most of the fact that it's only the two of us," I pointed out. "We don't often get this time to ourselves, what with Hunter and everything."

"Speaking of Hunter," She hesitated for a moment, "what's going to happen when we get back? With... well, with everyone?"

"I don't think we need to worry about that now," I soothed her gently. "Let's have a good time while we're here, and we can figure out the details when we get home, all right?"

"All right," she agreed, a weight seeming to lift from her face. The waiter approached with a pad in his hand.

"Ready to order?" he asked, and I nodded and picked up the menu.

The rest of the night was perfect. The food was great, the wine was delicious, and the view over the city was unforgettable. It felt so nice to be able to whisk my woman out on a real, bona fide date. I loved spending time with her and Hunter, but there was something luxurious and fun about the two of us kicking back as well. We talked about movies and books and work, gossiped about our friends, and I avoided the topic of Karla carefully to make sure I didn't let my ex throw a wrench into the works of the best date I'd had in years.

I paid the bill when we were done, and we slipped into a taxi to head back to the hotel. Autumn was leaning her head back against the seat, eyes closed, hands resting in her lap.

"You okay?" I asked her gently, and she opened her eyes and looked at me.

"Yeah, I'm great," she promised me. "Just don't want to forget any of this, that's all."

"Me neither," I agreed. I reached over and slipped my hand onto her bare thigh, just below the hem of her dress. I glanced over at her and found a small smile creeping across her face, and I knew the same thing on my mind was on her mind.

I paid the driver, and she led me to the hotel room, grabbing my hand and taking the elevator. She was a little shaky in her heels, and I wasn't sure if it was the booze or the promise of what we were about to do.

As soon as we were through the door, she wound her arms around me and looked deeply into my eyes.

"It's going to be okay, isn't it?" she asked me. "When we get back?"

"Of course, it will be," I promised her. "But we have a little time left here first, right?"

"Right," she agreed with a smile. I leaned down to kiss her, and as soon as our lips met, I knew where this was going.

56

AUTUMN

The moment I felt his hands on me, pushing up the hem of that red dress, I knew exactly what I wanted from him. What I needed from him. This night had been perfectly, gloriously romantic, and now I needed something a little dirtier to round it off. I knew exactly what I wanted to do to him.

He pressed me back against the wall, his hands all over me, gripping at the bare skin exposed wherever he could find it—my arms, my legs, my shoulders—his fingers brushing teasingly over my neck and my throat. The heels I had on meant I was actually nearly his height, so I could kiss him without having to stand up on tiptoes, but I didn't want to keep this height difference for long. No, I had something in mind that he was going to like.

"I think it's only fair I thank you for dinner, no?" I breathed in his ear, and he bit down softly on the lobe of my ear.

"And what exactly did you have in mind?" he asked. I grinned.

"Let me show you." I moved a little so I was no longer pressed back against the wall, and I sank to my knees before him. There was something so hot about getting on my knees for him. We had spent the whole night playing at being expensive, luxurious, classy adults, and now I wanted to show him that he would never be able to scrub out my dirty side. In this fancy dress, in this beautiful hotel room, I wanted to worship him and show him how much I still wanted him.

I unbuckled his pants and pulled out his cock, taking it into my hand and stroking it a couple of times to bring him to full hardness. He looked so good already, his beautiful suit enhancing his sharp edges. I looked up at him as I leaned forward to take him into my mouth.

"Mmm." He groaned as I twirled my tongue around the head of his cock. I could taste a little salty precome on my lips, and I loved the way it tasted, the way it filled my mouth. I kept my gaze fixed on him as I slid down a little farther, moving my mouth to take as much of him as I could. I shifted my hand up to cover the rest of the distance so I was taking care of every part of him at once and then moved my spare hand beneath his balls so I could play with them while I went down on him. He had shown me a perfect evening tonight, and the least I could do in return was prove to him how much I appreciated his efforts.

I moved my hand and mouth in time with each other, working my tongue up the underside of his cock as I went, making sure he was slick and wet enough for me to really fuck him with my mouth. I wanted to take him as deeply as I could, and he seemed in no rush to stuff his cock down my throat as so many guys were. No, when I looked up at him again, he was gazing down at me with complete helplessness, as though he wanted nothing more than for me to take control and do what I wanted with him. The pure desire in his eyes was a little intoxicating, even more so than the outrageously expensive wine I'd enjoyed earlier in the evening.

I began to move with a little more purpose, stroking his cock farther into my mouth, and I was starting to get seriously wet. Something about servicing him like this, where I was both powerful and submissive to him, was beyond erotic to me. I moved my hand between my legs, slipping it beneath the beautiful dress he had purchased for me, and began to play with myself as I went down on him. I couldn't wait to have him inside me, couldn't wait to feel his beautiful cock throbbing in my pussy as he fucked me.

I closed my eyes and lost myself to the task at hand. I'd forgotten how much fun it could be to go down like this, how much I enjoyed pleasuring him. He never pressured me to do more than I was comfortable with, and his gentleness with me made me feel safer in exploring things I might not have before—wrapping a hand around his thigh to pull him deep into my mouth, leaning down to suck on his balls, sucking and lapping at his tip alone for a moment. I could hear his breath growing harsher above me, and I knew he wouldn't be able to hold out for much longer. I would have been happy to let him come in my mouth if he'd wanted to, but he seemed to have something else in mind entirely.

He scooped me up off the ground suddenly, and it was clear that my turn in control was over. I giggled as he spun me around and unzipped my dress, letting it fall to the floor below me, and dropped to his knees to pull down my panties. He planted a kiss on each of my butt cheeks in turn, running his hands over my thighs and my ass as he did so.

"Fuck, you look so good," he murmured as he got back to his feet. He guided me toward the bed, and I bent over, still in my heels, and pushed my ass up into the air for him. I had never fucked in heels before, but I had always thought it sounded pretty sexy. Now was a prime opportunity to test my hypothesis.

I heard the rip of a condom wrapper behind me and then felt his cock pressing against my slit. It was clear he had no intention of waiting around, which I was glad for because I couldn't hold out much longer. He slipped into me with a long groan in one smooth motion, and my legs trembled dangerously in the heels as he penetrated me for the first time.

"You look amazing," he told me for what had to be the dozenth time that night. I loved it when he told me how beautiful I looked. I wasn't used to hearing such compliments from the guys I was dating, but Holden showered me with praise, with lust, with his adoration for my body and everything about it.

"Fuck me," I said with a groan, unable to wait any longer. Finally, he gave me what I wanted.

He didn't hold back for an instant, driving himself into me in long, deep strokes that sent shockwaves through my entire body. I planted my hands on the bed to keep myself from keeling over. It felt so good, so decadent, as though the luxury of the night was spreading over into this too. I flicked my gaze up and caught sight of the two of us in the window opposite the bed, his eyes closed as he fucked me, and the image at once burned itself onto my brain. We looked so right together, so good, as though we had been built to do this with each other. I had known from the first time we'd fucked that we had crazy chemistry, but I'd had no idea it would grow more and more intense as time passed, better each time we were together.

He moved his hand between my legs and began to play with my clit, picking up the pace of his thrusts a little and really burying himself all the way inside me. I couldn't get enough of the feeling of him taking me like that, my ass angled up thanks to the heels and allowing him even deeper access than normal. I closed my eyes and focused on the sensations, the way they seemed to burn up through my body, every nerve ending burning bright as I crested toward an orgasm.

"Fuck," I moaned. He slid his other hand over my back and wound it into the hair at the nape of my neck, tugging back softly. The prickling in my scalp, that mesh of pain and pleasure, was enough to put me over the edge, and within seconds, my pussy clenched around his cock as the orgasm tore through me.

I had fucked him before this, but this time was different. I had never felt anything as purely *good* as this before, the selfish pleasure rocking through my body and sending every muscle to jelly in a moment. I wasn't even sure the noises I made were fully human, but I didn't care. I just wanted him to know how good this was for me, how good *he* was for me.

A few moments later, he found his own release in my pussy, thrusting frantically a few more times before he came. He let out a deep groan-growl and slipped out of me, leaving me to crash forward onto the bed, still in my bra and my heels.

I lay there for a moment as I waited for him to join me, and he slipped onto the bed next to me just as I sat up to get fully undressed.

"No shoes on the bed, right?" I remarked as I kicked my heels off to land next to the dress he had ripped off me a few minutes before.

"That was amazing." He trailed his hand up my arm, sending a spiral of tingles along the skin. "You're amazing."

"Not so bad yourself." I giggled and then slipped onto the bed next to him. I should have gotten up to take my makeup off, but I didn't want to break the moment yet. I wanted to revel in this, in it being just the two of us for a little while longer. We didn't have much time before we had to return home, and when we did, we would have to face up to everything that came with that—his ex, Hunter, the friends who had supported us through our breakup. It was going to be weird to have to explain ourselves to people, and that was why it was so tempting to hole up in this hotel room and pretend the world at large didn't really exist.

He wrapped his arm around me and drew me in close, and I laid my hand on his chest to feel for the beat of his heart. I found it so comforting, so cooling, so grounding like it was bringing me back down to Earth—even though I still felt as like I was rotating up there with the stars.

57

HOLDEN

"What exactly are your intentions for my Autumn?" Zoe tapped her finger on her chin and eyed me from the other side of the cab. Autumn leaned back from the front seat to take my hand and gave me an apologetic look, but there was no need.

"Well, taking her back to Portland first," I told Zoe. "And then immediate marriage, two kids, everything. That sound acceptable to you?"

"As long as I get invited to the wedding," Zoe agreed, and Autumn laughed from the front seat.

"The two of you planning my entire future back there?" she teased.

"Well, someone needs to," Zoe replied, winking at me. I hadn't spent a lot of time with Autumn's best friend, but I liked her. She seemed to have Autumn's best interests at heart, which I could get behind.

"Fair point," Autumn agreed, and she grinned at her friend. "Sure you don't want to come back with us?"

"No, I'm going to stay for a few more days." Zoe flashed her a smile. "I have someone here now, remember? I want to spend a little more time with him before I go back."

"Ooh, keep me updated." Autumn tapped Zoe's knee.

"And you keep me updated on what it's like to fly around in a private jet," she shot back, raising her eyebrows at me. "I can't believe you actually have one of those, Holden. That's, like, crazy-rich stuff right there."

"Well, maybe one day I'll find an excuse to take you somewhere in it," I said. "All three of us could go somewhere maybe."

"Oh, you shouldn't have put that offer out in front of me." Zoe wagged her finger at me. "I might take you up on it when you least expect it."

"We're here," Autumn announced as we pulled into the airport. The private jet would be ready and waiting for us, and I was looking forward to getting back to see Hunter, though I would have been lying if I said I wasn't a little sad to be saying goodbye to this place as well. Vegas would always have a place in my heart after this, as the place were Autumn and I had connected with each other again. It had been a pretty special few days, and I was sad at the thought of bidding goodbye to them, even if it meant getting back to our real lives.

"Well, I guess I should let you guys get away." Zoe stretched and yawned, and while she turned the corners of her mouth down at the notion, I could tell she was looking forward to it. Things were going well with this new man she was seeing, or so Autumn told me, and she was likely glad to be getting some time with him to herself once more.

Before I got out of the car, Zoe grabbed my arm, and I turned to her. She raised her eyebrows at me and gave me a pointed look.

"I know it's a cliché for the best friend to say this," she told me, "but I have to come out with it. Autumn's an amazing woman, you know that. Please don't hurt her."

"I won't," I promised her, and she let go of my arm.

"Trust me, I know how amazing she is." I grinned at her. "I'm never going to forget it."

"I guess I can let you off for now then." Zoe nodded at me. "Have a safe flight home, all right?"

"Will do," I promised as she got out of the car to say goodbye to Autumn.

"Keep in touch," Autumn ordered her as she gave her a tight hug. "And be back by the time school starts again, okay?"

"I will be," Zoe agreed. "I'll message you when I get back in Portland. We can catch up then."

"See you soon." Autumn squeezed her friend one last time and walked toward the plane. Gathering our bags, I quickly followed her.

We settled into the plane—after the requisite amount of Autumn wandering around the place gaping at every little detail, stunned that anything so luxurious could exist in the real world, let alone her real world—and I offered her a glass of champagne as we took off to head back home.

"It's probably a bad idea." She giggled. "But why not?"

We toasted one another, and Autumn turned to look at the Earth retreating below us as we gained altitude. Just like that, the world we had been hiding inside for the last few days seemed to drop away as well. A furrow appeared on her brow, and I noticed a darkness flicker across her face. Leaning forward, I put my hand on her knee, and she turned her attention back to me.

"Something on your mind?" I asked gently, and she shook her head, took another sip of her champagne, and then nodded.

"Actually, there is," she admitted.

"What is it?" I pressed her, though I had a good idea what this was going to be about.

"You said the stuff with your ex was back in Portland," she reminded me. "Well, we're headed that way now. What do we do now that we have to deal with her again?"

"Nothing." I shook my head. "The ball's in her court now, and there's not a lot I can do about that for the time being. If she takes me to court, I can deal with it that way, but I doubt she's going to bother us personally anymore."

"And what if she does?" Autumn eyed me nervously. "What if she really wants to be part of his life, and she finds a way in? What then?"

"What exactly is it that you're worried about?" I asked, patient as I could be. I knew she didn't understand how terrible Karla had been when we had been together, the manipulation and cruelty she had inflicted on me.

"I'm worried that if she comes back, there'll be no place for me in the family anymore," she confessed, dropping her gaze down and fiddling with the hem of her dress. "She's his mother, after all. I don't know if I can compete with that."

"Autumn, please." I leaned forward and grabbed her hand, and she looked up at me at last. I hoped she could tell from the intensity in the way I was looking at her that I wasn't kidding. "She's never been a mother to Hunter. I know that might be hard to believe, but it's true."

"But she *is* his mother," Autumn pointed out, clearly not wrapping her head around the comment. "More than I ever will be. She gave birth to him."

"Yes, and that's all she did," I assured her. "That's where her involvement with our son comes to a dead halt. Do you understand what I'm saying?"

"I guess." She wrinkled up her nose, and I could tell she was struggling to wrap her head around what I was saying.

"I'm telling you, that woman had nothing to do with raising Hunter," I told her firmly. "She might have brought him into the world, sure, but that's it. I'm sorry, but that's not the kind of woman I would consider a mother, would you?"

She stared at me for a long moment, clearly trying to understand what I was saying to her. She pressed her lips together and took a deep breath.

"What happens if she does want to come back into his life?" she asked quietly. "What happens to me then? Won't I be unnecessary?"

"Autumn, that's never going to be the case with you." I squeezed her hand tightly. "Even if, by some fucking miracle, she does manage to convince me and a judge that she's serious about being in Hunter's life again, I don't give a damn. You're still important to me, and you'll still be important to Hunter."

She let her gaze drop downward, and it was like there was something she wanted to tell me but didn't quite know how to come out about it. But then she shook her head and managed a smile.

"I'm sorry I keep bringing it up," she said, sighing. "I want to be able to drop it as much as you do. I just can't seem to get it out of my head, that's all. What would happen if she did come back, properly."

"Well, the chances of that seem pretty fucking slim," I promised her. "And even if she does, Hunter's still going to adore you. You know how much he loves you, right?"

"He made me a card last week." She grinned at me. "He asked when I was going to be coming back."

"You want to come with me to pick him up from Raymond's?" I suggested. "I'm sure he'd be so happy to see you."

"You know what? Sure." She nodded. "Oh, speaking of Hunter, what else are you going to do with him now that you've got the rest of spring break to fill up?"

"I've been giving it some thought," I said. "I think I'm going to take him fishing. On the boat. He really enjoyed it when we went before, and I think it would be good for us to get out of the house for a little bit, you know? Both of us were hanging around there way too much after... after what happened between us."

"That sounds fun," she said, and I raised my eyebrows at her pointedly.

"You're totally coming too," I told her. "Hunter will love it if you come along."

"And you'll be what, pretty ambivalent about the matter?" she teased.

"Oh, I'm sure I would find a way to get through it," I agreed, and she leaned over and gave me a kiss.

"That sounds fun—if you don't mind me intruding."

"You're never intruding," I assured her. "You're part of the family now."

"Do I get a choice in the matter?" She pulled a playful face. I shook my head.

"No way," I replied, and I shifted so I was in the seat next to her. I looked down over the clouds below us and felt a wave of peace knowing I was soon going to be with my son. Even if I didn't miss him on an immediate level, there was something deep inside me that did, something that needed to be near him no matter what. And soon, I would be.

Despite the length of the flight and how tired we both were, we headed straight to Raymond's place as soon as we arrived to pick up Hunter. I had texted ahead to say the two of us were coming but had asked Raymond not to mention it to my son. I wanted to see the look on his face.

When he pulled the door open, I knew it had been worth it. He practically hurled himself at Autumn, wrapping his arms tightly around her and knocking all the air out of her as he clung to her. She laughed and patted his head softly.

"It's so good to see you," Hunter told her.

"You too," Autumn agreed, eventually extracting herself from his grasp. I looked down at the two of them. No matter what happened with Karla, these two were my family. These two and nobody else. That was all that mattered. As long as the three of us were together, we would find a way to work through anything the world decided to throw at us.

58

AUTUMN

A flutter of excitement hit me as we headed out to the dock. I had never fished before, and I had a feeling I was going to be useless at it, but that didn't mean I was any less eager to spend time with my two favorite guys in the world.

"So you're going to show me what I'm doing?" I asked Hunter, turning to him in the back seat of the car. Holden was driving us down from their place where we'd headed the night before after picking him up from Raymond's house. It had been beyond sweet to make breakfast with the two of them together before we headed out for our day on the boat.

"I'll try." Hunter nodded like it was some great and noble task he had landed, and he took it very seriously. "It's not hard when you get the hang of it, but most of it is about luck at the start."

"Well, that's good to hear," I said. "I've never been very good at outdoor pursuits."

"Don't worry. We'll show you everything you need to know." Holden flashed me a smile in the mirror, and I returned it. I couldn't believe I'd tried to walk away from this. Though I knew intellectually that I'd had my reasons, the thought of missing out on this, on anything I had shared with them over the last few days, made my heart ache. I was so glad to be here, and I would do my best to stem the roiling mess of insecurity swelling and threatening to take me over sometimes. I was going to have to get used to this stuff, given that Karla probably wasn't going to drop out of our lives like that, but I could hide from the thought of it for a little while in these happy moments where I really believed I could be a mother to Hunter, when I believed he could see me that way.

We arrived at the dock and headed down to the boat, and I let my mind drift back to the first time I had come down here, when Holden had taken me out on that private yacht of his to show off his life to me and how surprised he had seemed when I had told him that this kind of thing didn't impress me much. Not long afterward, he'd taken me on a real date, the first date we'd properly been on together, and he took into account every little detail of what I'd told him I wanted when he asked me for that counterpoint to his yacht.

And we were back here again as a family, not because he wanted to show this place off to me but because he knew his son would enjoy it. That was why I was so attracted to Holden, why I adored him so much. His family came first, and it seemed like I was a part of that now.

It was breezy out that day, and Holden loaned me a jacket from the yacht to keep me warm. He smiled at me as he draped it around my shoulders, and I felt that little frisson of attraction to him once more. There was something about seeing him with his son, his kindness and compassion that made him even more perfect to me. There was a maturity in him that I had never seen in anyone else I'd dated before.

"Come on, let's get out on the water." Holden went to take control of the boat, and Hunter grabbed my hand and led me down to the cabin where all the fishing equipment was.

"Okay, so what does that do?" I asked, pointing at the various sizes of hooks dangling off a rack on the wall. "Why are there different sizes?"

"It depends on what you're fishing for," he told me authoritatively. "You get one of the lines like this..."

I let Hunter guide me through the set-up and furrowed my brow as I tried to keep up. I had never done this before, and I didn't want to look like an idiot trying it out. Neither of them was going to judge me if I did end up goofing it up somehow, but still, I was at the stage of the relationship where I wanted to sweep in and prove my brilliance at every turn. Not that my personality really allowed for that, but a girl could dream.

Holden came down to join us and grabbed my hand as he led me up to the deck. The boat was still, the water calm around us, and I inhaled a deep lungful of the slightly salty air.

"A girl could get used to this," I said to Holden as Hunter went to clip our chairs into place.

"I sure hope a girl does," he replied, and glancing around to make sure his son wasn't looking, he planted a quick kiss on my lips.

"There!" Hunter exclaimed. We jumped apart as if we'd been caught at something, but when we looked over at him, he was pointing down at the water beneath him.

"There's loads of fish here," he told us excitedly, bounding over to join us. "We should get started."

"We should," Holden agreed, breaking away from me. A little heat was working up my neck, so I pulled up my jacket and hoped Hunter wouldn't notice my little flush.

A few moments later, Hunter and Holden were enthusiastically talking me through what I needed to do. I had my feet hooked around the base of the seat to keep from keeling over, and I was clutching the pole like it was the only thing keeping me secured. This was profoundly weird, and I had no idea what I was supposed to be doing.

"And now when you put the bait on, they all come around," Hunter told me, peering over into the water.

"Look! The line's moving! You've got a bite!" Holden exclaimed excitedly. I felt the rod twitch in my hands.

"What do I do?" I cried out, my body tensing. I wanted to let go of it, but I knew I had to keep a firm hold. I tightened my grasp, and

Holden moved behind me, covering my hands with his and guiding my slight shakiness into something more workable.

"Okay, so you just ease it up." He guided my arms up, and the rod pulled smoothly out of the water. I didn't know why, but I was surprised when I saw there was really a fish on the other end of it. Some part of me had been convinced I was only going to come up with an old boot or something like that, but there it was, the little fish wriggling on the other end of the line.

"You got one!" Hunter exclaimed triumphantly, and he tapped me on the shoulder in a celebration of my success.

"What happens now?" I asked as Holden began to reel in the line for me.

"I'll take it and put it on ice," he told me. "And we can take it by the butcher and get it ready for dinner this evening. How about that?"

"As long as I don't have to have anything to do with getting it ready." I made a face, and Hunter giggled.

"You won't," Holden assured me, carefully pulling the fish from the line and turning to head into the cabin.

Hunter hopped up in the seat beside me and set up his line. I watched him with amusement as he deftly lined the thing up and dropped it into the water, and then I climbed out of my seat so I could crouch behind him and watch.

"You enjoying your spring break so far?" I asked. I felt a little guilty that Holden had spent so much of it with me in Vegas, but Hunter seemed happy that we were all together now.

"Loads." He grinned at me, and he looked over his shoulder to check that his father was out of earshot. My heart dropped. The last time this had happened, he'd asked me about his mother, and the last thing I wanted was another conversation I didn't have the answers to.

"Can I ask you something?" He glanced at me as the line sat quietly in the water below us. I nodded.

"Of course."

"Do you love my dad?"

The question practically knocked me off my feet. I opened and closed my mouth a couple of times, gaping like a fish plucked from the water, and I strained my brain at double-speed to try and come up with a decent answer to that question. I had no idea how to respond.

"Uh, I like him very much." I nodded eventually. "And I really enjoy spending time with the two of you together. Why do you ask?"

"Because I think he loves you." He furrowed his brow. "He doesn't say it, but I think he does."

I fell silent for a moment. Honestly, my heart was so full at that moment, I could have leaped to my feet and punched the air. I had to remind myself that Hunter was a kid with a kid's understanding of love, and to him, any kind of relationship had to be true love because that's what he had been taught his whole life. But the words were so sweet coming out of his mouth, even if Holden himself hadn't said them yet.

"Bless your heart." I leaned over and gave him a big hug, nudging the rod a few inches to the left and out of the patch he had chosen to fish in. He didn't seem to care. He hugged me back, and I closed my eyes and felt a swell of what could only be described as maternal love for this little man right here. I hadn't been sure I could feel it until that moment, but there was no denying it.

"You guys okay?" Holden asked, and I released Hunter and returned to my seat. I didn't want Holden to hear what we'd been talking about. The last thing I wanted was for him to feel pressured into saying those words to me before he was ready. Still, it was a sweet little boost to hear them from someone and to know Hunter approved of our relationship enough to call it love.

"Great," I called to him, and he emerged from the cabin to join us, rubbing his hands together to ward off the cold.

"Let's see what else we can get for dinner tonight, huh?" he remarked as he settled into his seat, and I leaned back to watch the two of them fish. They were so alike when they were intently focused —that little furrow in their brow, their lips pressed together. It was so clear they were family. And I was starting to believe I could be part of that family too.

59

HOLDEN

"What do you guys want to do today?" I asked as I carefully slid the last pancake from the pan and onto the serving plate. Autumn grabbed it and carried it over to the breakfast table where Hunter was waiting, still in his pajamas with the sharks on them.

"Well, it's the last day of Hunter's spring break," Autumn pointed out. "I think we should let him decide, don't you?"

I grabbed the coffee I'd made for Autumn, and I went to join them for breakfast. The light was filtering in through the window, and I could tell it was going to be a warmer day than it had been before—not that the warmth in my heart wasn't more than enough right now.

"So what do you want to do today, Hunter?" I turned to my son as he tucked into his first pancake, slathering it in maple syrup the way he always did. I swear his appetite had increased the last few days like being around Autumn again had lifted a weight from his shoulders.

"There's a carnival by the pier," he told me once he'd chewed and swallowed, taking a sip of his orange juice to wash it down. "I saw a sign for it yesterday."

"We should totally go!" Autumn seemed excited by the thought. "I used to go to that one all the time. I think it's the same one. It used to run over the last weekend of spring break when I was a kid. It's cheesy, but it's really fun. And the food is great."

"Well, then it's decided." I grinned at them both. "Carnival it is."

We got dressed and cleaned up, and I drove the three of us across town to the carnival. I had never thought Hunter would be interested in something like that, but it seemed like he was getting better about opening up with what he really wanted now that Autumn was around. She was a great influence on him. I hoped these last few days had been enough to lift the worry in her mind that she wasn't enough for him—for us—because she was. She was exactly the kind of woman I had always dreamed of having in my life for Hunter. Kind, funny, gentle, understanding, smart. It was just a damned good bonus that we happened to like each other so much as well.

When we arrived, the place was already thronged with families. Where Hunter might have normally been a little wary about the huge crowds, he took off out of the car and toward the entrance at once, forcing Autumn to hurry to keep up with him. I watched for a moment as the two of them sped off together and then took up a dignified jog to catch up. I wanted to remember every little moment of this, of how good it felt to really have a full-blown family beyond me and Hunter.

I paid our entry fees, and Hunter paused for a moment as soon as he was through the gate. He seemed a little taken aback by how much there was, as though he had no idea where to get started. I had to admit, there was a lot going on here—a carousel, a chair swing, dozens of stalls selling toys or deep-fried treats, and others that were set up with simple games where you could win soft toys or pretend guns for your trouble.

"This is exactly like the one that was here when I was growing up," Autumn sighed as she looked around. "Man, I haven't been down here in so long. I should make more of an effort."

"Where do you recommend we start?" I asked, putting my hand on Hunter's shoulder to make sure he didn't go speeding off again. "As the woman in the know."

"Hmm." She tapped her finger against her chin ponderously. "How about we start with the rides? Then food and then the games so if we win something, we don't have to lug it around with us all day."

I nodded. "That sounds great. How's that for you, Hunter?"

"Sure," he agreed, clearly glad to have a little guidance in the face of all this fun stuff to do. He grabbed Autumn by the hand and headed straight for this crummy little rollercoaster that looked like it was about to give out at the seams, and I went after them.

We spent the first hour doing all the rides at least twice. Hunter loved every second of it, peering at the mechanics of the carousel as we waited in line and asking the man at the desk how it worked. Then we moved on to the food, which was ridiculously greasy and fatty and also ridiculously delicious. I hadn't eaten a funnel cake in years, and as soon as I took a bite, I was transported back to being Hunter's age, kicking my legs against a bench on the side of the pier one day in late Fall. Autumn smiled at me as I ate.

"Good?" she asked, and I nodded.

"Great," I replied. Hunter was trying to get his mouth around a huge cone of ice cream, and I quickly pressed a couple of napkins into his hand before things got out of control.

"We should do this all the time," Hunter said, sighing with satisfaction.

"Well, back to school tomorrow," I reminded him. "But we'll come here again next year, huh?"

"We could take some more time off," Hunter asked hopefully. "Maybe another week?"

I laughed and shook my head.

"Nice try, buddy, but I'm afraid it doesn't work like that." I ruffled his hair. "You have to go back to school, and we both have to go back to work. Right, Autumn?"

"Right." She made a face at Hunter in sympathy. "But I want to come back again next year."

"We could make it a tradition!" Hunter suggested excitedly. I glanced over at Autumn, who smiled back at me.

"Maybe we could," I agreed.

Next for us was taking on the game stalls. They were silly little games, mostly trying to shoot down balls to land in these certain little cartons, and at first, none of us had much luck with them, but soon enough, I managed to land a prize. I watched as the guy behind the counter dipped below the top of the stall, felt around for a little bit, and then seemed to pull out the first thing he laid his hands on. He planted a large, plush teddy bear on the stall in front of us.

I picked it up and held it out to Autumn, who looked down at Hunter first.

"You sure you don't want it?" she asked him, and Hunter shook his head.

"I think you should have it," he told her, and she reached out to take it from me, clutching the enormous thing to her chest and wrapping her arms all the way around it.

"It's perfect. Thank you." She grinned at me. "What do you want to have a go at next?"

The three of us continued around the carnival, taking in all the stalls, even as the sun started to dip a little over the water behind us. It was a tiny bit cold, and I draped my jacket around Autumn's shoulders as we rounded the last line of stalls and walked back toward the entrance. Hunter glanced up at me, and he seemed satisfied by my choice as if he liked it when I made an effort to be romantic. Well, he had to learn that shit from someone, didn't he? I wanted my son to be a gentleman when the time came.

"Man, I'm tired." Autumn stretched, the teddy bear tucked under one arm haphazardly. "You think we should be heading out of here? I could use something real to eat at your place."

"That's probably a good idea," I agreed. I had noticed that Hunter had fallen a little quiet in the last ten minutes or so, and I knew him well enough to suspect he was getting tired and could use the break himself.

"Come on then." I grabbed Hunter's hand, and the three of us turned to head back down to the car. Hunter was tired enough that he didn't try to pull away from me as he might have usually, and I felt a little swell of happiness holding his hand like this. It reminded me of when he had been really little, when he had really needed me, and I missed that so much sometimes. Autumn took my other hand and bumped her hip against mine as we walked, and warmth spread across my chest knowing that the whole family was together. I could have done this all day, just walked with them anywhere they wanted to go. It felt so right, the three of us all together like this, and I couldn't imagine it ever getting old.

As we reached the exit of the carnival, I saw her, and I froze to the spot.

For a second, I tried to convince myself there was no way it could be her, no way she was actually here. She had to have skipped town by now as soon as she'd realized I wasn't falling for her scheme. I hadn't heard from her in a while, and I'd assumed she made a break for it again, but there was no mistaking her. She was facing away from me, half-turned with her eyes narrowed in the opposite direction, but it seemed like she was looking for something. Or someone. Us?

"Holden, what's wrong?" Autumn asked, peering off into the direction I was staring, trying to make out what had caught my attention. I shook my head.

"Nothing," I muttered. "Come on. Let's get home."

I ducked my head down low and prayed to all things holy that she hadn't noticed any of us. How long had she been in there? The place was beginning to clear out now, and she could have spotted us earlier. Maybe the reason she was hanging by the exit was in the hope that she could intercept us and catch us before we got out of here. But to what end? What was Karla doing here? Was it coincidence, or had she followed us?

I hurried out of the carnival and back to the car, my heart pounding in my chest. I felt like I had seen some ghost from my past, someone raised from the dead to spook me beyond belief. As soon as we were all back in the car, I gripped the wheel and let out a long sigh. Hunter had his eyes closed and his head pressed to the window, so I don't think he even noticed my reaction, but Autumn sure as hell had.

"What was that about?" she asked quietly, and I shook my head.

"Nothing," I replied quickly, my voice harder than I had intended. "I just... I'm sorry. I'm tired, that's all. It's been a long few days."

"Let's get home, shall we?" Autumn smiled at me, placing her hand on my forearm. Her touch was enough to bring me back down to Earth, to remind me that Karla hadn't seen any of us and that we had made it out of there unscathed.

"Yeah, let's go home." I pulled out of the parking lot and started back toward the house, Autumn's hand still on my arm. It was at that moment that I realized she had referred to my place, for the first time, as home. That was enough to lift the stress of what had just happened long enough for me to get out a smile.

60

AUTUMN

"Well, well. You made it back in time, I see," I remarked as Zoe slipped into the room. She looked exhausted but satisfied, and she flopped into the tiny chair opposite my desk as soon as she was through the door.

"Did you have a good time?" I asked her as she pushed her fingers through her slightly messy hair and yawned.

"Oh, yeah," she agreed at last. "I had an incredible time there. But I lost all my savings."

"What the hell are you talking about?" I exclaimed. I hadn't heard much from Zoe since I had left with Holden a few days before, but I had assumed she had been hanging out with that hottie she had been hooking up with, not dropping all her cash.

"Oh, cool it. I don't remember doing it, so it doesn't count." She waved her hand and flashed me a wicked smile. "Besides, I'm pretty sure my new man was worth it."

"So you're actually dating now?" I asked, and she shrugged.

"Honestly, I have no idea, but I don't really care," she replied. "He lives a hundred miles or so from Portland, and he says he's going to come into town to visit as soon as he can. I'm *really* looking forward to it *if* you know what I mean."

"You can't wait to have sex with him again?" I filled in the blanks for her, and she pointed at me.

"Exactly."

I smiled at her. "Well, I'm glad you had a good time. How do you feel about being back?"

"It's nice to come back to reality," she confessed. "I loved all that stuff in Vegas, but I'm happy to be home too. What about you? How's it been since you guys got back? You officially back together now?"

"I would say so." I nodded, a smile on my face. "I mean, we spent the whole week together, all three of us, and I stayed over at their place the whole time, so I sure as hell would consider that getting back together. Wouldn't you?"

"Oh, I'm so happy for you." Zoe tapped me on the arm excitedly. "You guys make such a lovely couple. And Holden seems really sweet."

"You barely got to spend any time with him," I pointed out.

"So you're saying I got the wrong impression?" Zoe cocked an eyebrow, and I giggled and shook my head.

"No, I didn't mean that," I corrected myself. "I'm just saying I'd like you guys to get to know each other better, given that you're both such important parts of my life."

"Oh, you flatter me." She planted a hand over her heart and smiled. "I'd love to spend some more time with him. Maybe we could double-date when Kieran is back in town?"

"Sounds great," I said right as she checked the clock and jumped to her feet.

"Hey, I have to be getting out of here," she pointed out. "Need to get things set up for all the kids coming back."

"Good luck," I told her, and she pulled a face at me. She knew as well as I did that trying to wrangle kids coming back from a time off was one of the hardest things a teacher could do. She headed out, and I turned back to the lesson plan I had for the rest of the day. I found that if you pushed toward a really packed schedule, the kids wouldn't wind up too bored and antsy for their first day back.

A knock came at the door, and I glanced up, wondering why Zoe didn't walk in like she normally did, but I saw a woman I didn't recognize standing in the doorway instead. She was a little older than me with long dark hair and sharp eyes. I smiled at her.

"Can I help you?" I asked politely, and she glanced around and slipped over the threshold, pushing the door shut behind her.

"I'm really hoping you can," she replied, biting her lip and widening her eyes. She looked like she was the right age to be a parent of one of the kids from my classes, but I knew most of the parents by sight at least now, and I had no clue who the hell she was.

"Can I ask what this is about?" I pressed her. I wasn't sure why, but a rush of reprehension ran up the back of my neck, my body stiffening as she approached the table. I wasn't sure what this was, but there was something in me telling me it was wrong, kicking me into fight-or-flight mode.

"It's about..." She hesitated for a moment, sinking down gracefully into the seat in front of me before she spoke. "It's about Hunter."

My eyes widened. The pieces clicked into place before she explained herself.

"I'm his mother," she told me. "Karla. It's lovely to meet you."

She extended a hand toward me across the desk, and I took it without thinking, but as soon as our fingers met, I felt like I had betrayed Holden in some way. He hated this woman, hated that she was trying to get her claws into his son, and here I was playing the hostess to her. But I couldn't kick her out, could I? I didn't want to cause a scene, and part of me was intrigued to find out what she had to say. Well, and to find out exactly how it was that she'd found me and whether she was here because I was Hunter's teacher or because I was Holden's girlfriend.

"I came to you today," she sighed deeply and shook her head, as though she couldn't believe she was having to ask me for this kind of help, "because I need your help in seeing him again."

"I don't know what you mean," I lied, deciding to play the fool in the hopes of her telling me her side of the story.

She sighed again, this time more irritated, and eyed me as though I was an idiot before she went on.

She flicked her tongue across her lips and took a deep breath. "I mean, I have been kept from my son for years now. For *years*. Do you have children? Do you know what that's like?"

"No, I don't," I confessed, even though when she asked that question, Hunter popped up into my mind. Yes, he wasn't my son, but something maternal had begun to grow inside me for him, despite the facts.

"Then you couldn't possibly understand what I've been through." She shook her head again, touching her fingers to her cheeks as though wiping away tears, but I couldn't see anything. I shifted in my seat. This felt wrong, having this conversation without Holden here, but it wasn't like I had a panic button I could press to send him running to me, was it?

"His father has kept me out of his life." She leaned forward. "He's hidden him from me, basically, unfairly kept my son away. And I've had to take drastic measures to get him back. Do you understand what I mean?"

"What kind of measures?" I asked her, playing dumb.

"I need you to let me see him," she explained. "That's why I came here today. I knew someone neutral like you would be able to listen to reason and see how unfair it is that I'm still being kept from my son."

"I'm afraid we can't let any unauthorized adults see the children in our classes," I told her calmly. "Do you have a letter from Holden?"

"Holden would never let me see him, that's the entire *point*," Karla snapped back. This was clearly not going the way she had hoped it would, and I was having to bite back a little amusement at how frustrated she was getting over this. I knew it was cruel, but then, she was too. She was the one who had abandoned Hunter and Holden, and she was the one who had made her decision. She wasn't allowed to walk back into her son's life like nothing had happened. That wasn't how this worked, and I wasn't going to let her come flitting in here and trying to guilt-trip me into doing whatever it was she wanted.

"Okay, but we can't let you see any of the kids until you have authorization," I repeated myself. "Otherwise, anyone could come in here and claim any child they wanted. You see what I mean?"

"Can't you tell I'm his mother?" She shoved her face at me across the table, and I scanned it for a long moment. I could say without a shadow of a doubt, I would never have known she was Hunter's biological mother. Hunter had so much of Holden in him, not just in the way he looked but in the way he was, the way he moved, the way he spoke, the way he acted. This woman had clearly had nothing to do with that boy, and it showed. That only strengthened my resolve to keep her away from him at all costs as Holden had always wanted to.

"I'm afraid that until you can provide some legal documentation that confirms your relationship with Hunter, I'm going to have to ask you to leave." I got to my feet and pointed firmly to the door.

"I'm not going anywhere." She crossed her arms over her chest and looked at me expectantly.

"If you don't leave, I'm going to call the police," I told her. "We have the safety of all our students to consider, and I can't allow—"

"You have no idea who you're messing with." Karla rose to her feet, taking my threats seriously at last. "*No* clue. You really think you can keep me away from my son? You're just some teacher who's too invested. Hunter needs a mother in his life, and you couldn't understand that if you don't have children of your own—"

"Please, you need to leave." I pointed to the door once more, praying the shake in my voice wasn't audible to her. She struck me as the kind of woman who would pounce on any weakness she sensed and sink her claws into it, never letting go until she had exploited it to the furthest degree she could.

"I'll call security." I picked up the receiver on my desk phone, even though we didn't have a security team in the school for day-to-day classes. I prayed she wouldn't call my bluff, and though she lingered for a moment longer, she finally shook her head and backed toward the door.

"You're just a do-gooder teacher." She wagged her finger at me as she retreated. "You don't know what you're doing, and you don't know *who* you're dealing with."

I lifted the receiver to my ear, giving her a hard look, and finally, she stormed out the door and slammed it behind her. Hunter wouldn't be here yet—at least I could cling to that—so she wasn't going to run into him in the corridor and try to swipe him from there or something.

I slumped back into my seat, my heart racing. I couldn't believe I'd just done that. I had looked her in the eye, and I had turned her away. All those doubts I'd had, all that fear about her being Hunter's real mother, they had started to sink down, dulling and dimming inside me. Now that I had met her, I could see what Holden meant, that she hadn't a bone in her body that actually wanted to be a mother. Hunter was better off without her, no matter what she might have believed.

I had stood up for Holden and what he thought was right as well. I had protected Hunter where he needed it. It almost made me chuckle, the thought that Hunter was in the middle of all of this and didn't even know it. But it was best that he never found out, best that he never knew what he was the center of, and best that Holden and I worked to keep him as safe as we could. We had to keep that woman away from him at all costs.

Still, she had stepped things up by coming to the school. She had taken things to the next level. Who knew what she would be capable of next? My heart shuddered at the thought. I forced myself to return my attention to the plan in front of me and pull my mind away from Karla and the threat she had made toward me.

61

HOLDEN

The first day back after spring break, I knew I had to do something to make the transition a little easier for Hunter. So the two of us had come down to the diner not far from the school for some breakfast, and Hunter was happily chatting about how much he had enjoyed his break with Autumn and me.

"I'm so glad everything's back to normal," he said as he took a sip of his apple juice. I smiled at him.

"Me, too, son," I agreed. "Me too."

"Do you think Autumn's going to stick around this time?" he asked, the question simple but laced with meaning. I knew he didn't mean it that way, but it was impossible not to read it as that, as him trying to grope for a sense of security after the mess of everything that had happened.

"I think she will." I nodded, and he grinned.

"Do you think...?" He swallowed the words before he could say them.

"Do I think what?" I pressed him. I had noticed Hunter opening up a lot more than he usually did since Autumn had come back, and it made me pretty damn happy to see him speaking his mind more clearly than before.

"Do you think Autumn is going to be my mom?" he asked finally, and I smiled at him. That was about the sweetest thing I'd ever heard him come out with.

"You know, I don't—" Before I could continue, my phone buzzed against my hip, and I pulled it out of my pocket. A text from Autumn. I opened it up, assuming it was just going to be a "good morning" message, but my heart dropped when I saw what it really was.

I scanned the message three times before it really sank in. Karla had come to the school, trying to guilt-trip Autumn into letting her see Hunter. Autumn had turned her away, but Karla had seemed intent on letting her know she wasn't just going to vanish that easily. I switched off my phone and closed my eyes for a moment. She was getting closer. Had she seen us at the carnival? Had she followed us there?

"Dad?"

I opened my eyes and found my son sitting opposite me, the son I was trying my hardest to protect from all of this. My heart sank as I realized he had to know the truth. I couldn't keep hiding this from him. If she was moving in on his school, God only knew where else she might try to find him, and I needed him to be able to stand up for himself if she did turn up somewhere when we weren't expecting it.

"Hunter, there's something I need to tell you." I leaned toward him seriously. His eyes widened.

"Is it about Autumn?" he asked, and I shook my head.

"No, no, it's nothing to do with that," I assured him. "It's about... it's about your mother."

He sat there for a moment, staring at me. I had never really talked to him about his mother before, and I knew that was my fault. I should have sat him down before this, explained the truth to him instead of trying to duck it every time the question arose. Now I was in a place where I had no choice but to tell him what was going on— and no choice but to scare him with the knowledge that she was back in town.

"What about her?" he asked, his voice tiny. As I sat there opposite him, it struck me how small he was. I suddenly wanted to grab him and hug him close, promise him that nobody was ever going to get near him, promise that I was going to keep him safe from his mother no matter what. But I didn't know how I could do that. I needed him in on the situation so he could help me in protecting himself.

"When you were just born," I began, tracing the story all the way back to the start. "Your mother left us."

"Why?" His face dropped, and I felt instantly guilty for telling him about this. I had to swallow it down and tell him to watch out for Karla, not that she was his mother and that she wanted him back but that he couldn't be with her. It was too complex. But I had started already, and I was going to finish.

"There were a lot of reasons, son." I shook my head. "But none of it had to do with you. You understand that, right? She left because she wanted to, not because she didn't want you or like you."

"I don't understand." He shook his head, and I felt that punch of guilt once more. This was so much to put on him. But he needed to know the truth, or at least as much of it as he could handle, if we were going to keep him safe from Karla. She would use whatever she could to get to him, and the last thing I wanted was for him to believe she really did want him back when he was only another pawn in one of her sick little games.

"I don't either, Hunter," I replied. "It took me a long time to come to terms with the fact that she left. I never really understood why she did it. But eventually, I realized that it was for the best. She wasn't a good person, the woman who gave birth to you, and it was better that she was out of our lives. Even though it was hard sometimes, and I know it must have been hard for you, having these questions that never got answered."

"Why are you telling me this?" Hunter asked, and there was a helpless tone to his voice. I hated that he felt this way, hated that I was even forced to have this conversation with him, but there was no avoiding it. He needed to know what was going on. I couldn't risk Karla swooping in and exploiting his ignorance about her for her own personal gain. The thought of her getting her claws into him—no, I would never let that happen.

"Because..." I took a long, deep breath before I continued, knowing that I had to tell him the truth but hating that I had to weigh him down with it. "Because your mother came back into my life recently."

His eyes widened so far, it would have been comical if it hadn't been for the situation at hand. He stared at me for a long time, as though expecting me to take back what I said and admit it had been a joke. But I didn't. He looked down at the table, trying to process what he had heard, and then looked back up at me once more.

"What does she want?" he asked quietly. I shook my head.

"I don't know," I confessed. "At least, I'm not sure. I have some ideas, but I don't think she's back for any—I don't think it's good news, Hunter."

"What do I do?" His eyes widened again, and he looked so nervous, I wanted to drive him back home and lock the doors and spend the whole day making him feel safe again. But I couldn't do that. I couldn't let Karla use her influence to scare me into keeping my son on lockdown. I wasn't going to let her have that much power over either of us.

"If any woman approaches you when you're at school or you're out and about, you go to someone you trust right away, okay?" I told him. "Make sure you don't leave with her. I'm going to get you a phone with my number and Autumn's number on it, and you can call either of us, and we'll be there right away to pick you up, all right?"

"All right," he replied bravely, trying to keep his face set solid, but I could see the waver of panic in his eyes. I felt a swell of anger at Karla, anger at making us go through this, anger that she had forced my son to endure this kind of fear. She was no mother to him. She was using him, moving back into his life because there was some kind of personal gain in it for herself. And now she had made it to the school, to Autumn. She was making his life unsafe, and she probably still thought she was in the right about it.

"You're being so brave about this," I told him, reaching across to pat his arm. "But it's okay if it freaks you out too. Autumn and I are

going to take care of you every way we can. You understand
that, right?"

"Yes." He nodded, and I closed my eyes.

"Good," I replied, and I noticed that he had finished his breakfast.
"You want to go to school? Autumn's going to be there waiting
for you."

"Yeah, I do," he said, and I paid up and we headed out to the car. I
noticed that Hunter was sticking close by my side, looking around as
though he expected Karla to leap out from behind a car at any
moment. I hated that he had to feel that way, but at least it meant he
was going to be alert to the danger now. Better for him to know and
have some way to push back against it than it was for him to be innocent of everything that was going on and leave himself vulnerable to
her swooping in and sweet-talking him into leaving with her.

I switched the radio to the channel he liked in the car on the way
to school, but he kept his gaze fixed out of the window. I wanted to
talk to him, to ask what was going through his mind, but I had no
idea how to start that conversation. I should have discussed this stuff
with him years ago, should have known Karla would find some way
to come sliding back into our lives, but I supposed I would have to
work with what I had for the time being.

When I got to the school, Autumn was waiting next to the gate for
us as she told me she would be in her text. She smiled when she saw
us, but her arms were wrapped tight around herself like she was
protecting herself from something.

"Hey, Hunter!" she greeted him perkily. "You ready to start classes
again?"

"Yeah." Hunter nodded, subdued, and she shot me a look and
a smile.

"I'll talk to you more later," I told her quickly. "After school.
Thanks for letting me know."

"Of course," she said. She touched my arm briefly.

"It's going to be all right," she assured me. "We'll take care of him,
I promise. And I've told everyone to be on the lookout for her, so she's

not going to be able to make it onto school property again that easily."

"Thank you." I sighed, not realizing how much I had needed to hear that. "I'll see you soon."

"See you." She bid me farewell, and she led Hunter back toward the school. I planted my hands on my hips and watched them go. I was scared, really scared, for the first time in a long time. But I also knew Autumn would fight as hard as I would to protect him, and that was something. It was enough. For now. Until I could find a way to get Karla out of our lives for good.

62

AUTUMN

"All right, guys. As you know, no after-school activities today." I clapped my hands together and was met with a collective groan from the kids in front of me. "So pack up your stuff, and you can get going."

I watched as the children in my class chattered away and gathered their things. I had been forced to cancel all the after-school clubs I had been running for the following few weeks because I promised Holden I would bring Hunter home from school every evening to make sure Karla didn't get anywhere near him. We had played it off as a cute little bonding experience for Hunter and me, and I was keeping my fingers crossed that he hadn't figured out it had something to do with his nightmare of a biological mother.

The rest of the kids scattered out of the classroom, and I headed over to Hunter, who was peering down into his bag. All those friends he had made earlier, the ones he had hung out with after school, seemed to have dropped away now, much to my concern. He was starting to draw into himself once more, as though he was hiding from something. From Karla. He knew she was a presence in his life now, and I felt pretty fucking awful that he had wrapped his head around that fact. I wanted nothing more than to give him a big hug and tell him it was all going to be all right, but there was no way I could truly promise that and mean it. And that was the hardest thing in the world.

"Hey, Hunter." I crouched down in front of him and managed to put a big smile on my face, even though it felt false. "You think you're nearly ready to get going?"

"Yeah." Hunter nodded, and he hooked his bag over his shoulders and straightened up, his mouth set into a hard line. "Let's go."

I let him lead me out of the school and fired off a quick text to Holden to let him know I would be taking Hunter home that evening as we'd agreed. It wasn't that he didn't want to get him himself or couldn't be bothered but rather that Karla could have been following his car to figure out the details of Hunter's day, and the last thing we needed was to give her any more of a tip-off than she already had as to his whereabouts.

I opened the car door for Hunter, and he climbed inside, his face twisted downward as he was struggling to make sense of this. I frowned at him. I wanted things to go back to the way they had been before that woman had turned up. I wished I'd taken Holden seriously right off the bat, instead of assuming he was overstating the seriousness of the threat. It wasn't until I'd been looking her dead in the eyes that I'd known without a doubt that this woman meant business and that I would be in trouble if I stood in the way of her and her son. Which meant I was about to land myself in a whole damn heap of it, but it was worth it if I could keep Hunter safe.

"Ms. Becks?" Hunter asked suddenly as we turned on to the freeway, and I glanced down at him.

"What's up, Hunter?"

"Did my dad ever speak to you about my mom?"

I pressed my lips together. I never felt as though I was the one who should be having these conversations with Hunter, but as long as he kept springing them on me like this...

"Did he?" Hunter pressed, not happy with the long silence that followed his question. I chewed my lip.

"Yes, he talked to me about her a little bit," I admitted.

"And what did he say?" he pressed. "How did he... what did she do? When I was little?"

"I don't know everything," I warned him with a shake of my head. "I don't know if I can answer all the questions you have."

"That's okay," he replied eagerly. "You don't need to answer all of them. I just want to know the answer to some."

I glanced down at him and felt that sadness swell in me. Holden had been such an amazing dad to Hunter all those years, but at the same time, he had left so many questions unanswered, left so much unsaid, and now it was coming back to bite him in the ass. No matter if Karla had turned up or not, Hunter would clearly have had worries at the back of his mind about what had happened to his mother and if he had done anything to drive her away.

"Okay, fire away," I offered carefully. I was playing with fire, but what could I do, roll out of a moving car and hope he forgot about all of it?

"When did she go?"

"When you were very little," I replied. "A baby, I think. She barely even got to know you."

"Okay." Hunter nodded. "And when—have you met her? When she came back again?"

"Yes, I've met her," I replied, trying to keep my tone as neutral as possible. No matter how much a part of this family I became, I would never not feel a little angst talking to Hunter about his real mother. Things with Holden were so freshly back in place, and I didn't want to have to do anything to fuck that up.

"And what was she like?"

"Very different from your dad," I replied evasively. "And very different from you. Which makes sense."

"How long have you known her?"

"Not long." I shook my head again. "And I don't know her. We met one time."

"Where did you meet?" he asked, and I racked my brains for a believable lie. No way I could tell him his mother had showed up at the school—that would be far too unsettling for him.

"Oh, just around," I finally offered vaguely, hoping it would be enough. It seemed to satisfy him for the time being, and Hunter looked back out the window for a long moment, falling silent. I thought I had gotten away with it and those were the end of his questions, but then he turned back to me and hit me with a killer.

"Why did she leave?"

"What?" I almost screeched the car to a halt right then and there, I was so taken aback by what he had asked me.

"Why did she leave?" Hunter repeated simply. It was strange, the questions that seemed so impossible to understand as an adult sounded so simple coming out of the mouth of a child.

"Uh, I don't know." I shook my head. "There are a lot of reasons someone might do something like that."

"Was it because of me?" Hunter asked, his little brow furrowing. That was when I knew I needed to pull the car over and make sure he understood his place in all of this.

I pulled on to the side of the road, thankful that there was a rest stop we could talk in because I couldn't let something like that slide.

"Hunter, this is very important," I told him intently. "You did nothing wrong. Do you understand that? You were a baby. Nothing you did or that you've done since was what made your mother leave."

He stared at me for a long moment, and I could tell he wasn't quite sure if he believed me.

"Will you leave?" he asked quietly, and my stomach dropped. I reached over to give him a tight hug, not caring that it was probably an overstepping of my teacher boundaries. What I saw in front of me was a child in desperate need of some comfort, and I wasn't going to look that in the eye and turn it down, no matter what.

"Of course I won't," I told him firmly. "There's nothing you can do to get rid of me, you understand that? You're stuck with me."

He pulled back and looked at me, and I could tell he was scanning my statements for truth. I offered him a big smile, and he managed to return it at last. A swell of relief went through me, knowing I had managed to banish those thoughts from his mind at least.

"Come on. Let's get you home," I told him. "Your dad will be waiting for you."

I switched on the radio to the channel I knew Hunter liked—it was the one Holden had the radio in their car set to whenever I got in —and we drove the rest of the way down to Holden's place. I glanced over at the little boy beside me, and I felt it again, that swell of maternal instinct toward him. I wanted nothing more than to gather him up in my arms and tell him everything was going to work out. Which I supposed, in some ways, I had just done.

We arrived at the house, and I watched as Hunter hurried in ahead of me, giving his dad a big hug before plowing up the stairs to his bedroom. I smiled as I watched him go. Being around his father seemed to lift a weight off his mind, and it was a joy to see.

"What are you grinning about?" Holden greeted me, stealing a quick kiss while Hunter wasn't looking. I shook my head and smiled.

"It's good to be here, that's all," I told him. "I missed you. I missed this place."

"I missed you too," he assured me, planting another kiss on the corner of my mouth. "I appreciate what you're doing for Hunter, by the way. More than you know."

"Trust me, now that I've met her, I totally get where you're coming from." I made a face. "I wouldn't want her anywhere near my kid either."

He grinned. "Glad we're on the same page. But still. You don't have to do that, but you are. We both appreciate it so much."

I gazed at him for a moment, wondering if I should tell him the truth of what Hunter had been saying to me in the car. I thought better of it at the last minute. He didn't need to hear that. As though things weren't hard enough for him as it was.

"You want to stick around for dinner?" Holden asked hopefully, and I nodded.

"Well, I'm not doing all this taxiing around for free now, am I?" I pointed out, nudging him playfully. He laughed.

"And here I thought you were doing it out of the goodness of your own heart." He shook his head in faux disappointment. "Come on. I have a chicken curry cooking. I could use your palette to figure out what it's missing."

"Chili powder," I replied. "The answer to that is always more chili powder."

I followed him into the kitchen and paused for a moment to look up the stairs where Hunter had vanished to as soon as we had come in. I wanted nothing more than to go up there and reassure him that we were going to keep him safe and that most of all, none of this was his fault. This was all happening because Karla couldn't take no for an answer, not because of some poor innocent like Hunter.

But the best I could do for now was show him with my actions, not explain it with my words. He needed to see that I wasn't going anywhere, and I had every intention of proving it to him.

"Autumn?" Holden called through from the kitchen. "You coming?"

"Right there," I called back, pushing those thoughts out of my mind and following the beautiful scent wafting through from the kitchen to its source.

63

HOLDEN

With a smile on my face, I watched as Hunter hurried over to be with his friends. It was so good to see him socializing, and he seemed to have relaxed a little in the last few days. My presence and Autumn's had apparently been enough for him to start feeling safe again, which was all I'd really wanted. Karla would lose interest and back off soon enough, and for the time being, all that mattered was keeping focused on making sure Hunter felt loved and cared for.

I slipped inside the building and headed straight to Autumn's classroom. I was hoping for a sneaky make-out before work, but when I opened the door, I found her friend Zoe in there with her.

"Well, speak of the devil." Zoe planted her hands on her hips and looked at me.

"And what exactly have I done?" I grinned as I made my way over to Autumn and gave her a quick kiss on the cheek. She beamed up at me.

"We were actually talking about your new program," she told me. "The grading system? It's been so useful, we actually have our weekends back."

"If I'm not stealing them from you," I pointed out playfully. "They're doing the job, then?"

"Oh, they're perfect." Zoe nodded. "You need to roll it out across all the schools in the county. I can't think how much time this might save teachers who really need it, you know?"

"That sounds like a great idea," I said. "I'll need to speak to my people and figure out the details, but if you think it's worth it—"

"More than worth it," Zoe urged. "And it would be big for you if you could get this into all the schools in the county, right?"

"Sure would." I glanced at Autumn, who was beaming up at me delightedly. "But that's not why I did it."

"Yeah, yeah, I know you did it for *love* or something like that." She shook her head teasingly. I didn't meet Autumn's gaze. Neither of us had said that to each other yet, and I sure as hell wasn't going to let that word come out of my mouth as part of Zoe lightly roasting us.

"Anyway, class is getting ready to start." She glanced down at her watch. "I need to get out of here."

"So do I." I sighed apologetically to Autumn. "I want to head home and speak to the administrators about the program. If you like it so much, I want to get ahead of it before it spreads anywhere else."

"You should." Autumn waved her hand. "Have a good day. And I'll drive Hunter home this afternoon after class, all right?"

"All right." I nodded and then stole one last kiss before I ducked out of the door and started back to my car, waving at Hunter as I passed by. Heading back to the house, I ran through all my contacts in my head, figuring out who the best point of contact might be to get ahold of within the school district. Because I had something that could change everything for teachers like Autumn, and if it was working well, there was no reason to sit on it a moment longer.

I headed straight to my office when I was through the door and grabbed my phone. Though I had been something of a recluse when it came to my work for the last few weeks, I still had decent clout in the business, and I intended to take full advantage of that. A half hour of phone calls later, I ended up on the other end of the line with the woman who organized the resources for school teachers around the district.

"And you said that you've been testing this program with a couple of teachers?" she asked. I could hear the incredulity in her voice—and she didn't even know that the teacher I had tested this with was also the one I was dating. I decided to keep that on the down-low for the time being—to make sure my credibility wasn't totally shot.

"Yes, and they've both given me great feedback for the program as a whole," I replied enthusiastically. "They told me the program has saved them a lot of time. One of them has started running some after-school activities with the time she had to spare."

"I see." She sounded impressed. "And how much are you charging for this program? For, say, a ten-school rollout?"

"I'd be happy to give you a trial run for free," I told her eagerly. "Maybe six weeks? And if you like it, we can talk about packaging the program into the teacher's software across the district."

"That sounds fair to me," she agreed, and I could hear the grin on her face even through the phone.

"You know," she confessed. "I used to teach. And the grade curves were always my least favorite part of doing that. I always wondered why nobody put something together to make them easier! I suppose you saw a gap in the market, huh?"

"I suppose I did." I grinned. "And I'm delighted if I can help out the teachers in the district too."

"You have children at a school around here?"

"Yes, a son. Hunter."

"And any spare time the teachers have to focus on their students will benefit him as well," she rounded off for me. "Well, makes sense. Let me make a few calls and see where this program would be best suited to start out, okay? You'll hear from me soon."

"Looking forward to it," I replied. She hung up, leaving me feeling as though I could punch the air in victory. Things were starting to slide into place. I hadn't heard from Karla in a while, Hunter seemed like he was opening up again, and Autumn and I were getting closer and closer to dropping that all-important L-word.

And if I could pull off this project on top of everything else, that would be perfect. It could be huge if I pulled it off. Sure, it would be hard work getting off the ground and rolling out across the district, but it would be worth it. Not only would I be able to have a big impact on the world around me, and Hunter especially, but it could make me a lot of money. Maybe that was a little greedy, but every time I had a project like this one come through, I thought forward to what it could mean for Hunter—to everything I could do for him with that kind of money. I could send him to whatever college he wanted in the world. I could pay for any summer camp he wished to attend, could afford classes that would cover anything he wanted to learn. Every time I put this money aside, I was assuring a future for my son and the life I wanted him to have. And that made me happy.

I was about to go downstairs to make coffee and plan out exactly how to roll out the program when my phone buzzed again in my pocket. I grabbed it, assuming it would be the same woman I had been on the line with, maybe calling to mention something she'd forgotten the first time around. Instead, I saw a number I didn't recognize on the screen. Furrowing my brow, I lifted it to my ear and took the call.

"Hello?"

"Holden?"

I recognized the voice at once. My body tensed from top to bottom, and my heart felt frozen dead solid in my chest. *Karla.* But I had her number. Where the fuck was she calling from?

"Karla, what do you want?" I asked. I strained to hear what was in the background of the call, hoping it would give me an indicator of where she was. I could make out a little traffic, but nothing more than that. She must have been calling from a payphone somewhere. But why?

"I wanted to let you know I'm standing outside of Hunter's school right now," she told me. If I hadn't been scared before, I launched into full-blown panic mode when I heard those words come out of her mouth. *No.* I wanted to sprint down there, grab my son, and run as far away from the woman who claimed to be his mother as I could. I instantly went to grab my car keys, trying to keep her on the line.

"What the hell are you doing down there?" I demanded. I racked my brains for where she might be. There was a pay phone maybe two hundred feet down the street from the school. Perhaps she was there. I hurried out to the car as I waited for her to reply, but she seemed determined to make me wait for the response.

"I think that it's only fair Hunter know about his mother," she replied, and her voice was strangely calm as if this whole situation was almost funny to her. I wanted to scream down the line at her, tell her to get away from my son and never go near him again as long as she lived. But I needed to stay calm and get down there.

"Karla, don't do this," I warned her as I turned on the engine and pulled out of the driveway. "You know this is a bad idea. It's only going to make things worse."

"As if they could be any worse than they are right now," she shot back cruelly. "You're keeping me away from him, Holden, and you're letting some new woman into his life at the same time? You don't think that's hypocritical?"

Her voice was taunting now like she knew she had me where she wanted me. I clenched and unclenched my hands on the wheel. If only I could reach through the phone and drag her away from him, away from my son, away from whatever she had in mind.

"Karla—"

But before I could get another word out, the phone went dead. With an annoyed grunt, I tossed it to the side and dumped it in the seat next to me. All that mattered now was getting down there in time —before she had a chance to get to Hunter. I tried to soothe myself, reminding myself that Autumn was there and that she would do everything she could to take care of my kid any way she was able. That would be enough. It had to be. I had to believe, with everything in me, that it was as I sped through the streets of Portland and toward Karla, Autumn, and Hunter.

64

AUTUMN

"Hey, you having a good day?" I asked as Hunter approached me with a smile on his face. He nodded.

"Really good," he replied, and I couldn't help smiling. It was such a relief to see him looking happier and more relaxed than he had been in recent memory. It had been clear that the truth about his mother had been weighing heavily on him, but now things had calmed down a little bit, he seemed to be lightening up. I was still a little on edge, but it was my job to be. I was his teacher and more than that too. It would have been wrong if I wasn't a little overly involved.

It was break time at school, and I was on playground duty, hanging out by the gate to make sure nobody tried to slip out and grab something from the corner store across the street. Sometimes kids would head down there to get candy when they thought nobody was paying attention, but I was keeping an extra-close watch that day. Nobody was getting in or out of this school that I didn't know about, that was for damn sure.

"What have you been up to?" I asked, glancing around the street and inhaling a big lungful of air. It was starting to warm up now that the sun was high in the sky, and the day felt still and sweet, full of promise. As I looked across the street, a cold fear gripped my stomach. It couldn't be her. Could it?

I stared for a long moment, trying to figure out whether my mind was playing tricks on me. It had to be some kind of mirage, my mind filling in the blanks where there was nothing to see. Because there was no way in holy hell Karla was standing there, staring at the two of us from the other side of the street. She wouldn't have dared. Would she?

Then she started moving toward me, and I swiftly stepped in front of Hunter who stopped in midsentence.

"What's wrong?" he asked, his voice quivering with nervousness as he waited for me to respond. What the hell did I tell him? That the one woman who should have been nowhere close to him was making her way to us, staring me straight in the eye like she belonged there? I wanted to hustle him back into the school, but that might have given her time to slip through the gate, and getting her out was going to be a lot harder than keeping her at bay.

"Who's that lady?" Hunter asked curiously as she got closer, close enough that I could see the bile in her face.

"Hunter, go inside and find Zoe," I told him urgently, not bothering with her proper teacher name for that moment. He furrowed his brow at me, and I waved my hands at him.

"Go, now!" I ordered him, and his face dropped as he did as he was told. I hated speaking to him like that, but he needed to get out of there before something happened, something I couldn't put a stop to.

"Autumn?" Karla was suddenly right in front of me as I turned back around to check on her progress. My heart dropped.

"Karla, what the hell are you doing here?" I demanded. "Does Holden know you're here?"

"Yes, he does." She nodded. My eyes widened. Had he given her permission?

"Where's my son?" she demanded. "I saw him here with you a second ago. Where is he now?"

"He's in the school, and you're not getting anywhere near him," I told her firmly. "Please, just leave. Before I call the police."

"What for?" She tossed her hands in the air. "You don't have a restraining order against me. I want to see my son. That's all. You know how heartless you're being right now?"

I took a deep breath, trying to steady myself. She was manipulating me, and I couldn't let her get away with it. I couldn't let her get close.

"Karla, I'm going to ask you one more time," I warned her. "Get out of here. Leave."

"You can't tell me what to do." She pushed her face closer to mine, over the fence that was keeping us apart. The gate suddenly felt flimsy like it wasn't even sturdy enough to keep her where she needed to be.

"I work here, and I can tell you that we don't allow anyone on the property who hasn't been cleared by the school," I snapped back. "I don't care what you want. You need to get away from here. Speak to Holden, not to Hunter. He's a kid, and he doesn't need this—"

"You don't know what my son needs," she sneered. "I don't care what Holden's convinced you. You'll never be a parent to him. You can't be. You don't understand the connection we had."

Before, she had at least tried to sweet-talk me a little. Here, she was going for it, not holding back, not giving a shit how I felt or what my relationship with Hunter might have been. She only wanted to get under my skin, and I couldn't let her do that. I was the responsible adult here, and it was up to me to reject the bullshit she was dripping and remind myself that she was nothing more than a pathetic, manipulative bitch trying to get what she wanted. I could almost guarantee that if Holden had let her see Hunter with no restrictions, she would have grown tired of him by now and moved on. The fact that she had to fight it—that was what she was attracted to. That was what she wanted. She was making a point here, reminding anyone who would listen that she was the one in charge and she was the one who would get her way. No matter what the cost.

"You haven't been a mother to him his entire life," I shot back angrily. "You took ten years to come back into his life. Ten years! You really think he's done badly without you?"

"Well, I wouldn't know since everyone has been trying to keep me from him," she replied through gritted teeth. "I won't stand for this. I'll sue you, and I'll sue the school. Holden might have the money to deal with it, but you don't, do you?"

I stayed silent. She was right.

"That's why you went after someone like Holden," she taunted me. "You're after his money, aren't you? Well, you'll never have the connection with him that I do. You could never *dream* of it."

"Karla," I warned her as best I could. It was taking everything I had in me not to take a swing at this woman. I was deadly serious. I had never felt the urge to hurt another human being before, not seriously, but the way she was talking to me, the way she was looking at me like I was some kind of idiot, I wanted to yell at her. I wanted to prove she would never have the kind of relationship I had with Hunter and Holden—with either of them, but that would only prove her point. She wanted me to drop down to her level so she could show I wasn't worthy for her son. I wasn't going to give her that satisfaction. Not in a million years. Still, I found my fist clenched at my side, and I noticed her gaze slide down to take it in.

Suddenly, I heard a noise from behind me.

"Hunter, come back—"

I spun around to find Zoe standing in the doorway to the school, a pained expression on her face as Hunter broke away from her and hurried over to me.

"Autumn?" He grabbed my hand, and even though I knew he was just a little kid, his presence made me feel a bit better. He was on my side, and that was what mattered. In the whole mess of this nightmare, he was the only thing I cared about.

"Hunter, go back inside," I ordered him. Zoe went to stride over to us, but I held my hand up to keep her at bay. I knew that I had to handle this as it stood before things went any further.

"Is this her?" Hunter demanded, looking up at the woman before him. Karla was staring down at him with the most curious expression on her face. I couldn't have described it even if I'd tried. There was a whole lot going on there, but most of it looked like panic. As though she had been happy to talk a big game when she didn't think anyone would take her up on it, but now that he was here looking her in the face, she had no fucking clue how to react.

But all at once, she crouched down, wrapping her fingers around the bars of the gate and staring at Hunter intently.

"I'm your mommy, Hunter," she cooed to him, her voice sugary-sweet and clearly fake. I wanted to slap her away from him. My heart was pounding hard in my chest, and I looked down at Hunter, waiting for him to respond. He was eyeing his mother for a long time before he opened his mouth and then finally came out with it.

"I don't need you." He shook his head, his voice small but firm.

"But I'm your family, baby," she told him, her voice growing spiked around the edges. I pulled Hunter back an inch, making sure there was plenty of space between the gate and him. She could have reached through and grabbed him if I wasn't careful, and I wasn't about to let her any closer to him than she had already gotten.

"No, you're not." He shook his head. "Autumn is. And Dad. Not you."

Her face twisted into a mask of rage, and I could tell she hadn't envisioned this reaction, not in a million years. I smirked, despite myself. It might have been childish, but seeing her not getting what she wanted was so satisfying.

"I never wanted you anyway," she spat back at him. Her voice was full of spite, lashing out at this helpless child because he wouldn't go along with her crazy plan to suddenly be a family again after all that time apart. Something in her voice triggered a reaction in me, the kind of reaction I never imagined in a million years I would have to anyone.

It all came in such a rush that I hardly had time to process it. I dropped Hunter's hand and straightened up, grabbed Karla by the collar of her cheap shirt, and swung a fist at her. I hardly noticed the blur of pain punch through my hand as it made contact with her. It wasn't that hard. I didn't have it in me to hurt her badly, physically or mentally, but she went reeling back from the gate and staggered dramatically away from me.

Zoe sped forward and grabbed Hunter by the shoulders, pulling him back inside the school, and I stared as Karla went sprawling across the street. She was waving her arms around to attract the attention of anyone who would look, and I hurried around the gate to catch her before she wound up getting hit by a car or something.

"That woman!" she shrieked, pointing a shaking finger at me. "She hit me! And now she's coming after me! Please, someone help me!"

I stood there as a few passers-by intervened, pulling her off the road. I suppose one of them must have dialed 911 because moments later, the police had turned up at the school. I was still in such a total daze at what had happened that it took me a good long moment to realize they were there for me and not her.

"Miss, can you come with us, please?" An officer stepped toward me. Karla was cowering on the other side of the road, and I couldn't take my eyes off her. How had she pulled this off? How had she managed to make this happen? How had I been dumb enough to fall for her manipulation, to let myself believe I had no choice but to do that to her?

"Yeah, yeah," I muttered. As soon as I got down to the station, I could explain this, explain that I was protecting Holden's son, the kid who was starting to feel like my own. But what if they took her side? What if Holden had given her permission to come down there, and I had walked into the middle of it and caused an enormous mess?

"Autumn!"

Another familiar voice. I turned to see Holden clambering out of a car, hurrying toward me.

"Hunter's okay," I called to him. "He's inside with Zoe."

"Autumn—"

"Sir, please step away." One of the officers pushed Holden away from me firmly as he got closer, and he stared, wide-eyed, as they clapped handcuffs on me and pushed me down into the car. My body was numb, my brain switched off, my soul so far gone, I would be surprised if I ever found it again. But none of that mattered. What mattered was that I had defended Hunter when he'd needed it, that

I'd let him know I was there for him and that nothing his deadbeat mother tried to tell him was true. As they slammed the door behind me, I looked out at Holden's face beyond the window, shell-shocked, and I knew I would do it all again if I had to. Anything to ensure that my two boys stayed safe. Anything to ensure that woman stayed well away from them.

65

HOLDEN

I paced up and down outside the police station. I prayed it would be the last time I had to be anywhere like this for a long while. I couldn't believe I was there to keep my girlfriend from going to jail. How crazy was this?

This entire day had been batshit insane from start to finish, and I was glad the worst of it was over. Karla was in the hospital, probably swooning around acting like someone had attacked her with a baseball bat instead of throwing one measly punch. Hunter was with Raymond, where he was helping him decompress and relax after the seriousness of what had happened. And Autumn was in the cell at the local police station, but they had promised me she would be out soon enough, as soon as they could get the statements from the witnesses to confirm what they'd seen that morning.

I was still kind of in shock from seeing Autumn getting put into the back of the police car, but as soon as I spotted Karla wailing from the other side of the street, I guessed what had happened at once. It touched me more than Autumn could know that the first thing she had told me when she'd seen me was that Hunter was all right. Despite what was happening to her, she still had my son as a priority. That was the most important thing in the world to me.

Suddenly, the doors flew open, and an exhausted-looking Autumn crashed out onto the steps.

"Oh thank God, you're here." She waved to me. "I thought I was out here on my own."

"Not after you defended my honor like that." I grinned. "You punched someone for me. I don't think I can say that about anyone else."

"Well, don't get used to it," she warned. "I'm not exactly planning on making a habit of it anytime soon."

"No, no, of course not," I agreed. "Last thing I want is an amateur boxer on my hands."

"Who knows? Maybe I'll start craving it," she teased me. "Get the bloodlust, have to go out on the street to fulfill it."

"Yeah, I doubt that." I wrapped an arm around her shoulders and led her to the car. "You want to go back to my place?"

"Yeah, I could do with a long rest." She sighed and let out a long yawn. "I thought I was going to be in there a hell of a lot longer, though. I mean, I did punch her."

"I heard some of the cops talking, and it seems like most of them were on your side." I shrugged as we climbed into the car. "The witnesses, I mean. They all said she started it, more or less, and that you were inside the school gates doing what you had to in order to protect your students."

"Well, that's true enough," she agreed, and she rubbed her knuckles. "Still, I didn't think I would ever be the kind of person who would do something like that."

"What did she say that got you so mad?" I asked. "Hunter wouldn't tell me what it was."

"Hunter said he didn't want anything to do with her," she admitted and then hesitated before she came out with the next part. "And she told him she didn't even want him anyway."

"Damn." I shook my head. "I think I'd have done the same thing if I'd been in your situation."

"Yeah, I just saw red." She shook her head. "I don't really remember it happening. I'm not surprised someone called the cops."

"Wouldn't be surprised if she called them in advance or something, hoping to get someone to lash out at her so she could play the victim," I remarked. "She called me first, after all. Clearly wanted to get me riled up."

"Yeah, but I think that was so she could tell me that you knew she was there," she said with a sigh. "It made some twisted sense in her mind, I suppose."

"That's crazy." I turned on the engine, flicking down the radio so we could talk. "How was jail?"

"Boring." She shrugged. "Mostly boring. I guess I'm not cut out for the life of a hardened criminal."

"One punch does not a hardened criminal make," I teased her.

"Come on, you telling me the thought of a sexy ex-con girlfriend doesn't turn you on a little bit?" she asked. I laughed.

"Okay, maybe it's a little sexy," I agreed as the wind whipped through the car, washing the rest of the day thus far away at last.

"Yeah, I think so." She reached over to squeeze my leg.

"Hunter told me everything that happened. You were so brave, standing up to her like that."

"It was nothing on how brave *he* was," she replied at once. "I couldn't believe how he stood up to her."

"It was because you were right beside him helping him," I told her. "No way would he have had the nerve to do something like that if you weren't there to help."

She made a face. "I don't know. I was pretty fucking terrified. He was probably coming out there to provide some moral support, help me get through the worst of it."

"Well, you sure did that," I agreed. "Are there going to be any charges?"

"Not that I know of," she replied. "Everyone there seemed to go in my favor, and I don't think Karla wants to draw any more attention than strictly necessary to what the fuck she was doing at the school in the first place."

"That's a good point," I agreed. "You think she's going to try to come by there again?"

"I don't think so." Though she shook her head, uncertainty crossed her expression. "She'd have to be seriously dumb to try that again. I'm going to speak to the school about what happened, make sure they know what's going on. I don't want to land in any trouble from them after this."

"I'm sure you won't," I promised her. "I'll vouch for you if you need me to."

"I might," she agreed. "Maybe bribe them with the program you've been working on?"

"Oh, yeah, it looks like they're going to be testing it out soon," I replied. "I was on the phone with the head of the resource allocation for the area, and she seemed pretty keen to try it out. Don't know how many schools I'm going to be starting at, but it's something."

"Oh my God, that's amazing!" she exclaimed, slapping my arm excitedly. "I'm going to boast about that to anyone who'll listen."

"Fair warning, I don't think anyone's going to give a shit," I said. "Talk about designing programs and people tend to glaze over a little bit."

"Well, I'll use my new reputation as a bruiser to get them to do what I want." She flexed her muscles pointedly. "They'll listen to anything I have to say then."

I chuckled. "I'll believe it when I see it."

"Still, it's big news," she replied enthusiastically. "I'm so proud of you."

"Maybe we can celebrate later."

"Well, that, and the fact that your ex should have gotten the message loud and clear by now." She raised her eyebrows.

"Yeah, that too." I glanced down at my watch. "Hey, do you mind if we head around to Raymond's? I dropped Hunter off there after what happened. I think he'd like to see you."

"I don't know if I can look him in the eye after what happened. I punched someone in front of him! That's not how I'm supposed to behave."

"Yeah, well, he thinks you're a badass now," I assured her.

"Like he didn't think that before?" she fired back playfully. I grinned.

"Well, of course. But he'll want to make sure you're doing okay after what happened with Karla. And I'm sure he could use some comforting, too, given everything that went down."

"You're right," she conceded, and I took the turn that would lead us down to Raymond's place.

"Do they know what happened? Olivia and Raymond?" she asked, twisting her hands over and over in her lap. I nodded.

"And they think it's amazing," I assured her. "Remember, Raymond was there when everything happened with Karla the first time around. He's glad to know she's out of my life once and for all, I think."

She held her hands up. "Well, happy to oblige. I'm still a little embarrassed, though. I've never had that kind of reaction to anyone before. I've never wanted to do something like that in my life."

"That's what being a parent does to you," I said without thinking. "You'd do anything to protect the person you're looking after, things you didn't even know you were capable of."

She fell silent for a long moment, and it took me a second to realize I had referred to her as Hunter's mother. It was the first time I had even let myself use those words. Yes, I had thought for a long time that she would make an amazing parent to my son, but I had never allowed myself to think of her as his mother. But today, she had proven she was, that she could be. When things had been at their worst, she had been the one to step up and make sure no harm came to him, and that was about the most motherly thing I could imagine in the world.

"We're here." I turned into the driveway. She still hadn't said anything.

"Ready to go in and see Hunter?" I asked as I pulled the car to a halt. After a moment's pause, she nodded and reached over to squeeze my hand.

"Yeah, I am," she nodded. "I really am."

66

AUTUMN

I followed Holden up the steps to the house, and my heart was fluttering with nerves at the thought of seeing all of them. I was now a woman who had punched someone—punched someone?—right in the face. That wasn't who I was. It had never been who I was. Yet I was standing there outside the house, knowing I had landed a hit on the woman who had been hurting the most important little guy in the world to me. Holden had said none of them thought less of me, but I wasn't sure that was true of me—at least, not yet.

We knocked on the door, and Raymond opened it a second later. I hardly had time to blink before Hunter came speeding past his legs to throw his arms around my waist.

"Autumn!" he cried out. "You're okay!"

"Ms. Becks," I reminded him playfully, gently extracting him from around my waist. "And yes, I'm fine. Nothing to worry about with me."

"Except that left hook of yours," Raymond teased me, stepping aside to let us in. "Come on in. I have dinner on the table for us."

"You're a lifesaver, Ray." Holden slapped his friend on the

shoulder as we walked into the house. "The last thing I wanted was to have to cook after we got home tonight."

"Yeah, well, sounds like it's been a busy day," Olivia said from where she appeared in the doorway, wiping her hands on a towel and smiling at me.

"Baby's asleep." She pointed upstairs. "So just us five, yeah?"

"Sounds perfect," Holden agreed as she led us to the dining room. There was a large pot of soup sitting in the middle of the table, and Raymond began to serve up for us at once. Hunter was right behind me, practically clinging to my legs like he didn't want to let me out of his sight. I knew how he felt. He took the seat next to mine and shifted closer to me. Clearly, he had something he wanted to tell me.

"You were so cool today." He widened his eyes. "You hit her. I've never seen anyone hit somebody in real life before—"

"You should never use violence to solve your problems," I told him firmly. "You should always talk things out first. You shouldn't take my lead on stuff like this. You could land yourself in a lot of trouble. I know I nearly did."

"Yeah, of course." Hunter nodded, but he looked a little disappointed by my reaction. I noticed Holden and Raymond exchanging amused glances. They would never have said it out loud, not wanting to undercut my message, but I knew they felt I had done the right thing. I was even having a hard time believing what I was saying myself, to be honest. I couldn't think of any other way I could have gotten her to back off and stay that way without getting physical.

"Thank you so much for this." I glanced at Olivia and Raymond. "It's so kind of you."

"Well, we couldn't let the hero of the hour go without dinner now, could we?" Olivia remarked.

"I wouldn't go that far," I protested weakly, but the three adults exchanged glances.

"I would." Holden patted my hand, and my heart spun as soon as he laid his fingers on me. I couldn't believe he'd called me Hunter's mother in the car. Maybe it was the stress of the day, with so much happening it was hard to keep everything straight, but still, that was how he saw me. And I was beginning to believe it myself.

It was hard to remember a time when I had truly thought Karla might have been the best thing for Hunter. I was beginning to wrap my head around it now, the notion that because she was his biological parent didn't mean she had some deep connection to him. Hell, she didn't even seem to have a whole lot in the way of simple compassion for her son. The way she had spoken to him, the way she had looked into his eyes and told him she had never wanted him anyway —it sent a shiver down my spine, a flare of fury at the thought that she could speak that way to the boy she was supposed to love.

We settled in for dinner, and Olivia and Raymond chatted with us about the baby and what they had been up to lately. It felt good to revel in some normalcy after all the drama, and I was glad to absorb the news about their family. They seemed so happy, their eyes shining as they talked about their daughter, and I wondered if I would ever be in a similar place—delighted to tell people about Hunter, boasting about him and everything he had achieved. Looking at him now, engaging in the conversation where he could, was enough to get me to swell with pride. He had worked so hard to get where he was, to be able to communicate this way, and it was starting to pay off in a big way.

Olivia took Hunter off to see the baby after a while, leaving the three of us together to talk a little more. I was so tired, I could have keeled over on the spot right there and fallen asleep, but I was glad for the company to get my mind off the inevitable conversation I was going to have with everyone at the school when I got back there. I was pretty sure most of them didn't even know I was seeing Holden at the moment, and this wasn't exactly how I had imagined them finding out.

"What are you going to do now?" Raymond asked. "With Karla, I mean."

Holden sighed. "I honestly have no idea. It depends on if she tries to press charges for this or not."

"I'm thinking she's going to let it drop," I cut in, "given that most of the people there attested to the fact that she came up and started this shit with me."

"Well, fingers crossed that it's the last you see of her," Raymond said. "Might be worth taking out a restraining order, you know, to make sure she keeps her distance."

"Honestly, if she's willing to leave it alone from here, then I am too," Holden shook his head. "All of this has been so much stress on us, not to mention Hunter."

"He didn't seem very stressed today," Raymond pointed out playfully. "Seemed to think the whole thing was very exciting when he was recounting the story to us. And he told it about three times, so I know it pretty well now."

"Yeah, but she said some shitty stuff to him," I reminded him. "It might not have an impact now, but in the future, it could take a turn for the worse. I want to make sure he's taken care of and that he doesn't have to worry about Karla coming back into his life anytime soon."

"You'll fight her off if she does, right?" Raymond teased, and I rolled my eyes and laughed.

"I'm not going to become some kind of pro boxer after this, you know," I shot back. "I only did what I had to."

"I guarantee you're not the first person who's wanted to land one on her," Raymond replied. "And I doubt you'll be the last. Not a court in the land would get you in any trouble for that, not if they found out what she was trying to do. Aren't there rules about her coming onto school property, anyway?"

"Yeah, there are." I yawned, covering my mouth. "Sorry, I'm exhausted."

"I won't keep you here much longer," Raymond promised. "Just wanted to see that you were all right and fed before you went home."

"Well, consider us taken care of." I lifted my glass of water to him. "And thank you so much for this. You really helped me out."

He smiled at me. "Anytime. Anyone who'd punch Karla in the face is a friend of mine for life."

"You make it sound a lot more dramatic than it actually was." I laughed. "I got pissed and swung for her, that's all. Surprised I didn't miss, given my sense of balance."

"Even so." Holden squeezed my knee beneath the table.

"Hey, so I was thinking," Raymond leaned back in his seat, "you want us to take Hunter for tomorrow night? Maybe you guys could do with some time to talk things over, figure out what the best course of action going forward is."

"That's not a bad idea." Holden nodded, turning to me. "Maybe we could go out to dinner somewhere?"

"Celebrate the program getting a test run," I agreed with a smile. "That sounds perfect."

"Oh, the program stuff is going forward?" Raymond perked up. "That's great news. Even more reason to get out there and have a good time, right?"

"Sure is," I said. "I'm so proud of him."

"Well, you both have a lot to be proud of." Raymond smiled at us both.

"If you're okay taking him for another night, then that would be great," Holden agreed.

"Are you kidding?" Raymond raised his eyebrows. "He practically does all the childcare when he's around. He can't get enough of looking after her."

"Must have learned that from you." I nudged Holden, who gazed at me for a moment with a warm smile on his face.

"Must have," he echoed as he turned back to Raymond. "You want me to drop him off after school?"

"Sounds perfect," he replied. "And don't worry about hurrying back. We're happy to keep him for as long as you need."

"And it means that Karla can't get to him, even if she comes by the house," Holden said. "That's good news."

"Not that she'd dare take me on again." I nudged him playfully.

"Damn straight." Raymond nodded, and then Hunter and Olivia appeared back in the doorway.

"I think Hunter's getting pretty tired," she said as the boy next to her let out an enormous yawn. I echoed it almost at once.

ALI PARKER

"Yeah, let's get everyone home," Holden agreed, getting to his feet. "Thanks for dinner, guys. We owe you one."

"Anytime you need it," Olivia replied at once, and we said our goodbyes. She gave me an extra-tight hug as though silently thanking me for what I had done today. She was a mother. Maybe she understood better than anybody else why I had done what I'd done. Perhaps she would have done the same thing in my situation.

We climbed back into the car, and Hunter passed out as soon as we hit the road. He would have a lot to talk to his new friends about at school tomorrow. What had happened there with Karla and me would be the talk of the students and the teachers alike, I could already tell.

"Thank you for what you did today," Holden murmured, taking my hand as we headed back down to the center of the city. "I can't thank you enough."

"I should have done more." I shook my head. "I should have never spoken to her."

"You sound like a real parent." He grinned. "You'll always think you could have done more or that you should have. But trust me, you did enough today. More than enough. And we're both so grateful for it."

I leaned my head against the window and stared out on the street beyond, glad to know I had done something good today. Because I still wasn't sure about what I had done and I wasn't sure if I had made the right choice. At the end of the day, I had kept Hunter safe, and I hadn't suffered too badly as a result of it. I still had to see what the school would say about the actions I had taken, but once I filled them in—or if Zoe already had, which I wouldn't have been surprised to hear—I was sure they would understand where I was coming from. I was protecting a student, which was my duty, even if he happened to be the son of the man I was dating. The man I was in love with.

67

HOLDEN

I pulled into the parking lot of the school and drummed my fingers on the wheel. There was a big-ass smile on my face, and there was a damn good reason for that. Today couldn't have gone much better if I'd been outright trying to make it perfect, and I still had dinner with Autumn before the day was out.

Hunter was down at Raymond's, and Autumn had asked me to give her an hour after classes finished to make sure she had time to sort everything out before the weekend. I assumed she would have to speak to the administrators at the school after what had happened. I hadn't heard anything from her, so I was sincerely hoping that whatever happened, they had landed firmly on her side of the matter. I would be more than happy to step up and fight in her corner if I needed to, though I hoped it wouldn't come to that.

Autumn practically skipped out of the school toward me, wearing the very same dress I had purchased for her while she had been in Vegas. If anything, she looked even more beautiful in it now than she had then, my beautiful girlfriend, the woman I still had no idea what I had done to deserve.

"Well, good evening, good sir." She slipped into the car next to me and gave me a kiss. "And where might we be off to this fine evening?"

"There's a new Italian place not far from my house," I told her. "Thought we could use something hearty to earn back some energy from the last few days, don't you think?"

"I totally agree." She nodded with certainty. "Drive on."

The place was smaller than I had imagined it would be when we arrived, but I liked it well enough. In fact, the quietness felt intimate, allowed me a closeness with Autumn that I had been craving all week. I pulled out her chair for her, and she took her seat, grinning up at me as she did so.

"You remember our first date?" she asked. "When they set us up together?"

"I wouldn't exactly call that a date," I pointed out, chuckling. "You were pretty horrified to see me, as I remember."

"Hey, and you weren't much better," she shot back. "I was surprised you didn't get the fuck up and walk out of there as soon as you saw it was me."

"Trust me, I thought about it," I replied, and she giggled.

"Considering it again today?"

"Not so much." I leaned across the table to steal a brief kiss. We ordered—pasta for both of us, wine for her, and water for me—and she cocked her head at me across the table.

"I guess we have to get it out of the way." She made a face. "What's going on with Karla?"

"What do you mean?"

"I mean, do we have to worry about her anymore?" she asked, shaking her head. "I was on edge all day at school thinking we were going to see her again, but she didn't turn up, so I assumed..."

"You're okay," I promised her gently. "I know it's scary, but she's dealt with."

"Like how?"

"It turns out the cops had her on hold for a few different crimes out of the state." I raised my eyebrows. "Fraud mostly. Which explains why she didn't follow through on taking me to court, even after what she said. But they have her now, got her when they brought her in for questioning, so you have nothing to worry about."

"Thank goodness," she said with a sigh, planting her hand on her chest. "Well, the stuff with the school turned out all right as well. When I explained to them what was going on, they seemed to come around to my side pretty quickly, which was a relief."

"So you're not going to lose your job?"

"No, looks like I'll hang on to it yet." She grinned, lifting her glass to me. "Toast to that?"

"Toast to it indeed." I touched my water to her wine.

"So what happens now?" she asked me, her voice tinged with nervousness.

"In what sense?" I asked, and she cocked her head at me.

"You know, now that Karla is out of the picture, but Hunter knows about her. What happens now?"

"I honestly have no idea." I shook my head and half-snorted with amusement at my own inability to answer that question. "I never planned for something like this. I never thought I would meet anyone who made me feel the way you do. I never thought I would find a person who... I never thought there would be anyone but me I trusted with Hunter, you know?"

"Oh, trust me, I get it." She raised her hands. "I didn't expect to slide into your lives like that. I know it's going to take time, even after everything that's happened."

"Hunter chose you," I reminded her simply. "It might be hard for you to accept, but it's true. He wanted you. More than her. Even when he had Karla right in front of him, you were the only one he gave a damn about. And that's..."

I didn't know quite how to put it into words. How could I? I wanted to tell her she had changed everything—not only for me but for my son, for our family. Until a few months ago, I could never have imagined embracing a true family like this, but here she was, reminding me every day that there was hope for me, that I wasn't as shut off as I had always imagined. All the sadness and solitude in my soul seemed to have fallen away as soon as I kissed her for the first time, and, as long as she stuck around, I couldn't see it returning.

"That's all that matters," I told her at last. "That you're here, that you're with us. We want you around as long as you'll have the both of us."

"Hmm." She tapped her finger against her bottom lip playfully. "I'll have to see if I have room in my schedule for you among all my other lovers."

"We'd appreciate that," I replied as the waiter turned up with our food. She beamed at me across the table as the two of us tucked in and shared the stories about our days and our work. Of course, there was a little surprise I had up my sleeve for her with regard to the work side of things, but she didn't need to hear about that yet.

The food was good, fresh and authentic, and I joked about flying her out to Italy one day to try the real thing in person. She had never traveled to Europe before, and I instantly made a mental note of it in my head so I could whisk her off on some adventure, all three of us, perhaps over the summer break. I could bring my work with me while Autumn and Hunter explored Italy and ate all the food they could get their hands on. It would be utterly perfect.

"Mmm, that was amazing." Autumn leaned back from the table and closed her eyes, and I watched her with a smile. I loved how peaceful she looked after she'd eaten, how much she seemed to genuinely enjoy the food we shared together. There was so much I loved about her, so much that looking at her filled my heart with joy. The warmth, her kindness, her patience that she had shown with Hunter and me, those were what made her who she was. I was proud to be with her.

We finished up—she reached for her wallet, but I tapped her hand away and insisted on covering the meal myself—and we slipped away to the car to drive back to my place.

"We have the whole evening to ourselves," she said, letting her teeth rest on her bottom lip as though she was already anticipating how much fun it was going to be.

"Why do you think we skipped dessert?"

"Oh, there I was thinking you were a cheapskate," she teased, and I reached over to squeeze her knee, letting her know what was in store for the two of us. I wanted to affirm my love for her every way I knew how, including with my body. I wanted to hold her so close that it would feel as though we were merging into one being, that there was no gap between her body and mine. We fit together like we had been made that way, and I needed to remind myself of that fact.

We arrived at the house, and I helped her out of the car and to the door.

"I didn't have that much wine, you know," she said as I took her hand and opened the front door.

"Yeah, yeah." I waved my hand. "But in that dress, I want to make sure no one swipes you before I have a chance to get my hands on you."

"Oh?" She tripped over the doorstep, letting me catch her. "And what exactly did you have in mind for that?"

"I'm more of a show guy, not tell," I murmured as I rounded on her, wrapping my arms around her waist and pushing the door shut behind her. She wound her arms around my shoulders and grinned, and my heart picking up the pace from being this close to her. How could our chemistry still be so good, so intense, even after all this time? It didn't make any sense. Was there ever going to be a moment where I didn't want to touch her, kiss her, fuck her? It seemed so far off as to be impossible.

"Show away," she breathed, and I leaned forward and pressed my mouth to her neck, guiding her against the wall so she had something to lean on. She ran her fingers lightly through my hair, trailing them gently over my skin and touching me as though there was nothing more she wanted in the world than this. I knew how she felt. Getting time away from Hunter was rare, and it was going to get rarer as he got more attached to Autumn and wanted to spend more time around her, so any moments we got to ourselves were to be savored as much as they could be.

"You feel so good," she moaned into my ear, and I tucked my hands down beneath her butt and hitched her up. She squealed and hooked her legs around my waist and allowed me to carry her to the stairs and up to the bedroom. I remembered that time in Vegas when she had been wearing the very same dress and I had fucked her as though it was the only thing in the world that mattered. Tonight, I wanted something different. Tonight I wanted to make love to her, to tell her without words that my feelings were deep and real and that I had never shared them with anyone else before.

"Holden..." She moaned into my ear, and for a second, I thought she was going to say the words. But then she turned her head and kissed me. I closed my eyes and lost myself to the comfort of her embrace, knowing this was all I needed from her, all I would ever need.

68

AUTUMN

I guided his mouth to mine again. Kissing him felt like coming home—as though this was what I had been searching for all along, something that ran deeper than anything I had felt before, even with him. He pushed my dress up a few inches over my thighs, tracing shapes on my skin.

"You look incredible in this dress," he breathed in my ear, and I giggled.

"You got it for me," I reminded him. "You must have good taste."

"Well, I'm here with you, aren't I?"

"Guess there's no accounting for every choice." I grinned into our next kiss, and he wrapped his arms around me and held me even tighter than before. I couldn't get over how good his body felt on top of mine. After the mess of the last few days, feeling something so secure, so certain, so safe, was everything I needed. I kissed him slowly, in no rush, tasting every part of him. His mouth was so soft and yielding, even with the strength and the weight of his body on top of me.

He pushed my dress up a little farther and slipped his fingers down and between my legs, finding the soft pair of black panties I had slipped into that morning with precisely this night in mind. He brushed his fingers lightly along the very outside of the fabric, the pressure so mild it was almost worse than none at all. The taunt of something more, the tease, was so deliciously perfect, I could hardly bear it.

"Mmm." I sighed as he brushed his mouth across my throat.

"I think we need to get you naked," he murmured.

"You do the honors," I suggested, and he lifted me up so I was kneeling upright on the bed and peeled the dress up slowly over my body. Drawing me close, he unclipped my bra and tossed it aside and then moved back from me to run his hands over my bare flesh.

"You're so gorgeous," he said. I closed my eyes and let his touch communicate the same thing as his words. No man had ever made me feel that wanted, that needed before. Because it wasn't just my body he was talking about. No, I knew it ran deeper than that, far deeper than anything I had shared with anyone prior to him.

"I think it's only fair we get you naked too." I moved toward him, unbuttoning his shirt with slightly shaky fingers and pulling it open so I could run my hands over his chest. His skin was warm to the touch, familiar by now, but I could never imagine getting tired of it. He closed his eyes as I carefully undressed him, stripping him down until he was in nothing but his boxers. We lay down on the bed opposite each other, propping our heads up on the pillows so we could look at each other and exchanged smiles that said so much more than anything our words ever could.

He moved toward me suddenly, pushing his hand over my belly and up across my breasts as he kissed me once more. The sudden roughness of his touch sent my head spinning in infinity, and I held on to him for dear life as he massaged my breasts and pushed his tongue into my mouth.

He pulled me on top of him, and I pressed my hands to his chest, feeling his erection against my pussy through my panties. His warm skin against mine, the contours of his muscles beneath it, was enough to bring me back down to Earth. All of this felt so unreal and yet specific at the same time, as though my body was working hard to commit all of this to memory, to fantasy, even as it was happening.

He moved his hand down again, tangling our legs together as he pushed his hand beneath my panties at last. His deft fingers found my clit in an instant, and I squirmed on top of him, parting my legs even further than before. I wanted his cock inside me, but I would take anything I could get at that moment.

"Mmm, you're so wet already," he growled, sounding pleased with himself, and his hint of arrogance was enough to send a flood of need for him through me once more. There was something about overconfidence deployed at the right moments that made my heart dance in my chest. He was in control of this now, and I wanted it that way, couldn't imagine it any other way.

Holden let his fingers trail down and against my slit, stroking soft circles against my entrance as though letting me know what I was in store for. I closed my eyes and buried my face into his shoulder, urging him on, urging me to give him more.

"I want to make love to you," he murmured and, after everything we had been through, I wasn't sure we could do it any other way. We had fucked so much before this—that kind of raw, hungry need for each other best expressed with our bodies in an urgency I needed to work out before it filled me to bursting—but now it was different. We had time, and I wanted to take advantage of it, wanted to lose myself in it.

"Make love to me then," I moaned in his ear, pressing my hips down to him and rocking them back and forth for a moment. He didn't need telling twice. He reached for a condom and opened it, sheathing himself as he kicked off his boxers. I shifted back, giving him room to get them off, and then he drew me back on top of him. He peeled off my panties slowly, letting his fingertips graze against my skin as he did so, and then pulled me back to him.

He was sitting up with me astride him as I lowered myself down onto his cock, winding his arms so tightly around me, I couldn't believe he never wanted to let me go. I began to move on top of him, guiding him into me as deeply as he would go. My hips were grinding with purpose against his body, and I had enveloped him inside me, letting him push all the way into me. He was running his hands all over my back, tracing his fingers eagerly over the skin as though he was writing his love for me every way he could think how.

"You feel incredible," he said as I rode him, and all I could do was cling to him and rock back and forth against him. The pleasure already began to swell in me, to consume me and roll through me, the power of it arcing and rising through my body like it was the only feeling in the world that existed. But it was more than simple pleasure, more than simple desire. It ran deeper than anything I'd ever felt with him. And that was because of him and the way he had opened himself up to me and allowed me into his life, the way he'd drawn me in and filled my life with so much love and so much purpose that I had never known. It was so much what I'd wanted before I met him.

He kissed me again, softly, almost chaste had it not been for what was going on between my legs – it was the kind of kiss that a groom might have given the bride at the end of the ceremony in front of the congregation, and it made my heart swell with adoration for him, as if it hadn't already gone far enough in that direction.

"Oh." I panted in his ear, as the intensity of what we were sharing suddenly built and crested within me. The orgasm rolled through me like a rising tide, washing everything away but this moment, this man, this mutual exchange of love and lust. I buried my head into his shoulder, inhaling his scent greedily, loving the way he smelled, tasted, felt. I was addicted to him, well and truly, and nothing was ever going to change that. Nothing.

Moments later, he moved into me one last time, driving his cock deep into my pussy as it contracted with his own orgasm, and he sank his teeth softly into my skin as it hit him. He held himself still for a long while as though any sort of movement would be enough to break the spell at this second. I knew how he felt. I never wanted to pull apart from him, never wanted to let this go, and found myself rocking ever so slightly against him for a few minutes more, squeezing the last out of him that I could.

Eventually, he pulled back and planted a soft kiss on the corner of my mouth before slowly lifting me off his lap and heading to dispose of the condom. Utterly spent, I sprawled out on the bed and lay there bare-ass naked and feeling like I never wanted to put clothes on again as long as I lived.

I was grinning when he returned to the bedroom, slipping down the bed toward me and running his hand up my back. He was leaving an imprint on me, branding himself into my skin. Not that I would have minded if the whole damn world knew I was his and that he was mine.

"That was amazing," he murmured, and I nodded.

"It really was," I agreed. "Never... you know, made love before."

"Well, get used to it," he teased. "Because if it's that good—"

He interrupted himself with a yawn and lay back on the bed, and I snuggled up next to him and stroked his hair.

"You should get some rest," I told him firmly. "It's been a busy few days. You need it."

"Same goes for you," he said through a yawn. "Come here."

He held his arms out to me, and I cuddled in close to him. I watched as he closed his eyes and drifted off to sleep. I smiled as his chest rose and fell, and he settled into a decent rest. I didn't even want to think how hard these last few days had been for him. Yet he had still made the time for me, despite it all.

"I love you," I whispered to him, knowing he was asleep. Even if he hadn't been, my words were so quiet, he would have barely been able to make them out. But what mattered was, they were out there and were in his mind because they were true. I did love him. I didn't know when I would have the nerve to tell him in person when he was awake, but that day would come. I could hardly wait for it. But for now, enough had already happened, and we both needed some time to gather ourselves. As long as I was there in his arms to do it, I didn't mind one little bit.

EPILOGUE
AUTUMN

One Week Later

"Ooh, can I chat with you for a minute?" Zoe ducked her head into my classroom and glanced around. "I know Holden's here soon, but I wanted to speak to you."

"What's going on?" I asked with a smile. It had to be good news. After a test period, Holden was going to find out that day whether they had picked up his idea for the grade curve program, and he was stopping by as soon as he found out to tell me.

"Nothing. I wanted to see if Holden had come by yet." She shrugged. "Anything from him yet?"

"Nothing yet," I replied, shaking my head. "I have everything crossed for him, though. I think it could help out so many teachers too. Imagine all the time it would free up."

Zoe waved her hand. "Tell me about it. I actually got to have a real-life fling because of the time he saved me. He has no idea how much that means to me."

"How are things going with this mystery Vegas man?" I cocked my head with interest, and she tapped her nose.

"Let's just say he's passing through town next weekend," she replied mysteriously. "And we're going to see how things go from there."

"Oh, the romance." I planted my hand on my chest. "Why don't you get set up on a blind date, turn him down, become friends with him, and then date him, and punch his ex like a normal person?"

"Well, I guess we can't all be as traditional as you, Autumn," she said. "Jesus, I was so glad when I heard the school isn't going to do anything about the charges. I was worried they might try and pin you for something, but everyone came out for you."

"Yeah, it's nice to know so many people in this place have my back," I agreed. They'd had to launch a formal investigation, even though the principal had pretty much waved away this whole thing as soon as he'd heard the details of it. Even with a proper investigation into what happened, everyone had backed me up, no question. The fact that Karla had some outstanding charges against her as well helped undermine her credibility, and once it was clear to anyone paying attention that I had been out there trying to keep Hunter and the rest of the children safe no matter what, nobody had really cared too much at what I'd done. I had no intention of doing anything like it again, that was for sure, and I hoped I would never have to.

"I sure as hell have your back." She grinned, reaching over the table to pat my hand. "I thought you were so damn brave that day. I've never seen anything like it before."

"Well, that's what dating Holden has done to me."

"And there you were saying you would never date a guy with kids of his own already," she teased. "How long ago was that? Seven, eight months?"

"If that." I shook my head. "I know. So much has changed since then."

"But you're happy?" Zoe asked, and I nodded without hesitation.

"Yeah, I'm happy," I assured her. "Really happy, actually."

"Mind if I cut in?"

We both turned to see where the source of the voice was coming from, and I beamed when I saw Holden in the doorway.

"I suppose you can." I nodded, and Zoe slipped away, grinning at Holden as she brushed by him.

"So you hear about the program yet?" I asked him, and he waited until Zoe was out of the room and closed the door behind her. My heart sank. It had to be because there was bad news, and he didn't want Zoe to overhear it.

"Not good?" I made a face, but before he answered my question, he walked around my desk, clasped my shoulders, and planted a big kiss on my lips.

"All right, so a little good?" I laughed as he pulled back, checking that the door was shut. Hunter was at an after-school club, one of the ones the other teachers ran, and I didn't want him walking in on me and his father.

"Autumn, I can't believe it." He shook his head. "They want to roll it out across the whole state next semester. The whole *state!*"

"Oh my God!" I exclaimed, practically jumping up and down on the spot. "You're kidding me. The whole state?"

"The whole thing," he said, and the thrill of excitement in his voice was obvious to anyone paying attention. He might have tried to play it cool most of the time, but I could tell when he was thrilled, and right now, he was spinning among the clouds.

"They're buying the rights for the program from me," he explained. "So we're going to be... well, whenever you want to take a trip to Vegas next, we'll be able to afford the best of everything."

"Wait, we?" I held my hand up to stop him. We weren't sharing finances yet. We were pretty far removed from that as far as I was concerned. What was he talking about? Then I saw a smile spread out across his face, and I knew this was going to be good.

"Okay, so I have something to admit." He brushed a strand of hair back from my face. "When I registered the copyright to the program, I put your name on it too."

"What the hell are you talking about?" I gasped.

"Without you, I wouldn't have been able to come up with it at all," he pointed out. "Zoe has a few shares, too, since she helped me test it. And now that we've sold it..."

I stared at him for a long moment, trying to process this, trying to make sense of it. He was beaming at me, but it took me a moment to let everything sink in.

"How much—"

"A whole hell of a lot," he replied. "I can talk to you about the exact numbers later, but suffice it to say, you have enough to live on for the next decade. Comfortably."

"Holy shit," I murmured. "Holy *shit*. Please tell me I can be the one to break this news to Zoe?"

"I think it's only right that you do," he said. I stared at him for another moment, waiting for him to pull the rug out from underneath me. But he didn't, and he never would have been that cruel, never would have led me to believe something so exciting when it was false. He was telling me the truth. I was rich. Like him.

"I can't believe you did this." I shook my head again. My thoughts were battering back and forth in my brain, unable to process it all. I had money now. Real money. I could do whatever I wanted.

"I wanted you to be able to have any kind of life you wanted." He held me close, and I looked into his eyes and saw a sincerity glowing in there. This wasn't some kind of empty gesture to show off. This was him offering me a lifestyle of my choice.

"I only want to share it with you," I murmured, and he planted a kiss on my lips. When I pulled back, I looked deeply into his eyes, and I opened my mouth to say the words—but before I could, he said them first.

"I love you too." He brushed his nose against mine.

I widened my eyes. "You heard me last night?"

"Sure did," he replied with a grin. "But I wanted to be properly awake when I said it to you for the first time."

"I love you," I said the words to him, rolling them off my tongue as though they had been waiting there for a lifetime. I closed my eyes and let my head rest against his, letting the warmth pass between us. How had I waited so long to say those words? How long had I felt them and tried to hide from them? Looking back, it was so clear that from the very moment we met, it had been leading to this moment, to this admission that we loved one another. And that was never going to change. He completed me in a way that I had never felt before in my life.

"I'm going to be saying that a lot in the next few days," he said, not pulling back from me. I didn't care if anyone walked in on us at that moment. In fact, I wanted the whole world to see and hear those words, to know we were finally together and in love and at peace with everything that was going on and everything that we had been through.

"Me too," I replied. "Making up for lost time."

"I was so nervous to say it to anyone," he confessed. "I've known it for a long time. Since I saw you again in Vegas, I knew it."

"That trip was amazing." I sighed. "We should do that again sometime soon."

"Well, you can afford to go anywhere in the world now," he pointed out. "Where do you want to start out?"

"Oh my God." I gasped. "I really can go anywhere, can't I? I don't know where to start."

"I was thinking the three of us could take a trip to Italy," he suggested. "Maybe try out some of that authentic Italian food? See how it compares to what we have over here?"

"That sounds amazing," I said, beaming. "Me, you, and Hunter."

"A proper family vacation," he replied, the smile spreading wider over his face. "That would be perfect."

"We're a real family now," I murmured. "The three of us. Aren't we?"

"You're going to be an amazing mother to him," Holden promised me. "You already have been, you know. With everything that happened with Karla—"

"That's behind us now," I assured him. "We get to look forward now. Not back."

"You're right. I can't wait."

"Well, I can't wait to celebrate properly tonight." I cocked an eyebrow at him playfully, and he laughed.

"Hmm, well, now that you mention it." He leaned in and planted another kiss on my lips. That familiar warmth spread through my entire body, boiling down in my belly, ready for more. I couldn't wait to get him home, have dinner together, and then head to the bedroom and—

"Gross." A voice came from behind us, and we sprang apart. Hunter was standing in the doorway with Zoe, and I smiled at him, a little embarrassed that he'd caught us in the act. But I supposed there was nothing to hide from him anymore since we were truly a couple now, since Holden had called me Hunter's mother. The thought of that was enough to fill me near to bursting with total joy.

"Hey, come on now." Holden strolled over to join Hunter. "Not that bad, right?"

"I guess." He made a disgusted face.

"You ready to head home?" Holden asked his son, and Hunter nodded.

"I guess I'll see you tomorrow," Zoe said with a grin, and I waved her closer.

"Oh, give me a minute. There's something I need to tell you," I replied casually, winking at Holden. Zoe glanced between us, cocking an eyebrow.

"Something I should know?"

I nodded. "Yeah, there is."

She grinned widely, and she looked to Holden and wagged her finger at him. "I told you, you're supposed to ask my permission before you propose," she joked, and he chuckled.

"When the time comes, you'll be the first person I ask," he promised her.

"Okay, you guys head out. I'll meet you there in a minute." I waved to Hunter and Holden.

"Can we go out for dinner tonight?" Hunter asked hopefully.

"I don't see why not," Holden agreed. "We're celebrating, after all."

"Are we?" Zoe asked keenly.

"Come on. I'll catch you up on everything," I promised her.

"See you in a second." Holden nodded to me, and I watched them

go. We would move in together soon, when the moment was right. I
had no doubt about it.

A smile lifted my lips. Zoe was practically hopping from foot to
foot with excitement, but I took a moment to watch them leave—
Holden and Hunter, my two boys, the family I had never known I
needed. We were celebrating tonight, celebrating so much. The
program, sure, but more than that too. We were celebrating us,
together at last, and the promise of a future together that I could
already hardly wait to get to.

A future that was everything I never knew I wanted. Funny
enough, I'd been right under his nose the whole time. Lucky boy!

The End

ABOUT THE AUTHOR

Ali Parker is a full-time contemporary and new adult romance writer with more than a hundred and twenty books behind her. She loves coffee, watching a great movie and hanging out with her hubs. By hanging out, she means making out. Hanging out is for those little creepy elves at Christmas. No tight green stockings for her.

She's an entrepreneur at heart and loves coming up with more ideas than any one person should be allowed to access. She lives in Texas with her hubs and three kiddos and looks forward to traveling the world in a few years. Writing under eleven pen names keeps her busy and allows her to explore all genres and types of writing.

Other books by Ali Parker

Baited

Second Chance Romances
Jaded
Jaded Christmas

Justified
Justified Christmas

Judged
Judge Christmas

Alpha Billionaire Series
His Demands, Book 1
His Needs, Book 2
His Forever, Book 3

Bad Money Series
Blood Money
Dirty Money
Hard Money
Cash Money

Forbidden Fruit Series
Forgotten Bodyguard

Bright Lights Billionaire
Stage Left
Center Stage
Understudy
Improv
Final Call

Pro-U Series
Breakaway
Offside
Rebound
Homerun
Freeststyle

The Rules
Making the Rules
Bending the Rules
Breaking the Rules

My Creative Billionaire

Money Can't Buy Love

My Father's Best Friend

The Lost MC Series
Ryder
Axel
Jax
Sabian
Derek

The Dawson Brothers Series
Always on my Mind
Wild as the Wind
Mine Would Be You
Don't Close Your Eyes

Made in the USA
Monee, IL
03 January 2024

51109254R00246